KRISTIN LAVRANSDATTER

III: THE CROSS

Sigrid Undset (1882–1949) was born in Denmark, the eldest daughter of a Norwegian father and a Danish mother, and moved with her family to Oslo two years later. She published her first book, *Fru Marta Oulie (Mrs. Marta Oulie)*, in 1907, and her second, *Den lykkelige alder (The Happy Age)*, in 1908. The following year came her first work set in the Middle Ages, *Fortællingen om Viga-Ljot og Vigdis* (later translated into English under the title *Gunnar's Daughter* and now available in Penguin Twentieth-Century Classics). More novels and stories followed, including *Jenny* (1911, translated 1920), *Fattige skjæbner (Fates of the Poor*, 1912), *Vaaren (Spring*, 1914), *Splinten av troldspeilet* (1917, translated in part as *Images in a Mirror*, 1938), and *De kloge jomfruer (The Wise Virgins*, 1918). Most of these early works have never been translated into English. In 1920 Undset published the first volume of *Kristin Lavransdatter*, the medieval trilogy that would become her most famous work. *Kransen (The Wreath)* was followed by *Husfrue (The Wife)* in 1921 and *Korset (The Cross)* in 1922. Beginning in 1925 she published the four-volume *Olav Audunssøn i Hestviken* (translated into English under the title *The Master of Hestviken)*, also set in the Middle Ages. In 1928 Sigrid Undset won the Nobel Prize for Literature. During the 1930s she published several more novels, notably the autobiographical *Elleve aar* (1934, translated as *The Longest Years*, 1935). She was also a prolific essayist on subjects ranging from Scandinavian history and literature to the Catholic Church (to which she became a convert in 1924) and politics. During the Nazi occupation of Norway, Undset lived as a refugee in New York City. She returned home in 1945 and lived in Lillehammer until her death in 1949.

Tiina Nunnally has translated all three volumes of *Kristin Lavransdatter* for Penguin Twentieth-Century Classics. She won the PEN/Book-of-the-Month Club Translation Prize for the third volume, *The Cross*. Her translations of the first and second volumes, *The Wreath* and *The Wife*, were finalists for the PEN Center USA West Translation Prize, and *The Wife* was also a finalist for the PEN/Book-of-the-Month Club Translation Prize. She won the Lewis Galantière Prize, given by the American Translators Association, for her translation of Peter Høeg's novel *Smilla's Sense of*

Snow. She is known for her translations of novels and short stories from Danish, Norwegian, and Swedish, including the works of Jens Peter Jacobsen, Tove Ditlevsen, and Knut Hamsun. She won the PEN Center USA West Translation Award for Jacobsen's *Niels Lyhne*, and the American-Scandinavian Foundation Translation Prize for Ditlevsen's *Early Spring*. She has also published three novels, *Fate of Ravens*, *Runemaker*, and *Maija*. She holds an M.A. in Scandinavian Studies from the University of Wisconsin–Madison. She lives in Seattle, Washington.

Sherrill Harbison is a lecturer at Trinity College, Hartford, and an Associate of the Five Colleges (Amherst, Smith, Mount Holyoke, Hampshire, and the University of Massachusetts). She received her B.A. in Art History from Oberlin College and her Ph.D. in English from the University of Massachusetts at Amherst. Her work on Sigrid Undset has been supported by the Fulbright Association and the Norwegian Marshall Fund, and she is a three-time winner of the Aurora Borealis Prize, awarded by the Five Nordic Governments. She has published articles on Undset, Willa Cather, and William Faulkner and has translated some of Undset's shorter works. She is the editor of the Penguin Twentieth-Century Classics editions of Undset's *Gunnar's Daughter* and Cather's *The Song of the Lark*; she also wrote the introduction to *Kristin Lavransdatter II: The Wife*.

KRISTIN LAVRANSDATTER III: THE CROSS

SIGRID UNDSET

TRANSLATED WITH NOTES
BY TIINA NUNNALLY

INTRODUCTION
BY SHERRILL HARBISON

PENGUIN BOOKS

PENGUIN BOOKS
Published by the Penguin Group
Penguin Group (USA) Inc., 375 Hudson Street, New York, New York 10014, U.S.A.
Penguin Books Ltd, 80 Strand, London WC2R 0RL, England
Penguin Books Australia Ltd, 250 Camberwell Road, Camberwell, Victoria 3124, Australia
Penguin Books Canada Ltd, 10 Alcorn Avenue, Toronto, Ontario, Canada M4V 3B2
Penguin Books India (P) Ltd, 11 Community Centre, Panchsheel Park, New Delhi – 110 017, India
Penguin Books (N.Z.) Ltd, Cnr Rosedale and Airborne Roads, Albany, Auckland, New Zealand
Penguin Books (South Africa) (Pty) Ltd, 24 Sturdee Avenue,
Rosebank, Johannesburg 2196, South Africa

Penguin Books Ltd, Registered Offices: 80 Strand, London WC2R 0RL, England

This translation first published in Penguin Books 2000

7 9 10 8

Translation and notes copyright © Tiina Nunnally, 2000
Introduction copyright © Sherrill Harbison, 2000
All rights reserved

Originally published in Norwegian as *Korset*
by H. Aschehoug & Company, Oslo, 1922.

LIBRARY OF CONGRESS CATALOGING-IN-PUBLICATION DATA
Undset, Sigrid, 1882–1949.
[Korset.   English]
The Cross / Sigrid Undset ; translated with notes by Tiina Nunnally;
introduction by Sherrill Harbison.
p.   cm. — (Penguin twentieth-century classics)
(Kristin Lavransdatter : 3)
ISBN 0 14 11.8235 0
I. Nunnally, Tiina, 1952–   II. Title.   III. Series.
PT8950.U5K6413   2000
839.8'2372—dc21
99–048568

Printed in the United States of America
Set in Sabon
Designed by Mia Risberg
Maps by Virginia Norey

CONTENTS

INTRODUCTION

Kristin Lavransdatter is a remarkably durable novel, for at least two reasons that appear to be contradictory. Its narrative style and familiar domestic subject matter make it accessible even to the unsophisticated reader, and yet its rich textual subtleties—including allusions to unfamiliar, even arcane medieval works—show no signs of being exhausted by scholars. These are not, in fact, contradictory qualities, but the combination is difficult to achieve. The early poetry of William Butler Yeats, for example, which draws on Irish lore and legends, is hauntingly beautiful but remains obscure even to the initiated; Margaret Mitchell's *Gone with the Wind*, on the other hand, is a gripping story but lacks literary resonance. What is unusual about *Kristin Lavransdatter* is that its accessibility is actually a feature of its complexity. This is due to the nature of Undset's literary models.

Kristin Lavransdatter absorbs, transforms, and echoes countless other texts, including such Norse works as sagas, ballads, lays, poems, sermons, folktales, and prayers, as well as a wide variety of material from England and the Continent, including romances, minnesong, tales, religious legends, visionary poems, philosophical and theological treatises, and works by writers such as Geoffrey Chaucer, whom Undset especially admired. The ideas about love, marriage, and family life in *Kristin Lavransdatter* derive from these medieval sources, which are themselves unfamiliar to most readers; but the concepts and values advanced in those early texts have become so much a part of Western culture that few are aware of their medieval origin. This sense of recognition—however vague—is one reason the novel is so accessible to the general reader.

Another reason is Undset's narrative method. She is, above all, a master storyteller whose earliest inspiration came from Icelandic sagas and Scandinavian ballads, both rooted in oral tradition. Oral narratives demand certain dramatic devices if listeners are to follow along—logical sequencing, formulaic transitions, and cadenced speech, for example. Undset uses this inheritance both to have intertextual conversations with her sources and to serve her readers.

Undset's attitudes and tastes were marked in fundamental ways by her Icelandic models, beginning with her choice of historical fiction itself. The sagas are histories of the early Norwegian kings and Icelandic families from the Viking era, histories that began in oral tradition and were finally recorded in the twelfth and thirteenth centuries. Several scholars have described their mingling of fact, creative speculation, and national pride as a prototype of the historical novel. Thus it is no accident that revived interest in these old texts was an outgrowth of nineteenth-century national romanticism, or that it coincided with Sir Walter Scott's invention of the historical novel in Scotland (once a Viking colony) early in that same century.

Undset announces her intellectual debt to the sagas in the opening paragraph of *Kristin Lavransdatter* by reciting genealogical histories pertinent to her heroine—the way all sagas begin. As in the sagas, too, action in the trilogy revolves around families and the obligations of kinship. Undset had been profoundly impressed in childhood by the sagas' unvarnished psychological portraits of individuals whose driving passions were both generous and destructive, and her own characterizations owe much to their example. Her stubborn, unforgiving heroine is endowed with what is called *"et stridt sinn"* in Old Norse (she is quick to take offense and long to hold resentments), marking Kristin as heir both to Undset's own earlier heroine Vigdis Gunnarsdatter and to such passionate, goading saga women as Gudrun Osvifsdottír of *Laxdæla Saga*. Undset's psychological realism achieves its purpose: Kristin, Erlend, Lavrans, Ragnfrid, and Simon are believable and sympathetic precisely because they are not sentimentalized. The sagas are blunt, too, in describing such unsavory physical events as death and dismemberment, and Undset's writing about violent death and the progress of disease rivals theirs. She also broke new ground by extending the same unflinching gaze to labor and childbirth, subjects that never had been described by male writers.

Undset first encountered the sagas at age ten; at eighteen she had a second literary epiphany: Svend Grundtvig and Axel Olrik's *Danmarks gamle folkeviser*, a collection of Danish ballads that she immediately described as "the book of my books and source of eternal life." In their number, breadth, and variety, ballads are a major Scandinavian contribution to medieval literature, but unlike other genres, they are creations of both men and women from all classes of society. They were not superficial entertainment: beneath the surface narratives of love, domestic tragedy, and supernatural happenings, they treat familial ties and tensions, the most fundamental transitions and conflicts of the human psyche in both love and maturation.

Undset's incorporation of ballad themes and narrative strategies is thus another way she makes *Kristin Lavransdatter* both accessible and sophisticated, especially for Scandinavian readers familiar with the ballad legacy. But this literary device helps make the novel seem familiar to non-Scandinavian readers as well, both because ballads tell entertaining stories, and because, like fairy tales, they revolve around archetypal scripts that appear in variants in the folklore of other cultures. Even those who don't know a particular story recognize its type.

Undset includes all of the six major Scandinavian ballad types—historical, legendary, heroic, chivalric, supernatural, and jocular—in the text of *Kristin Lavransdatter*. She uses stories of abduction and rescue (Kristin and Bentein, Kristin and Erlend, Gaute and Jofrid), tragic love (Ragnfrid, Arne, Eline, Simon), folk and Christian legends (Brother Edvin's talking animals at the Nativity), idylls (Kristin and Erlend in the rose garden, Kristin as Madonna with Child), supernatural events (the elf maiden, Kristin's vision of Brother Edvin's waving glove), and saints' lives (Saint Olav, Saint Thomas à Becket). In a few cases she incorporates ballad texts directly, as when dances are performed at feasts and festivals, but more often she alludes to them in dialogue or incident, or merely suggests them with characteristic motifs, rhythms, or formulas. During the years she was writing this novel she corresponded regularly with the Danish painter Agnes Slott-Møller, who was also using ballad subjects for her paintings and murals; Slott-Møller's painting of the tragic love ballad of Ebbe Skammelsen hung over Undset's bed while she worked on *Kristin*.

Several scholars have observed that the entire first volume of the trilogy works as a ballad. The novel's governing motif is that of the elf maiden, who in Norwegian folklore is associated with abduction and erotic abandon; her mischief is to lure young girls into the mountain for orgies with the mountain king. The elf maiden (and Kristin's name) is found in the ballad about "Liti Kjersti," who is captured and carried to the mountain. When Kjersti later visits home, her mother notices milk spurting from her breasts, and Kjersti confesses her condition. But her abductor then fetches her back, silencing her with a drink that makes her forget her past, and Kjersti stays with the mountain king forever. Both the ballad and the novel include episodes in which the garlanded heroine gazes dizzily at her reflection in the water.

This imagery becomes a leitmotif for a major theme in *Kristin Lavransdatter*: the tension between sacred and profane love. The saintly Brother Edvin and the elf maiden (later personified as Fru Aashild) represent the two poles, and beginning with the fateful childhood journey in the first two chapters, when Kristin meets them both, ballad imagery ripples through the text. In the months before Kristin's marriage, for example, Ragnhild puts her arm around her daughter's waist, and Kristin, who has not confided her pregnancy, shrieks in terror of Ragnhild's suspicions. Later, when she is crowned for her wedding and Fru Aashild bids her to admire her reflection in the water, Kristin nearly faints at her shadowy memory of the elf maiden. The theme returns in *The Cross* when Kristin and Erlend experience a late-life reprise of their early, besotted love on the mountain at Haugen, Fru Aashild's retreat, which had been the scene of their crime against Eline. As Erlend entreats Kristin to abandon Jørundgaard and remain with him forever, she feels she is being bewitched by the mountain king.

The elf-maiden episode is symbolic not only of Kristin's personal conflict but also of continuing tensions in medieval Norway between paganism and Christianity. The Church had arrived late in the North—Norway's official conversion dates to the reign of Olav Trygvessøn (995–1000), but the process took several centuries. By Kristin's lifetime most pagan beliefs survived only as folk superstitions—though very powerful ones. Lavrans's fear for his seven-year-old daughter's safety is real; his crucifix is the only talisman strong enough to ward off the mountain spirit. Fru Aashild is shunned because she is suspected of witchcraft, and Kristin's midnight venture to fetch graveyard turf for Simon's ailing son remains a shameful secret. Even more sinister is the reversion to human sacrifice that occurs in this final volume, a desperate attempt to ward off the Black Death.

In *Kristin Lavransdatter* Undset illustrates many of the changes Christianity brought to women's lives, particularly those affecting courtship and marriage. Pagan marriages in the North had been strictly men's business arrangements involving matters of kinship and property alliances. Personal attraction between partners was not presumed, and wives were expected to tolerate concubines. When King Olav Haraldssøn (Saint Olav) instituted Christian law in 1024, women gained some advantages never available to them before. For the first time a woman's consent was required for a marriage to be valid (a ruling that invited Kristin's conflict with Lavrans over her betrothal). Sexual fidelity was expected of both spouses, which reduced conflicts and jealousies between wives, concubines, and their offspring. Women could also choose not to marry at all, to live in female communities under the protection of the Church (as the Nonneseter and Rein cloisters offer refuge for Kristin at troubled times in her life).

An equally important revolution in women's status, however, came with the introduction of the code of courtly love, an intense, idealized form of sexual passion invented by poets in France in the twelfth century, which was both an expression of and a challenge to Christian teachings. The troubadour poets overturned the ancient idea of eros as a troublesome illness that interferes with manly pursuits, designating it instead a divine mystery, a high spiritual experience on a physical plane. A woman who inspired passion became a goddess worthy of adoration, and a knight who pledged to protect and serve his lady in *trouthe* and *curtesie* was expressing not baser instincts, but nobler ones.

This idea was, understandably, very popular with women, who enjoyed their new power and the more peaceful, gracious way of life the courtly ethic fostered. And clearly the chivalric ideal had great strengths. In addition to elevating the status of women, it shifted emphasis away from aggression and vengeance (the Viking code of honor), toward diplomatic and "court-eous" behavior, an ideal that survives today. But it also had serious flaws—chiefly, inherent tendencies toward narcissism and anarchy—which are amply documented in medieval romance narratives such as the Arthurian legends, which Undset published in her own Norwegian version in 1915.

Both narcissism and anarchy were encouraged by the *Liber de arte honeste amandi et reprobatione inhonesti amoris* (*The Art of Courtly Love*), a compilation of rules and courtly etiquette for lovers recorded in the twelfth century by Andreas Capellanus. According to the code, darkness and secrecy were requirements for passion. Jealousy and obstacles—either legal or moral—enhanced it, while the light of public exposure killed it. It was largely the lovers' isolation that encouraged narcissism: Couples hidden away from sober judgments and everyday responsibilities could imagine themselves identical with the flattering image reflected in their lover's eyes. The courtly code also made romance and marriage theoretically incompatible: All great love affairs—unless they were platonic—were illicit. Thus, despite its heroic rules and civilizing manners, the game of courtly love could operate only in a labyrinth of deceit, allowing all the precepts of noble conduct— honesty, chastity, charity, courtesy, the very rules it aspired to teach—to be broken for the sake of its own rule of love. Classic medieval examples were Tristan and Iseult, who in keeping their troth broke the law and caused undeserved suffering to themselves and others; or Lancelot and Guinevere, whose betrayal of King Arthur led to the collapse of the chivalrous values the Round Table had stood for. The tragic paradox was that, according to the courtly code, this erotic anarchy was justified.

The narcissism of lovers was hardly a new theme for Sigrid Undset. It had informed all of her contemporary stories, starting with *Fru Marta Oulie* in 1907, and the anarchic force of passion had ruled the sorry destinies of her modern heroines Jenny Winge (*Jenny*, 1911) and Harriet Waage (*Splinten av troldspeilet*, 1917). She revisits these issues with Kristin and Erlend, who, like Tristan and Iseult, feel their illicit love as an irresistible force sanctified by their own secret pledge. Erlend's narcissism—his inflated sense of self—leads him to imagine that his love for and protection of an innocent girl can rescue him from past failures and moral compromises. But in fact secret love does not ennoble him; it only sullies

Kristin, whose initiation to passion propels her to acts of deceit and cruelty of which she had not known herself capable.

By carrying Kristin and Erlend's story beyond the courtship stage, when love is burnished by secrecy and suspense, and taking them through a marriage in which they are subject to the very visibility and public responsibility Andreas Capellanus had warned lovers to avoid, Undset attempts to address the moral issues raised by the courtly code. Her idea was not original—like everything else in the novel, it is historically grounded, reflecting the changing views of love found in the philosophy, theology, and literature of the Middle Ages.

It was clear that a society based on feudal vows and Christian ethics could not long accommodate a competing code that undermined its core values. Here it is important to remember that the Church in the Middle Ages was the most powerful and elastic it has ever been, and knowledge of the flesh was one of its strengths before it became one of its weaknesses. Once it recognized the need to harness the explosive force of sexual desire, it attempted to divert erotic energy toward moral development and works of Christian charity. The Church was fortunate not to be alone in this ambitious project—by the thirteenth century, poets, too, had wearied of the theme of self-absorbed sensuality and were seeking more realistic ways to write about love.

In their effort to accommodate courtly love to changing needs and tastes, many poets turned to classical literature, selecting the image of Narcissus—with its emblem of the reflecting well or mirror—as their primary tool. The development of the Narcissus theme in courtly poetry reflects a changing understanding of the stages of self-knowledge necessary for the capacity to love—from the "narcissistic" love of a mere reflection, a watery image that dissolves at the touch, to a "courtly" infatuation with a person one believes to mirror one's own best qualities, and finally to an active, engaged love for a separate, very human being with an identity and integrity of his or her own.

A famous example of this development is the *Roman de la rose*, a controversial allegory of love that held a central position in French literature for some two hundred years, and that exerted a greater influence on Chaucer (who translated it) than any other vernacular literary work in either French or English. Undset absorbed its ideas, therefore, not just from her reading of French sources but through Chaucer's literary transcription of the poem and his conversations with it in his own work, notably *The Legend of Good Women* and *The Canterbury Tales*.

The controversy aroused by the *Roman de la rose* was inherent in the text: The poem was left unfinished by Guillaume de Lorris at his death in 1237, and was completed by Jean de Meun in a very different spirit forty years later. Its split personality is worth examining for the light it sheds on changing views of love, human nature, and the physical world in the later Middle Ages, views reflected in the world Undset re-created for *Kristin Lavransdatter*.

The authors of the *Roman de la rose* assumed their readers' knowledge of Ovid's tale of Narcissus, who falls in love with his own image in the water, declines the affection of the nymph Echo, and finally dies because without an external object his love is sterile and hopeless. (In some versions of the legend, he drowns after plunging into the pool to embrace his reflection.) In the *Roman de la rose* the hero's adventures take place in a dream. The Dreamer is led through a garden to what he knows to be the well of Narcissus, but he is determined not to repeat Narcissus' mistake. After deciding that his wisdom should protect him from folly, he gazes down and sees, not a reflection of himself in the water's surface, but a beautiful Rose, reflected in crystals lying deeper at the bottom of the pool. He realizes (again from Narcissus' mistake) that it is wrong and futile to resist loving another, so he willingly accepts his duty to serve the Rose above all else. The purpose of the Dreamer's quest is to become educated in the pleasures and rewards of love, but his quest has just begun when the first part of the narrative ends.

Many ideas and images from this section of the allegory appear in *The Wreath*, interwoven with echoes of other medieval sources in a way typical of Undset. Merging the allegory's concerns with the ballad about Kjersti, she establishes the Narcissus theme in the elf-maiden episode. Later, the young Kristin is rescued by a handsome knight with whom she falls in love, although she is (like the famous Iseult) betrothed to another. Convinced (like the Dreamer) that resisting true love would be both wrong and futile, she and Erlend secretly pledge their troth in a rose garden—a scene resonating not only with the allegorical Rose, but with countless symbolic paintings of the Virgin Mary in a rose garden. In this setting Erlend imagines that his devotion to a pure and innocent virgin can raise his moral profile (later he will engrave her wedding ring not with *K* but with *M* for Mary). The well of Narcissus returns when Kristin stands dressed in her wedding finery and swoons at her reflection in the water.

When Guillaume de Lorris died in 1237, Jean de Meun, who would complete the earlier writer's work, was not yet born. Jean came of age later in the century, and when he took up the poem he designed a curriculum for the Dreamer that would adapt love to the more realistic needs and tastes of his own day. Using a popular device called the "palinode," or retraction, he revised the assumptions of the earlier writer in order to rescue the poem for a newly dubious audience. His strategy was twofold: to de-idealize women, to remove them from their unrealistic pedestals and bring them down to earth by means of stories that defamed their character and motives, and to domesticate eros—to depart from the courtly convention of illicit liaisons and propose a genuinely naturalistic view of sex as something honest and good in its proper context. The discussion is begun by the allegorical figure of Reason (presented as a rival mistress), whose role is to persuade the Dreamer that secret passion impairs intelligence, judgment, and the ability to take advice, as the ancients had always known; in an extreme case one could lose one's life altogether, as Narcissus had done. The discussion is then taken up by Nature and her priest Genius (the god of reproduction), who hold forth in a triumphal hymn to regeneration and to the beauty and energy of nature. The object of love is not self-absorbed erotic sensation, they maintain, but human fecundity, the critical and never-ending race of life against death.

The allegory concludes with a meditation on the mystical parallel of human and divine love. The garden the Dreamer had entered was actually a poor copy of the garden of Paradise, and the well of Narcissus a flawed counterpart to the biblical well of eternal life. Because earthly love was a pale reflection of divine love, it was wrong to expect (as Narcissus had) that a lover should reflect an idealized image of oneself, as only God could do that. According to Augustine, the chief objective of earthly love was to imitate the

Creator by propagating the race; human lovers were thus bound to each other not by personal inclination (as the troubadour poets had claimed), but by God's law, to be responsible for and to love one another in His name. This view of sexuality as the human correlate to God's creative energy changed two things: It modified the Church's earlier ideal of celibacy (which it had previously recommended even in marriage), and it discredited the courtly code of illicit love.

Volumes II and III of *Kristin Lavransdatter* best reflect these ideas from the later portion of the allegory. As Andreas Capellanus had warned, public life and mundane responsibilities reveal Undset's lovers to be flawed and human, but even after bitterness consumes them, Kristin and Erlend remain bound to each other, both by their children and by their initial vows, whose fulfillment they regard as a high and holy obligation. For Undset, as for Jean de Meun, fertility was inextricably linked to the power and beauties of nature, which is both a vividly living and a rich symbolic presence in the novel. Kristin's deep contentment in maternity reflects the new doctrine of procreation as the highest expression of erotic feeling, and maternal nurturing as the noblest female calling.

But Kristin and Erlend quarrel about her repeated pregnancies, which sap her energy, fade her beauty, and interfere with her sexual desire. After one bitter episode she confides in Erlend's brother Gunnulf, only to protest when he admonishes her: "You can't know how much I loved Erlend. And my children!" Gunnulf's reply echoes the lessons of the allegory:

> *Dear sister—all other love is merely a reflection of the heavens in the puddles of a muddy road. You will become sullied too if you allow yourself to sink into it. But if you always remember that it's a reflection of the light from that other home, then you will rejoice at its beauty and take good care that you do not destroy it by churning up the mire at the bottom.* (The Wife, 151)

Despite such earnest sermons from Kristin's spiritual advisers— and she had several—*Kristin Lavransdatter* resonates the most of all Undset's novels with the heightened physical and emotional experience of a woman in love. Kristin, Ragnhild, Aashild, and Eline all sacrifice their moral integrity for carnal joys, and nothing in their stories suggests that Undset thought passion was not worth claiming, even at such high cost. In essays written during the 1910s, Undset acknowledged that most people at some time experience emotions that may cause them to break society's rules, and erotic passion could be one such emotion. But this did not mean, as some of her contemporaries were arguing, that society's rules should be abolished in favor of "free love." Rules were established to protect innocent people, and were evidence of advanced civilization. It did mean that people must be prepared to pay the price for their transgressions—and that price may be high. As Fru Aashild, who had lost her position at the royal court for her illicit escapade with Herr Bjørn, explains to the young Kristin, "the grandest of days are costly indeed," but she cannot be so naive as to complain that she is left only with "sour, watered-down milk" after she has "drunk up all [her] wine and ale" (I.49).

Undset believed that this complex moral dilemma, which especially affected women, had inspired medieval chivalry. Because women controlled family bloodlines they had enormous power, but, paradoxically, it was a power that placed them under male control. In a 1919 essay she wrote:

Medieval literature was chivalrous in the sense that it was full of understanding and sympathy for woman, who was placed by nature in a uniquely difficult position: . . . [as a wife] she was destined to be subject to another person, and yet she was a freeborn soul with the same responsibility for her own doom or salvation as any man. Because medieval writers saw the world from this point of view, they portrayed the abused or betrayed woman with the utmost pathos, and the unfaithful wife with sympathy. . . . It is true, for example, that the Romance of the Rose, *which was long one of the favorite books of the Middle Ages, says many unattractive things about women. But Chaucer, who translated it to English, later acknowledged to Cupid and his ladies-in-waiting that this was sinful slander, and took upon himself the task of creating a legendarium of women martyred to love.*

This "legendarium" was *The Legend of Good Women*, Chaucer's palinode for Jean de Meun's discourtesies. But the "querelle de la *Roman de la rose*" (as French literary historians term the medieval debate about the book) did not end there for Chaucer; he was too much of a realist for simple solutions. His discussion of female sexuality and women's character continued from every possible angle in his later works, including *The Canterbury Tales*, from which Undset drew many details of character and incident for *Kristin Lavransdatter*.

Kristin Lavransdatter, too, ends with a palinode, in which Kristin reevaluates her life, the nature of love, her marriage, and her relation to God. It closely resembles Chaucer's use of the device in his greatest romance, *Troilus and Criseyde*, from the 1380s. As Chaucer's translator Nevill Coghill observes, "*Troilus & Criseyde* is a poetical study of natural human love, fully romantic, fully sexual; but in the last moments, in what is called 'the palinode' this sexual human love is suddenly placed in the context of a higher love, the love of God."

In Undset's version of the palinode, Kristin ponders on her deathbed which of her two remaining earthly treasures—her father's crucifix or her wedding ring—she should donate for masses for the dead. She chooses to give the ring, but when it is gone she feels its engraved *M* still imprinted on her flesh. In this moment, the ring and the cross—both symbols and titles of the trilogy's framing volumes—arch and meet across the center volume, titled *The Wife*. However impatient, stubborn, and rebellious Kristin has been, she suddenly understands that full engagement in her earthly marriage has indelibly marked her as God's own.

This discussion of *Kristin Lavransdatter*'s intertextual conversations is only one of dozens possible, yet the trilogy (like Undset's other novels about the Middle Ages) remains surprisingly little studied outside Norway. Especially in the English-speaking countries, Undset's work has been seriously neglected since her death in 1949. There seem to be several explanations for this.

In the first part of the century, Anglo-American academic critics favored Modernist writers, a category to which Undset does not belong. (Nor do most of her Norwegian contemporaries: Due to differences in historical circumstances, the Modernist movement had little impact on Norwegian literature until after World War II.) Nor does Undset fit comfortably into today's favored categories. Her interest in medieval theology and her own conversion to Catholicism underscored her resistance to social determinism—a red flag for many Marxists, feminists, and others suspicious of the Church's politics and power. (This objection, however, is not new; during the 1910s and 1920s, Undset's fiercely anti-Catholic countrymen were already calling her reactionary.) As the scholar Otto Reinert wryly observes, Undset is "unfashionable" because her novels are "product and not process literature," because they neither "invite deconstruction into multiple meanings held in suspension" nor mirror "the shattered certainties and the bottomless self-reflexiveness of postmodernism." Undset's stories about the lives of her contemporaries do mirror "shattered certainties" and "bottomless self-reflexiveness," to be sure, but her historical works about the Middle Ages were imagined as an anodyne to those modern forms of pain.

Kristin Lavransdatter has also suffered from waning interest in the historical novel (in the United States especially), as Hollywood has increasingly usurped its role. Blockbuster films and docudramas—forms that have established and regulated the shorter attention span of recent generations—now feed most popular interest in historical fiction. The status of English as today's international language is yet another factor; few Americans are familiar with the Scandinavian languages and literary traditions, which closes off some avenues of research to them and makes judging translations difficult.

All this probably does not matter to readers embarking on this final volume of the trilogy, who are already gripped by Undset's narrative power and can doubtless supply better reasons for reviving interest in *Kristin Lavransdatter* than for continuing its neglect. One of the most obvious reasons would be renewed interest in narratology—the sophisticated analysis of the relations within a story—which has grown with attention to alternative traditions such as women's writing and oral literature, which have always relied heavily on storytelling. In addition, realistic historical novels like *Kristin Lavransdatter* (and the Icelandic sagas as well) deserve a place in modern debates over the blurred line between fact and fiction which so occupies historians, biographers, journalists, textbook writers, filmmakers—everyone responsible for narratives about actual occurrences in the past.

This new English translation, the first since the 1920s, is itself sufficient reason to reassess Undset's finest novel. Translating Undset is a special challenge, because her scrupulous historical accuracy extended to her use of language. Already in 1900, in her first efforts at historical fiction, she struggled to find ways to give her text a tone of the past while still keeping the sound of natural speech. After much experimenting, she found the effect she wanted by limiting her vocabulary to words based on Old Norse roots, and by retaining Old Norse syntax—the order of subject and verb, arrangement of adjectives, and use of coordinating conjunctions. Twenty years later she had finely honed this method, which the scholar Einar Haugen documented in a 1942 study. Calling her achievement an "unusually extended linguistic tour de force," Haugen found virtually no foreign material in her usage, except (deliberately) Church Latin. (For example, she carefully excludes modern abstracts, which in Norwegian are mostly of Germanic origin.) By rejecting obtrusive dialect and keeping spelling and grammar ordinary, she creates a readable, natural-sounding prose with subtle reminiscences of Old Norse, more like a musical undertone than an imitation.

The vigorousness of this style does not translate easily to English, where the flowery chivalric tradition (as in Sir Thomas Malory's *Morte d'Arthur*) and its later imitators (William Morris, for example), with their fondness for superfluous rhetorical adornment, have interfered with Anglo-Saxon directness. Translators must strike a balance between the falsely archaic and the falsely modern, while still trying to respect Undset's careful usage. Whereas it is easy to make the English sound too quaintly antique, it is also easy to "correct" Undset's evocative syntax, to flatten her rhythms and make her language too modern and ungraceful.

Until now, *Kristin Lavransdatter* has been available only in Charles Archer's original translation, which buries her forthright style under fussy Victorian archaisms. Archer also leaves out a great many passages of the text. Some omissions, such as Gunnulf's long, two-part story of his youthful experiences in Rome in Volume II, seem arbitrary and editorial—dubiously so, as the excision leaves Gunnulf a more colorless and marginal character than

Undset meant him to be. Others, such as details of Kristin and Erlend's lovemaking at Brynhild Fluga's house of ill-repute in Volume
I, may have been deemed too sexually explicit for Anglo-American
audiences in the 1920s. In one case—the removal of the name of
King Magnus's "secret sin" in Volume II—such prudery makes following the story difficult.

The strengths of Tiina Nunnally's translation are precisely the
weaknesses of Archer's: She has restored the complete text, and
she has pruned it of the false ring of English archaisms ("I trow,"
"methinks") so favored by Victorian medievalists. Readers must
judge the results for themselves, but comparing Archer's and Nunnally's versions of this short passage—soon to be encountered on
the first page of *The Cross*—may help.

Archer:
> *But elsewhere in the Dale 'twas not the use for the mas-
> ter's womenfolk of the great manors to abide themselves at
> the sæters. Kristin knew that if she did it, there would be talk
> and wonderment among the folks.*
> *—In God's name, then, they must even talk. Sure it was
> that they gossiped about her and hers whether or no.*

Nunnally:
> *But elsewhere it wasn't customary for the women of the
> gentry on the large estates to go up to the pastures. Kristin
> knew that if she did so, people would be surprised and
> would gossip about it.*
> *In God's name, then, let them talk. No doubt they were
> already talking about her and her family.*

May this edition of *Kristin Lavransdatter* keep us "talking about
her and her family" for many generations more.

Sherrill Harbison
Amherst, Massachusetts
August 1999

SUGGESTIONS FOR FURTHER READING

RESOURCES FOR SIGRID UNDSET

This list focuses on works relevant to *Kristin Lavransdatter*. For a more complete list of works by and about Undset (up to 1963), see Ida Packness, *Sigrid Undset Bibliografi* (Norsk Bibliografisk Bibliotek, Bd. 22, Universitetsforlaget, Oslo, 1963).

Allen, W. Gore. *Renaissance in the North* (New York: Sheed & Ward, 1936).

Amadou, Anne-Lisa. *Å gi kjærligheten et språk: Syv studier i Sigrid Undsets forfatterskap* (Oslo: H. Aschehoug & Co., 1994).

Anderson, Gidske. *Sigrid Undset, et liv* (Oslo: Gyldendal, 1989).

Bang, Elisabeth Wikborg. *Sigrid Undset og "Kristin Lavransdatter": En mesterverk blir til* (Drammen, Norway: Harald Lyche & Co., n.d.).

Bayerschmidt, Carl. *Sigrid Undset* (New York: Twayne, 1970).

Bliksrud, Liv. "Narcissisme som litterært og psykologisk motiv hos Sigrid Undset," in *Andre Linjer*, eds. Kari Ellen Vogt and Liv Bliksrud (Oslo: Solum, 1982), pp. 133–43.

———. *Natur og normer hos Sigrid Undset* (Oslo: H. Aschehoug & Co., 1988).

———. *Sigrid Undset* (Oslo: Gyldendal, 1997).

———. "Sigrid Undset og ættesagaen," in *Atlantisk dåd og drøm, 17 essays om Island/Norge,* ed. Asbjørn Aarnes (Oslo: H. Aschehoug & Co., 1998).

Blom, Ådel. "Sigrid Undset og bruken av ballader i *Kristin Lavransdatter,*" *Nordisk Tidskrift* vol. 58, no. 1 (1982), pp. 229–48.

Bovenizer, David A. "Mr. Lytle's *Kristin,*" in *Sigrid Undset on Saints and Sinners, New Translations and Studies,* Papers Presented at a Conference Sponsored by the Wethersfield Institute, New York City, April 24, 1993, ed. Deal W. Hudson (San Francisco: Ignatius Press, 1993), pp. 148–64.

Brøgger, Niels Christian. *Korset og rosen: En studie i Sigrid Undsets middelalderdiktning* (Oslo: H. Aschehoug & Co., 1952).

Danbolt, Gunnar. "En atterglans av Guds rikes herlighet: Noen tanker om Sigrid Undset og middelalderens billedkunst," in *Sigrid Undset og middelalderen—og vor egen tid*, ed. Inge Eidsvåg, Nansenskolens årbok 1994 (Oslo: Universitetsforlaget, 1994), pp. 25–52.

Deschamps, Nicole. *Sigrid Undset, ou la morale de la passion* (Montreal: Montreal University Press, 1966).

Dyade. Special number, ed. Carl Henrik Grøndal, "Sigrid Undset vurdert i utlandet," vol. 14, no. 2 (1982).

Emerson, Katherine T. "A Chaucer Borrowing in *Kristin Lavransdatter*," *Notes and Queries*, new series, vol. 2, no. 9 (September 1955), pp. 370–71.

Engelstad, Carl Fredrik. *Mennesker og makter: Sigrid Undsets middelalderromaner* (Oslo: H. Aschehoug & Co., 1940).

Eriksen, Trond Berg. "Sigrid Undset og middelaldermennesket," in *Sigrid Undset og middelalderen—og vor egen tid*, Nansenskolens årbok 1994, ed. Inge Eidsvåg (Oslo: Universitetsforlaget, 1994), pp. 13–24.

Gustafson, Alrik. *Six Scandinavian Novelists* (Princeton: Princeton University Press, 1940).

Harbison, Sherrill. "Medieval Aspects of Narcissism in Sigrid Undset's Modern Novels," *Scandinavian Studies*, vol. 63, no. 4 (Autumn 1991), pp. 464–73.

Haugen, Einar. *Norwegian Word Studies*, vol. 1: *On the Vocabularies of Sigrid Undset and Ivar Aasen* (Madison: University of Wisconsin Press, 1942).

Heltoft, Bente. *Livssyn og diktning: Strukturgrundlaget i Sigrid Undsets romaner* (Oslo: H. Aschehoug & Co., 1985).

Krane, Borghild. *Sigrid Undset, liv og meninger* (Oslo: Gyldendal, 1970).

Larsen, Hanna Astrup. "Sigrid Undset: II, Medieval Works," *American-Scandinavian Review* (July 1929), pp. 406–14.

Lytle, Andrew. *Kristin: A Reading* (Columbia: University of Missouri Press, 1992).

McFarlane, James Walter. *Ibsen and the Temper of Norwegian Literature* (London and New York: Oxford University Press, 1960).

Michaud, Ginette. "Merveilleux/Langue/Histoire: Le chemin sauvage d'une saga historique," *Liberté*, vol. 21, no. 1 (1979), pp. 96–117.

Moen, Hanne Helliesen. *Opplysninger til Sigrid Undsets Middelalderromaner* (Oslo: H. Aschehoug & Co., 1950).

Mørkhagen, Sverre. *Kristins verden: Om norsk middelalder på Kristin Lavransdatters tid* (Oslo: Cappelens, 1995).

Ørjasæter, Tordis. *Menneskenes hjerter: Sigrid Undset, en livshistorie* (Oslo: H. Aschehoug & Co., 1993).

Paasche, Fredrik. "Sigrid Undset og norsk middelalder," *Samtiden* 1929, pp. 1–12.

Paasche, Stina. "Fredrik Paasche, Sigrid Undset, och *Kristin Lavransdatter*," *Edda* 1975:6, pp. 377–82.

Reinert, Otto. "Unfashionable Kristin Lavransdatter," *Scandinavian Studies*, vol. 71, no. 1 (Spring 1999), pp. 67–80.

Rønning, Helge. "Middelalderens lys—mellomkrigstidens lyst—Om den historiske roman som genre og Sigrid Undsets middelalderromaner," *Vinduet* 37:3 (1983), pp. 48–55.

Ruch, Velma. "Sigrid Undset's *Kristin Lavransdatter*: A Study of Its Literary Art and Reception in America, England, and Scandinavia," diss., University of Wisconsin, Madison, 1957.

Schacht, C. "Condition féminine et vie chrétienne: Relire Christine Lavransdatter," *La vie spirituelle*, 63 année, n. 654 (1983), pp. 179–93.

Solberg, Olav. *Tekst møter tekst: Kristin Lavransdatter og mellomalderen* (Oslo: H. Aschehoug & Co., 1997).

Steen, Ellisiv. *Kristin Lavransdatter: En estetisk studie*, 2nd. ed. (Oslo: H. Aschehoug & Co., 1969).

Svarstad, Christianne Undset. "Disposisjonen til *Kristin Lavransdatter*," *Edda* 1955, pp. 349–52.

Thorn, Finn. *Sigrid Undset: Kristentro og kirkesyn* (Oslo: H. Aschehoug & Co., 1975).

Undset, Sigrid. "En bok som blev et vendepunkt i mitt liv," in *Artikler og essays om litteratur*, ed. Jan Fr. Daniloff (Oslo: H. Aschehoug & Co., 1986), pp. 300–308.

———. *Et kvinnesynspunkt* (1919) (Oslo: H. Aschehoug & Co., 1982).

————. *Gunnar's Daughter*. Trans. Arthur G. Chater; ed., Introduction and Notes Sherrill Harbison (New York: Penguin, 1998).

————. *Kjære Dea*. Ed. Christianne Undset Svarstad (Oslo: Cappelens, 1979).

————. "Klosterlivet," in *Norsk kulturhistorie, Billedet av folkets dagligliv gjennem årtusener*, eds. Anders Bugge and Sverre Steen, vol. 2, *Fra tunet til bystredet* (Oslo: J. W. Cappelens, 1939), pp. 385–432.

————. *Kristin Lavransdatter. I: The Wreath* (1920), *II: The Wife* (1921), trans. Tiina Nunnally (New York: Penguin, 1997, 1999).

————. *The Master of Hestviken* (1925–27), trans. Arthur G. Chater (1928) (New York: Knopf/Plume, 1978).

————. "Om folkeviser," in *Artikler og essays om litteratur*, ed. Jan Fr. Daniloff (Oslo: H. Aschehoug & Co., 1986), pp. 232–83.

————. "Pilgrimmene," *Den norske turistforenings årbok* (n.p., 1930), pp. 65–71.

————. *Saga of Saints*, trans. E. C. Ramsden (New York: Longmans Green, 1934).

————. Trans., *Tre sagaer om Islændinger* (Christiania, Norway: H. Aschehoug & Co., 1923).

————. Ed., Introduction, *True and Untrue, and Other Norse Tales* (New York: Knopf, 1945).

Whitehouse, J. C. "Religion as Fulfilment in the Novels of Sigrid Undset," *Renascence*, vol. 38, no. 1 (1986), pp. 2–12.

Winsnes, A. H. *Sigrid Undset: A Study in Christian Realism*, trans. P. G. Foote (1953) (Westport, Conn.: Greenwood Press, 1970).

Ystad, Vigdis. "Ideologikritisk og/eller vitenskapelig? Helge Rønnings fortolkning av Sigrid Undset," *Vinduet* 38:1 (1984), pp. 60–65.

————. "Kristin Lavransdatter og historien," in *Sigrid Undset idag*, Forord av Pål Espolin Johnson (Oslo: H. Aschehoug & Co., 1982), pp. 101–32.

————. "Sensualisme og ordenstrang: Liv og lov i Sigrid Undsets diktning," *Nytt norsk tidskrift*, vol. 5, no. 1 (1988), pp. 63–81.

RELATED WORKS

Brundage, James A. *Law, Sex and Christian Society in Medieval Europe* (Chicago and London: University of Chicago Press, 1987).

Capellanus, Andreas. *The Art of Courtly Love by Andreas Capellanus*, trans. John F. Parry, Columbia University Records of Civilization: Sources and Studies No. 33 (New York: Columbia University Press, 1941).

Chaucer, Geoffrey. *The Works of Geoffrey Chaucer*, ed. F. N. Robinson (Cambridge, England: Riverside Press, 1957).

———. *Troilus and Criseyde*, trans. Nevill Coghill (Harmondsworth, England: Penguin, 1971).

The Complete Sagas of Icelanders, 5 vols., gen. ed. Viðar Hreinsson, Introduction Robert Kellogg (Rejkjavík: Leifur Eiriksson Publishing Co., 1997).

Duby, Georges. *The Knight, The Lady, and The Priest: The Making of Modern Marriage in Medieval France*, trans. Barbara Bray (New York: Pantheon, 1983).

Fischer, Gerhard. *Oslo under Eikaberg: 1050, 1624, 1950* (Oslo: H. Aschehoug & Co., 1950).

Goldin, Frederick. *The Mirror of Narcissus in the Courtly Love Lyric* (Ithaca, N.Y.: Cornell University Press, 1967).

Jonsson, Bengt R., Svale Solheim, and Eva Danielson, eds. *The Types of Scandinavian Medieval Ballad*, Institute for Comparative Research in Human Culture, Oslo, in collaboration with Mortan Nolsøe and W. Edson Richmond (Oslo/Bergen/Tromsø: Universitetsforlaget, 1978).

Lewis, C. S. *The Allegory of Love* (Oxford University Press, 1936).

Lorris, Guillaume de, and Jean de Meun. *The Romance of the Rose*, trans. Harry W. Robbins (New York: Dutton, 1962).

Naess, Harald, ed. *A History of Norwegian Literature* (Lincoln and London: University of Nebraska Press, in cooperation with the American Scandinavian Foundation, 1993).

Olrik, Alex, ed. *A Book of Danish Ballads*, trans E. M. Smith-Dampier (1939) (Freeport, N.Y.: Books for Libraries Press, 1968).

Pulsiano, Phillip J., and Kirsten Wolf, eds. *Medieval Scandinavia: An Encyclopedia* (Hamden, Conn.: Garland, 1993).

Sawyer, Birgit, and Peter Sawyer. *Medieval Scandinavia: From Conversion to Reformation, Ca. 800–1500* (Minneapolis: University of Minnesota Press, 1993).

Schia, Erik. *Oslo innerst i viken: Liv og verk i middelalderbyen* (Oslo: H. Aschehoug & Co., 1991).

Slott-Møller, Agnes. *Folkevisebilleder* (København: H. Aschehoug & Co., 1923).

Syndergaard, Larry E. *English Translations of the Scandinavian Medieval Ballads: An Analytical Guide and Bibliography* (Turku, Finland: Nordic Institute of Folklore, 1995).

A NOTE ON THE TRANSLATION

This translation is based on the original Norwegian edition of *Korset*, published in 1922 by H. Aschehoug & Company, Oslo.

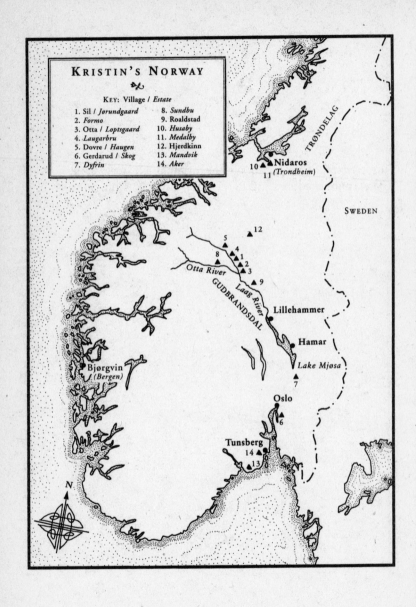

KRISTIN'S NORWAY

KEY: Village / *Estate*

1. Sil / *Jørundgaard*
2. *Formo*
3. Otta / *Loptsgaard*
4. *Laugarbru*
5. Dovre / *Haugen*
6. Gerdarud / *Skog*
7. *Dyfrin*
8. *Sundbu*
9. Roaldstad
10. *Husaby*
11. *Medalby*
12. *Hjerdkinn*
13. *Mandvik*
14. *Aker*

TRØNDELAG

SWEDEN

10 Nidaros
11 (Trondheim)

12

5
4
8 1
2
Otta River 3
9

Laag River

GUDBRANDSDAL

Lillehammer

Hamar

Lake Mjøsa

7

Bjørgvin
(Bergen)

Oslo

6

Tunsberg
14
13

N

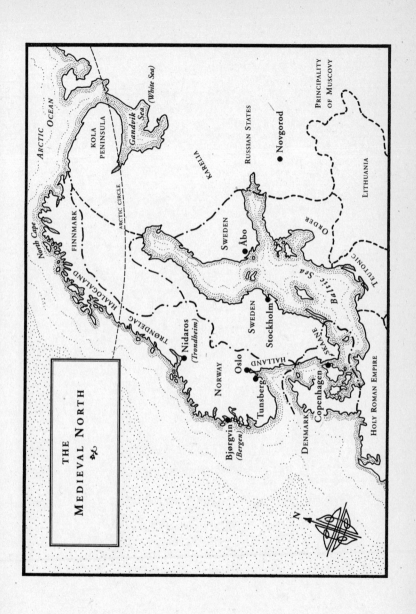

PART I

HONOR AMONG KIN

CHAPTER 1

DURING THE SECOND year that Erlend Nikulaussøn and Kristin Lavransdatter lived at Jørundgaard, Kristin decided to spend the summer up in the mountain pastures.

She had been thinking about this ever since winter. At Skjenne it had long been the custom for the mistress herself to stay in the mountain pastures; in the past a daughter from the manor had once been lured into the hills, and afterward her mother insisted on living in the mountains each summer. But in many ways they had their own customs at Skjenne; people in the region were used to it and expected as much.

But elsewhere it wasn't customary for the women of the gentry on the large estates to go up to the pastures. Kristin knew that if she did so, people would be surprised and would gossip about it.

In God's name, then, let them talk. No doubt they were already talking about her and her family.

Audun Torbergssøn owned nothing more than his weapons and the clothes on his back when he was wed to Ingebjørg Nikulausdatter of Loptsgaard. He had been a groom for the bishop of Hamar. It was back when the bishop came north to consecrate the new church that Ingebjørg suffered the misfortune. Nikulaus Sigurdssøn took it hard at first, swearing by God and man that a stableboy would never be his son-in-law. But Ingebjørg gave birth to twins, and people said with a laugh that Nikulaus evidently thought it would be too much to support them on his own. He allowed his daughter to marry Audun.

This happened two years after Kristin's wedding. It had not been forgotten, and people probably still thought of Audun as a stranger to the region; he was from Hadland, of good family, but his lineage had become quite impoverished. And the man himself was not well liked in Sil; he was obstinate, hardheaded, and slow to forget either bad or good, but he was a most enterprising farmer, with a fair knowledge of the law. In many ways Audun Torbergssøn was now a respected man in the parish and a man with whom people were loath to become foes.

Kristin thought about Audun's broad, tanned face with the thick, curly red hair and beard and those sharp, small blue eyes of his. He looked like many other men she had seen; she had seen such faces among their servants at Husaby, among Erlend's men and ship's crew.

She sighed. It must be easier for such a man to assert himself as he sat there on his wife's ancestral estate since he had never ruled over anything else.

All winter and spring Kristin spent time talking to Frida Styrkaarsdatter, who had come with them from Trøndelag and was in charge of all her other maids. Again and again she would tell the woman that such and such was the way they did things here in the valley during the summer, this was what the haymakers were used to getting, and this was how things were done at harvest time. Surely Frida must remember how Kristin had done things the year before. For she wanted everything on the manor to be just as it was during Ragnfrid Ivarsdatter's time.

But to come right out and say that she would not be there on the farm during the summer, that was hard for her to do. She had been the mistress of Jørundgaard for two winters and a summer, and she knew that if she went up to the mountain pastures now, it would be the same as running away.

She realized that Erlend was in a terribly difficult position. Ever since the days when he sat on his foster mother's knee, he had never known anything other than that he was born to command and rule over everything and everyone around him. And if the man had allowed himself to be ruled and commanded by others, at least he had never been aware of this himself.

He couldn't possibly feel the way he outwardly seemed. He must be unhappy here. She herself . . . Her father's estate at the bottom of the quiet, closed-in valley, the flat fields along the curve of the gleaming river through the alder woods, the farms on the cultivated land far below at the foot of the mountain, and the steep slopes above, with the gray clefts against the sky overhead,

pale slides of scree and the spruce forest and leafy woods clamber-
ing upward through the meadows from the valley—no, this no
longer seemed to her the most beautiful and safest home in the
world. It felt closed off. Surely Erlend must think that it was ugly
and confining and unpleasant.

But no one could tell anything from his appearance except that
he seemed content.

On the day when they let out the livestock at Jørundgaard, she finally managed to speak of it, in the evening as they ate their supper. Erlend was picking through the fish platter in search of a good
piece; in surprise he sat there with his fingers in the dish while he
stared at his wife. Then Kristin added quickly that it was mostly
because of the throat ailment that was rampant among the children in the valley. Munan wasn't strong; she wanted to take him
and Lavrans along with her up to the mountains.

Well, said Erlend. In that case it would be advisable for Ivar and
Skule to go with her too.

The twins leaped up from the bench. During the rest of the meal
they both chattered at once. They wanted to go with Erling, who
would be camping north among the Gray Peaks with the sheep.
Three years before, the sheepherders from Sil had caught a
poacher and killed him near his stone hut in the Boar Range; he
was a man who had been banished to the forest from Østerdal. As
soon as the servants got up from the table, Ivar and Skule brought
into the hall all the weapons they owned and sat down to tinker
with them.

A little later that evening Kristin set off southward with Simon
Andressøn's daughters and her own sons Gaute and Lavrans.
Arngjerd Simonsdatter had been at Jørundgaard most of the winter. The maiden was now fifteen years old, and one day during
Christmas at Formo, Simon had mentioned that Arngjerd ought to
learn something more than what they could teach her at home; she
was just as skilled as the serving maids. Kristin had then offered to
take the girl home with her and teach her as best she could, for she
could see that Simon dearly loved his daughter and worried a great
deal about her future. And the child needed to learn other ways
than those practiced at Formo. Since the death of his wife's parents
Simon Andressøn was now one of the richest men in the region.

He managed his properties with care and good sense, and he oversaw the farm work at Formo with zeal and intelligence. But indoors things were handled poorly; the serving women were in charge of everything. Whenever Simon noticed that the disarray and slovenliness in the house had surpassed all bounds, he would hire one or two more maids, but he never spoke of such things to his wife and seemed neither to wish nor to expect that she should pay more attention to the housekeeping. It was almost as if he didn't yet consider her to be fully grown up, but he was exceedingly kind and amenable toward Ramborg and was constantly showering her and the children with gifts.

Kristin grew fond of Arngjerd after she got to know her. The maiden was not pretty, but she was clever, gentle, good-hearted, nimble-fingered, and diligent. When the young girl accompanied her around the house or sat by her side in the weaving room in the evenings, Kristin often thought that she wished one of her own children had been a daughter. A daughter would spend more time with her mother.

She was thinking about that on this evening as she led Lavrans by the hand and looked at the two children, Gaute and Arngjerd, who were walking ahead of her along the road. Ulvhild was running about, stomping through the brittle layer of nighttime ice on the puddles of water. She was pretending to be some kind of animal and had turned her red cloak around so that the white rabbit fur was on the outside.

Down in the valley in the dusk the shadows were deepening across the bare brown fields. But the air of the spring evening seemed sated with light. The first stars were sparkling, wet and white, high up in the sky, where the limpid green was turning blue, moving toward darkness and night. Above the black rim of the mountains on the other side of the valley a border of yellow light still lingered, and its glow lit up the scree covering the steep slope that towered above them as they walked. At the very top, where the snowdrifts jutted out over the ridges, the snow glistened, and underneath glittered the glaciers, which gave birth to the streams rushing and splashing everywhere down through the scree. The sound of water completely filled the air of the countryside; from below reverberated the loud roar of the river. And the singing of birds came from the groves and leafy shrubbery on all sides.

Once Ulvhild stopped, picked up a stone, and threw it toward the sound of the birds. Her big sister grabbed her arm, and she walked on calmly for a while. But then she tore herself away and ran down the hill until Gaute shouted after her.

They had reached the place where the road headed into the forest; from the thickets came the ringing of a steel bow. Inside the woods snow lay on the ground, and the air smelled cold and fresh. A little farther on, in a small clearing, stood Erlend with Ivar and Skule.

Ivar had taken a shot at a squirrel; the arrow was stuck high up in the trunk of a fir tree, and now he was trying to get it down. He pitched stone after stone at it; the huge mast tree resonated when he struck the trunk.

"Wait a minute. I'll try to see if I can shoot it down for you," said his father. He shook his cape back over his shoulders, placed an arrow in his bow, and took aim rather carelessly in the uncertain light among the trees. The string twanged; the arrow whistled through the air and buried itself in the tree trunk right next to the boy's. Erlend took out another arrow and shot again; one of the two arrows sticking out of the tree clattered down from branch to branch. The shaft of the other one had splintered, but the point was still embedded in the tree.

Skule ran into the snow to pick up the two arrows. Ivar stood and stared up at the treetop.

"It's mine—the one that's still up there, Father! It's buried up to the shaft. That was a powerful shot, Father!" Then he proceeded to explain to Gaute why he hadn't hit the squirrel.

Erlend laughed softly and straightened his cape. "Are you going to turn back now, Kristin? I'm setting off for home; we're planning to go after wood grouse early in the morning, Naakkve and I."

Kristin told him briskly no, that she wanted to accompany the maidens to their manor. She wanted to have a few words with her sister tonight.

"Then Ivar and Skule can go with Mother and escort her home if I can stay with you, Father," said Gaute.

Erlend lifted Ulvhild Simonsdatter up in his arms in farewell. Because she was so pretty and pink and fresh, with her brown curls under the white fur hood, he kissed her before he set her back down and then turned and headed for home with Gaute.

Now that Erlend had nothing else to occupy him, he was always in the company of a few of his sons. Ulvhild took her aunt's hand and walked on a bit; then she started running again, rushing in between Ivar and Skule. Yes, she was a beautiful child, but wild and unruly. If they had had a daughter, Erlend would have no doubt taken her along and played with her too.

At Formo Simon was alone in the house with his little son when they came in. He was sitting in the high seat[1] in the middle of the long table, looking at Andres. The child was kneeling on the outer bench and playing with several old wooden pegs, trying to make them stand on their heads on the table. As soon as Ulvhild saw this, she forgot about greeting her father. She climbed right up onto the bench next to her brother, grabbed him by the back of the neck, and pounded his face against the table while she screamed that they were *her* pegs; Father had given them to *her*.

Simon stood up to separate the children; then he happened to knock over a little pottery dish standing near his elbow. It fell to the floor and shattered.

Arngjerd crawled under the table and gathered up the pieces. Simon took them from her and looked at them, greatly dismayed. "Your mother is going to be angry." It was a pretty little flower-painted dish made of shiny white ceramic that Sir Andres Darre had brought home from France. Simon explained that Helga had inherited it, but she had given it to Ramborg. The women considered it a great treasure. At that moment he heard his wife out in the entryway, and he hid his hands, holding the pottery shards, behind his back.

Ramborg came in and greeted her sister and nephews. She took off Ulvhild's cloak, and the maiden ran over to her father and clung to him.

"Look how fine you are today, Ulvhild. I see that you're wearing your silver belt on a workday." But he couldn't hug the child because his hands were full.

Ulvhild shouted that she had been visiting her aunt Kristin at Jørundgaard; that was why Mother had dressed her so nicely in the morning.

"Yes, your mother keeps you dressed so splendid and grand;

they could set you up on the shrine on the north side of the church, the way you look," said Simon, smiling. The only work Ramborg ever did was to sew garments for her daughter; Ulvhild was always magnificently clothed.

"Why are you standing there like that?" Ramborg asked her husband.

Simon showed her the pottery pieces. "I don't know what you're going to say about this—"

Ramborg took them from him. "You didn't have to stand there looking like such a fool because of this."

Kristin felt ill at ease as she sat there. It was true that Simon had looked quite ridiculous as he stood there hiding the broken pieces in such a childish manner, but Ramborg didn't need to mention it.

"I expected you to be mad because your dish was broken," said her husband.

"Yes, you always seem to be so afraid that something will make me mad—and something so frivolous," replied Ramborg. And the others saw that she was close to tears.

"You know quite well, Ramborg, that's not the only way I act," said Simon. "And it's not just frivolous things either . . ."

"I wouldn't know," replied his wife in the same tone of voice. "It has never been your habit, Simon, to talk to me about important matters."

She turned on her heel and walked toward the entryway. Simon stood still for a moment, staring after her. When he sat down, his son Andres came over and wanted to climb onto his father's lap. Simon picked him up and sat there with his chin resting on the child's head, but he didn't seem to be listening to the boy's chatter.

After a while Kristin ventured, a little hesitantly, "Ramborg isn't so young anymore, Simon. Your oldest child is already seven winters old."

"What do you mean?" asked Simon, and it seemed to her that his voice was unnecessarily sharp.

"I mean nothing more than that . . . perhaps my sister thinks you find her too young to . . . maybe if you could try to let her take charge of things more here on the estate, together with you."

"*My* wife takes charge of as much as she likes," replied Simon heatedly. "I don't demand that she do more than she wants to do, but I've never refused to allow Ramborg to manage anything here at Formo. If you think otherwise, then it's because you don't know—"

"No, no," said Kristin. "But it has seemed to me, brother-in-law, that now and then you don't consider Ramborg to be any older than when you married her. You should remember, Simon—"

"*You* should remember—" he set the child down and jumped to his feet—"that Ramborg and I came to an agreement; you and I never could." His wife came into the room at that moment, carrying a container of ale for the guests. Simon quickly went over to her and placed his hand on her shoulder. "Did you hear that, Ramborg? Your sister is standing here saying that she doesn't think you're happy with your lot." He laughed.

Ramborg looked up; her big dark eyes glittered strangely. "Why is that? I got what I wanted, just as you did, Kristin. If we two sisters can't be happy, then I don't know . . ." And she too laughed.

Kristin stood there, flushed and angry. She refused to accept the ale bowl. "No, it's already late; time for us to head back home now." And she looked around for her sons.

"Oh no, Kristin!" Simon took the bowl from his wife and drank a toast. "Don't be angry. You shouldn't take so much to heart every word that falls between the closest kin. Sit down for a while and rest your feet and be good enough to forget it if I've spoken to you in any way that I shouldn't have."

Then he said, "I'm tired," and he stretched and yawned. He asked how far they had gotten with the spring farm work at Jørundgaard. Here at Formo they had plowed up all the fields north of the manor road.

Kristin left as soon as she thought it was seemly. No, Simon didn't need to accompany her, she said when he picked up his hooded cape and axe; she had her big sons with her. But he insisted and also asked Ramborg to walk along with them, at least up through the fenced fields. She didn't usually agree to this, but tonight she went with them all the way up to the road.

Outdoors the night was black and clear with glittering stars. The faint, warm and pleasant smell of newly manured fields gave a springtime odor to the night frost. The sound of water was everywhere in the darkness around them.

Simon and Kristin walked north; the three boys ran on ahead. She could sense that the man at her side wanted to say something, but she didn't feel like making it easier for him because she was still quite furious. Of course she was fond of her brother-in-law, but there had to be a limit to what he could say and then brush aside afterward—as merely something between kinsmen. He had to realize that because he had stood by them so loyally during their troubles, it wasn't easy for her when he grew quick-tempered or rude. It was difficult for her to take him to task. She thought about the first winter, not long after they had arrived in the village. Ramborg had sent for her because Simon lay in bed with boils in his throat and was terribly ill. He suffered from this ailment now and then. But when Kristin arrived at Formo and went in to see the man, he refused to allow her to touch him or even look at him. He was so irate that Ramborg, greatly distressed, begged her sister's forgiveness for asking her to come. Simon had not been any kinder toward her, she said, the first time he fell ill after they were married and she tried to nurse him. Whenever he had throat boils, he would retreat to the old building they called the Sæmund house, and he couldn't stand to have anyone near him except for a horrid, filthy, and lice-ridden old man named Gunstein, who had served at Dyfrin since before Simon was born. Later Simon would no doubt come to see his sister-in-law to make amends. He didn't want anyone to see him when he was ill like that; he thought it such a pitiful shortcoming for a full-grown man. Kristin had replied, rather crossly, that she didn't understand—it was neither sinful nor shameful to suffer from throat boils.

Simon accompanied her all the way up to the bridge, and as they walked, they exchanged only a few words about the weather and the farm work, repeating things they had already said back at the house. Simon said good night, but then he asked abruptly, "Do you know, Kristin, how I might have offended Gaute that the boy should be so angry with me?"

"Gaute?" she said in surprise.

"Yes, haven't you noticed? He avoids me, but if he can't help meeting me, he barely opens his mouth when I speak to him."

Kristin shook her head. No, she hadn't noticed, "unless you said something in jest and he took it wrong, child that he is."

He heard in her voice that she was smiling; then he laughed a bit and said, "But I can't remember anything of the sort."

And with that he again bade her good night and left.

It was completely quiet at Jørundgaard. The main house was dark, with the ashes raked over the fire in the hearth. Bjørgulf was awake and said that his father and brothers had left some time ago.

Over in the master's bed Munan was sleeping alone. Kristin took him in her arms after she lay down.

It was so difficult to talk about it to Erlend when he didn't seem to realize himself that he shouldn't take the older boys and run off with them into the woods when there was more than enough work to be done on the estate.

That Erlend himself should walk behind a plow was not something she had ever expected. He probably wouldn't be able to do a proper job of it either. And Ulf wouldn't like it much if Erlend interfered in the running of the farm. But her sons could not grow up in the same way as their father had been allowed to do, learning to use weapons, hunting animals, and amusing himself with his horses or poring over a chessboard with a priest who would slyly attempt to cajole the knight's son into acquiring a little knowledge of Latin and writing, of singing and the playing of stringed instruments. She had so few servants on the estate because she thought that her sons should learn even as children that they would have to become accustomed to farm work. It now looked doubtful that there would be any knighthood for Erlend's sons.

But Gaute was the only one of the boys who had any inclination for farming. Gaute was a hard worker, but he was thirteen years old, and it could only be expected that he would rather go with his father when Erlend came and invited him to come along.

It was difficult to talk to Erlend about this because it was Kristin's firm resolve that her husband should never hear from her a single word that he might perceive as a criticism of his behavior or a complaint over the fate that he had brought upon himself and his sons. That meant it wasn't easy to make the father understand that his sons had to get used to doing the work themselves on their estate. If only Ulf would speak of it, she thought.

When they moved the livestock from the spring pastures up to Høvringen, Kristin went along up to the mountains. She didn't want to take the twins with her. They would soon be eleven years old, and they were the most unruly and willful of her children; it was even harder for her to handle them because the two boys stuck together in everything. If she managed to get Ivar alone, he was good and obedient enough, but Skule was hot-tempered and stubborn. And when the brothers were together, Ivar said and did everything that Skule demanded.

ONE DAY EARLY in the fall Kristin went outside about the time of midafternoon prayers. The herdsman had said that a short distance down the mountainside, if she followed the riverbed, there was supposed to be an abundance of mulleins on a cleared slope.

Kristin found the spot, a steep incline baking in the direct glare of the sun; it was the very best time for picking the flowers. They grew in thick clumps over the heaps of stones and around the gray stubble. Tall, pale yellow stalks, richly adorned with small open stars. Kristin set Munan to picking raspberries in among some brushwood from which he wouldn't be able to escape without her help; she told the dog to stay with him and keep watch. Then she took out her knife and began cutting mulleins, constantly casting an eye at the little child. Lavrans stayed at her side and cut flowers too.

She was always fearful for her two small children in the mountains. Otherwise she was not afraid of the people up there anymore. Many had already gone home from the pastures, but she was thinking of staying until after the Feast of the Birth of Mary. It was pitch black at night now, and vile when the wind blew hard—vile if they had to go outside late at night. But the weather had been so fine up in the heights, while down below, the countryside was parched this year and the grazing was poor. The men would have to stay up in the mountains during both the late fall and winter, but her father had said that he had never noticed anyone haunting their high pastures during the winter.

Kristin stopped under a solitary spruce tree in the middle of the hillside; she stood with her hands wrapped around the heavy weight of the flower stalks that were draped over her arm. From here she could look northward and see halfway to Dovre. In many places the grain was gathered in shocks in the fields.

The hillsides were yellow and sun-scorched over there too. But it was never truly green here in the valley, she thought, not as green as in Trøndelag.

Yes, she longed for the home they had had there: the manor that stood so high and magnificent on the broad breast of the ridge, with fields and meadows spreading out all around, extending below to the cluster of leafy woods that sloped down toward the lake at the bottom of the valley. The vast view across low, forested hills that undulated, wave upon wave, south toward the Dovre Range. And the lush meadows so thick and tall in the summer, red with crimson flowers beneath the red evening sky, the second crop of hay so succulent and green in the autumn.

Yes, sometimes she even felt a longing for the fjord. The skerries of Birgsi, the docks with the boats and ships, the boathouses, the smell of tar and fishing nets and the sea—all those things she had disliked so much when she first went north.

Erlend must be longing for that smell, and for the sea and the sea wind.

She missed everything that she had once found so wearisome: all the housekeeping, the scores of servants, the clamor of Erlend's men as they rode into the courtyard with clanging weapons and jangling harnesses, the strangers who came and went, bringing them great news from all over the land and gossip about people in the town and countryside. Now she realized how quiet her life had become when all this had been silenced.

Nidaros with its churches and cloisters and banquets at the great estates in town. She longed to walk through the streets with her own servingman and maid accompanying her, to climb the loft stairs to the merchants' shops, to choose and reject wares, to step aboard the boats on the river to buy goods: English linen hats, elegant shawls, wooden horses with riders that would thrust out their lances if you pulled a string. She thought about the meadows outside town near Nidareid where she used to walk with her children, looking at the trained dogs and bears of the wandering minstrels, buying gingerbread and walnuts.

And there were times when she longed to dress in her finery again. A silk shift and a delicate, fine wimple. The sleeveless surcoat made of pale blue velvet that Erlend had bought for her the winter before the misfortune befell them. It was edged with marten

fur along the deep cut of the bodice and around the wide arm-
holes, which reached all the way down to her hips, revealing the
belt underneath.

And occasionally she longed for . . . oh no, she should be sensible and be happy about *that*—happy as long as she was free from
having any more children. When she fell ill this autumn after the
great slaughtering . . . It was best that it happened that way. But
she had wept a little, those first few nights afterward.

It seemed an eternity since she had held an infant. Munan was
only four winters old, but she had been forced to give him into the
care of strangers before he was even a year. When he came back to
her, he could already walk and talk, and he didn't know her.

Erlend. Oh, Erlend. Deep in her heart she knew that he wasn't
as nonchalant as he seemed. This man who was always restless,
now he seemed always so calm. Like a stream that finally runs up
against a steep cliff and lets itself be diverted, trickling out into the
peat to become a calm pool with marshlands all around. He wandered about Jørundgaard, doing nothing, and then he would find
one or another of his sons to keep him company in his idleness. Or
he would go out hunting with them. Once in a while he would go
off to tar and repair one of the fishing boats they kept at the lake.
Or he would set about breaking in one of the young colts, although he never had much success; he was far too impatient.

He kept to himself and pretended not to notice that no one
sought out his company. His sons followed their father's example.
They were not well liked, these outsiders who had been driven to
the valley by misfortune and who still went about like proud
strangers, never inquiring about the customs of the region or its
people. Ulf Haldorssøn was outright despised. He was openly
scornful of the inhabitants of the valley, calling them stupid and
old-fashioned; people who hadn't grown up near the sea weren't
proper folks at all.

As for Kristin herself . . . She knew that she didn't have many
friends here in her own valley either. Not anymore.

She straightened her back in the peat-brown homespun dress,
shading her eyes with her hand against the golden flood of afternoon sunlight.

To the north she caught a glimpse of the valley along the pale
green ribbon of the river and then the crush of mountainous

shapes, one after the other, grayish yellow with scree and moss-covered plateaus; toward the center, snowdrifts and clouds melded into one another in the passes and ravines. Right across from her the Rost Range jutted out its knee, closing off the valley. The Laag River had to bend its course; a distant roar reached her from the river, which cut deep through the rocky cliffs below and tumbled in a roiling froth from ledge to ledge. Just beyond the mossy slopes at the top of the range towered the two enormous Blue Peaks, which her father had compared to a woman's breasts.

Erlend must think this place hemmed in and hideous, find it difficult to breathe.

It was a little farther to the south, on this same hillside, but closer to the familiar slopes, that she had seen the elf maiden when she was a small child.

A gentle, soft, pretty child with lush silken hair framing her round, pink-and-white cheeks. Kristin closed her eyes and turned her sunburned face up toward the flood of light. A young mother, her breasts bursting with milk, her heart churned up and fecund like a newly plowed field after the birth of her child—yes. But with someone like herself there should be no danger: They wouldn't even try to lure her inside.[1] No doubt the mountain king would find the bridal gold ill suited to such a gaunt and worn-out woman. The wood nymph would have no desire to place her child at Kristin's withered teats. She felt hard and dry, like the spruce root under her foot that curved around stones and clung to the ground. Abruptly she dug her heel into the root.

The two little boys who had come over to their mother rushed to do as she did, kicking the tree root with all their might and then asking eagerly, "Why are you doing that, Mother?"

Kristin sat down, placed the mulleins in her lap, and began tearing off the open blossoms to put in the basket.

"Because my shoe was pinching my toes," she replied so much later that the boys had forgotten what they had asked. But this didn't bother them; they were used to the way their mother seemed not to listen when they spoke to her or the way she would wake up and give an answer after they had long forgotten their own question.

Lavrans helped tear off the flowers; Munan wanted to help too, but he merely shredded the tufts. Then Kristin took the mulleins away from him without a word, showing no anger, completely absorbed in her own thoughts. After a while the boys began playing and fighting with the bare stalks that she had cast aside.

They were making a loud ruckus next to her knee. Kristin looked at the two small, round heads with brown hair. They still looked much alike; their hair was the same light brown color, but from various faint little traits and hastily glimpsed signs, their mother could tell they would grow up to be quite different. Munan was going to look like his father; he had those pale blue eyes and such silky hair, which curled in thick, soft tendrils on his narrow head. It would grow as dark as soot with time. His little face was still so round in the chin and cheeks that it was a pleasure to cup her hands around its tender freshness; his face would become thin and lean when he grew older. He would also have the high, narrow forehead with hollowed temples and the straight, jutting triangle of a nose that was narrow and sharp across the ridge with thin, flaring nostrils, just as Naakkve already had and the twins clearly showed signs of having too.

Lavrans had had flaxen, curly hair as fine as silk when he was small. Now it was the color of a hazelnut, but it gleamed like gold in the sun. It was quite straight and still soft enough, although somewhat coarser and heavier than before, close and thick when she buried her fingers in it. Lavrans looked like Kristin; he had gray eyes and a round face with a broad forehead and a softly rounded chin. He would probably retain his pink-and-white complexion long after he became a man.

Gaute too had that fresh coloring; he looked so much like her father, with a long, full face, iron-gray eyes, and pale blond hair.

Bjørgulf was the only one in whom she could see no resemblance. He was the tallest of her sons, with broad shoulders and heavy, strong limbs. Curly locks of raven-black hair fell low over his broad white forehead; his eyes were blue-black but oddly without luster, and he squinted badly when he looked up. She didn't know when he had actually started doing this, because he was the child to whom she had always paid the least attention. They took him away from her and gave him to a foster mother right after his birth. Eleven months later she had Gaute, and Gaute had been in poor health during the first four years of his life. After the birth of the twins she had gotten out of bed, still ailing and with a pain in her back, and resumed caring for the older child, carrying him around and tending to him. She barely had time to look at the two new children except when Frida brought her Ivar, who was crying and thirsty. And Gaute would lie there screaming while she sat and nursed the infant. She hadn't had the strength . . . Blessed Virgin Mary, you know that I *couldn't* manage to pay more attention to Bjørgulf. And he preferred to keep to himself and do things alone, solitary and quiet as he always had been; he never seemed to like it when she caressed him. She had thought he was the strongest of her children; a young, stubborn, dark bull is how she thought of him.

Gradually she realized that his eyesight was quite poor. The monks had done something for his eyes when he and Naakkve were at Tautra, but it hadn't seemed to help.

He continued to be taciturn; it did no good for her to try to draw Bjørgulf closer. She saw that he was just the same with his father. Bjørgulf was the only one of their sons who didn't warm to Erlend's attention the way a meadow receives the sunlight. Only toward Naakkve was Bjørgulf any different, but when Kristin tried to talk to Naakkve about his brother, he refused to say anything. She wondered whether Erlend had any better luck in those quarters, since Naakkve's love for Erlend was so great.

Oh no, Erlend's offspring readily bore witness to who their father was. She had seen that child from Lensvik when she was in Nidaros the last time. She had met Sir Baard in the Christ Church courtyard. He was coming out the door, accompanied by many men and women and servants; a maid carried the swaddled infant. Baard Aasulfssøn greeted Kristin with a nod of his head, silent and courteous, as they walked past her. His wife was not with him.

She had seen the child's face, just a single glance. But that was enough. He looked like the tiny infant faces that she had held to her own breast.

Arne Gjavvaldssøn was with her, and he couldn't keep from talking—that's just the way he was. Sir Baard's other heirs were not pleased when the child was born the previous winter. But Baard had had him baptized Aasulf. Between Erlend Nikulaussøn and Fru Sunniva there had never been any other friendship than what everyone knew; that's what Baard claimed never to doubt. Indiscreet and reckless as Erlend was, he had probably let too much slip when he was bantering with Sunniva, and it was nothing more than her duty to warn the king's envoys when she became suspicious. But if they had been *too* friendly, then Sunniva must have also known that her brother was involved in Erlend's plans. When Haftor Graut took his own life and forfeited his salvation in prison, she was greatly distraught. No one could know how much she blamed herself during that time. Sir Baard had placed his hand on the hilt of his sword and stared at everyone as he spoke of this, said Arne.

Arne had also mentioned the matter to Erlend. One day when Kristin was up in one of the lofts, the men were standing beneath the gallery, unaware that she could hear their conversation. The Lensvik knight was overjoyed about the son his wife had given birth to the winter before; he never doubted that he himself was the father.

"Yes, well, Baard must know best about that," Erlend had replied. She knew that tone of voice of his; now he would be standing there with lowered eyes and a little smile tugging at the corner of his mouth.

Sir Baard bore such rancor toward his kinsmen who would have been his heirs if he had died childless. But people were now saying this was unfair. "Well, the man himself must know best," said Erlend again.

"Yes, yes, Erlend, but that boy is going to inherit more than the seven sons you have with your wife."

"I will provide for *my* seven sons, Arne."

Then Kristin went downstairs; she couldn't bear to hear them talk anymore about this subject. Erlend was a little startled when he saw her. Then he went over and took her hand, standing behind her so that her shoulder touched his body. She understood that as he stood there, gazing down at her, he was repeating without words what he had just affirmed, as if he wanted to give her strength.

Kristin became aware that Munan was staring up at her a bit anxiously. She had apparently smiled, though not in a pleasant way. But when his mother looked down at him, the boy smiled back, hesitant and uncertain.

Impetuously she pulled him onto her lap. He was little, little, still so little, her youngest . . . not too big to be kissed and caressed by his mother. She winked one eye at him; he wanted to wink back, but try as he might, *both* his eyes kept winking. His mother laughed loudly, and then Munan laughed too, chortling as Kristin hugged him in her arms.

Lavrans had been sitting with the dog on his lap. They both turned toward the woods to listen.

"It's Father!" First the dog and then the boy bounded down the steep slope.

Kristin stayed where she was for a moment. Then she stood up and walked forward to the precipice. Now they appeared on the path below: Erlend, Naakkve, Ivar, and Skule. They shouted greetings up to her, merry and boisterous.

Kristin greeted them in return. Were they on their way up to get the horses? No, Erlend replied. Ulf planned to send Sveinbjørn after them that evening. He and Naakkve were off to hunt reindeer, and the twins had wanted to come along to see her.

She didn't reply. She had realized this even before she asked. Naakkve had a dog on a tether; he and his father were dressed in gray-and-black dappled homespun tunics that were hard to see against the scree. All four were carrying bows.

Kristin asked about news from the manor, and Erlend chatted as they climbed upward. Ulf was in the midst of the grain harvesting. He seemed pleased enough, but the hay was stunted, and the grain in the rest of the fields had ripened too early in the drought; it was falling off the stalks. And the oats would soon be ready to harvest; Ulf said they would have to work fast. Kristin walked along, nodding, without saying a word.

She went to the cowshed herself to do the milking. She usually enjoyed the time she sat in the dark next to the bulging flank of the cow, smelling the sweet breath of the milk as it reached her nose. A spurting sound echoed from the darkness where the milkmaid and herdsman were milking. It created such a calm feeling: the strong, warm smell of the shed, the creaking sounds of the osier door hasps, horns butting against wood, a cow shifting her hooves in the soft muck of the floor and swatting her tail at the flies. The wagtails that had made their nests inside during the summer were gone now.

The cows were restless tonight. Bluesides set her foot down in the milk pail. Kristin gave her a slap and scolded her. The next cow began acting refractory as soon as Kristin moved over to her side. She had sores on her udder. Kristin took off her wedding ring and milked the first spurts through the ring.

She heard Ivar and Skule down by the gate. They were shouting and throwing stones at the strange bull that always followed her cows in the evening. They had offered to help Finn milk the goats in the pen, but they had soon grown bored.

A little later, when Kristin walked up the hill, they were teasing the pretty white calf that she had given to Lavrans, who was standing nearby and whimpering. She put down her pails, seized the two boys by the shoulder and flung them aside. They should leave the calf alone if their brother, who was its owner, told them to do so.

Erlend and Naakkve were sitting on the doorstep. They had a fresh cheese between them, and they were eating sliver after sliver as they fed some to Munan, who was standing between Naakkve's knees. He had put her horsehair sieve on the little boy's head, saying that now Munan would be invisible, because it wasn't really a sieve but a wood nymph's hat. All three of them laughed, but as soon as Naakkve saw his mother, he handed her the sieve, stood up, and took the milk pails from her.

Kristin lingered in the dairy shed. The upper half of the door stood open to the outer room of the hut; they had put plenty of wood on the hearth. In the warm flickering glow, they sat around the fire and ate: Erlend, the children, her maid, and the three herdsmen.

By the time she came in they had finished eating. She saw that the two youngest had been put to bed on the bench along the wall; they were already asleep. Erlend had crawled up into the bed. She stumbled over his outer garments and boots and picked them up as she walked past and then went outside.

The sky was still light, with a red stripe above the mountains to the west. Several dark wisps of clouds hovered in the clear air. It looked as if they would have fair weather the next day too, since it was so calm and biting cold now that night had begun to fall. No wind, but an icy gust from the north, a steady breath from the bare gray slopes. Above the hills to the southeast the moon was rising, nearly full, huge, and still a pale crimson in the slight haze that always lingered over the marshes in that direction.

Somewhere up on the plateau the strange ox was bellowing and carrying on. Otherwise it was so quiet that it hurt—only the roar of the river from below their pasture, the little trickling creek on the slope, and a languid murmuring in the woods—a rustling through the boughs as they moved, paused for a moment, and then moved again.

She busied herself with some milk pans and trenchers that stood next to the wall of the hut. Naakkve and the twins came out, and their mother asked them where they were going.

They were going to sleep in the barn; there was such a foul smell in the dairy shed from all the cheeses and butter and from the goats that slept inside.

Naakkve didn't go to the barn at once. His mother could still see his pale gray figure against the green darkness of the hayfield down at the edge of the woods. A little later the maid appeared in the doorway; she gave a start when she saw her mistress standing near the wall.

"Shouldn't you go to bed now, Astrid? It's getting late."

The maid muttered that she just had to go behind the cowshed. Kristin waited until she saw the girl go back inside. Naakkve was now in his sixteenth year. It was some time ago that his mother had begun keeping an eye on the serving maids on the manor whenever they flirted with the handsome and lively young boy.

Kristin walked down to the river and knelt on a rock protruding out over the water. Before her the river flowed almost black into a wide pool with only a few rings betraying the current, but a short distance above, it gushed white in the darkness with a great roar and cold gusts of air. By now the moon had risen so high that it shone brightly; it glittered here and there on a dewy leaf. Its rays caught on a ripple in the stream.

Erlend called her name from right behind her. She hadn't heard him come down the slope. Kristin dipped her arm in the icy water and fished up a couple of milk pans weighted with stones that were being rinsed by the river. She got to her feet and followed her husband back, with both her hands full. They didn't speak as they clambered upward.

Inside the hut Erlend undressed completely and climbed into bed. "Aren't you coming to bed soon, Kristin?"

"I'm just going to have a little food first." She sat down on her stool next to the hearth with some bread and a slice of cheese in her lap. She ate slowly, staring at the embers, which gradually grew dark in the stone-rimmed hollow in the floor.

"Are you asleep, Erlend?" she whispered as she stood up and shook out her skirt.

"No."

Kristin went over and drank a ladleful of curdled milk from the basin in the corner. Then she went back to the hearth, lifted a stone, and laid it down flat, sprinkling the mullein blossoms on top to dry.

But then she could find no more tasks to do. She undressed in the dark and lay down in the bed next to Erlend. When he put his arms around her, she felt weariness wash over her whole body like a cold wave; her head felt empty and heavy, as if everything inside it had sunk down and settled like a knot of pain in the back of her neck. But when he whispered to her, she dutifully put her arms around his neck.

She woke up and didn't know what time of night it was. But through the transparent hide[2] stretched over the smoke vent she could see that the moon must still be high.

The bed was short and cramped so they had to lie close to each other. Erlend was asleep, breathing quietly and evenly, his chest moving faintly as he slept. In the past she used to move closer to his warm, healthy body when she woke up in the night and grew frightened that he was breathing so silently. Back then she thought it so blissfully sweet to feel his breast rise and fall as he slept at her side.

After a while she slipped out of bed, got dressed in the dark, and crept out the door.

The moon was sailing high over the world. The moss glistened with water, and the rocky cliffs gleamed where streams had trickled during the day—now they had turned to ice. Up on the plateaus frost glittered. It was bitterly cold. Kristin crossed her arms over her breasts and stood still for a moment.

Then she set off along the creek. It murmured and gurgled with the tiny sounds of ice crystals breaking apart.

At the top of the meadow a huge boulder rose up out of the earth. No one ever went near it unless they had to, and then they would be certain to cross themselves. People poured cream under it whenever they went past. Otherwise she had never heard that anyone had ever witnessed anything there, but such had been the custom in that pasture ever since ancient times.

She didn't know what had come over her that she would leave the house this way, in the middle of the night. She stopped at the boulder and set her foot in a crevice. Her stomach clenched tight, her womb felt cold and empty with fear, but she refused to make the sign of the cross. Then she climbed up and sat on top of the rock.

From up there she could see a long, long way. Far into the ugly bare mountains in the moonlight. The great dome near Dovre rose up, enormous and pale against the pale sky. Snowdrifts gleamed white in the pass on the Gray Peaks. The Boar Range glistened with new snow and blue clefts. The mountains in the moonlight were more hideous than she could have imagined; only a few stars shone here and there in the vast, icy sky. She was frozen to the very marrow and bone; terror and cold pressed in on her from all sides. But defiantly she stayed where she was.

She refused to get down and lie in the pitch dark next to the warm, slumbering body of her husband. She could tell that for her there would be no more sleep that night.

As sure as she was her father's daughter, her husband would never hear his wife reproach his actions. For she remembered what she had promised when she beseeched the Almighty God and all the saints in heaven to spare Erlend's life.

That was why she had come out into this troll night to breathe when she felt about to suffocate.

She sat there and let the old, bitter thoughts rise up like good friends, countering them with other old and familiar thoughts—in feigned justification of Erlend.

He had certainly never demanded this of her. He had not asked her to bear any of the things she had taken upon her own shoulders. He had merely conceived seven sons with her. "I will provide for *my* seven sons, Arne." God only knew what Erlend had meant by those words. Maybe he meant nothing; it was simply something he had said.

Erlend hadn't asked her to restore order to Husaby and his other estates. He hadn't asked her to fight with her life to save him. He had borne it like a chieftain that his property would be dispersed, that his life was at stake, and that he would lose everything he owned. Stripped and empty-handed, with chieftainlike dignity and calm he had accepted the misfortune; with chieftainlike calm and dignity he lived on her father's manor like a guest.

And yet everything that was in her possession lawfully belonged to her sons. They lawfully owned her sweat and blood and all her strength. But then surely she and the estate had the right to make claims on them.

She hadn't needed to flee to the mountain pastures like some kind of poor leaseholder's wife. But the situation was such at home that she felt pressed and hemmed in from all sides—until she felt as if she couldn't breathe. Then she had felt the need to prove to herself that she *could* do the work of a peasant woman. She had toiled and labored every hour and every day since she had arrived at the estate of Erlend Nikulaussøn as his bride—and realized that *someone* there would have to fight to protect the inheritance of the one she carried under her heart. If the father couldn't do it, then *she* must. But now she needed to be certain. For that matter, she had demonstrated before to her nursemaids and servant women that there wasn't any kind of work she wasn't capable of doing with her own hands. It was a good day up here if she didn't feel an ache in her flanks from standing and churning. It felt good in the morning when she would go along to let out the cattle; the animals had grown fat and glossy in the summer. The tight grip on her heart eased when she stood in the sunset and called to the cows coming home. She liked to see food growing under her own hands; it felt as if she were reaching down into the very foundation from which the future of her sons would be rebuilt.

Jørundgaard was a good estate, but it was not as good as she had thought. And Ulf was a stranger here in the valley; he made mistakes, and he grew impatient. As people saw it in the region, they always had plenty of hay at Jørundgaard. They had the hay meadows along the river and out on the islands, but it wasn't *good* hay, not the kind that Ulf was used to in Trøndelag. He wasn't used to having to gather so much moss and foliage, heath and brushwood as they did here.

Her father had known every patch of his land; he had possessed all the farmer's knowledge about the whims of the seasons and the way each particular strip of field handled rain or drought, windy summers or hot summers; about livestock that he himself had bred, raised, foddered, and sold from, generation after generation—the very sort of knowledge that was needed here. She did not have that kind of knowledge of her estate. But she would acquire it, and her sons would too.

And yet Erlend had never demanded this of her. He hadn't married her in order to lead her into toil and travail. He had married her so she could sleep in his arms. Then, when her time came, the child lay at her side, demanding a place on her arm, at her breast, in her care.

Kristin moaned through clenched teeth. She was shivering with cold and anger.

"*Pactum serva*—in Norwegian it means 'keep thy faith.'"

That was back when Arne Gjavvaldssøn and his brother Leif of Holm had come to Husaby to take her possessions and the children's belongings to Nidaros. This too Erlend had left for her to handle; he had taken lodgings at the monastery at Holm. She was staying at their residence in town—now owned by the monks—and Arne Gjavvaldssøn was with her, helping her in word and deed. Simon had sent him letters about it.

Arne could not have been more zealous if he had been trying to salvage the goods for himself. On the evening he arrived in town with everything, he wanted both Kristin and Fru Gunna of Raasvold, who had come to Nidaros with the two small boys, to come out to the stable. Seven splendid horses—people wanted to be fair with Erlend Nikulaussøn, and they agreed to Arne's claim that the five oldest boys each owned a horse and that one belonged to the mistress herself and one to her personal servant. He could testify that Erlend had given the Castilian, his Spanish stallion, to his son Nikulaus, even though this had been done mostly in jest. Not that Arne thought much of the long-legged animal, but he knew that Erlend was fond of the stallion.

Arne thought it a shame to lose the magnificent armor with the great helmet and gold-chased sword; it was true that these things were of real use only in a tournament, but they were worth a great deal of money. But he had managed to keep Erlend's coat of mail made of black silk with the embroidered red lion. And he had demanded his English armor for Nikulaus; it was so splendid that Arne didn't think its equal could be found in all of Norway—at least to those who knew how to *see*—although it was in disrepair. Erlend had used his weapons far more than most sons of noblemen at the time. Arne caressed each piece: the helmet, shoulder collar, the leather arm and leg coverings, the steel gloves made of the finest plates, the corselet and skirt made of rings, so light and comfortable and yet so strong. And the sword . . . It had only a plain steel hilt, and the leather of the handle was worn, but the likes of such a blade were rarely seen.

Kristin sat and held the sword across her lap. She knew that Erlend would embrace it like a much-loved betrothed; it was the only one he had used of all the swords he owned. He had inherited it in his early youth from Sigmund Torolfssøn, who had been his bedmate when he first joined the king's retainers. Only once had Erlend ever mentioned this friend of his to Kristin. "If God had not been so hasty to take Sigmund away from this world, many things would have doubtless been different for me. After his death I was so unhappy at the royal palace that I managed to beg permission from King Haakon to go north with Gissur Galle that time. But then I might never have won you, my dear; then I probably would have been a married man for many years before you were a grown maiden."

From Munan Baardsøn she had heard that Erlend nursed his friend day and night, the way a mother cares for her child, getting no more sleep than short naps at the bedside of the ailing man during that last winter when Sigmund Torolfssøn lay vomiting up bits of his heart's blood and lungs. And after Sigmund was buried at Halvard Church, Erlend had constantly visited his grave, lying prostrate on the gravestone to grieve. But to Kristin he had mentioned the man only once. She and Erlend had arranged to meet several times in Halvard Church during that sinful winter in Oslo. But he had never told her that his dearest friend from his youth lay buried there. She knew he had mourned his mother in the same way, and he had been quite frantic with grief when Orm died. But he never spoke of them. Kristin knew that he had gone into town to see Margret, but he never mentioned his daughter.

Up near the hilt she noticed that some words had been etched into the blade. Most of them were runes, which she couldn't read; nor could Arne. But the monk picked up the sword and studied it for a moment. "*Pactum serva*," he said finally. "In Norwegian it means 'keep thy faith.' "

Arne and his brother Leif talked about the fact that a large part of Kristin's properties in the north, Erlend's wedding gifts to her, had been mortgaged and dispersed. They wondered whether there was any way to salvage part of them. But Kristin refused. Honor was the most important thing to salvage; she didn't want to hear of any disputes over whether her husband's dealings had been lawful. And she was deadly tired of Arne's chatter, no matter how well intentioned it was. That evening, when he and the monk bade her good night and went to their sleeping chambers, Kristin had thrown herself to her knees before Fru Gunna and buried her head in her lap.

After a moment the old woman lifted her face. Kristin looked up. Fru Gunna's face was heavy, yellowish, and stout, with three deep creases across her forehead, as if shaped out of wax; she had pale freckles, sharp and kind blue eyes, and a sunken, toothless mouth shadowed by long gray whiskers. Kristin had had that face above her so many times. Fru Gunna had been at her side each time she gave birth, except when Lavrans was born and she was at home to attend her father's deathbed.

"Yes, yes, my daughter," said the woman, putting her hands at Kristin's temples. "I've given you help a few times when you had to sink to your knees, yes, I have. But in this trouble, my Kristin, you must kneel down before the Mother of God and ask her to help you through."

Oh, she had already done that too, thought Kristin. She had said her prayers and read some of the Gospels every Saturday; she had observed the fast days as Archbishop Eiliv had enjoined her to do when he granted her absolution; she gave alms and personally served every wanderer who asked for shelter, no matter how he might look. But now she no longer felt any light inside her when she did so. She knew that the light outside did exist, but it felt as if shutters had closed her off inside. That must be what Gunnulf had spoken of: spiritual drought. Sira Eiliv said that was why no soul should lose courage; remain faithful to your prayers and good deeds, the way the farmer plows and spreads manure and sows. God would send the good weather for growing when it was time. But Sira Eiliv had never managed a farm himself.

She had not seen Gunnulf during that time. He was living north in Helgeland, preaching and collecting gifts for the monastery. Well, yes, that was one of the knight's sons from Husaby, while the other . . .

But Margret Erléndsdatter came to visit Kristin several times at the town residence. Two maids accompanied the merchant's wife. She was beautifully dressed and glittering with jewelry. Her father-in-law was a goldsmith, so they had plenty of jewelry at home. She seemed happy and content, although she had no children. She had received her inheritance from her father just in time. God only knew if she ever gave any thought to that poor cripple Haakon, out at Gimsar. He could barely manage to drag himself around the courtyard on two crutches, Kristin had heard.

And yet she thought that even back then she had not had bitter feelings toward Erlend. She seemed to realize that for Erlend, the worst was still ahead when he became a free man. Then he had taken refuge with Abbot Olav. Tend to the moving or show himself in Nidaros now—that was more than Erlend Nikulaussøn could bear.

Then came the day when they sailed across Trondheim Fjord, on the Laurentius boat, the same ship on which Erlend had transported all the belongings she had wanted to bring north with her after they had won permission to marry.

A still day in late autumn; a pale, leaden gleam on the fjord; the whole world cold, restless, white-ribbed. The first snow blown into streaks along the frozen acres, the chill blue mountains white-striped with snow. Even the clouds high overhead, where the sky was blue, seemed to be scattered thin like flour by a wind high up in the heavens. Heavy and sluggish, the ship pulled away from the land, the town promontory. Kristin stood and watched the white spray beneath the cliffs, wondering if she was going to be seasick when they were farther out in the fjord.

Erlend stood at the railing close to the bow with his two eldest sons beside him. The wind fluttered their hair and capes.

Then they looked across Kors Fjord, toward Gaularos and the skerries of Birgsi. A ray of sunlight lit up the brown and white slope along the shore.

Erlend said something to the boys. Then Bjørgulf abruptly turned on his heel, left the railing, and walked toward the stern of the ship. He fumbled along, using the spear that he always carried and used as a staff, as he made his way between the empty rowing benches and past his mother. His dark, curly head was bent low over his breast, his eyes squinting so hard they were nearly closed, his lips pressed tight. He walked under the afterdeck.

Kristin glanced forward at the other two, Erlend and his eldest son. Then Nikulaus knelt, the way a page does to greet his lord; he took his father's hand and kissed it.

Erlend tore his hand away. Kristin caught a glimpse of his face, pale as death and trembling, as he turned his back to the boy and walked away, disappearing behind the sail.

They put in at a port down by Møre for the night. The sea swells were more turbulent; the ship tugged at its ropes, rising and pitching. Kristin was below in the cabin where she was to sleep with Erlend and the two youngest children. She felt sick to her stomach and couldn't find a proper foothold on the deck, which rose and fell beneath her feet. The skin-covered lantern swung above her head, its tiny light flickering. And she stood there struggling with Munan, trying to get him to pee in between the planks. Whenever he woke up, groggy with sleep, he would both pee and soil their bed, raging and screaming and refusing to allow this strange woman, his mother, to help him by holding him over the floor. Then Erlend came below.

She couldn't see his face when he asked in a low voice, "Did you see Naakkve? His eyes were just like yours, Kristin." Erlend drew in a breath, quick and harsh. "That's the way your eyes looked on that morning out by the fence in the nuns' garden—after you had heard the worst about me—and you pledged me your trust."

That was the moment when she felt the first drop of bitterness rise up in her heart. God protect the boy. May he never see the day when he realizes that he has placed his trust in a hand that lets everything run through its fingers like cold water and dry sand.

A few moments ago she thought she heard distant hoofbeats somewhere on the mountain heights to the south. Now she heard them again, closer. Not horses running free, but a single horse and rider; he rode sharply over the rocky slopes beneath the hillside.

Fear seized her, icy cold. Who could be traveling about so late? Dead men rode north under a waning moon; didn't she hear the other horsemen accompanying the first one, riding far behind? And yet she stayed sitting where she was; she didn't know if this was because she was suddenly bewitched or because her heart was so stubborn that night.

The rider was coming toward her; now he was fording the river beneath the slope. She saw the glint of a spearpoint above the willow thickets. Then she scrambled down from the boulder and was about to run back to the hut. The rider leaped from his horse, tied it to the gatepost, and threw his cape over its back. He came walking up the slope; he was a tall, broad man. Now she recognized him: it was Simon.

When he saw her coming to meet him in the moonlight, he seemed to be just as frightened as she had been before.

"Jesus, Kristin, is that you? Or . . . How is it that you're out at this time of night? Were you waiting for me?" he asked abruptly, as if in great dread. "Did you have a premonition of my journey?"

Kristin shook her head. "I couldn't sleep. Brother-in-law, what is it?"

"Andres is so ill, Kristin. We fear for his life. So we thought . . . We know you are the most practiced woman in such matters. You must remember that he's the son of your own sister. Will you agree to come home with me to tend to him? You know that I wouldn't come to you in this manner if I didn't think the boy's life was in peril," he implored her.

He repeated these words inside the hut to Erlend, who sat up in bed, groggy with sleep and quietly surprised. He tried to comfort Simon, speaking from experience. Such young children grew easily feverish and jabbered deliriously if they caught the least cold; perhaps it was not as dangerous as it looked.

"You know full well, Erlend, that I would not have come to get

Kristin at such an hour of the night if I hadn't clearly seen that the child is lying there, struggling with death."

Kristin had blown on the embers and put on more wood. Simon sat and stared into the fire, greedily drinking the milk she offered him but refusing to eat any food. He wanted to head back down as soon as the others arrived. "If you are willing, Kristin." One of his men was following behind with a widow who was a servant at Formo, an able woman who could take over the work up here while she was away. Aasbjørg was most capable, he said again.

After Simon had lifted Kristin up into the saddle, he said, "I'd prefer to take the shortcut to the south if you're not averse to it."

Kristin had never been on that part of the mountain, but she knew there was supposed to be a path down to the valley, cutting steeply across the slope opposite Formo. She agreed, but then his servant would have to take the other road and ride past Jørundgaard to get her chest and the pouches of herbs and bulbs. He should wake up Gaute; the boy knew best about these things.

At the edge of a large marsh they were able to ride side by side, and Kristin asked Simon to tell her again about the boy's illness. The children of Formo had had sore throats around Saint Olav's Day, but they had quickly recovered. The illness had come over Andres suddenly, while he seemed in the best of health—in the middle of the day, three days before. Simon had taken him along, and he was going to ride on the grain sledge down to the fields. But then Andres complained that he was cold, and when Simon looked at the boy, he was shivering so hard that his teeth were rattling in his mouth. Then came the burning fever and the coughing; he vomited up such quantities of loathsome brown matter and had such pain in his chest. But he couldn't tell them much about where it hurt most, the poor little boy.

Kristin tried to reassure Simon as best she could, and then she had to ride behind him for a while. Once he turned around to ask whether she was cold; he wanted her to take his cape over her cloak.

Then he spoke again of his son. He had noticed that the boy wasn't strong. But Andres had grown much more robust during the summer and fall; his foster mother thought so too. The last few days before he fell ill he had acted a little strange and skittish. "Scared," he had said when the dogs leaped at him, wanting to play. On the day when the fever seized him, Simon had come home in the first rays of dawn with several wild ducks. Usually the boy liked to borrow the birds his father brought home and play with them, but this time Andres screamed loudly when his father swung the bundle toward him. Later he crept over to touch the birds, but when he got blood on his hands, he grew quite wild with terror. And now, this evening, he lay whimpering so terribly, unable to sleep or rest, and then he screamed something about a hawk that was after him.

"Do you remember that day in Oslo when the messenger arrived? You said, 'It will be your descendant who will live on at Formo after you're gone.' "

"Don't talk like that, Simon. As if you think you will die without a son. Surely God and His gentle Mother will help. It's unlike you to be so disheartened, brother-in-law."

"Halfrid, my first wife, said the same thing to me after she gave birth to our son. Did you know that I had a son with her, Kristin?"

"Yes. But Andres is already in his third year. It's during the first two years that it's the most difficult to protect a child's life." But even to her these words seemed to offer little help. They rode and rode; the horses plodded up a slope, nodding and casting their heads about so the harnesses jangled. Not a sound in the frosty night except the sound of their own passage and occasionally the rush of water as they crossed a stream, and the moon shining on everything. The scree and the rocky slopes glistened as hideously as death as they rode along beneath the cliffs.

Finally they reached a place where they could look down into the countryside. The moonlight filled the whole valley; the river and marshes and lake farther south gleamed like silver; the fields and meadows were pale.

"Tonight there's frost in the valley too," said Simon.

He dismounted and walked along, leading Kristin's horse down the hillside. The path was so steep in many places that she hardly dared look ahead. Simon supported her by keeping his back against her knee, and she held on by putting one hand behind on the horse's flank. A stone would sometimes roll from under the horse's hooves, tumbling downward, pausing for a moment, and then continuing to roll, loosening more on the way and carrying them along.

Finally they reached the bottom. They rode across the barley fields north of the manor, between the rime-covered shocks of grain. There was an eerie rustling and clattering in the aspen trees above them in the silent, bright night.

"Is it true," asked Simon, wiping his face with his sleeve, "that you had no premonition?"

Kristin told him it was true.

He went on, "I've heard that it does happen; a premonition can appear if a person yearns strongly for someone. Ramborg and I talked about it several times, that if you had been home, you might have known—"

"None of you has entered my thoughts all this time," said Kristin. "You must believe me, Simon." But she couldn't see it gave him much solace.

In the courtyard a couple of servants appeared at once to take their horses. "Things are just as you left them, Simon—not any worse," one of them said quickly. He had glanced up at the master's face. Simon nodded. He walked ahead of Kristin toward the women's house.

Kristin could see that there was indeed grave danger. The little boy lay alone in the large, fine bed, moaning and gasping, ceaselessly tossing his head from side to side on the pillows. His face was fiery hot and dark red; he lay with his glistening eyes partially open, struggling to breathe. Simon stood holding Ramborg's hand, and all the women of the estate who had gathered in the room crowded around Kristin as she examined the boy.

But she spoke as calmly as she could and comforted the parents as best she could. It was probably lung fever. But this night would soon be over without any turn for the worse; it was the nature of this illness that it usually turned on the third or sixth or ninth night before the rooster crowed. She told Ramborg to send all the servingwomen to bed except for two, so that she would always have rested maids to help her. When the servant returned from Jørundgaard with her healing things, she brewed a sweat-inducing potion for the boy and then lanced a vein in his foot so the fluids would be drawn away from his chest.

Ramborg's face blanched when she saw her child's blood. Simon put his arm around her, but she pushed her husband away and sat down on a chair at the foot of the bed. There she stayed, staring at Kristin with her big dark eyes while her sister tended to the child.

Later in the day, when the boy seemed to be a little better, Kristin persuaded Ramborg to lie down on a bench. She arranged pillows and blankets around the young woman and sat near her head, stroking her forehead gently. Ramborg took Kristin's hand.

"You only wish us well, don't you?" she asked with a moan.

"Why shouldn't I wish you well, sister? The two of us, living here in our village once again, the only ones remaining of our kinsmen . . ."

Ramborg uttered several small, stifled sobs from between her tightly pressed lips. Kristin had seen her young sister cry only once, when they stood at their father's deathbed. Now a few swift little tears rose up and trickled down her cheeks. Ramborg lifted Kristin's hand and stared at it. It was big and slender, but reddish brown now, and rough.

"And yet it's more beautiful than mine," she said. Ramborg's hands were small and white, but her fingers were short and her nails square.

"Yes, it is," she said, almost angrily when Kristin shook her head and laughed lightly. "And you're still more lovely than I have ever been. Our father and mother loved you more than me, all their days. You caused them sorrow and shame; I was docile and obedient and set my sights on the man they most wanted me to marry. And yet they loved you more."

"No, sister. They were just as fond of you. Be happy, Ramborg, that you never gave them anything but joy; you cannot know how heavy the other is to bear. But they were younger back when I was young; perhaps that was why they talked to me more."

"Yes, I think everybody was younger back when you were young," said Ramborg, and sighed again.

A short time later she fell asleep. Kristin sat and looked at her. She had known her sister so little; Ramborg was a child when she herself was wed. It seemed to her that in some ways her sister had remained a child. As she sat beside her ill son she looked like a child, a pale, scared child who was trying stubbornly to fend off terror and misfortune.

Sometimes an animal would stop growing if it had young ones too soon. Ramborg was not even sixteen when she gave birth to her daughter, and ever since she had never seemed to grow properly again; she continued to be slender and small, lacking in vigor and fertility. She had given birth only to the one boy since then, and he was oddly weak—with a handsome face, fair and fine, but so pitifully frail and small. He had learned to walk late, and he still talked so poorly that only those who were with him every day could understand any of his chatter. He was also so shy and peevish with strangers that Kristin had hardly even touched her nephew until now. If only God and Holy Olav would grant her the joy to save this poor small boy, she would thank them for it all her days. The mother was such a child herself that she wouldn't be able to bear losing him. And Kristin realized that for Simon Darre it would also be terribly difficult to bear if his only son were taken from him.

That she had become deeply fond of her brother-in-law became most apparent to her now as she saw how much he was suffering from fear and grief. No doubt she could understand her own father's great love for Simon Andressøn. And yet she wondered whether he might have done wrong by Ramborg when he was in such haste to arrange this marriage. For as she gazed down at her little sister, she thought that Simon must be both too old and much too somber and steadfast to be the husband of this young child.

CHAPTER 3

THE DAYS PASSED, and Andres remained ill in bed; there were no great changes, either for the worse or for the better. The worst thing was that he got almost no sleep. The boy would lie with his eyes half open, seeming not to recognize anyone, his thin little body racked by coughs, gasping for breath, the fever rising and falling. One evening Kristin had given him a soothing drink, and then calm descended on him, but after a while she saw that the child had turned pale blue and his skin felt cold and clammy. Quickly she poured warm milk down his throat and placed heated stones at the soles of his feet. Then she didn't dare give him any more sleeping potions; she realized that he was too young to tolerate them.

Sira Solmund came and brought the sacred vessels from the church to him. Simon and Ramborg promised prayers, fasts, and alms if God would hear them and grant their son his life.

Erlend stopped by one day; he declined to get down from his horse and go inside, but Kristin and Simon came out to the courtyard to talk to him. He gave them a look of great distress. And yet that expression of his had always annoyed Kristin in an oddly vague and unclear way. No doubt Erlend felt aggrieved whenever he saw anyone either sad or ill, but he seemed mostly perplexed or embarrassed; he looked genuinely bewildered when he felt sad for someone.

After that, either Naakkve or the twins would come to Formo each day to ask about Andres.

The sixth night brought no change, but later the following day the boy seemed a little better; he was not quite as feverish. Simon and Kristin were sitting alone with him around midday.

The father pulled out a gilded amulet he wore on a string around his neck under his clothing. He bent down over the boy, dangling the amulet before his eyes and then putting it in the child's hand, closing the small fingers around it. But Andres didn't seem to take any notice.

Simon had been given this amulet when he himself was a child, and he had worn it ever since; his father had brought it back from France. It had been blessed at a cloister called Mont Saint Michel, and it bore a picture of Saint Michael with great wings. Andres liked to look at it, Simon explained softly. But the little boy thought it was a rooster; he called the greatest of all the angels a rooster. At long last Simon had managed to teach the boy to say "angel." But one day when they were out in the courtyard, Andres saw the rooster screeching at one of the hens, and he said, "The angel's mad now, Father."

Kristin looked up at the man with pleading eyes; it cut her to the heart to listen to him, even though Simon was speaking in such a calm and even voice. And she was so worn out after keeping vigil all these nights; she realized that it would not be good for her to begin weeping now.

Simon stuck the amulet back inside his shirt. "Ah, well. I will give a three-year-old ox to the church on the eve of Saint Michael's Day every autumn for as long as I live if he will wait a little longer to come for this soul. He'd be no more than a bony chicken on the balance scale, Andres, as small as he is—" But when Simon tried to laugh, his voice broke.

"Simon, Simon!" she implored.

"Yes, things will happen as they must, Kristin. And God Himself will decide; surely He knows best." The father said no more as he stood gazing down at his son.

On the eighth night Simon and one of the maids kept watch as Kristin dozed on a bench some distance away. When she woke up, the girl was asleep. Simon sat on the bench with the high back, as he had on most nights. He was sitting with his face bent over the bed and the child.

"Is he sleeping?" whispered Kristin as she came forward.

Simon raised his head. He ran his hand over his face. She saw that his cheeks were wet, but he replied in a calm, quiet voice, "I don't think that Andres will have any sleep, Kristin, until he lies under the turf in consecrated ground."

Kristin stood there as if paralyzed. Slowly her face turned pale beneath the tan until it was white all the way to her lips.

Then she went back to her corner and picked up her outer garments.

"You must arrange things so that you are alone in here when I come back." She spoke as if her throat and mouth were parched. "Sit with him, and when you see me enter, don't say a word. And never speak of this again—not to me or to anyone else. Not even to your priest."

Simon got to his feet and slowly walked over to her. He too had grown pale.

"No, Kristin!" His voice was almost inaudible. "I don't dare . . . for you to do this thing. . . ."

She put on her cloak, then took a linen cloth from the chest in the corner, folded it up, and hid it in her bodice.

"But I dare. You understand that no one must come near us afterward until I call; no one must come near us or speak to us until he wakes up and speaks himself."

"What do you think your father would say of this?" he whispered in the same faint voice. "Kristin . . . don't do it."

"In the past I have done things that my father thought were wrong; back then it was merely to further my own desire. Andres is his flesh and blood too—my own flesh, Simon—my only sister's son."

Simon took in a heavy, trembling breath; he stood with his eyes downcast.

"But if you don't want me to make this last attempt . . ."

He stood as before, with his head bowed, and did not reply. Then Kristin repeated her question, unaware that an odd little smile, almost scornful, had appeared on her white lips. "Do you not want me to go?"

He turned his head away. And so she walked past him, stepped soundlessly out the door, and closed it silently behind her.

It was pitch dark outside, with small gusts of wind from the south making all the stars blink and flicker uneasily. She had reached no farther than the road up between the fences when she felt as if she had stepped into eternity itself. An endless path both behind her and up ahead. As if she would never emerge from what she had entered into when she walked out into this night.

Even the darkness was like a force she was pressing against. She plodded through the mud; the road had been churned up by the carts carrying unthreshed grain, and now it was thawing in the south wind. With every footstep she had to pull herself free from the night and the raw chill that clung to her feet, swept upward, and weighted down the hems of her garments. Now and then a falling leaf would drift past her, as if something alive were touching her in the dark—gentle but confident of its superior power: Turn back.

When she came out onto the main road, it was easier to walk. The road was covered with grass, and her feet did not get stuck in the mire. Her face felt as rigid as stone, her body tensed and taut. Each step carried her mercilessly toward the forest grove through which she would have to pass. A feeling rose up inside her like an inner paralysis: She couldn't possibly walk through that patch of darkness. But she had no intention of turning around. She couldn't feel her body because of her terror, yet all the while she kept moving forward, as if in her sleep, steadily stepping over stones and roots and puddles of water, unconsciously careful not to stumble or break her steady stride and thus allow fear to overwhelm her.

Now the spruce trees rustled closer and closer in the night; she stepped in among them, still as calm as a sleepwalker. She sensed every sound and hardly dared blink because of the dark. The drone of the river, the heavy sighing of the firs, a creek trickling over stones as she walked toward it, passed by it, and then continued on. Once a rock slid down the scree, as if some living creature were moving about up there. Sweat poured from her body, but she did not venture either to slow or to speed her step because of it.

Kristin's eyes had now grown so accustomed to the dark that when she emerged from the woods, she could see much better; a glint came from the ribbon of the river and from the water on the marshes. The fields became visible in the blackness; the clusters of buildings looked like clumps of earth. The sky was also beginning to lighten overhead; she could feel it, although she didn't dare look up at the black peaks towering above. But she knew that it would soon be time for the moon to rise.

She tried to remind herself that in four hours it would be daytime; people would be setting about their daily chores on all the farms throughout the countryside. The sky would grow pale with dawn; the light would rise over the mountains. Then it wouldn't seem far to go; in the daylight it wasn't far from Formo to the church. And by then she would have returned home long ago. But it was clear that she would be a different person.

She knew that if it had been one of her own children, she would not have dared make this last attempt. To turn away God's hand when He reached out for a living soul. When she kept watch over her own ill children, back when she was young and her heart bled with tenderness, when she thought she would collapse in anguish and torment, she had tried to say: Lord, you love them better than I do, let thy will be done.

But now on this night she was walking along, defying her own terror. This child who was not her own—she *would* save him, no matter what fate she was saving him for. . . .

Because you too, Simon Darre, acquiesced when the dearest thing you possessed on earth was at stake; you agreed to more than anyone can accept with full honor.

Do you not want me to go? He hadn't been man enough to answer. Deep in her heart she knew that if the child died, Simon would have the strength to bear this too. But she had struck at the only moment when she ever saw him on the verge of breaking down; she had seized hold of that moment and carried it off. She would share that secret with him, the knowledge that she had also witnessed *him* when he once stood unsteady on his feet.

For he had learned too much about her. She had accepted help from the man she had spurned every time it was a matter of saving the one she had chosen. This suitor whom she had cast aside—he was the man she had turned to each time she needed someone to protect her love. And never had she asked for Simon's help in vain. Time after time he had stepped forward, covering her with his kindness and his strength.

So she was undertaking this nighttime errand to rid herself of a little of the debt; until that hour, she hadn't fully realized how heavy a burden it was.

Simon had forced her to see at last that he was the strongest: stronger than she was and stronger than the man to whom she had chosen to give herself. No doubt she had realized this from the moment all three of them met, face-to-face, in that shameful place in Oslo. And yet she had refused to accept it then: that such a plump-cheeked, stout, and gaping young man could be stronger than . . .

Now she was walking along, not daring to call on a good and holy name; she took upon herself this sin in order to . . . She didn't know what. Was it revenge? Revenge because she had been forced to see that he was more noble-minded than the two of them?

But now you too understand, Simon, that when the life of the one you love more than your own heart is at stake . . . Then the poor person grasps for anything, anything.

The moon had risen over the mountain ridge as she walked up the hill to the church. Again she felt as if she had to overcome a new wave of terror. The moonlight lay like a delicate spiderweb over the tar-timbered edifice. The church itself looked terrifying and ominously dark beneath the thin veil. Out on the green she saw the cross, but for the first time she didn't dare approach to kneel before the blessed tree. She crept over the churchyard wall at the place where she knew the sod and stone were the lowest and most easily breached.

Here and there a gravestone glistened like water down in the tall, dewy grass. Kristin walked straight across the cemetery to the graves of the poor, which lay near the south wall.

She went over to the burial place of a poor man who had been a stranger in the parish. One winter the man had frozen to death on the mountainside. His two motherless daughters had been taken in by one farm after another,[1] until Lavrans Bjørgulfsøn had offered to keep them and bring them up, for the sake of Christ. When they were full grown and had turned out well, Kristin's father had found honorable, hardworking husbands for them and married them off with cows and calves and sheep. Ragnfrid had given them bedding and iron pots. Now both women were well provided for, as befitted their station. One of them had been Ramborg's maid, and Ramborg had carried the woman's child to be baptized.

So you must grant me a bit of the turf covering you, Bjarne, for Ramborg's son. Kristin knelt down and pulled out her dagger.

Drops of ice cold sweat prickled her brow and upper lip as she dug her fingers under the dew-drenched sod. The earth resisted . . . it was only roots. She sliced through them with the dagger.

In return, the ghost must be given gold or silver that had been passed down through three generations. She slipped off the little gold ring with the rubies that had been her grandmother's betrothal ring.

The child is my father's descendant.

She pushed the ring as far down into the earth as she could, wrapped the piece of sod in the linen cloth, and then spread peat and leaves over the spot where she had removed it.

When she stood up, her legs trembled under her, and she had to pause for a moment before she could turn around. If she looked under her arm right now, she would be able to see them.

She felt a terrible tugging inside her, as if they would force her to do so. All the dead who had known her before in this world. Is that you, Kristin Lavransdatter? Are you coming here in this way?

Arne Gyrdsøn lay buried outside the west entrance. Yes, Arne, you may well wonder—I was not like this, back when you and I knew each other.

Then she climbed over the wall again and headed down the slope.

The moon was now bright over the countryside. Jørundgaard lay out on the plain; the dew glittered in the grass on all the rooftops. She stared in that direction, almost listlessly. She felt as if she herself were dead to that home and all the people there; the door was closed to her, to the woman who had wandered past, up along the road on this night.

The mountains cast their shadows over her nearly the whole way back. The wind was blowing harder now; one gust of wind after another came straight toward her. Withered leaves blew against her, trying to send her back to the place she had just left.

Nor did she believe that she was walking along unaccompanied. She heard the steady sound of stealthy footsteps behind her. Is that you, Arne?

Look back, Kristin, look under your arm, it urged her.

And yet she didn't feel truly afraid anymore. Just cold and numb, sick with desire to give up and sink down. After this night she could never be afraid of anything else in the world.

Simon was sitting in his usual place at the head of the bed, leaning over the child, when she opened the door and stepped inside. For a brief moment he looked up; Kristin wondered if she had grown as worn out and haggard and old as he had during these days. Then Simon bowed his head and hid his face with his arm.

He staggered a bit as he got to his feet. He turned his face away from her as he walked past and over to the door, his head bowed, his shoulders slumped.

Kristin lit two candles and set them on the table. The boy opened his eyes slightly and looked up, his gaze strangely unseeing; he whimpered a bit and tried to turn his head toward the light. When Kristin straightened out his little body, the way a corpse is laid out, he tried to change position, but he seemed too weak to move.

Then she covered his face and chest with the linen cloth and placed the strip of sod on top.

At that moment the terror seized her again, like a great sea swell.

She had to sit down on the bed. The window was right above the short bench, and she didn't dare sit with her back to it. Better to look them in the eyes if anyone should be standing outside and looking in. She pulled the high-backed chair over to the bed and sat down facing the windowpane. The stifling black of the night pressed against it; one of the candles was reflected in the glass. Kristin fixed her eyes on it, clutching the arms of the chair so that her knuckles grew white; now and then her arms trembled. She couldn't feel her own legs, as chilled and wet as they were. She sat there with her teeth chattering from horror and cold, and the sweat ran like ice water down her face and back. She sat without moving, merely casting now and then a quick glance at the linen cloth, which faintly rose and fell with the child's breath.

Finally the pale light of dawn appeared in the windowpane. The rooster crowed shrilly. Then she heard men out in the courtyard. They were heading for the stable.

She slumped against the back of the chair, shuddering as if with convulsions, and tried to find a position for her legs so they wouldn't twitch and jerk around from the shaking.

There was a strong movement under the linen cloth. Andres pushed it away from his face, whimpering crossly. He seemed partially conscious since he grunted at Kristin when she jumped to her feet and leaned over him.

She grabbed the cloth and sod, rushed over to the fireplace, and stuffed twigs and wood inside it; then she threw the ghostly goods into the fresh, crackling fire. She had to stand still for a moment, holding on to the wall. The tears poured down Kristin's face.

She took a ladleful of milk from the little pot that stood near the hearth and carried it over to the child. Andres had fallen asleep again. He seemed to be slumbering peacefully now.

Then she drank the milk herself. It tasted so good that she had to gulp down two or three more ladlefuls of the warm drink.

Still, she didn't dare speak; the boy hadn't yet said a comprehensible word. But she sank to her knees next to the foot of the bed and recited mutely to herself:

Convertere, Domine, aliquantulum; et deprecare super servos tuos. Ne ultra memineris iniquitatis nostræ: ecce respice; populus tuus omnes nos.[2]

Yes, yes, yes. This was a terrible thing she had done. But he was their only son. While she herself had seven! Shouldn't she try *everything* to save her sister's only son?

All the thoughts she had had during the night—they were merely ramblings of the night. She had done it only because she couldn't stand to see this child die in her hands.

Simon—the man who had never failed her. The one who had been loyal and good toward every child she had ever known and most of all toward herself and her own. And this son whom he loved above all else—shouldn't she use every measure to save the boy's life? Even if it was a sin?

Yes, it was sinful, but let the punishment fall on me, God. That poor, beautiful, innocent son of Simon and Ramborg. God would not allow Andres to be punished.

She went back and leaned over the bed, breathing on the tiny, waxen hand. She didn't dare kiss it; he mustn't be wakened.

So fair and blameless.

It was during the nights of terror when they were left alone at Haugen that Fru Aashild had told her about it—told her about her own errand to the cemetery at Kongunahelle. "That, Kristin, was surely the most difficult task I have ever undertaken." But Bjørn Gunnarssøn was not an innocent child when he lay there after Aashild Gautesdatter's cousins had come too close to his heart with their swords. He had slain one man before he was brought down himself, and the other man never regained his vigor after the day he exchanged blows with Herr Bjørn.

Kristin stood at the window and looked out into the courtyard. Servants were moving from building to building, going about the day's chores. Several young calves were roaming about the yard; they were so lovely.

Many different thoughts rise up in the darkness—like those gossamer plants that grow in the lake, oddly bewitching and pretty as they bob and sway; but enticing and sinister, they exert a dark pull as long as they're growing in the living, trickling mire. And yet they're nothing but slimey brown clumps when the children pull them into the boat. So many strange thoughts, both terrifying and enticing, grow in the night. It was probably Brother Edvin who once said that those condemned to Hell had no wish to give up their torment: hatred and sorrow were their pleasures. That was why Christ could never save them. Back then this had sounded to her like wild talk. An icy shiver ran through her; now she was beginning to understand what the monk had meant.

She leaned over the bed once more, breathing in the smell of the little child. Simon and Ramborg were not going to lose him. Even though she had done it out of a need to prove herself to Simon, to show him that she could do something other than take from him. She had needed to take a risk on his behalf, to repay him.

Then she knelt again, repeating over and over as much as she could remember from the prayer book.

That morning Simon went out and sowed winter rye in the newly plowed field south of the grove. He had decided he must act as if

this were merely reasonable, because the work on the estate had to
continue as usual. The serving maids had been greatly surprised
when he went in to them during the night to tell them that Kristin
wanted to be alone with the boy until she sent word. He said the
same to Ramborg when she got up: Kristin had requested that no
one should go near the women's house that day.

"Not even you?" she asked quickly, and Simon said no. That
was when he went out to get the seed box.

But after the midday meal he stayed up at the manor; he didn't
have the heart to go far from the buildings. And he didn't like the
look in Ramborg's eyes. A short time after the noonday rest it happened. He was standing down by the grain barn when he saw his
wife racing across the courtyard. He rushed after her. Ramborg
threw herself at the door to the women's house, pounding on it
with her fists and screaming shrilly for Kristin to open up.

Simon put his arms around her, speaking gently. Then she bent
down as fast as lightning and bit him on the hand. He saw that she
was like a raging beast.

"He's *my* child! What have the two of you done to my son?"

"You know full well that your sister wouldn't do anything to
Andres except what might do him good." When he put his arms
around her again, Ramborg struggled and screamed.

"Come now, Ramborg," said her husband, making his voice
stern. "Aren't you ashamed in front of our servants?"

But she kept on screaming. "He's mine—that much I know. You
weren't with us when I gave birth to him, Simon," she shouted.
"We weren't so precious to you back then."

"You know what I had on my hands at the time," replied her
husband wearily. He dragged her across to the main house; he had
to use all his strength.

After that he didn't dare leave her side. Ramborg gradually
calmed down, and when evening came, she obediently allowed her
maids to help her undress.

Simon stayed up. His daughters were asleep over in their bed,
and he had sent the servingwomen away. Once when he stood up
and walked across the room, Ramborg asked from her bed where
he was going; her voice sounded wide awake.

"I was thinking of lying down with you for a while," he said after a moment. He took off his outer garments and shoes and then

crawled under the blanket and woolen coverlet. He put his arm around his wife's shoulders. "I realize, my Ramborg, that this has been a long and difficult day for you."

"Your heart is beating so hard, Simon," she said a little later.

"Well, I'm afraid for the boy too, you know. But we must wait patiently until Kristin sends us word."

He sat up abruptly in bed, propping himself up on one elbow. In bewilderment he stared at Kristin's white face. It was right above his own, glistening wet with tears in the candlelight; her hand was on his chest. For a moment he thought . . . But this time he wasn't merely dreaming. Simon threw himself back against the head-board, and with a stifled moan he covered his face with his arm. He felt sick; his heart was hammering inside him, furious and hard.

"Simon, wake up!" Kristin shook him again. "Andres is calling for his father. Do you hear me? It was the first thing he said." Her face was beaming with joy as her tears fell steadily.

Simon sat up, rubbing his face several times. Surely he hadn't spoken in confusion when she woke him. He looked up at Kristin, who was standing next to the bed with a lantern in her hand.

Quietly, so as not to wake Ramborg, he crept out of the room with her. The loathsome nausea was still lodged in his chest. He felt as if something were about to burst inside him. Why couldn't he stop having that dreadful dream? He who in his waking hours struggled and struggled to drive all such thoughts from his mind. But when he lay asleep, powerless and defenseless, he would have that dream, which the Devil himself must have sent. Even now, while she sat and kept watch over his deathly ill son, he dreamed like some kind of demon.

It was raining, and Kristin had no idea what time of night it might be. The boy had been half conscious, but he hadn't spoken. And it was only when night came and she thought he was sleeping comfortably and soundly that she dared lie down for a moment to rest—with Andres in her arms so she would notice if he stirred. Then she had fallen asleep.

The boy looked so tiny as he lay alone in the bed. He was terri-bly pale, but his eyes were clear, and his face lit up with a smile when he saw his father. Simon dropped to his knees beside the bed, but when he reached out to lift the small body into his embrace, Kristin grabbed him by the arm.

"No, no, Simon. He's soaked with sweat, and it's cold in here." She pulled the covers tighter around Andres. "Lie down next to him instead, while I send word for a maid to keep watch. I'll go back to the main house now and get into bed with Ramborg."

Simon crept under the covers. There was a warm hollow where she had lain and the faint, sweet scent of her hair on the pillowcase. Simon quietly uttered a moan, and then he gathered up his little son and pressed his face against the child's damp, soft hair. Andres had become so small that he felt like nothing in Simon's arms, but he lay there contentedly, occasionally saying a word or two.

Then he began tugging and poking at the opening of his father's shirt; he stuck his clammy little hand inside and pulled out the amulet. "The rooster," he said happily. "There it is."

On the day of Kristin's departure, as she made ready to leave, Simon came to see her in the women's house and handed her a little wooden box.

"I thought this was something you might like to have."

Kristin knew from the carving that it was the work of her father. Inside, wrapped in a soft piece of glove leather, was a tiny gold clasp set with five emeralds. She recognized it at once. Lavrans had worn it on his shirt whenever he wanted to look particularly fine.

She thanked Simon, but then she turned blood red. She suddenly remembered that she had never seen her father wear this clasp since she had come home from the convent in Oslo.

"When did Father give this to you?" She regretted the question the moment she asked it.

"He gave it to me as a farewell gift one time when I was leaving the estate."

"This seems to me much too great a gift," she said softly, looking down.

Simon chuckled and replied, "You're going to need many such things, Kristin, when the time comes for you to send out all your sons with betrothal gifts."

Kristin looked at him and said, "You know what I mean, Simon—those things that my father gave you . . . You know that I'm as fond of you as if you had been his own son."

"Are you?" He placed the back of his hand against her cheek and gave it a fleeting caress as he smiled, an odd little smile, and spoke as if to a child, "Yes, yes, Kristin. I know that."

CHAPTER 4

LATER THAT FALL Simon Andressøn had business with his brother at Dyfrin. While he was there, a suitor was proposed for his daughter Arngjerd.

The matter was not settled, and Simon felt rather uneasy and apprehensive as he rode northward. Perhaps he ought to have agreed; then the child would have been well provided for, and he could stop all his worrying about her future. Perhaps Gyrd and Helga were right. It was foolish of him not to seize hold with both hands when he received such an offer for this daughter of his. Eiken was a bigger estate than Formo, and Aasmund himself owned more than a third of it; he would never have thought of proposing his son as a suitor for a maiden of such birth as Arngjerd—of lowly lineage and with no kin on her mother's side—if Simon hadn't held a mortgage on a portion of the estate worth three marks in taxes. The family had been forced to borrow money from both Dyfrin and the nuns in Oslo when Grunde Aasmundssøn happened to slay a man for the second time. Grunde grew wild when he was drunk, although he was otherwise an upright and well-meaning fellow, said Gyrd, and surely he would allow himself to be guided by such a good and sensible woman as Arngjerd.

But the fact was that Grunde was not many years younger than Simon himself. And Arngjerd was young. And the people at Eiken wanted the wedding to take place as early as spring.

It hung on like a bad memory in Simon's mind; he tried not to think of it if he could avoid it. But now that Arngjerd's marriage had come under discussion, it kept cropping up. He had been an unhappy man on that first morning when he woke up at Ramborg's side. Certainly he had been no more giddy or bold than a bridegroom ought to be when he went to bed—although it had

52

made him feel strange and reckless to see Kristin among the bride's attendants, and Erlend, his new brother-in-law, was among the men who escorted him up to the loft. But when he woke up the next morning and lay there looking at his bride, who was still asleep, he had felt a terrible, painful shame deep in his heart—as if he had mistreated a child.

And yet he knew that he could have spared himself this sorrow. But *she* had laughed when she opened her big eyes.

"Now you're *mine*, Simon." She ran her hands over his chest. "My father is your father, and my sister is your sister." And he grew cold with anguish, for he wondered whether she knew that his heart had given a start at her words.

Otherwise he was quite content with his marriage—this much he firmly believed. His wife was wealthy, of distinguished lineage, young and lively, beautiful and kind. She had borne him a daughter and a son, and that was something a man valued after he had tried living among riches without producing any children who could keep the estate together after the parents were gone. Two children, and their position was assured. He was so rich that he could even obtain a good match for Arngjerd.

He would have liked to have another son; yes, he wouldn't be sad if one or two more children were born on Formo. But Ramborg was probably happy as long as she was spared all that. And that was worth something too. For he couldn't deny that things were much more comfortable at home when Ramborg was in good humor. He might well have wished that she had a more even temperament. He didn't always know how he stood with his wife. And more attention could have been paid to the housekeeping in his home. But no man should dare expect to have all his bowls filled to the brim, as the saying goes. This is what Simon kept telling himself as he rode homeward.

Ramborg was to travel to Kruke during the week before Saint Clement's Day; it always cheered her up to get away from home for a while.

God only knew how things would go over there this time around. Sigrid was now carrying her eighth child. Simon had been shocked when he paid a visit to his sister on his way south; she didn't look as if she could stand much more.

He had offered four thick wax tapers to the ancient image of the Virgin Mary at Eyabu, which was supposed to be particularly powerful in effecting miracles, and he had promised many gifts if Sigrid made it through with her life and her health. How things would go with Geirmund and all their children if the mother died and left them behind . . . No, he couldn't think about that.

They lived together so well, Sigrid and Geirmund. Never had she heard an unkind word from her husband, she said; never had he left anything undone that he thought might please her. When he noticed that Sigrid was wasting away with longing for the child she had borne in her youth with Gjavvald Arnessøn, he had asked Simon to bring the boy to visit so the mother could spend some time with him. But Sigrid had reaped only sorrow and disappointment from the reunion with that spoiled, rich man's son. Since then Sigrid Andresdatter had clung to her husband and the children she had with him, the way a poor, ailing sinner clings to her priest and confession.

Now she seemed fully content in many ways. And Simon understood why. Few men were as pleasant to be with as Geirmund. He had such a fine voice that even if he was only talking about the narrow-hoofed horse that had been foisted upon him, it was almost like listening to harp music.

Geirmund Hersteinssøn had always had a strange and ugly face, but in the past he had been a strong man, with a handsome build and limbs, the best bowman and hunter, and better than most in all sports. Three years ago he had become a cripple, after he returned to the village from a hunting expedition, crawling on his hands and one knee, with the other leg crushed and dragging behind him. Now he couldn't walk across the room without a cane, and he couldn't mount a horse or hobble around the steep slopes of the fields without help. Misfortune constantly plagued him, such an odd and eccentric man as he was, and ill prepared for safeguarding his property or welfare. Anyone who had the heart for it could fool him in trade or business dealings. But he was clever with his hands, an able craftsman in both wood and iron, and a wise and skilled speaker. And when this man took his harp on his lap, Geirmund could make people laugh or cry with his singing and playing. It was almost like listening to the knight in Geirmund's song who could entice the leaves from the linden tree and the horn from the lively cattle with his playing.

Then the older children would take up the refrain and sing along with their father. They were more lovely to hear than the chiming of all the bells in the bishop's Hamar. The next youngest child, Inga, could walk if she held on to the bench, although she had not yet learned to talk. But she would hum and sing all day long, and her tiny voice was so light and delicate, like a little silver bell.

They lived crowded together in a small, dark old hearth house: the man and his wife, the children, and the servants. The loft, which Geirmund had talked of building all these years, would now probably never be built. He had barely managed to put up a new barn to replace the one that had burned the previous year. But the parents couldn't bear to part with a single one of their many children. Every time he visited Kruke, Simon had offered to take some of them in and raise them; Geirmund and Sigrid had thanked him but declined.

Simon sometimes thought that perhaps she was the one among his siblings who had found the best life, after all. Although Gyrd did say that Astrid was quite pleased with her new husband; they lived far south in Ry County, and Simon hadn't seen them since their wedding. But Gyrd had mentioned that the sons of Torgrim were constantly quarreling with their stepfather.

And Gudmund was very happy and content. But if that was man's happiness, then Simon thought it would not be a sin to thank God that their father hadn't lived to see it. As soon as it could be decently permitted after Andres Darre's death, Gudmund had celebrated his wedding to the widow whom his father wouldn't allow him to marry. The knight of Dyfrin thought that since he had sought out young, rich, and beautiful maidens of distinguished families and unblemished reputation for his two eldest sons, and this had led to little joy for either Gyrd or Simon, then it would mean pure misery for Gudmund if his father allowed him to follow his own foolish wishes. Tordis Bergsdatter was much older than Gudmund, moderately wealthy, and she had had no children from her first marriage. But afterward she had given birth to a daughter by one of the priests at the Maria Church in Oslo, and people said that she had been much too amenable toward other men as well—including Gudmund Darre, as soon as she became acquainted with him. She was as ugly as a troll, and much too rude and coarse in speech for a woman, thought Simon. But she was lively and witty, intelligent and good-natured. He knew that he would have been fond of Tordis himself, if only she hadn't married into their lineage. Now Gudmund was flourishing, and it was dreadful to witness; he was almost as stout and portly as Simon. And that was not Gudmund's nature; in his youth he had been slender and handsome. He had grown so flabby and indolent that Simon felt an urge to give the boy a thrashing every time he saw him. But it was true that Gudmund had been a cursed simpleton all his days. And the fact that his children took their wits from their mother but their looks from him was at least one bit of luck in this misfortune. And yet Gudmund was thriving.

So Simon didn't need to fret as much as he did over his brother. And in some ways it was probably also needless for him to lament on Gyrd's behalf. But each time he went home to his father's manor and saw how things now stood there, he felt so dreadfully overwhelmed that his heart ached when he left.

The wealth of the estate had increased; Gyrd's brother-in-law, Ulf Saksesøn, now enjoyed the king's full favor and grace, and he had drawn Gyrd Andressøn into the circle of men who possessed the most power and advantages in the realm. But Simon didn't care for the man and saw that Gyrd apparently didn't either. Reluctantly and with little joy, Gyrd of Dyfrin followed the course that his wife and her brother had set for him in order to have some peace in his house.

Helga Saksesdatter was a witch. But it was Gyrd's two sons who caused him to look as careworn as he did. Sakse, the older one, must be sixteen winters old by now. Nearly every night his personal servant had to heave the whelp into bed, dead drunk. He had already ruined his mind and his health with liquor; no doubt he would drink himself to death before he reached the age of a man. It would be no great loss; Sakse had acquired an ugly reputation in the region for coarseness and insolence, in spite of his youth. He was his mother's favorite. Gyrd loved Jon, his younger son, better. He also had more of the temperament needed for him to bring honor to his lineage, if only he hadn't been . . . Well, he was a bit misshapen, with hunched shoulders and a crooked back. And he had some kind of inner stomach complaint and was unable to tolerate any food other than gruel and flat bread.

* * *

Simon Andressøn had always taken secret refuge in a feeling of community with his family whenever his own life seemed to him . . . well, troublesome, or whatever he might call it. When he met with adversity, it bothered him less if he could remember the good fortune and well-being of his siblings. If only things had been the same at Dyfrin as during his father's time, when peace, contentment, and prosperity reigned, then Simon thought there would have been much to ease his secret distress. He felt as if the roots of his own life were intertwined with those of his brothers and sisters, somewhere deep down in the dark earth. Every blow that struck, every injury that ate away at the marrow of one of them was felt by all.

He and Gyrd, at any rate, had felt this way, at least in the past. Now he wasn't so sure that Gyrd felt the same anymore.

He had been most fond of his older brother and of Sigrid. He remembered when they were growing up: He could sit and feel such joy for his youngest sister that he had to do *something* to show it. Then he would pick a quarrel with her, tease and needle her, pull on her braids, and pinch her arm—as if he couldn't show his affection for her in any other way without feeling ashamed. He had to tease her so that without embarrassment he could give her all the treasures he had stashed away; he could include the little maiden in his games when he built a millhouse at the creek, built farms for her, and cut willow whistles for the little girls in the springtime.

The memory of that day when he learned the full extent of her misfortune was like a brand scorched onto his mind. All winter long he had seen the way Sigrid was grieving herself into the grave over her dead betrothed, but he didn't know any more than that. Then one Sunday in early spring he was standing on the gallery at Mandvik, feeling cross with the women for not appearing. The horses were in the courtyard, outfitted with their church saddles, and the servants had been waiting a long time. Finally he grew angry and went into the women's house. Sigrid was still in bed. Surprised, he asked whether she was ill. His wife was sitting on the edge of the bed. A tremor passed over her gentle, withered face as she looked up.

"Ill she is indeed, the poor child. But even more than that, I think she's frightened . . . of you and your kinsmen . . . and how you will take the news."

His sister shrieked loudly, throwing herself headlong into Halfrid's arms and clinging to her, wrapping her thin, bare arms around her sister-in-law's waist. Her scream pierced Simon to the heart, so he thought it would stop and be drained of all blood. Her pain and her shame coursed through him, robbing him of his wits; then came the fear, and the sweat poured out. Their father—what would he do with Sigrid now?

He was so frightened as he struggled through the thawing muck on the journey home to Raumarike that at last the servant, who was traveling with him and knew nothing of the matter, began joking about the way Simon constantly had to get down from his horse. He had been a full-grown married man for many years, and yet he was so terrified at the thought of the meeting with his father that his stomach was in upheaval.

Then his father had barely uttered a word. But he had fallen apart, as if his roots had been chopped in half. Sometimes when he was about to doze off, Simon would recall that image and be wide awake at once: his father sitting there, rocking back and forth, with his head bowed to his chest, and Gyrd standing beside him with his hand on the arm of the high seat, a little paler than usual, his eyes downcast.

"God be praised that she wasn't here when this came out. It's a good thing she's staying with you and Halfrid," Gyrd had said when the two of them were alone.

That was the only time Simon heard Gyrd say anything that might indicate he didn't put his wife above all other women.

But he had witnessed how Gyrd seemed to fade and retreat ever since he had married Helga Saksesdatter.

During the time he was betrothed to her Gyrd had never said much, but each time he caught sight of his bride, Gyrd had looked so radiantly handsome that Simon had felt uneasy when he glanced at his brother. He had seen Helga before, Gyrd told Simon, but he had never spoken to her and could not have imagined that her kinsmen would give such a rich and beautiful bride to him.

Gyrd Darre's splendid good looks in his youth had been something that Simon regarded as a kind of personal honor. He was handsome in a particularly appealing way, as if everyone must see that goodness, gentility, and a courageous and noble heart resided in this fine, quiet young man. Then he was wed to Helga Saksesdatter, and it was as if nothing more ever came of him.

He had always been taciturn, but the two brothers were constantly together, and Simon managed to talk enough for both of them. Simon was garrulous, well liked, and considered sensible. For drinking bouts and bantering, for hunting and skiing expeditions, and for all manner of youthful amusements, Simon had countless friends, all equally close and dear. His older brother went along, saying little but smiling his lovely, somber smile, and the few words he did say seemed to count all the more.

Now Gyrd Andressøn was as silent as a locked chest.

The summer when Simon came home and told his father that he and Kristin Lavransdatter had agreed that they both wished to have the agreement retracted which had been made on their behalf . . . back then Simon knew that Gyrd understood most of what lay behind this matter: that Simon loved his betrothed, but there was some reason why he had given up his right, and this reason was such that Simon felt scorched inside with rancor and pain. Gyrd had quietly urged his father to let the matter drop. But to Simon he had never hinted with a single word that he understood. And Simon thought that if he could possibly have greater affection for his brother than he had felt all his days, it was then, because of his silence.

Simon *tried* to be happy and in good spirits as he rode north toward home. Along the way he stopped in to visit his friends in the valley, greeting them and drinking merrily. And his friends saddled up their horses to accompany him to the next manor, where other friends lived. It was so pleasant and easy to ride when there was frost but no snow.

He rode the last part of the journey in the twilight. The flush of the ale had left him. His men were wild and raucous, but their master seemed to have run dry of laughter and banter; he must be tired.

Then he was home. Andres tagged after his father, wherever he stood or walked. Ulvhild hovered around the saddlebags; had he brought any presents home for her? Arngjerd brought in ale and food. His wife sat down next to him as he ate, chattering and asking for news. When the children had gone to bed, Simon took Ramborg on his knee as he passed on greetings to her and spoke of kinsmen and acquaintances.

He thought it shameful and unmanly if he could not be content with such a life as he had.

The next day Simon was sitting in the Sæmund house when Arngjerd came over to bring him food. He thought it would be just as well to speak to her of the suitor while they were alone, and so he told his daughter about his conversation with the men from Eiken.

No, she was not very pretty, thought her father. He looked up at the young girl as she stood before him. Short and stocky, with a small, plain, pale face; her grayish blond hair was blotchy in color, hanging down her back in two thick braids, but over her forehead it fell in lank wisps in her eyes, and she had a habit of constantly brushing her hair back.

"It must be as you wish, Father," she said calmly when he was done speaking.

"Yes, I know that you're a good child, but what do you think about all this?"

"I have nothing to say. You must decide about this matter, dear Father."

"This is how things stand, Arngjerd: I would like to grant you a few more free years, free from childbirth and cares and responsibilities—all those things that fall to a woman's lot as soon as she is married. But I wonder if perhaps you might be longing to have your own home and to take charge yourself?"

"There is no need for haste on my account," said the girl with a little smile.

"You know that if you moved to Eiken through marriage, you would have your wealthy kinsmen nearby. Bare is the brotherless back." He noticed the glint in Arngjerd's eyes and her fleeting smile. "I mean Gyrd, your uncle," he said quickly, a little embarrassed.

"Yes, I know you didn't mean my kinswoman Helga," she said, and they both laughed.

Simon felt a warmth in his soul, in gratitude to God and the Virgin Mary, and to Halfrid, who had made him acknowledge this daughter as his own. Whenever he and Arngjerd happened to laugh together in this way, he needed no further proof of his paternity.

He stood up and brushed off some flour that she had on her sleeve. "And the suitor—what do you think of the man?" he asked.

"I like him well enough, the little that I've seen of him. And one shouldn't believe everything one hears. But you must decide, Father."

"Then we'll do as I've said. Aasmund and Grunde can wait a while longer, and if they're of the same mind when you're a little older . . . Otherwise, you must know, my daughter, that you may decide on your marriage yourself, insofar as you have the sense to choose in your own best interest. And your judgment is sound enough, Arngjerd."

He put his arms around her. She blushed when her father kissed her, and Simon realized that it had been a long time since he had done this. He was usually not the kind of man who was afraid to embrace his wife in the light of day or to banter with his children. But it was always done in jest, and Arngjerd . . . . It suddenly dawned on Simon that his young daughter was probably the only person at Formo with whom he sometimes spoke in earnest.

He went over and pulled the peg out of the slit in the south wall. Through the small hole he gazed out across the valley. The wind was coming from the south, and big gray clouds were piling up where the mountains converged and blocked out the view. When a ray of sun broke through, the brilliance of all the colors deepened. The mild weather had licked away the sallow frost; the fields were brown, the fir trees blue-black, and high on the mountain crests the light gleamed with a golden luster where the bare slopes began, covered with lichen and moss.

Simon felt as if he could glean a singular power from the autumn wind outside and the shifting radiance over the countryside. If they had a lasting thaw for All Saints' Day, there would be mill water in the creeks, at least until Christmas. And he could send men into the mountains to gather moss. It had been such a dry fall; the Laag was a meager, small stream running through the fish traps made of yellow gravel and pale stones.

Up in the north end of the valley only Jørundgaard and the parsonage had millhouses on the river. He had little desire to ask permission to use the Jørundgaard mill. No doubt everyone in the region would be taking their grain there, since Sira Eirik charged a mill fee. And people thought he gained too good an idea of how much grain they had; he was so greedy about demanding tithes. But Lavrans had always allowed people to grind their grain at his mill without charge, and Kristin wanted things to continue in the same way.

If he so much as thought of her, his heart would begin trembling, sick and anguished.

It was the day before both Saint Simon's Day and the Feast of Saint Jude, the day when he always used to go to confession. It was to search his soul, to fast and to pray, that he was sitting there in the Sæmund house while the house servants were doing the threshing in the barn.

It took no time at all to go over his sins: He had cursed; he had lied when people asked about matters that were not their concern; he had shot a deer long after he had seen by the sun that the Sabbath had begun on a Saturday evening; and he had gone hunting on Sunday morning when everyone else in the village was at mass.

What had happened when the boy lay ill—that was something he must not and dared not mention. But this was the first time in his life that he reluctantly kept silent about a sin before his parish priest.

He had thought much about it and suffered terribly over it in his heart. Surely this must be a great sin, whether he himself had used sorcery to heal or had directly lured another person into doing so.

But he wasn't able to feel remorse when he thought about the fact that otherwise his son would now be lying in the ground. He felt fearful and dejected and kept watch to see if the child had changed afterward. He didn't think he could discern anything.

He knew it was true of many kinds of birds and wild animals. If human hands touched the eggs or their young, the parents wanted no more to do with them but would turn away from their offspring. A man who had been granted the light of reason by God could not do the same. For Simon the situation had become such that when he held his son, he almost felt as if he couldn't let the child out of his hands because he had grown so fearful for Andres. Sometimes he could understand why the heathen dumb beasts felt such loathing for their young because they had been *touched*. He too felt as if his child had been in some way infected.

But he had no regrets, did not wish that it hadn't happened. He merely wished it had been someone other than Kristin. It was difficult enough for him that they lived in the same region.

Arngjerd came in to ask for a key. Ramborg didn't think she had gotten it back after her husband had used it.

There was less and less order to the housekeeping on the manor. Simon remembered giving the key back to his wife; that was before he journeyed south.

"Well, I'm sure I'll find it," said Arngjerd.

She had such a nice smile and wise eyes. She wasn't truly ugly either, thought her father. And her hair was lovely when she wore it loose, so thick and blond, for holy days and feasts.

The daughter of Erlend's paramour had been pretty enough, and nothing but trouble had come of it.

But Erlend had had that daughter with a fair and highborn woman. Erlend had probably never even glanced at a woman like Arngjerd's mother. He had sauntered jauntily through the world, and beautiful, proud women and maidens had lined up to offer him love and adventure.

Simon's only sin of that kind—and he didn't count the boyish pranks when he was at the king's court—might have had a little more grandeur to it when he finally decided to betray his good and worthy wife. And he hadn't paid her any more heed, that Jorunn; he couldn't even remember how it happened that he first came too near the maid. He had been out carousing with friends and acquaintances a good deal that winter, and when he came home to his wife's estate, Jorunn would always be waiting there, to see that he got into bed without causing any accidents with the hearth.

It had been no more splendid an adventure than that.

He had deserved even less that the child should turn out so well and bring him such joy. But he shouldn't dwell on such thoughts now, when he was supposed to be thinking about his confession.

It was drizzling when Simon walked home from Romundgaard in the dark. He cut across the fields. In the last faint glimmer of daylight the stubble shone pale and wet. Over by the old bathhouse wall something small and white lay shining on the slope. Simon went over to have a look. It was the pieces of the French bowl that had been broken in the spring; the children had set a table made from a board placed across two stones. Simon struck at it with his axe and it toppled over.

He regretted his action at once, but he didn't like being reminded of that evening.

As if to make amends for the fact that he had kept silent about a sin, he had talked to Sira Eirik about his dreams. It was also because he needed to ease his heart—at least from *that*. He had been ready to leave when it suddenly occurred to him that he needed to talk about it. And this old, half-blind priest had been his spiritual father for more than twelve years.

So he went back and knelt again before Sira Eirik.

The priest sat motionless until Simon had finished talking. Then he spoke, his powerful voice now sounding old and veiled from inside the eternal twilight: It was not a sin. Every limb of the struggling church had to be tested in battle with the Fiend; that's why God allowed the Devil to seek out a man with many kinds of temptations. As long as the man did not cast aside his weapons, as long as he refused to forsake the Lord's banner or, fully alert and aware, refused to surrender to the visions with which the impure spirit was trying to bewitch him, then the sinful impulses were not a sin.

"No!" cried Simon, ashamed at the sound of his own voice.

He had *never* surrendered. He was tormented, tormented, tormented by them. Whenever he woke up from these sinful dreams, he felt as if he himself had been violated in his sleep.

Two horses were tied to the fence when he entered the courtyard. It was Soten, who belonged to Erlend Nikulaussøn, and Kristin's horse. He called for the stableboy. Why hadn't they been led inside? Because the visitors had said it wasn't necessary, replied the boy sullenly.

He was a young lad who had taken a position with Simon now that he was home; before, he had served at Dyfrin. There everything was supposed to be done according to courtly custom; that's what Helga had demanded. But if this fool Sigurd thought he could grumble at his master here at Formo because Simon preferred to jest and banter with his men and didn't mind a bold reply from a servant, then the Devil would . . . Simon was about to scold the boy roundly, but he refrained; he had just come from confession after all. Jon Daalk would have to take the newcomer in hand and teach him that good peasant customs were just as acceptable as the refined ways at Dyfrin.

He merely asked in a relatively calm voice whether Sigurd was fresh out of the mountains this year and told him to put the horses inside. But he was angry.

The first thing he saw as he entered the house was Erlend's laughing face. The light from the candle on the table shone directly on him as he sat on the bench and fended off Ulvhild, who was kneeling beside him and trying to scratch him or whatever she was doing. She was flailing her hands at the man's face and laughing so hard that she hiccupped.

Erlend sprang to his feet and tried to push the child aside, but she gripped the sleeve of his tunic and hung on to his arm as he walked across the room, erect and light-footed, to greet his brother-in-law. She was nagging him for something; Erlend and Simon could barely get a word in.

Her father ordered her, rather harshly, to go out to the cookhouse with the maids; they had just finished setting the table. When the maiden protested, he took her hard by the arm and tore her away from Erlend.

"Here!" Ulvhild's uncle took a lump of resin out of his mouth and stuck it into hers. "Take it, Ulvhild, my little plum cheeks! That daughter of yours," he said to his brother-in-law with a laugh as he gazed after the maiden, "is not going to be as docile as Arngjerd!"

Simon hadn't been able to resist telling his wife how well Arngjerd had handled the marriage matter. But he hadn't intended for her to tell the people of Jørundgaard. And it was unlike Ramborg to do so; he knew that she had little affection for Erlend. He didn't like it. He didn't like the fact that Ramborg had spoken of this matter, or that she was so capricious, or that Ulvhild, little girl though she was, seemed so charmed by Erlend—just as all women were.

He went over to greet Kristin. She was sitting in the corner next to the hearth wall with Andres on her lap. The boy had grown quite fond of his aunt during the time she nursed him when he was recovering from his illness the previous fall.

Simon realized that there must be some purpose for this visit since Erlend had come too. He was not one to wear out the doorstep at Formo. Simon couldn't deny that Erlend had handled the difficult situation admirably—considering how things had turned out between the brothers-in-law. Erlend avoided Simon as much as he could, but they met as often as necessary so that gossip wouldn't spread about enmity between kinsmen, and then they always behaved like the best of friends. Erlend was quiet and a bit reticent whenever they were together but still displayed a free and unfettered manner.

When the food had been brought to the table and the ale set out, Erlend spoke, "I think you're probably wondering about the reason for my visit, Simon. We're here to invite you and Ramborg to a wedding at our manor."

"Surely you must be jesting? I didn't think you had anyone of marrying age on your estate."

"That depends on how you look at it, brother-in-law. It's Ulf Haldorssøn."

Simon slapped his thigh.

"Next I'll expect my plow oxen to produce calves at Christmastime!"

"You shouldn't call Ulf a plow ox," said Erlend with a laugh. "The unfortunate thing is that the man has been far too bold . . ."

Simon whistled.

Erlend laughed again and said, "Yes, you can well imagine that I didn't believe my own ears when they came to the estate yesterday—the sons of Herbrand of Medalheim—and demanded that Ulf should marry their sister."

"Herbrand Remba's? But they're nothing but boys; their sister can't be old enough that Ulf would . . ."

"She's twenty winters old. And Ulf is closer to fifty. Yes." Erlend had turned somber. "You realize, Simon, that they must consider him a poor match for Jardtrud, but it's the lesser of two evils if she marries him. Although Ulf is the son of a knight and a well-to-do man; he doesn't need to earn his bread on another man's estate, but he followed us here because he would rather live with his kinsmen than on his own farm at Skaun . . . after what happened. . . ."

Erlend fell silent for a moment. His face was tender and handsome. Then he continued.

"Now we, Kristin and I, intend to celebrate this wedding as if he were our brother. That's why Ulf and I will ride south in the coming week to Musudal to ask for her hand at Medalheim. For the sake of appearances, you understand. But I thought of asking you a favor, brother-in-law. I remember, Simon, that I owe you a great deal. But Ulf is not well liked here in the villages. And you are so highly respected; few men are your equal . . . while I myself . . ." He shrugged his shoulders and laughed a little. "Would you be willing, Simon, to ride with us and act as spokesman on Ulf's behalf? He and I have been friends since we were boys," pleaded Erlend.

"That I will, brother-in-law!" Simon had turned crimson; he felt oddly embarrassed and powerless at Erlend's candid speech. "I will gladly do anything I can to honor Ulf Haldorssøn."

Kristin had been sitting in the corner with Andres; the boy wanted his aunt to help him undress. Now she came forward into the light, holding the half-naked child, who had his arms around her neck.

"That's kind of you, Simon," she said softly, holding out her hand. "For this we all thank you."

Simon lightly clasped her hand for a moment.

"Not at all, Kristin. I have always been fond of Ulf. You should know that I do this gladly." He reached up to take his son, but Andres pretended to fret, kicking at his father with his little bare feet, laughing and clinging to Kristin.

Simon listened to the two of them as he sat and talked to Erlend about Ulf's money matters. The boy suddenly started giggling; she knew so many lullabies and nursery rhymes, and she laughed too, a gentle, soft cooing sound from deep in her throat. Once he glanced in their direction and saw that she had made a kind of stairway with her fingers, and Andres's fingers were people walking up it. At last she put him in the cradle and sat down next to Ramborg. The sisters chatted to each other in hushed voices.

It was true enough, he thought as he lay down that night: He had always been fond of Ulf Haldorssøn. And ever since that winter in

Oslo when they had both struggled to help Kristin, he had felt himself bound to the man with a kind of kinship. He never thought that Ulf was anything but his equal, the son of a nobleman. The fact that he had no rights from his father's family because he had been conceived in adultery meant only that Simon was even more respectful in his dealings with Ulf. Somewhere in the depths of his own heart there was always a prayer for Arngjerd's well-being. But otherwise this was not a good situation to get involved with: a middle-aged man and such a young child. Well, if Jardtrud Herbrandsdatter had strayed when she was at the *ting*[1] last summer, it was none of his concern. He had done nothing to offend these people, and Ulf was the close kinsman of his brother-in-law.

Unasked, Ramborg had offered to help Kristin by overseeing the table at the wedding. He thought this kind of her. When it mattered, Ramborg always showed what lineage she was from. Yes indeed, Ramborg was a good woman.

CHAPTER 5

THE DAY AFTER Saint Catherine's Day, Erlend Nikulaussøn celebrated the wedding of his kinsman in a most beautiful and splendid fashion. Many good people had gathered; Simon Darre had
seen to that. He and his wife were exceedingly well liked in all the
surrounding villages. Both priests from the Olav Church were in
attendance, and Sira Eirik blessed the house and the bed. This was
considered a great honor since nowadays Sira Eirik only said mass
on the high holy days and performed other priestly duties only for
those few who had been coming to him for confession for many
years. Simon Darre read aloud the document detailing Ulf's
betrothal and wedding gifts to his bride, and Erlend gave an ad-
mirable speech to his kinsman at the table. Ramborg Lavransdatter oversaw the serving of the food along with her sister, and
she was also present to help the bride undress in the loft.

And yet it was not a truly joyous wedding. The bride was from
an old and respected family there in the valley; her kinsmen and
neighbors could not possibly think she had won an equal match
since she had to make do with an outsider and one who had served
on another man's estate, even though it belonged to a kinsman.
Neither Ulf's birth, as the son of a wealthy knight and his maid,
nor his kinship with Erlend Nikulaussøn seemed to impress the
sons of Herbrand as any great honor.

Apparently the bride herself was not content either, considering
how she had behaved. Kristin sounded quite despondent when she
spoke to Simon about this. He had come to Jørundgaard to take
care of some matters several weeks after the wedding. Jardtrud
was urging her husband to move to his property at Skaun. Weeping, she had said within Kristin's earshot that the worst thing she
could imagine was that her child should be called the son of a servant. Ulf had not replied. The newly married couple lived in the

building known as the foreman's house because Jon Einarssøn had
lived there before Lavrans bought all of Laugarbru and moved him
out there. But this name displeased Jardtrud. And she resented
keeping her cows in the same shed as Kristin's; no doubt she was
afraid that someone might think she was Kristin's servingwoman.
That was reasonable enough, thought Kristin. She would have a
shed built for the foreman's house if Ulf didn't decide to take his
wife and move to Skaun. But perhaps that might be best after all.
He was no longer so young that it would be easy for him to
change the way he lived; perhaps it would be less difficult for him
in a new place.

Simon thought she might be right about that. Ulf was greatly
disliked in the region. He spoke scornfully about everything there
in the valley. He was a capable and hardworking farmer, but he
was unaccustomed to so many things in that part of the country.
He took on more livestock in the fall than he could manage to feed
through the winter, and when the cows languished or he ended up
having to slaughter some of the starving beasts toward spring, he
would grow angry and blame the fact that he was unused to the
meager ways of the region, where people had to scrape off bark
for fodder as early as Saint Paal's Day.

There was another consideration: In Trøndelag the custom had
gradually developed between the landowner and his tenants that
he would demand as lease payment the goods that he needed
most—hay, skins, flour, butter, or wool—even though certain
goods or sums had been specified when the lease was settled. And
it was the landowner or his envoys who recalculated the worth of
one item in replacement for another, completely arbitrarily. But
when Ulf made these demands upon Kristin's leaseholders around
the countryside, people called them injurious and grievously unlawful, as they were, and the tenants complained to their mistress.
She took Ulf to task as soon as she heard of the matter, but Simon
knew that people blamed not only Ulf but Kristin Lavransdatter as
well. He had tried to explain, wherever talk of this arose, that
Kristin hadn't known about Ulf's demands and that they were
based on customs of the man's own region. Simon feared this had
done little good, although no one had said as much to his face.

For this reason he wasn't sure whether he should wish for Ulf to
stay or to leave. He didn't know how Kristin would handle things

without her diligent and loyal helper. Erlend was completely incapable of managing the farmwork, and their sons were far too
young. But Ulf had turned much of the countryside against her,
and now there was this: He had seduced a young maiden from a
wealthy and respected family in the valley. God only knew that
Kristin was already struggling hard enough, as the situation now
stood.

And they were in difficult straits, the people of Jørundgaard. Erlend was no better liked than Ulf. If Erlend's overseer and kinsman
was arrogant and surly, the master himself, with his gentle and
rather indolent manner, was even more irksome. Erlend Nikulaussøn probably had no idea that he was turning people against
him; he seemed unaware of anything except that, rich or poor, he
was the same man he had always been, and he wouldn't dream
that anyone would call him arrogant for that very reason. He had
plotted to incite a group of rebels against his king even though he
was Lord Magnus's kinsman, vassal, and retainer; then he himself
had caused the downfall of the plan through his own foolish recklessness. But he evidently never thought that he might be branded
a villain in anyone's eyes because of these matters. Simon couldn't
see that Erlend gave much thought to anything at all.

It was hard to figure the man out. If one sat and conversed with
Erlend, he was far from stupid, thought Simon, but it was as if he
could never take to heart the wise and splendid things he often
said. It was impossible to remember that this man would soon be
old; he could have had grandchildren long ago. Upon closer study,
his face was lined and his hair sprinkled with gray, yet he and
Nikulaus looked more like brothers than father and son. He was
just as straight-backed and slender as when Simon had seen him
for the first time; his voice was just as young and resonant. He
moved among others with the same ease and confidence, with that
slightly muted grace to his manner. With strangers he had always
been rather quiet and reserved; letting others seek him out instead
of seeking their company himself, during times of both prosperity
and adversity. That no one sought his company now was something that Erlend didn't seem to notice. And the whole circle of noblemen and landowners all along the valley, intermarried and
closely related with each other as they were, resented the way this
haughty Trøndelag chieftain, who had been cast into their midst

by misfortune, nevertheless considered himself too highborn and
noble to seek their favor.

But what had caused the most bad blood toward Erlend Nikulaussøn was the fact that he had drawn the men of Sundbu into
misfortune along with him. Guttorm and Borgar Trondssøn had
been banished from Norway, and their shares of the great Gjesling
estates, as well as their half of the ancestral manor, had been seized
by the Crown. Ivar of Sundbu had to buy himself reconciliation
with King Magnus. The king gave the confiscated properties—not
without demanding compensation, it was said—to Sir Sigurd Erlendssøn Eldjarn. Then the youngest of the sons of Trond, Ivar and
Haavard, who had not known of their brothers' treasonous plans,
sold their shares of the Vaage estates to Sir Sigurd, who was their
cousin as well as the cousin of the daughters of Lavrans. Sigurd's
mother, Gudrun Ivarsdatter, was the sister of Trond Gjesling and
Ragnfrid of Jørundgaard. Ivar Gjesling moved to Ringheim at
Toten, a manor that he had acquired from his wife. His children
would do well to live where they had inheritance and property
rights from their mother's family. Haavard still owned a great deal
of property, but it was mostly in Valdres, and with his marriage he
had now come into possession of large estates in the Borge district.
But the inhabitants of Vaage and northern Gudbrandsdal thought
it the greatest misfortune that the ancient lineage of landowners
had lost Sundbu, where they had lived and ruled the countryside
for as far back as people could remember.

For a short time Sundbu had been in the hands of King Haakon
Haakonssøn's loyal retainer Erlend Eldjarn of Godaland at Agder.
The Gjeslings had never been warm friends with King Sverre or his
noblemen, and they had sided with Duke Skule when he rallied the
rebels against King Haakon.[1] But Ivar the Younger had won
Sundbu back in an exchange of properties with Erlend Eldjarn and
had given his daughter Gudrun to him in marriage. Ivar's son,
Trond, had not brought honor of any kind to his lineage, but his
four sons were handsome, well liked, and intrepid men, and people took it hard when they lost their ancestral estate.

Before Ivar moved away from the valley, an accident occurred
that made people even more sorrowful and indignant about the
fate of the Gjeslings. Guttorm was unmarried, but Borgar's young
wife had been left behind at Sundbu. Dagny Bjarnesdatter had al-

ways been a little slow-witted, and she had openly shown that she loved her husband beyond all measure. Borgar Trondssøn was handsome but had rather loose ways. The winter after he had fled from the land, Dagny fell through a hole in the ice of Vaage Lake and drowned. It was called an accident, but people knew that grief and longing had robbed Dagny of the few wits she had left, and everyone felt deep pity for the simple, sweet, and pretty young woman who had met with such a terrible end. That's when the rancor became widespread toward Erlend Nikulaussøn, who had brought such misfortune upon the best people of the region. And then everybody began to gossip about how he had behaved when he was to marry the daughter of Lavrans Lagmandssön. She too was a Gjesling, after all, on her mother's side.

The new master of Sundbu was not well liked, even though no one had anything specific to say against Sigurd himself. But he was from Egde, and his father, Erlend Eldjarn, had quarreled with everyone in this part of the land with whom he had had any dealings. Kristin and Ramborg had never met this cousin of theirs. Simon had known Sir Sigurd in Raumarike; he was the close kinsman of the Haftorssøns, and they in turn were close kinsmen of Gyrd Darre's wife. But as complicated as matters now were, Simon avoided meeting Sir Sigurd as much as possible. He never had any desire to go to Sundbu anymore. The Trondssøns had been his dear friends, and Ramborg and the wives of Ivar and Borgar used to visit each other every year. Sir Sigurd Erlendssøn was also much older than Simon Andressøn; he was a man of almost sixty.

Things had become so tangled up because Erlend and Kristin were now living at Jørundgaard that although the marriage of their overseer could not be called important news, Simon Darre thought it was enough to make the situation even more vexed. Usually he would not have troubled his young wife if he was having any difficulties or setbacks. But this time he couldn't help discussing these matters a bit with Ramborg. He was both surprised and pleased when he saw how sensibly she spoke about them and how admirably she tried to do all that she could to help.

She went to see her sister at Jørundgaard much more often than she had before, and she gave up her sullen demeanor with Erlend. On Christmas Day, when they met on the church hill after the mass, Ramborg kissed not only Kristin but her brother-in-law as well. In the past she had always fiercely mocked these foreign customs of his: the fact that he used to kiss his mother-in-law in greeting and the like.

It suddenly occurred to Simon when he saw Ramborg put her arms around Erlend's neck that he might do the same with his wife's sister. But then he realized that he couldn't do it after all. He had never been in the habit of kissing the wives of his kinsmen; his mother and sisters had laughed at him when he suggested trying it when he came home after he had been at court, in service as a page.

For the Christmas banquet at Formo, Ramborg seated Ulf Haldorssøn's young wife in a place of honor, showing both of them such respect as was seemly toward a newly married couple. And she went to Jørundgaard to be with Jardtrud when she gave birth.

That took place a month after Christmas—two months too soon, and the boy was stillborn. Then Jardtrud flew into a fury. If she had known that things might go this way, she would never have married Ulf. But now it was done and could not be helped.

What Ulf Haldorssøn thought about the matter, no one knew. He didn't say a word.

During the week before Mid-Lent, Erlend Nikulaussøn and Simon Andressøn rode south together to Kvam. Several years before Lavrans died, he and a few other farmers had purchased a small estate in the village there. Now the original owners of the manor wanted to buy it back, but it was rather unclear how things had been handled in the past as far as offering the land to the heirs,[2] or whether the kinsmen of the sellers had claimed their rights in lawful fashion. When Lavrans's estate had been settled after his death, his share in this farm had been excluded, along with several other small properties that might involve legal proceedings over proof of ownership. The two sisters then divided up the income from them. That was why both of Lavrans's sons-in-law were now appearing on behalf of their wives.

A good number of people had gathered, and because the tenant's wife and children lay sick in bed in the main house, the men had to make do with meeting in an old outbuilding on the farm. It was drafty and in terrible disrepair; everyone kept on his fur cape. Each man placed his weapons within reach and kept his sword on his belt; no one had a desire to stay any longer than necessary. But they would at least have a bite to eat before they parted, and so at the time of midafternoon prayers, when the discussion was over, the men took out their bags of provisions and sat down to eat, with the packets lying next to them on the benches or in front of them on the floor. There was no table in the building.

The parish priest of Kvam had sent his son, Holmgeir Moi-sessøn, in his stead. He was a devious and untrustworthy young man, whom few people liked. But his father was greatly admired, and his mother had belonged to a respected family. Holmgeir was a tall and strong fellow, hot-blooded and quick to turn on people, so no one wished to quarrel with the priest's son. There were also many who thought him an able and witty speaker.

Simon hardly knew him and didn't like his looks. He had a long, narrow face with pale freckles and a thin upper lip, which made his big yellow front teeth gleam like a rat's. But Sira Moises had been Lavrans's good friend, and for a time the son had been raised at Jørundgaard, partly as a servant and partly as a foster son, until his father had acknowledged him as his own.[3] For this reason Simon was always friendly when he met Holmgeir Moi-sessøn.

Now Holmgeir had rolled a stump over to the hearth and was sitting there, sticking slices of meat—roasted thrush with pieces of bacon—on his dagger and heating them in the fire. He had been ill and had been granted fourteen days' indulgence, he told the others, who were chewing on bread and frozen fish as the fragrant smell of Holmgeir's meat rose up to their noses.

Simon was in a bad humor—not truly angry but slightly dejected and embarrassed. The whole property matter was difficult to sort out, and the documents he had received from his father-in-law were very unclear; and yet when he left home, he thought that he understood them. He had compared them with other documents, but now when he heard the statements of the witnesses and saw the other evidence that was put forth, he realized that his view of the matter wouldn't hold up. But none of the other men had any better grasp of it—particularly not the sheriff's envoy, who was also present. It was suggested that the case would have to be brought up before a *ting*. Then Erlend suddenly spoke and asked to see the documents.

Up to that moment he had sat and listened, almost as if he had no interest in the matter. Now he seemed to wake up. He carefully read through all the documents, a few of them several times. Then he explained the situation, clearly and briefly: Such and such were the provisions of the lawbooks, and in such a way they could be interpreted. The vague and clumsy phrases in the documents had to mean either this or that. If the case were brought before a *ting*, it would be decided in either this or that manner. Then he proposed a solution with which the original owners might be satisfied but which was not entirely to the detriment of the present owners.

Erlend stood up as he spoke, with his left hand resting lightly on the hilt of his sword, his right hand carelessly holding the stack of documents. He acted as if he were the one in charge of the meeting, although Simon could see that he wasn't aware of this himself. He was used to standing up and speaking in this manner when he used to hold sheriff *tings* in his county. When he turned to one of the others to ask if something was so and if the man understood what he was explaining, he spoke as if he were interrogating a witness—not without courtesy and yet as if it were his place to ask the questions and the other man's place to answer. When he was done speaking, he handed the documents to the envoy as if the man could be his servant and sat down. While the others discussed the matter and Simon also stated his opinion, Erlend listened, but in such a fashion as if he had no stake in the case. His replies were curt, clear, and instructive if anyone happened to address him, but all the while he scraped his fingernail on some grease spots that had appeared on his tunic, straightened his belt, picked up his gloves, and seemed to be waiting rather impatiently for the conversation to come to an end.

The others agreed to the arrangement that Erlend had proposed, and it was one that Simon could be tolerably satisfied with; he would have been unlikely to win anything more from a court case.

But he had fallen into a bad mood. He knew full well that it was childish of him to be cross because his brother-in-law had understood the matter while he had not. It was reasonable that Er-

lend should be better able to interpret the word of law and decipher confusing documents, since for years it had been his role to
explain the statutes to people and settle disputes. But it had come
upon Simon quite unexpectedly. The night before at Jørundgaard,
when he talked to Erlend and Kristin about the meeting, Erlend
hadn't mentioned any opinion; he seemed to listen with only half
an ear. Yes, it was clear that Erlend would be better versed in the
law than ordinary farmers, but it was as if the law were no concern of his as he sat there and counseled the others with friendly
indifference. Simon had a vague feeling that in some way Erlend
had never respected the law as a guide in his own life.

It was also strange that he could stand up in that manner, completely untroubled. He had to be aware that this made the others
think about who and what he had been and what his situation
now was. Simon could feel the others thinking about this; some
probably resented this man, who never seemed to care what other
people thought of him. But no one said anything. When the blue-
frozen clerk who had come with the envoy sat down and put the
writing board on his lap, he addressed all his questions to Erlend,
and Erlend spelled things out for him as he sat holding a few
pieces of straw, which he had picked up from the floor, twining
them around his long tan fingers and weaving them into a ring.
When the clerk was finished, he handed the calfskin to Erlend,
who tossed the straw ring into the hearth, took the letter, and read
it half aloud:

" 'To all men who see or hear this document, greetings from
God and from Simon Andressøn of Formo, Erlend Nikulaussøn of
Jørundgaard, Vidar Steinssøn of Klaufastad, Ingemund and
Toralde Bjørnssøn, Bjørn Ingemundssøn of Lundar, Alf Einarssøn,
Holmgeir Moisessøn . . .'

"Do you have the wax ready?" he asked the clerk, who was
blowing on his frozen fingers. " 'Let it be known that in the year
of our Lord, one thousand three hundred and thirty-eight winters,
on the Friday before Mid-Lent Sunday, we met at Granheim in the
parish of Kvam . . .'

"We can take the chest that's standing in the alcove, Alf, and
use it as a table." Erlend turned to the envoy as he gave the document back to the scribe.

Simon remembered how Erlend had been when he was in the

company of his peers up north. Easy and confident enough; he
wasn't lacking in that regard. Impetuous and rash in his speech,
but always with something slightly ingratiating about his manner.
He was not in the least indifferent to what others thought of him if
he considered them his peers or kinsmen. On the contrary, he had
doubtless put great effort into winning their approval.

With an oddly fierce sense of bitterness, Simon suddenly felt al-
lied with these farmers from here in the valley—men whom Erlend
respected so little that he didn't even wonder what they might
think of him. He had done it for Erlend's sake. For his sake Simon
had parted with the circles of the gentry and well-to-do. It was all
very well to be the rich farmer of Formo, but he couldn't forget
that he had turned his back on his peers, kinsmen, and the friends
of his youth. Because he had assumed the role of a supplicant
among them, he no longer had the strength to meet them, hardly
had the strength to think of it at all. For this brother-in-law of his
he had as good as denied his king and departed from the ranks of
royal retainers. He had revealed to Erlend something that he found
more bitter than death to recall whenever it entered his thoughts.
And yet Erlend behaved toward him as if he had understood nothing and remembered nothing. It didn't seem to trouble the fellow
at all that he had wreaked havoc with another man's life.

At that moment Erlend said to him, "We should see about leaving, Simon, if we want to make it back home tonight. I'll go out
and see to the horses."

Simon looked up, feeling a strange ill will at the sight of the
other man's tall, handsome figure. Under the hood of his cape Erlend wore a small black silk cap that fit snugly to his head and was
tied under his chin. His lean dark face with the big pale blue eyes
sunk deep in the shadow of his brow looked even younger and
more refined under that cap.

"And pack up my bag in the meantime," he said from the door
as he went out.

The other men had continued to talk about the case. It was
quite peculiar, said one of them, that Lavrans hadn't been able to
arrange things better; the man usually knew what he was doing.
He was the most experienced of farmers in all matters regarding
the purchase and sale of land.

"It's probably my father who is to blame," said Holmgeir, the priest's son. "He said as much this morning. If he had listened to Lavrans back then, everything would have been plain and clear. But you know how Lavrans was. . . . Toward priests he was always as amenable and submissive as a lamb."

Even so, Lavrans of Jørundgaard had always guarded his own welfare, said someone else.

"Yes, and no doubt he thought he was doing so when he followed the priest's advice," said Holmgeir, laughing. "That can be the wise thing to do, even with earthly matters—as long as you're not eyeing the same patch that the Church has set its sights on."

Lavrans had been a strangely pious man, thought Vidar. He had never spared either property or livestock with regard to the Church or the poor.

"No," said Holmgeir thoughtfully. "Well, if I'd been such a rich man, I too might have had a mind to pay out sums for the peace of my soul. But I wouldn't have given away my goods with both hands, the way he did, and then walk around with red eyes and white cheeks every time I'd been to see the priest to confess my sins. And Lavrans went to confession every month."

"Tears of remorse are the fair gifts of grace from the Holy Spirit, Holmgeir," said old Ingemund Bjørnssøn. "Blessed is he who can weep for his sins here in this world; all the easier it will be for him to enter the other. . . ."

"Then Lavrans must have been in Heaven long ago," said Holmgeir, "considering the way he fasted and disciplined his flesh. I've heard that on Good Friday he would lock himself in the loft above the storeroom and lash himself with a whip."

"Hold your tongue," said Simon Andressøn, trembling with bitterness; his face was blood red. Whether Holmgeir's remark was true or not, he didn't know. But when he was cleaning up his father-in-law's belongings, he had found a small, oblong wooden box in the bottom of his book chest, and inside lay a silk whip that the cloisters called a flagellum. The braided strips of leather bore dark spots, which might have been blood. Simon had burned it, with a feeling of sad reverence. He realized that he had come upon something in the other man's life that Lavrans had never wanted a living soul to see.

"I don't think he would talk about such things to his servants, in any case," said Simon when he trusted himself to speak.

"No, it's just something that people have made up," replied Holmgeir. "Surely he didn't have such sins to repent that he would need to—" The man gave a little sneer. "If I had lived as blameless and Christian a life as Lavrans Bjørgulfsøn, and been married to a mournful woman like Ragnfrid Ivarsdatter, I think I would have wept for the sins that I *hadn't* committed—"

Simon leaped up and struck Holmgeir in the mouth so the man tumbled back toward the hearth. His dagger fell to the floor, and in the next instant he grabbed it and tried to stab the other man. Simon shielded himself with his arm holding his cape as he seized Holmgeir's wrist with his other hand and tried to wrest the dagger away. In the meantime the priest's son aimed a number of blows at his face. Simon then gripped him by both arms, but the young man sank his teeth into Simon's hand.

"You dare to bite me, you dog!" Simon let go, took several steps back, and pulled his sword from its sheath. He fell upon Holmgeir so that his young body arched back, with a few inches of steel buried in his chest. A moment later Holmgeir's body slipped from the sword point and fell heavily, halfway in the hearth fire.

Simon flung his sword away and was about to lift Holmgeir out of the blaze when he saw Vidar's axe raised to strike right above his head. He ducked and lunged to the side, seized hold of his sword again, and just managed to fend off the blade of the envoy, Alf Einarssøn; he whirled around and again had to shield himself from Vidar's axe. Out of the corner of his eye he saw behind him that the Bjørnssøns and Bjørn of Lunde were aiming spears at him from the other side of the hearth. He then drove Alf in front of him over to the opposite wall but sensed that Vidar was coming for him from behind. Vidar had dragged Holmgeir out of the fire; they were cousins, those two. And the louts from Lunde were approaching from around the hearth. He stood exposed on all sides, and in the midst of it all, even though he had more than enough to do to save his life, he felt a vague, unhappy sense of surprise that the men were all against him.

At the next moment Erlend's sword flashed between the Lunde men and Simon. Toralde reeled aside and fell against the wall. Quick as lightning, Erlend shifted his sword to his left hand and struck Alf's weapon away so that it slid with a clatter across the floor, while with his right hand he grabbed the shaft of Bjørn's spear and pressed it downward.

"Get outside," he told Simon, breathing hard and shielding his brother-in-law from Vidar. Simon ground his teeth together and raced across the room toward Bjørn and Ingemund. Erlend was at his side, screaming over the tumult and clanging of swords: "Get outside! Do you hear me, you fool? Head for the door—we have to get out!"

When Simon realized that Erlend meant for both of them to go out, he began moving backward, still fighting, toward the door. They ran through the entryway, and then they were out in the courtyard, Simon a few steps farther away from the building, and Erlend right in front of the door with his sword half raised and his face turned toward those who were swarming after them.

For a moment Simon felt blinded; the winter day was so dazzling bright and clear. Under the blue sky the mountains arched white-gold in the last rays of the sun; the forest was weighted down with snow and frost. The expanse of fields glittered and gleamed like gemstones.

He heard Erlend say, "It will not make amends for the misfortune if more deaths occur. We should use our wits, good sirs, so there is no more bloodshed. Things are bad enough as they are, with my brother-in-law having slain a man."

Simon stepped to Erlend's side.

"You killed my cousin without cause, Simon Andressøn," said Vidar of Klaufastad, who was standing in front of the others in the doorway.

"It was not entirely without cause that he fell. But you know, Vidar, that I won't refuse to pay the penance for this misfortune I've brought upon you. All of you know where you can find me at home."

Erlend talked a little more to the farmers. "Alf, how did it happen?" He went indoors with the other men.

Simon stayed where he was, feeling strangely numb. Erlend came back after a moment. "Let's go now," he said as he headed for the stable.

"Is he dead?" asked Simon.

"Yes. And Alf and Toralde and Vidar all have wounds, but none

is serious. Holmgeir's hair was singed off the back of his head."
Erlend had spoken in a somber voice, but now he abruptly burst
out laughing. "*Now* it certainly smells like a damn roasted thrush
in there, you'd better believe me! How the Devil could all of you
get into such a quarrel in such a short time?" he asked in astonishment.

A half-grown boy was holding their horses. Neither of the men
had brought his own servant along on this journey.

Both were still carrying their swords. Erlend picked up a hand-
ful of hay and wiped the blood from his. Simon did the same.
When he had rubbed off the worst of it, he stuck his sword back in
its sheath. Erlend cleaned his sword very thoroughly and then pol-
ished it with the hem of his cape. Then he made several playful little thrusts into the air and smiled, fleetingly, as if at a memory. He
tossed the sword high up, caught it by the hilt, and stuck it back in
its sheath.

"Your wounds . . . We should go up to the house, and I'll bandage them for you."

Simon said they were nothing. "But you're bleeding too, Erlend!"

"It's nothing dangerous, and my skin heals fast. I've noticed
that heavyset people always take longer to heal. And with this
cold . . . and we have such a long way to ride."

Erlend got some salve and cloths from the tenant farmer and
carefully tended to the other man's wounds. Simon had two flesh
wounds right next to each other on the left side of his chest; they
bled a great deal at first, but they weren't serious. Erlend had been
slashed on the thigh by Bjørn's spear. That would make it painful
to ride, said Simon, but his brother-in-law laughed. It had barely
made a scratch through his leather hose. He dabbed at it a bit and
then wrapped it tightly against the frost.

It was bitterly cold. Before they reached the bottom of the hill on
which the farm stood, their horses were covered with rime and the
fur trim on the men's hoods had turned white.

"Brrr." Erlend shivered. "If only we were home! We'll have to
ride over to the manor down here and report the slaying."

"Is that necessary?" asked Simon. "I spoke to Vidar and the
others after all . . ."

"It would be better if you did so," said Erlend. "You should report the news yourself. Don't let them have anything to hold against you."

The sun had slipped behind the ridge now; the evening was a pale grayish blue but still light. They rode along a creek, beneath the branches of birch trees that were even more shaggy with frost than the rest of the forest. There was a stink of raw, icy fog in the air, which could make a man's breath stick in his throat. Erlend grumbled impatiently about the long period of cold they had had and about the chill ride that lay before them.

"You're not getting frostbite on your face, are you, brother-in-law?" He peered anxiously under Simon's hood. Simon rubbed his hand over his face; it wasn't frostbitten, but he had grown quite pale as he rode. It didn't suit him, because his large, portly face was weather-beaten and ruddy, and the paleness appeared in gray blotches, which made his complexion look unclean.

"Have you ever seen a man spreading manure with his sword the way Alf did?" asked Erlend. He burst out laughing at the memory and leaned forward in his saddle to imitate the gesture. "What a splendid envoy he is! You should have seen Ulf playing with his sword, Simon—Jesus, Maria!"

Playing . . . Well, now he'd seen Erlend Nikulaussøn playing at that game. Over and over again he saw himself and the other men tumbling around the hearth, the way farmers chop wood or toss hay. And Erlend's slender, lightning-swift figure among them, his gaze alert and his wrist steady as he danced with them, quick-witted and an expert swordsman.

More than twenty years ago he himself had been considered one of the foremost swordsmen among the youth of the royal retainers, when they practiced out on the green. But since then he hadn't had much opportunity to use his knightly skills.

And here he was now, riding along and feeling sick at heart because he had killed a man. He kept seeing Holmgeir's body as it fell from his sword and sank into the fire; he heard the man's abrupt, strangled death cry in his ears and saw, again and again, images of the brief, furious battle that followed. He felt dejected, pained, and confused; they had turned on him suddenly, all those men with whom he had sat and felt a sense of belonging. And then Erlend had come to his aid.

He had never thought himself a coward. He had hunted down six bears during the years he had lived at Formo, and twice he had put his life at risk in the most reckless manner. With only the thin trunk of a pine tree between him and a raging, wounded female, with no other weapon than his spearpoint on a shaft a scant hand's breadth long . . . The tenseness of the game had not disturbed his steadiness of thought, action, or instinct. But now, in that outbuilding . . . he didn't know if he had been afraid, but he certainly had been confused, unable to think clearly.

When he was back home after the bear hunt, with his clothes thrown on haphazardly, with his arm in a sling, feverish, his shoulder stiff and torn, he had merely felt an overwhelming joy. Things might have gone worse; how much worse, he didn't dwell on. But now he kept thinking about it, ceaselessly: how everything might have ended if Erlend hadn't come to his aid just in time. He hadn't been afraid, but he had such a peculiar feeling. It was the expressions on the faces of the other men . . . and Holmgeir's dying body.

He had never killed a man before.

Except for the Swedish horseman he had felled . . . It was during the year when King Haakon led an incursion into Sweden to avenge the murder of the dukes.[4] Simon had been sent out on a scouting mission; he had taken along three men, and he was to be their chieftain. How bold and cocky he was. Simon remembered that his sword had gotten stuck in the steel helmet of the horseman so that he had to pry and wriggle it loose. There was a nick in the blade when he looked at it the next morning. He had always thought about that incident with pride, and there had been eight Swedes. He had gotten a taste of war at any rate, and that wasn't the lot of everyone who joined the king's men that year. When daylight came, he saw that blood and brains had splattered over his coat of mail; he tried to look modest and not boastful as he washed it off.

But it did no good to think about that poor devil of a horseman now. No, that was not the same thing. He couldn't get rid of a terrible feeling of remorse about Holmgeir Moisessøn.

There was also the fact that he owed Erlend his life. He didn't yet know what import this would have, but he felt as if everything would be different, now that he and Erlend were even.

In that way they were even at least.

The brothers-in-law had been riding in near silence. Once Erlend said, "It was foolish of you, Simon, not to think of getting out right from the start."

"Why is that?" asked Simon rather brusquely. "Because you were outside?"

"No . . ." There was the hint of a smile in Erlend's voice. "Well, because of that too. I hadn't thought about that. But through that narrow door they couldn't follow you more than one at a time. And it's always astounding how quickly people regain their senses when they come out under the open sky. It seems to me a miracle that there weren't more deaths."

A few times Erlend inquired about his brother-in-law's wounds. Simon said he hardly noticed them, even though they were throbbing terribly.

They reached Formo late that evening, and Erlend went inside with his brother-in-law. He had advised Simon to send the sheriff a report of the incident the very next day in order to arrange for a letter of reprieve[5] as soon as possible. Erlend would gladly compose the letter for Simon that night since the wounds on his chest would no doubt hamper his writing hand. "And tomorrow you must keep to your bed; you may have a little wound fever."

Ramborg and Arngjerd were waiting up for them. Because of the cold, they had settled on the bench on the warm side of the hearth, tucking their legs underneath them. A board game lay between them; they looked like a couple of children.

Simon had barely uttered a few words about what had happened before his young wife flew to his side and threw her arms around his neck. She pulled his face down to hers and pressed her cheek against his. And she crushed Erlend's hands so tightly that he laughingly said he had never thought Ramborg could have such strong fingers.

She begged her husband to spend the night in the main house so that she could keep watch over him. She implored him, almost in tears, until Erlend offered to stay and sleep with Simon if she would send a man north to Jørundgaard to take word. It was too late for him to ride home anyway, "and a shame for Kristin to sit up so late in this cold. She waits up for me too; you're both good wives, you daughters of Lavrans."

While the men ate and drank, Ramborg sat close to her husband. Simon patted her arm and hand; he was both a little embarrassed and greatly touched that she showed so much concern and love for him. Simon was sleeping in the Sæmund house during Lent, and when the men went over there, Ramborg went with them and put a large kettle of honey-ale to warm near the hearthstone.

The Sæmund house was an ancient little hearth building, warm and snug; the timbers were so roughly hewn that there were only four beams to each wall. Right now it was cold, but Simon threw a great armful of resinous pine onto the fire and chased his dog up into the bed. The animal could lie there and warm it up for them. They pulled the log chair and the high-backed bench all the way up to the hearth and made themselves comfortable, for they were frozen to the bone after their ride, and the meal in the main house had only partially thawed them.

Erlend wrote the letter for Simon. Then they proceeded to undress. Simon's wound began to bleed again when he moved his arms too much, so his brother-in-law helped him pull the outer tunic over his head and take off his boots. Erlend limped a bit from his wounded leg; it was stiff and tender after the ride, he said, but it was nothing. Then they sat down near the fire again, half dressed. The room had grown pleasantly warm, and there was still plenty of ale in the kettle.

"I can see that you're taking this much too hard," Erlend said once. They had been dozing and staring into the fire. "He was no great loss to the world, that Holmgeir."

"That's not what Sira Moises will think," said Simon quietly. "He's an old man and a good priest."

Erlend nodded somberly.

"It's a bad thing to have made enemies with such a man. Especially since he lives so near. And you know that I often have business in that parish."

"Yes, well . . . This kind of thing can happen so easily—to any of us. They'll probably sentence you to a fine of ten or twelve marks of gold. And you know that Bishop Halvard is a stern master when he has to hear the confession of an assailant, and the boy's father is one of his priests. But you'll get through whatever is required."

Simon did not reply.

Erlend continued. "No doubt I'll have to pay fines for the injuries." He smiled to himself. "And I own no other piece of Norwegian land than the farm at Dovre."

"How big of a farm *is* Haugen?" asked Simon.

"I don't remember exactly; it says in the deed. But the people who work the land harvest only a small amount of hay. No one wants to live there; I've heard that the buildings are in great disrepair. You know what people say: that the dead spirits of my aunt and Herr Bjørn haunt the place.

"But I know that I will win thanks from my wife for what I did today. Kristin is fond of you, Simon—as if you were her own brother."

Simon's smile was almost imperceptible as he sat there in the shadows. He had pushed the log chair back a bit and had put his hand up to shield his eyes from the heat of the flames. But Erlend was as happy as a cat in the heat. He sat close to the hearth, leaning against a corner of the bench, with one arm resting along its back and his wounded leg propped up on the opposite side.

"Yes, she had such charming words to say about it one day this past fall," said Simon after a moment. There was an almost mocking ring to his voice.

"When our son was ill, she showed that she was a loyal sister," he said somberly, but then that slightly jesting tone was back. "Well, Erlend, we have kept faith with each other the way we swore to do when we gave our hands to Lavrans and vowed to stand by each other as brothers."

"Yes," said Erlend, unsuspecting. "I'm glad for what I did today too, Simon, my brother-in-law." They both fell silent for a while. Then Erlend hesitantly stretched out his hand to the other man. Simon took it. They clasped each other's fingers tightly, then let go and huddled back in their seats, a little embarrassed.

Finally Erlend broke the silence. For a long time he had been sitting with his chin in his hand, staring into the hearth, where only a tiny flame now flickered, flaring up, dancing a bit, and playing over the charred pieces of wood, which broke apart and collapsed with brittle little sighs. Soon there would be only black coals and glowing embers left of the fire.

Erlend said quite softly, "You have treated me so magnanimously, Simon Darre, that I think few men are your equal. I . . . I haven't forgotten . . ."

"Silence! You don't know, Erlend . . . Only God in Heaven knows everything that resides in a man's mind," whispered Simon, frightened and distraught.

"That's true," said Erlend in the same quiet and somber tone of voice. "We all need Him to judge us . . . with mercy. But a man must judge a man by what he *does*. And I . . . I . . . May God reward you, brother-in-law!"

Then they sat in dead silence, not daring to move for fear of being shamed.

Suddenly Erlend let his hand fall to his knee. A fiery blue ray of light flashed from the stone on the ring he wore on his right index finger. Simon knew that Kristin had given it to Erlend when he was released from the prison tower.

"But you must remember, Simon," he said in a low voice, "the old saying: Many a man is given what was intended for another, but no one is given another man's fate."

Simon raised his head sharply. Slowly his face flushed blood red; the veins at his temples stood out like dark, twisted cords.

Erlend glanced at him for a moment but quickly withdrew his eyes. Then he too turned crimson. A strangely delicate and girlish blush spread over his tan skin. He sat motionless, embarrassed and confused, with his little, childish mouth open.

Simon stood up abruptly and went over to the bed.

"You'll want to take the outside edge, I presume." He tried to speak calmly and with nonchalance, but his voice quavered.

"No, I'll let you decide," said Erlend numbly. He got to his feet. "The fire?" he asked, flustered. "Should I cover the ashes?" He began raking the hearth.

"Finish that and then come to bed," said Simon in the same tone. His heart was pounding so hard that he could barely talk.

In the dark Erlend, soundless as a shadow, slipped under the covers on the outer edge of the bed and lay down, as quiet as a forest creature. Simon thought he would suffocate from having the other man in his bed.

CHAPTER 6

EVERY YEAR DURING Easter week Simon Andressøn held an ale feast for the people of the village. They came to Formo on the third day after mass and stayed until Thursday.

Kristin had never particularly enjoyed these banquets with their bantering and pleasantry. Both Simon and Ramborg seemed to think that the more commotion and noise there was, the better. Simon always invited his guests to bring along their children, their servants, and the children of their servants—as many as could be spared from home. On the first day everything proceeded in a quiet and orderly manner; only the gentry and the elders would converse, while the youth listened and ate and drank, and the little children kept mostly to a different building. But on the second day, from early in the morning on, the host would urge the lively young people and the children to drink and make merry, and before long the teasing would grow so wild and unrestrained that the women and maidens would slip away to the corners and stand there in clusters, giggling and ready to flee. But many of the more high-standing wives would seek out Ramborg's women's house, which was already occupied by the mothers who had rescued the youngest children from the tumult of the main building.

One game that was a favorite among the men was pretending to hold a *ting*. They would read summons documents, present grievances, proclaim new laws and modify old ones, but they always twisted the words around and said them backward. Audun Torbergssøn could recite King Haakon's letter to the merchants of Bjørgvin:[1] what they could charge for men's hose and for leather soles on a woman's shoes, about the men who made swords and big and small shields. But he would mix up the words until they were all jumbled and sheer babble. This game always ended with the men not having any idea what they were saying. Kristin remembered from her childhood that her father would never allow the jesting to turn to ridicule of anything related to the Church or divine services. But otherwise Lavrans thought it great fun when he and his guests would compete by jumping up on the tables and benches while they merrily shouted all manner of coarse and unseemly nonsense.

Simon was usually most fond of games in which a man was blindfolded and had to search through the ashes for a knife, or two people had to bob for pieces of gingerbread in a big bowl of ale. The other guests would try to make them laugh, and the ale would spray all around. Or they were supposed to use their teeth to dig a ring out of a flour bin. The hall would soon take on the look of a pigsty.

But this year they had such surprisingly glorious spring weather for Easter. On Wednesday by early morning it was already sunny and warm, and right after breakfast everyone went out to the courtyard. Instead of making a noisy ruckus, the young people played with balls, or shot at targets or had tugs-of-war with a rope. Later they played the stag game or the woodpile dance,[2] and afterward they persuaded Geirmund of Kruke to sing and play his harp. Soon everyone, both young and old, had joined the dance. Snow still covered the fields, but the alder trees were brown with buds, and the sun shone warm and lovely on all the bare slopes. When the guests came outside after supper, there were birds singing everywhere. Then they made a bonfire in the field beyond the smithy, and they sang and danced until late into the night. The next morning everyone stayed in bed a long time and left the banquet manor much later than usual. The guests from Jørundgaard were normally the last to depart, but this time Simon persuaded Erlend and Kristin to stay until the following day. Those from Kruke were to stay at Formo until the end of the week.

Simon had accompanied the last of his guests up to the main road. The evening sun was shining so beautifully on his estate, spread out over the hillside. He was warm and in high spirits from the drinking and noise of the feast. He walked back between the fences, homeward to the calm and pleasant goodwill that prevails when a small circle of close kin remains after a great banquet. He felt so light of heart and happier than he had been for a long time.

Down in the field near the smithy they had lit another bonfire:

Erlend's sons, Sigrid's older children, Jon Daalk's sons, and his own daughters. Simon leaned over the fence for a moment to watch. Ulvhild's scarlet feast day gown gleamed and rippled in the sun. She ran back and forth, dragging branches over to the fire, and suddenly she was stretched out full length on the ground! Her father shouted merrily, but the children didn't hear him.

In the courtyard two serving maids were tending to the smallest of the children. They were sitting against the wall of the women's house, basking in the sun. Above their heads the evening light gleamed like molten gold on the small glass windowpane. Simon picked up little Inga Geirmundsdatter, tossed her high in the air, and then held her in his arms. "Can you sing for your uncle today, pretty Inga?" Then her brother and Andres both fell upon Simon, wanting to be tossed up in the air too.

Whistling, he climbed the stairs to the great hall in the loft. The sun was shining into the room so splendidly; they had let the door stand open. A wondrous calm reigned over everyone. At the end of the table Erlend and Geirmund were bent over the harp, on which they were putting new strings. They had the mead horn standing near them on the table. Sigrid was in bed, nursing her youngest son. Kristin and Ramborg were sitting with her, and a silver mug stood on a footstool between the sisters.

Simon filled his own gilded goblet to the brim with wine, went over to the bed, and drank a toast to Sigrid. "I see that all have quenched their thirst, except you, my sister!"

Laughing, she propped herself up on her elbow and accepted the goblet. The infant began howling crossly at being disturbed.

Simon sat down on the bench, still whistling softly, and listened with half an ear to what the others were saying. Sigrid and Kristin were talking about their children; Ramborg was silent, fiddling with a windmill that belonged to Andres. The men at the table were strumming the harp, trying it out; Geirmund picked out a melody on the harp and sang along. They both had such charming voices.

After a while Simon went out to the gallery, leaned against the carved post, and gazed out. From the cowshed came the eternally hungry lowing. If this weather held on for a time, perhaps the spring shortages wouldn't last as long this year.

Kristin was approaching. He didn't have to turn around; he recognized her light step. She stepped forward and stood at his side in the evening sun.

So fair and graceful, she had never seemed to him more beautiful. And all of a sudden he felt as if he had somehow been lifted up and were swimming in the light. He let out a long breath. Suddenly he thought: It was simply good to be alive. A rich and golden bliss washed over him.

She was his own sweet love. All the troubled and bitter thoughts he had had seemed nothing more than half-forgotten foolishness. My poor love. If only I could comfort you. If only you could be happy again. I would gladly give up my life if it would help you.

Oh yes, he could see that her lovely face looked older and more careworn. She had an abundance of fine, little wrinkles under her eyes, and her skin had lost its delicate hue. It had become coarser and tan from the sun, but she was pale under the tan. And yet to him she would surely always be just as beautiful. Her big gray eyes, her fine, calm mouth, her round little chin, and her steady, subdued demeanor were the fairest he knew on earth.

It was a pleasure to see her once again dressed in a manner befitting a highborn woman. The thin little silk wimple covered only half of her golden brown tresses; her braids had been pinned up so they peeked out in front of her ears. There were streaks of gray in her hair now, but that didn't matter. And she was wearing a magnificent blue surcoat made of velvet and trimmed with marten fur. The bodice was cut so low and the sleeve holes so deep that the garment clung to her breast and shoulders like the narrow straps of a bridle. It looked so lovely. Underneath there was a glimpse of something sand yellow, a gown that fit snugly to her body, all the way up to her throat and down to her wrists. It was held closed with dozens of tiny gilded buttons, which touched him so deeply. God forgive him—all those little golden buttons gave him as much joy as the sight of a flock of angels.

He stood there and felt the strong, steady beat of his own heart. Something had fallen away from him—yes, like chains. Vile, hateful dreams—they were just phantoms of the night. Now he could see the love he felt for her in the light of day, in full sunlight.

"You're looking at me so strangely, Simon. Why are you smiling like that?"

The man gave a quiet, merry laugh but did not reply. Before them stretched the valley, filled with the golden warmth of the evening sun. Flocks of birds warbled and chirped metallically from the edge of the woods. Then the full, clear voice of the song thrush rang out from somewhere inside the forest. And here she stood, warmed by the sun, radiant in her brilliant finery, having emerged from the dark, cold house and the rough, heavy clothing that smelled of sweat and toil. My Kristin, it's good to see you this way again.

He took her hand, which lay before him on the railing of the gallery, and lifted it to his face. "The ring you're wearing is so lovely." He turned the gold ring on her finger and then put her hand back down. It was reddish and rough now, and he didn't know how he could ever make amends to it—so fair it had once been, her big, slender hand.

"There's Arngjerd and Gaute," said Kristin. "The two of them are quarreling again."

Their voices could be heard from underneath the loft gallery, shrill and angry. Now the maiden began shouting furiously, "Go ahead and remind me of that. It seems to me a greater honor to be called my father's bastard daughter than to be the lawful son of yours!"

Kristin spun on her heel and ran down the stairs. Simon followed and heard the sound of two or three slaps. She was standing under the gallery, clutching her son by the shoulder.

The two children had their eyes downcast; they were red-faced, silent, and defiant.

"I see you know how to behave as a guest. You do us such honor, your father and me."

Gaute stared at the ground. In a low, angry voice he said to his mother, "She said something . . . I don't want to repeat it."

Simon put his hand under his daughter's chin and tilted her face up. Arngjerd turned even brighter red, and her eyes blinked under her father's gaze.

"Yes," she said, pulling away from him. "I reminded Gaute that his father was a condemned villain and traitor. But before that he called you . . . He said that you, Father, were the traitor, and that it was thanks to Erlend that you were now sitting here, safe and rich, on your own manor."

"I thought you were a grown-up maiden by now. Are you going to let childish chatter provoke you so that you forget both your manners and honor among kin?" Angrily he pushed the girl away, turned toward Gaute, and asked calmly, "What do you mean, Gaute, my friend, that I betrayed your father? I've noticed before that you're cross with me. Now tell me: What do you mean?"

"You know what I mean!"

Simon shook his head.

Then the boy shouted, his eyes flashing with bitterness, "The letter they tortured my father on the rack for, trying to make him say who had put their seal on it—I saw that letter myself! I was the one who took it and burned it."

"Keep silent!" Erlend broke in among them. His face was deathly white, all the way to his lips; his eyes blazed.

"No, Erlend. It's better that we clear up this matter now. Was my name mentioned in that letter?"

"Keep silent!" Furiously Erlend seized Gaute by the shoulder and chest. "I trusted you. You, my son! It would serve you right if I killed you now."

Kristin sprang forward, as did Simon. The boy tore himself loose and took refuge with his mother. Beside himself with rage, he screamed furiously as he hid behind Kristin's arm, "I picked it up and looked at the seals before I burned it, Father! I thought the day might come when I could serve you by doing so. . . ."

"May God curse you!" A brief dry sob racked Erlend's body.

Simon too had turned pale and then dark red in the face, out of shame for his brother-in-law. He didn't dare look in Erlend's direction; he thought he would suffocate from the other's humiliation.

Kristin stood as if bewitched, still holding her arms protectively around her son. But one thought followed another, in rapid succession.

Erlend had had Simon's private seal in his possession for a short time during that spring. The brothers-in-law had jointly sold Lavrans's dock warehouse at Veøy to the cloister on Holm. Erlend had mentioned that this was probably unlawful, but surely no one would question it. He had shown her the seal and said that Simon should have had a finer one carved. All three brothers had acquired a copy of their father's seal; only the inscriptions were different. But Gyrd's was much more finely etched, said Erlend.

Gyrd Darre . . . Erlend had brought her greetings from him after both of his last journeys to the south. She remembered being surprised that Erlend had visited Gyrd at Dyfrin. They had met only once, at Ramborg's wedding. Ulf Saksesøn was Gyrd Darre's brother-in-law; Ulf had been part of the plot. . . .

"You were mistaken, Gaute," said Simon in a low, firm voice.

"Simon!" Unawares, Kristin gripped her husband's hand. "Keep in mind . . . there are other men than yourself who bear that emblem on their seal."

"Silence! Will you too—" Erlend tore himself away from his wife with a tormented wail and raced across the courtyard toward the stable. Simon set off after him.

"Erlend . . . Was it my brother?"

"Send for the boys. Follow me home," Erlend shouted back to his wife.

Simon caught up with him in the stable doorway and grabbed him by the arm. "Erlend, was it Gyrd?"

Erlend didn't reply; he tried to wrench his arm away. His face looked oddly stubborn and deathly pale.

"Erlend, answer me. Did my brother join you in that plan?"

"Perhaps you too would like to test your sword against mine?" Erlend snarled, and Simon could feel the other man's body trembling as they struggled.

"You know I wouldn't." Simon let go and sank back against the doorframe. "Erlend, in the name of Christ, who suffered death for our sakes: Tell me if it's true!"

Erlend led Soten out, and Simon had to step aside from the doorway. An attentive servant brought his saddle and bridle. Simon took them and sent the man away. Then Erlend took them from Simon.

"Erlend, surely you can tell me *now*! You can tell *me*!" He didn't know why he was begging as if for his very life. "Erlend, answer me. On the wounds of Christ, I beseech you. Tell me, man!"

"You can keep on thinking what you thought before," said Erlend in a low and cutting voice.

"Erlend, I didn't think . . . anything."

"I *know* what you thought." Erlend swung himself into the saddle. Simon grabbed the harness; the horse shifted and pranced uneasily.

"Let go, or I'll run you down," said Erlend.

"Then I'll ask Gyrd. I'll ride south tomorrow. By God, Erlend, you have to tell me. . . ."

"Yes, I'm sure *he* will give you an answer," said Erlend scornfully, spurring the stallion so that Simon had to leap aside. Then Erlend galloped off from the estate.

Halfway up the courtyard Simon met Kristin. She was wearing her cloak. Gaute walked at her side, carrying their clothing sack. Ramborg followed her sister.

The boy glanced up for a moment, frightened and confused. Then he withdrew his gaze. But Kristin fixed her big eyes directly on Simon's face. They were dark with sorrow and anger.

"Could you truly believe that of Erlend? That he would betray you in such a manner?"

"I didn't believe anything," said Simon vehemently. "I thought the boy was just babbling nonsense and foolishness."

"No, Simon, I don't want you to come with me," said Kristin quietly.

He saw that she was unspeakably offended and grieved.

That evening, when Simon was alone with his wife in the main house, as they undressed and their daughters were already asleep in the other bed, Ramborg suddenly asked, "Didn't you know anything about this, Simon?"

"No. Did you?" he asked tensely.

Ramborg came over and stood in the glow of the candle standing on the table. She was half undressed, in her shift and laced bodice; her hair fell in loose curls around her face.

"I didn't know, but I had a feeling. . . . Helga was so strange . . ." Her features twisted into an odd sort of smile, and she looked as if she were freezing. "She talked about how new times would be coming to Norway. The great chieftains would acquire the same rights here as in other lands." Ramborg gave a crooked, almost contorted smile. "They would be called knights and barons again.

"Later, when I saw that you took up their affairs with such zeal, and you were away from home almost a whole year . . . and didn't even feel that you could come north to be with me at Ringheim when I was staying on a stranger's estate, about to give birth to your child . . . I thought perhaps you knew that it concerned others than Erlend."

"Ha! Knights and barons!" Simon gave an angry laugh.

"Then was it merely for Kristin's sake that you did it?"

He saw that her face was pale, as if from frostbite; it was impossible to pretend that he didn't understand what she meant. Out of spite and despair, he exclaimed, "Yes."

Then he thought that she must have gone mad, and he was mad too. Erlend was mad; they had all lost their wits that day. But now there had to be an end to it.

"I did it for your sister's sake, yes," he said soberly. "And for the sake of the children who had no other man closer in family or kinship to protect them. And for Erlend's sake, since we should be as loyal to each other as brothers. So don't start behaving foolishly, for I've seen more than enough of that here on the estate today," he bellowed, and flung the shoe he had just taken off against the wall.

Ramborg went over and picked it up; she looked at the timber it had struck.

"It's shameful that Torbjørg didn't think of it herself, to wash off the soot in here before the feast. I forgot to mention it to her." She wiped off the shoe. It was Simon's best, with a long toe and red heel. She picked up its mate and put both of them into his clothes chest. But Simon noticed that her hands were shaking badly as she did so.

Then he went over and took her in his arms. She twined her thin arms around her husband as she trembled with stifled sobs and whispered to him that she was so tired.

Seven days later Simon and his servant rode through Kvam, heading north. They fought their way through a blizzard of great wet snowflakes. At midday they arrived at the small farm on the public road where there was an alehouse.

The proprietress came out and invited Simon to come into their home; only commoners were shown into the tavern. She shook out his outer garment and hung it up to dry on the wall peg near the hearth as she talked. Such awful weather . . . hard on the horses . . . and he must have had to ride the whole way around . . . it wasn't possible to go across Lake Mjøsa now, was it?

"Oh yes, if a man was sick enough of his life . . ."

The woman and her children standing nearby all laughed agreeably. The older ones went about their chores, bringing in wood and ale, while the younger ones huddled together near the door. They usually received a few *penninger* from Simon, the master of Formo, whenever he stayed there, and if he was bringing home treats for his own children from Hamar, he would often give them a tidbit too. But today he didn't seem to notice them.

He sat on the bench, leaning forward, with his hands hanging over his knees, staring into the hearth fire, and replied with a word or two to the woman's incessant chatter. Then she mentioned that Erlend Nikulaussøn happened to be at Granheim. It was the day on which the ancestral owners were to place the first payment in the hands of the former owners. Should she send one of the children over to his brother-in-law with a message so that they could ride home together?

No, said Simon. She could give him a little food, and then he would lie down and sleep for a while.

He would see Erlend in good time. What he had to say he wanted to say in front of Gaute. But he would prefer not to speak of the matter more than once.

His servant, Sigurd, had sought refuge in the cookhouse while the woman prepared the food. Yes, it had been a wearisome journey, and his master had been like an angry bull almost the whole way. Normally Simon Andressøn liked to hear whatever news from his home district his servants could glean while they were at Dyfrin. He usually had one or more people from Raumerike in his service. Folks would come to him to ask for work whenever he was home, for he was known as a well-liked and generous man who was merry and not high-handed with his servants. But on this journey about the only answer that he, Sigurd, had received from his master was "Keep silent!"

He had apparently had a great quarrel with his brothers; he hadn't even stayed the night at Dyfrin. They had taken lodgings on a tenant farm farther out in the countryside. Sir Gyrd—yes, for he could tell her that the king had made his master's brother a knight at Christmastime—well, Sir Gyrd had come out to the courtyard and warmly entreated Simon to stay, but Simon had given his brother a curt reply. And they had roared and bellowed and shouted, all those gentlemen up in the high loft—Sir Ulf Saksesøn and Gudmund Andressøn had been on the estate as well—so that everyone was terribly frightened. God only knew what it was that had made them foes.

Simon came past the cookhouse, paused for a moment, and peered inside. Sigurd announced quickly that he would get an awl and a strap to make proper repairs to the harness that had been torn in the morning.

"Do they have those kinds of things in the cookhouse on this farm?" Simon flung over his shoulder as he left. Sigurd shook his head and nodded to the woman when Simon had disappeared from sight.

Simon pushed his plate aside but stayed seated. He was so tired that he could hardly even get up. At last he got to his feet and threw himself onto the bed, still wearing his boots and spurs, but then thought better of it. It was a good, clean bed for the house of a commoner. He sat up and pulled off his boots. Stiff and worn out as he was, surely he would be able to sleep now. He was soaked through and freezing, but his face burned after the long ride in the storm.

He crawled under the coverlet, twisting and turning the pillows; they smelled so strangely of fish. Then he stretched out, half reclining, propped up on one elbow.

His thoughts began circling again. He had been thinking and thinking these past few days, the way an animal plods around a tether.

Even if Erling Vidkunssøn had known that the welfare of Gyrd and Gudmund Darre might also be at stake if Erlend Nikulaussøn had been broken and talked . . . well, that didn't make it any worse that Simon had seized upon all means to win the help of the Bjarkø knight. Quite the opposite. Surely a man was obligated to stand by his own brothers, even to the death if need be. But he still wished that he knew whether Erling had known about it. Simon weighed the matter for and against. Erling couldn't possibly have been entirely ignorant that a rebellion was brewing. But what exactly had he known? Gyrd and Ulf, at any rate, didn't seem to know whether the man was aware of their complicity. But Simon remembered that Erling had mentioned the Haftorssøns and had advised him to seek their help, for it was most likely their friends who would need to be afraid. The Haftorssøns were cousins of Ulf Saksesøn and Helga. The nose is right next to the eyes!

But even if Erling Vidkunssøn believed that he was also thinking of his own brothers, surely that didn't make what he had done any worse. And Erling might have realized that he knew nothing about his brothers' peril. Besides, he had said himself that . . . He remembered he had told Stig that he didn't think they could torture Erlend into talking.

They might still have reason to fear Erlend's tongue. He had kept silent through the torture and imprisonment, but he was the kind of man who might let it slip out afterward through some chance remark. It would be just like him.

And yet . . . Simon thought this was the one thing he could be certain that Erlend would never do. He was as silent as a rock every time the conversation touched on the matter, precisely because he was afraid of being lured into some slip of the tongue. Simon understood that Erlend had a fierce, almost childish terror of breaching a promise. Childish because the fact that he had given away the whole plan to his lover clearly did not seem to Erlend to have tarnished his honor in any significant way. He apparently thought that such could happen to the best of men. As long as he himself held his tongue, he considered his shield unblemished and his promise unbroken. And Simon had noticed that Erlend was sensitive about his honor, as far as his own understanding of honor and reputation went. He had nearly lost his wits from desperation and anger at the mere thought that any of his fellow conspirators might be exposed—even now, so much later and in such a manner that it couldn't possibly make any difference to the men whom he had protected with his life, as well as with his honor and his property. All because of a child talking to the closest kinsman of these men.

Erlend wanted to handle it in such a way that if things went wrong, he would be the one to pay the price for all of them. That's what he had vowed on the crucifix to every man who had joined him in the plot. But to think that grown-up, sensible men would put their faith in such an oath, when it was not entirely within

Erlend's control . . . Now that Simon had learned everything about
the plan, he thought it was the greatest foolishness he had ever
heard. Erlend had been willing to let his body be torn apart, limb
from limb, in order to keep his sworn oath. All the while the secret
lay in the hands of a ten-year-old boy; Erlend himself had seen to
that. And it was evidently no thanks to him that Sunniva Olavsdatter didn't know more than she did. Could anyone ever make
sense of such a man?

If, for a moment, he had believed . . . well, what Erlend and his
wife thought he had believed. . . . God only knew how close to the
truth such a thought was when Gaute started talking about seeing
his seal on the treasonous letter. The two of them might remember
that he knew a few things about Erlend Nikulaussøn so that he,
more than most other men, had little reason to believe the best of
that gentleman. But they had probably forgotten long ago how he
had once come upon them and witnessed the depths of their
shamelessness.

So there was little reason for him to lie here, berating himself
like a dog because he had wrongly accused Erlend in his mind.
God knew it was not because he wanted to think ill of his brother-
in-law; it only made him unhappy to have such thoughts. He was
fully aware that it was a wildly foolish notion; he would have realized at once, even without Kristin's words, that things *couldn't*
have happened that way. As quickly as the suspicion occurred to
him—that Erlend might have misused his seal—he had dismissed
it. No, Erlend couldn't possibly have done that. Erlend had never
in his life committed a dishonorable act that had been thought out
in advance or with some specific purpose in mind.

Simon tossed and turned in bed, moaning. They had made him
half mad with all this madness. He felt so tormented when he
thought about how Gaute had gone around for years, believing
this of him. But it was unreasonable for him to take it so hard.
Even though he was fond of the boy, fond of all of Kristin's sons,
they were still hardly more than children. Did he need to be so
concerned about how they might judge him?

To think he could be so furious with rage when he thought
about the men who had placed their hands on the hilt of Erlend's
sword and sworn to follow their chieftain. If they were such sheep
to allow themselves to be dazzled by Erlend's persuasive and bold

manner and to believe that he was a suitable chieftain, then it was only to be expected that they would behave like frightened sheep when the whole venture went awry. And yet he felt dazed when he thought about what he had learned at Dyfrin: that so *many* men had dared entrust the peace of the land and their own welfare into Erlend's hands. Even Haftor Olavssøn and Borgar Trondssøn! But not *one* of them had the courage to step forward and demand of the king that Erlend should be granted an honorable reconciliation and a reprieve for his ancestral estates. There were so many of them that if they had joined forces, it could easily have been accomplished. Apparently there was less wisdom and courage among the noblemen of Norway than he had thought.

Simon was also angry because he had been entirely kept out of these plans. Not that they would have been able to enlist *him* in such a foolhardy enterprise. But that both Erlend and Gyrd had gone behind his back and concealed everything . . . Surely he was just as good a nobleman as any of the others, and not without some influence in the regions where people knew him.

In some ways he agreed with Gyrd. Considering the manner in which Erlend had squandered his position as chieftain, the man couldn't reasonably demand that his fellow conspirators should step forward and declare their allegiance with him. Simon knew that if he had found Gyrd alone, he would not have ended up parting with his brothers in such a fashion. But there sat that knight, Sir Ulf, stretching out his long legs in front of him and talking about Erlend's lack of sense—after it was all over! And then Gudmund spoke up. In the past neither Gyrd nor Simon had let their younger brother take a position against them. But ever since he had married the priest's paramour, who then became his own paramour, the boy had grown so swaggering and cocky and independent. Simon had sat there glaring fiercely at Gudmund. He spoke so arrogantly and his round, red face looked so much like a child's backside that Simon's hands itched to give it a swat. In the end he hardly knew what he was saying to the three men.

And now he had broken with his brothers. He felt as if he would bleed to death when he thought about it, as if bonds of flesh and blood had been severed. He was the poorer for it. Bare is the brotherless back.

But however things now stood, in the midst of the heated exchange of words he had suddenly realized—he didn't know exactly why—that Gyrd's closed and stony demeanor wasn't solely due to the fact that he was hard pressed to find any peace at home. In a flash Simon saw that Gyrd still loved Helga; that was what made him so strangely fettered and powerless. And in some secretive, incomprehensible way, this aroused his fury over . . . well, over life itself.

Simon hid his face in his hands. Yes, in that sense they had been good, obedient sons. It had been easy for Gyrd and him to feel love for the brides whom his father announced he had chosen for them. The old man had made a long, splendid speech to them one evening, and afterward they had both sat there feeling abashed. About marriage and friendship and faithfulness between honorable, noble spouses; in the end their father even mentioned prayers of intercession and masses. It was too bad their father hadn't given them advice on how to forget as well—when the friendship was broken and the honor dead and the faithfulness a sin and a secret, disgraceful torment, and there was nothing left of the bond but the bleeding wound that would never heal.

After Erlend was released, an odd feeling of calm came over Simon—if only because a man can't continue to endure the kind of pain he had suffered during that time in Oslo. Either something happens, or it gets better of its own accord.

Simon had not been pleased when Kristin moved to Jørundgaard with her husband and all their children so that he had to see them more often and keep up their friendship and kinship. But he consoled himself that it would have been much worse if he had been forced to live with her in a fashion that is unbearable for a man: to live with a woman he loves when she is not his wife or his kinswoman by blood. He chose to ignore what had occurred between his brother-in-law and himself on that evening when they celebrated Erlend's release from the tower. Erlend had probably understood only half of it and surely hadn't given it much thought. Erlend had such a rare talent for forgetting. And Simon had his own estate, a wife whom he loved, and his children.

He had found some semblance of peace with himself. It was not his fault that he loved his wife's sister. She had once been his betrothed, and he was not the one who had broken his promise. Back when he had set his heart on Kristin Lavransdatter, it had simply been his duty to do so, because he thought she was intended to be his wife. The fact that he married her sister . . . that was Ramborg's doing, and her father's. Lavrans, as wise a man as he was, hadn't thought to ask whether Simon had forgotten. But he knew that he couldn't have stood to be asked that question by Lavrans.

Simon wasn't good at forgetting. He was not to blame for that. And he had never spoken a single word that he ought to have withheld. But he couldn't help it if the Devil plagued him with impulses and dreams that violated the bonds of blood; he had never willingly indulged in sinful thoughts of love. And he had always behaved like a loyal brother toward her and her kin. Of that he was certain.

At last he had managed to be tolerably content with his lot.

But only as long as he knew that he was the one who had served those two: Kristin and the man she had chosen in his stead. They had always been in need of his support.

Now this had changed. Kristin had risked her life and soul to save the life of his son. It felt as if all the old wounds had opened up ever since he allowed that to happen.

Later he became indebted to Erlend for his own life.

And then, in return, he had affronted the man—not intentionally, and only in his thoughts, but still . . .

"*Et dimitte nobis debita nostra, sicut et nos dimittibus debitoribus nostris.*" It was strange that the Lord hadn't also taught them to pray: "*sicut et nos dimittibus creditoribus nostris.*" He didn't know whether this was proper Latin; he had never been particularly good at the language. But he knew that in some way he had always been able to forgive his debtors. It seemed much harder to forgive anyone who had bound a debt around *his* neck.

But now they were even: he and those two. He felt all the old resentments, which he had trampled underfoot for years, rip open and come to life.

He could no longer shove Erlend aside in his thoughts as a foolish chatterer who couldn't see or learn or remember or ponder anything at all. Now the other man weighed on his mind precisely because no one knew *what* Erlend saw or thought or remembered; he was completely unfathomable.

Many a man is given what was intended for another, but no one is given another man's fate.

How truly spoken.

Simon had loved his young betrothed. If he had won her, he would certainly have been a contented man; surely they would have lived well together. And she would have continued to be as she was when they first met: gentle and seemly, intelligent enough that a man would gladly seek her counsel even on important matters, a bit headstrong about petty things, but otherwise amenable, accustomed as she was to accepting from her father's hands guidance and support and protection. But then that man had seized hold of her: a man incapable of restraining himself, who had never offered protection to anything. He had ravaged her sweet innocence, broken her proud calm, destroyed her womanly soul, and forced her to stretch and strain to the utmost every faculty she possessed. She had to defend her lover, the way a tiny bird protects its nest with a trembling body and shrill voice when anyone comes too close. It had seemed to Simon that her lovely, slender body was created to be lifted up and fervently shielded by a man's arms. He had seen it tense with wild stubbornness, as her heart pounded with courage and fear and the will to fight, and she battled for her husband and children, the way even a dove can turn fierce and fearless if she has young ones.

If he had been her husband, if she had lived with his honorable goodwill for fifteen winters, he was certain that she would have stood up to defend him too if he had landed in misfortune. With shrewdness and courage she would have stood by his side. But he would never have seen that stony face she turned toward him on the evening in Oslo when she told him that she had been over to take a look around in that house. He would never have heard her scream his own name in such desperate need and distress. And it was not the honorable and just love of his youth that had answered in his heart. The ardor that rose up and cried out toward her wild spirit . . . he would never have known that such feeling could reside in his own heart if things had happened between them as their fathers had intended.

Her expression, as she walked past him and went out into the night to find help for his child . . . She would not have dared to take those measures if she had not been Erlend's wife and had grown accustomed to acting fearlessly, even when her heart trembled with anguish. Her tear-streaked smile when she woke him up and said the boy was calling for his father . . . A smile of such heartbreaking sweetness was possible only for someone who knew what it meant both to lose a battle and to win.

It was Erlend's wife whom he loved—the way he loved her now. But that meant his love was sinful, and that was why things stood as they did and why he was unhappy. He was so unhappy that sometimes he felt only a great astonishment that he was the one this had befallen, and he could see no way out of his distress.

When he trampled on his own honor and noble decorum and reminded Erling Vidkunssøn of things that no honorable man would have imagined that he knew, he had done it not for his brothers or kinsmen but for her alone. It was for her sake that he had dared plead with the other man, just like the lepers who begged at the church doors in town, displaying their hideous sores.

He had thought that someday he would tell her about it. Not everything, not how deeply he had humbled himself. But after they had both grown old, he thought that he would say to Kristin: I helped you as best I could because I remembered how sincerely I loved you, back when I was your betrothed.

But there was one thing he didn't dare touch on with his thoughts. Had Erlend said anything to Kristin? Yes, he had thought that one day she should hear it from his own lips: I never forgot that I loved you when we were young. But if she already knew, and if she had learned it from her husband . . . No, then he didn't think he could go on.

He had intended to tell only her . . . someday, a long time from now. Then he thought about that moment when he had revealed it himself, when Erlend unwittingly happened to see what he thought he had hidden in the most secret part of his soul. And Ramborg knew—although he didn't understand how she had found out.

His own wife . . . and her husband—they both knew.

Simon gave a wild, stifled scream and abruptly flung himself onto the other side of the bed.

May God help him! Now he was the one who lay here, flayed naked, violated, bleeding with torment and trembling with shame.

The proprietress peeked around the door and met Simon's feverish, dry, and sharply glittering eyes from the bed. "Didn't you sleep? Erlend Nikulaussøn was just riding past with two men; no doubt two of his sons were traveling with him." Simon mumbled something in reply, angry and incomprehensible.

He wanted to give them a good head start. But he too would soon have to see about setting off for home.

As soon as Simon entered the main house at Formo and took off his outer garments, Andres would seize hold of his leather cap and try it on. While the boy straddled the bench and rode off to see his uncle at Dyfrin, the big cap would slip down, first over his small nose and then back over his lovely blond curls. But it did little good for Simon to try to remember such things now. God only knew when the boy would be visiting his uncle at Dyfrin again.

Instead the memory of his other son rose up: Halfrid's child. The tiny, pale blue body of an infant. He had seen little of the boy during the few days he lived; he had to sit at the bedside of the dying mother. If the child had survived, or if he had lived longer than his mother, then Simon would have kept Mandvik. Then he probably would have looked for a new wife there in the south. Occasionally he might have come north to the valley to see to his estate up here. Then surely he would have . . . not *forgotten* Kristin; she had led him into much too strange a dance for him to do that. By the Devil, a man should be allowed to remember it as a peculiar adventure: that he had been forced to rescue his betrothed, a highborn young maiden, reared in Christian and seemly behavior, from a house of ill repute and another man's bed. But then he wouldn't have been able to think of her in such a way that it troubled him and robbed the taste from everything good that life had to offer.

His son Erling . . . He would have been fourteen winters old by now. When Andres one day reached so near the age of a man, he himself would be old and feeble.

Oh, yes, Halfrid . . . You weren't very happy with me, were

you? I'm not entirely without blame that things have gone as they have for me.

Erlend Nikulaussøn might well have had to pay with his life for his impetuousness. And Kristin would now be living as a widow at Jørundgaard.

And he himself might have then regretted that he was a married man. Nothing seemed so foolish anymore that he didn't think himself capable of it.

The wind had died down, but great wet flakes of springtime snow were still falling when Simon rode out of the alehouse courtyard. And now, toward evening, birds began whistling and warbling in the grove of trees, defying the snowfall.

Just as a gash in the skin can reopen from too sudden a movement, a fleeting memory caused him pain. Not long ago, at his Easter banquet, several guests were standing outside, basking in the midday sun. High above them in the birch tree sat a robin, whistling into the warm blue air. Geirmund came limping around the corner of the house, dragging himself along with his cane, his other hand resting on the shoulder of his oldest son. He looked up, stopped, and imitated the bird. The boy also pursed his lips and whistled. They could mimic nearly all the birdsongs. Kristin was standing a short distance away, with several other women. Her smile had been so charming as she listened.

Now, toward sunset the clouds began to disperse in the west, tumbling golden over the white mountain slopes, filling the passes and small valleys like gray mist. The river gleamed dully like brass; the dark currents, free of ice, rushed around the rocks in the riverbed, and on each rock lay a little white pillow of new snow.

They made slow progress on the weary horses through the heavy snow. It was a milky white night with a full moon, which peeked out from the drifting haze and clouds as Simon rode down the slopes to the Ula River. When he had crossed the bridge and reached the flat expanses of pine forest, through which the winter road passed, the horses began moving faster. They knew they were approaching the stable. Simon patted Digerbein's steaming wet neck. He was glad this journey would soon be over. Ramborg had probably gone to bed long ago.

At the place where the road turned sharply and emerged from

the woods, there stood a small house. He was nearly upon it when he noticed that men on horseback were stopped in front of the door. He heard Erlend's voice shout, "Then it's agreed that you'll come to visit the day after Sunday? Can I tell my wife as much?"

Simon called out a greeting. It would seem much too strange not to stop and continue on in their company, but he told Sigurd to ride on ahead. Then he rode over to join them; it was Naakkve and Gaute. Erlend was just stepping out of the entryway.

They greeted each other again, the three others in a somewhat strained fashion. Simon could see their faces, although not very clearly in the fading light. He thought their expressions seemed uncertain—both tense and begrudging at the same time. So he said at once, "I've come from Dyfrin, my brother-in-law."

"Yes, I heard that you had traveled south." Erlend stood with his hand on the saddlebow, his eyes downcast. "You've made good time," he added, as if the silence were uncomfortable.

"No, wait a bit," said Simon to the young boys who were about to ride off. "You should hear this too. It was my brother's seal that you saw on the letter, Gaute. And I know you must think they showed poor loyalty to your father, both he and the other gentlemen who had affixed their seals on the letter to Prince Haakon, which your father was to carry to Denmark."

The boy looked down in silence.

Erlend said, "There was one thing you probably didn't think about, Simon, when you went to see your brother. I paid dearly for the safety of Gyrd and the others who joined me; it cost me all I owned except for my reputation as a loyal man who keeps his word. Now Gyrd Darre must think that I couldn't save even my reputation."

Shamefully Simon bowed his head. He hadn't thought about that.

"You might have told me this, Erlend, when I said that I was going to Dyfrin."

"You must have seen for yourself that I was so desperate and furious that I was beyond thinking or reasoning when I rode away from your manor."

"I wasn't particularly levelheaded myself, Erlend."

"No, but I thought you might have had time to come to your senses during the long ride. And I couldn't very well ask you not to talk to your brother without revealing things I had sworn a sacred oath to conceal."

Simon fell silent for a moment. At first he thought that Erlend was right. But then it occurred to him: No, Erlend was being quite unreasonable. Was he supposed to submit to having Kristin and the boys think so ill of him? He mentioned this rather vehemently.

"I have never uttered a word about this, kinsman—not to my mother or to my brothers," said Gaute, turning his handsome, fair face toward his uncle.

"But in the end they found out about it just the same," replied Simon obstinately. "I thought, after everything that happened on that day at my estate, we needed to clear up the matter. And I don't understand why it should take your father so unawares. You're still not much older than a child, my Gaute, and you were so young when you were mixed up in this . . . secret plot."

"Surely I should be able to trust my own son," replied Erlend angrily. "And I had no other choice when I needed to save the letter. I either had to give it to Gaute or let the sheriff find it."

Simon thought it pointless to discuss the matter any further. But he couldn't resist saying, "I wasn't happy when I heard what the boy has been thinking of me these past four years. I've always been fond of you, Gaute."

The boy urged his horse forward a few paces and stretched out his hand; Simon saw that his face had darkened, as if he were blushing.

"You must forgive me, Simon!"

Simon clasped the boy's hand. At times Gaute looked so much like his grandfather that Simon felt strangely moved. He was rather bowlegged and slight in build, but he was an excellent rider, and on the back of a horse he was as handsome a youth as any father could want.

All four of them began riding north; the boys were in front, and when they were beyond earshot, Simon continued.

"You must understand, Erlend . . . I don't think you can rightfully blame me for seeking out my brother and asking him to tell me the truth about this matter. But I know that you had reason to be angry with me, both you and Kristin. Because as soon as this strange news came out . . ." He fumbled for words. "What Gaute said about my seal . . . I can't deny that I thought . . . I know both of you believed that I thought . . . what I should have had sense enough to realize was unthinkable. So I can't deny that you have reason to be angry," he repeated.

The horses splashed through the slushy snow. It took a moment before Erlend replied, and then his voice sounded gentle and subdued. "I don't know what else you could have thought. It was almost inevitable that you should believe—"

"Oh, no. I should have known it wasn't possible," Simon interrupted, sounding aggrieved. After a moment he asked, "Did you think that I knew about my brothers? That I tried to help you for their sake?"

"No!" said Erlend in surprise. "I realized you couldn't possibly know. I knew that *I* hadn't said anything. And I thought I could safely rely on your brothers not to talk." He laughed softly. Then he grew somber and said gently, "I knew you did it for the sake of our father-in-law and because you're a good man."

Simon rode on in silence for a while.

"I imagine you must have been bitterly angry," he then said.

"Well . . . when I had time to think about it . . . I didn't see that there was any other way you could interpret things."

"What about Kristin?" asked Simon, his voice even lower.

"Kristin!" Erlend laughed again. "You know she won't stand for anyone censuring me—except for herself. She seems to think she can handle that well enough all alone. It's the same with our children. God save me if I should chastise them with a single word! But you can rest assured that I've brought her around."

"You have?"

"Yes, well . . . with time I'll manage to convince her. You know that once Kristin gives it some thought, she's the sort of person who will remember you've shown us such loyal friendship that . . ."

Simon, agitated and distraught, felt his heart trembling. He found it unbearable. The other man seemed to think that they could now dismiss this matter from their minds. In the pale moonlight Erlend's face looked so genuinely peaceful. Simon's voice quavered with emotion as he spoke again. "Forgive me, Erlend, but I don't see how I could have believed—"

"I told you I understand it." The other broke in rather impatiently. "It seems to me that you couldn't have thought anything else."

"If only those two foolish children had never spoken," said Simon heatedly.

"Yes. Gaute has never received such a beating before in his life. And the whole thing started because they were quarreling about their ancestors: Reidar Birkebein and King Skule and Bishop Nikolas." Erlend shook his head. "But let's not think about this anymore, kinsman. It's best if we forget about it as soon as we can."

"I can't do that!"

"But, Simon!" This was spoken in reproach, with mild astonishment. "It's not worth it to take this so seriously."

"I can't—don't you understand? I'm not as good a man as you are."

Erlend gave him a bewildered look. "I don't know what you mean."

"I'm not as good a man as you are. I can't so easily forgive those I have wronged."

"I don't know what you mean," repeated Erlend in the same tone of voice.

"I mean . . ." Simon's face was contorted with pain and desperation. His voice was low, as if he were stifling an urge to scream out the words. "I mean that I've heard you speaking kindly of Judge Sigurd of Steigen, the old man whose wife you stole. I've seen how you loved Lavrans with all the love of a son. And I've never noticed that you bore any grudge toward me because you . . . enticed my betrothed away from me. I'm not as noble-minded as you think, Erlend. I'm not as noble-minded as you are. I . . . I do bear a grudge toward the man whom I have wronged."

His cheeks flecked with white from the strain, Simon stared into the eyes of his companion. Erlend had listened to him with his mouth agape.

"I've never realized this until now! Do you *hate* me, Simon?" he whispered, overwhelmed.

"Don't you think I have reason to do so?"

Unawares, both men had reined in their horses. They sat and stared at each other. Simon's small eyes glittered like steel. In the hazy white light of the night, he saw that Erlend's lean features were twitching as if something had broken inside him: an awakening. He looked up from beneath half-closed lids, biting his quivering lower lip.

"I can't bear to see you anymore," said Simon.

"But that was twenty years ago, man!" exclaimed Erlend, overcome and confused.

"Yes. But don't you think she's . . . worth thinking about for twenty years?"

Erlend pulled himself erect in the saddle. He met Simon's eyes with a steady, open gaze. The moonlight lit a blue-green spark in his big, pale blue eyes.

"Yes, yes, I do. May God bless her!"

For a moment he sat motionless. Then he spurred his horse and galloped off through the puddles so the water sprayed up behind him. Simon held Digerbein back; he was almost thrown to the ground because he reined in the horse so sharply. He waited there at the edge of the woods, struggling with the restless animal, for as long as he could hear hoofbeats in the slush.

Remorse had overwhelmed him as soon as he said it. He felt regret and shame, as if in senseless anger he had struck the most defenseless of creatures—a child or a delicate, gentle, and witless beast. His hatred felt like a shattered lance; he was shattered himself from the confrontation with the man's foolish innocence. That bird of misfortune, Erlend Nikulaussøn, understood so little that he seemed both helpless and without guile.

Simon swore and cursed to himself as he rode. Without guile . . . The man was well past forty; it was about time that he could handle a conversation man to man. If Simon had wounded himself, then by the Devil it should be considered worth the price if for once he had managed to strike Erlend a blow.

Now he was riding home to her. May God bless her, Simon thought ruefully. And so it was over: the plodding around in that sibling love. The two of them over there, and he and his family. He would never have to meet Kristin Lavransdatter again.

The thought took his breath away. Just as well, by the Devil. If your eye offends you, then pluck it out, said the priests. He told himself that the main reason he had done this was to escape the sister-brother love with Kristin. He couldn't bear it anymore.

He had only one wish now: that Ramborg would not be awake when he came home.

But when he rode in among the fences, he saw someone wearing a dark cloak standing beneath the aspen trees. The white of her wimple gleamed.

She said that she had been waiting for him ever since Sigurd returned home. The maids had gone to bed, so Ramborg herself ladled up the porridge that stood on the edge of the hearth, keeping warm. She placed bacon and bread on the table and brought in newly tapped ale.

"Shouldn't you go to bed now, Ramborg?" asked her husband as he ate.

Ramborg did not reply. She went over to her loom and began threading the colorful little balls of wool in and out of the warp. She had set up the loom for a tapestry before Christmas, but she hadn't made much progress yet.

"Erlend rode past, heading north, some time ago," she said, with her back turned. "From what Sigurd said, I thought you would be riding together."

"No, it didn't turn out that way."

"Erlend had a greater longing for his bed than you did?" She laughed a little. When she received no answer, she said again, "I suppose he always longs to be home with Kristin when he has been away."

Simon was silent for a good while before he replied, "Erlend and I did not part as friends."

Ramborg turned around abruptly. Then he told her what he had learned at Dyfrin and about the first part of the conversation with Erlend and his sons.

"It seems to me rather unreasonable that you should quarrel over such a matter when you've been able to remain friends until now."

"Perhaps, but that's how things went. And it will take too long to discuss the whole matter tonight."

Ramborg turned back to her loom and busied herself with her work.

"Simon," she said suddenly, "do you remember a story that Sira

Eirik once told us . . . from the Bible? About a maiden named Abishag the Shunammite?"[3]

"No."

"Back when King David was old and his vigor and manhood were beginning to fade—" Ramborg began, but Simon interrupted her.

"My Ramborg, it's much too late at night; this is no time to start telling sagas. And now I do remember the story about the woman you mentioned."

Ramborg pushed up the reed of the loom and fell silent for a while. Then she spoke again. "Do you remember the saga my father knew—about the handsome Tristan and fair Isolde and dark Isolde?"

"Yes, I remember." Simon pushed his plate aside, wiped the back of his hand across his mouth, and got up. He went over to stand in front of the fireplace. With one foot resting on the edge, his elbow on his knee, and his chin in his hand, he stared into the fire, which was about to die out inside the stone-lined hollow. From the loom over in the corner came Ramborg's voice, fragile-sounding and close to tears.

"When I listened to those stories, I always thought that men like King David and Sir Tristan . . . It seemed to me so foolish, and cruel, that they didn't love the young brides who offered them their maidenhood and the love of their hearts with gentleness and seemly graciousness but preferred instead such women as Fru Bathsheba or fair Isolde, who had squandered themselves in other men's arms. I thought that if I had been a man, I wouldn't have been so lacking in pride . . . or so heartless." Overcome, she fell silent. "It seems to me the most terrible fate: what happened to Abishag and poor Isolde of Bretland." Abruptly she turned around, walked quickly across the room, and stood before her husband.

"What is it, Ramborg?" Simon reluctantly asked in a low voice. "I don't know what you mean by all this."

"Yes, you do," she replied fiercely. "You're a man just like that Tristan."

"I find it hard to believe"—he tried to laugh—"that I should be compared with the handsome Tristan. And the two women you mentioned . . . If I remember right, they lived and died as pure maidens, untouched by their husbands." He looked at his wife. The little triangle of her face was pale, and she was biting her lip.

Simon set his foot down, straightened up, and put both hands on her shoulders.

"My Ramborg, you and I have two children," he said softly.

She didn't reply.

"I've done my best to show you my gratitude for that gift. I thought . . . I've tried to be a good husband to you."

When she didn't speak, he let her go, went over to a bench, and sat down. Ramborg followed and stood before him, looking down at her husband: his broad thighs in the wet, muddy hose, his stout body, his heavy reddish-brown face. Her lip curled with displeasure.

"You've grown so ugly over the years, Simon."

"Well, I've never thought myself to be a handsome man," he said calmly.

"But I'm young and pretty. . . ." She sat down on his lap, the tears pouring from her eyes as she held his head in her hands. "Simon, look at me. Why can't you reward me for this? Never have I wanted to belong to anyone but you. It's what I dreamed of ever since I was a little maiden: that my husband would be a man like you. Do you remember how we were once allowed to follow along with you, both Ulvhild and I? You were going with Father to the west pasture, to look at his foals. You carried Ulvhild over the creek, and Father was going to lift me up, but I cried that I wanted you to carry me too. Do you remember?"

Simon nodded. He remembered paying a great deal of attention to Ulvhild because he thought it so sad that the lovely child was crippled. Of the youngest daughter he had no memory, except that he knew there was a girl younger than Ulvhild.

"You had the most beautiful hair. . . ." Ramborg ran her fingers through the lock of wavy light-brown hair that fell over her husband's forehead. "And there's still not a single streak of gray. Erlend's hair will soon be as much white as black. And I always loved to see the deep dimples in your cheeks when you smiled . . . and the fact that you had such a merry voice."

"Yes, no doubt I looked a little better back then than I do now."

"No," she whispered fiercely. "When you look at me tenderly . . . Do you remember the first time I slept in your arms? I was in bed, whimpering over a toothache. Father and Mother were asleep, and it was dark in the loft, but you came over to the bench where we lay, Ulvhild and I, and asked me why I was crying. You told me to hush and not wake the others; then you lifted me in your arms. You lit a candle and cut a splinter of wood and then poked at my gums around the aching tooth until you drew blood. Then you said a prayer over the splinter, and the tooth didn't hurt anymore. And I was allowed to sleep in your bed, and you held me in your arms."

Simon placed his hand on her head, pressing it to his shoulder. Now that she spoke of it, he remembered. It was when he had come to Jørundgaard to tell Lavrans that the bond between him and Kristin had to be broken. He had slept very little that night. And now he recalled that he had gotten up to tend to little Ramborg, who lay fretting over a toothache.

"Have I ever behaved toward you in such a way, my Ramborg, that you thought it right to say that I didn't love you?"

"Simon . . . don't you think I might deserve that you loved me more than Kristin? She was wicked and dishonest toward you, while I have stayed with you like a little lapdog all these years."

Gently Simon lifted her off his lap, stood up, and took her hands in his.

"Speak no more of your sister, Ramborg—not in that manner. I wonder whether you even realize what you're saying. Don't you think that I fear God? Can you believe that I would be so unafraid of shame and the worst of sins, or that I wouldn't think of my children and all my kinsmen and friends? I'm your husband, Ramborg. Don't forget that, and don't talk of such things to me."

"I know you haven't broken any of God's commandments or breached any laws or code of honor."

"Never have I spoken a word to your sister or touched her with my hand in any way that I cannot defend on the Day of Judgment. This I swear before God and the apostle Saint Simon."

Ramborg nodded silently.

"Do you think your sister would have treated me as she has all these years if she thought, as you do, that I love her with sinful desire? Then you don't know Kristin."

"Oh, she has never thought about whether any man might desire her, except for Erlend. She hardly notices that the rest of us are flesh and blood."

"Yes, what you say is probably true, Ramborg," replied Simon calmly. "But then you must realize how senseless it is for you to torment me with your jealousy."

Ramborg pulled her hands away.

"I didn't mean to do so, Simon. But you've never loved me the way you love her. She is still always in your thoughts, but you seldom think of me unless you see me."

"I'm not to blame, Ramborg, if a man's heart is created in such a fashion that whatever is inscribed on it when it's young and fresh is carved deeper than all the runes that are later etched."

"Haven't you ever heard the saying that a man's heart is the first thing to come alive in his mother's womb and the last thing to die inside him?" replied Ramborg quietly.

"No . . . Is there such a saying? That might well be true." Lightly he caressed her cheek. "But if we're going to get any sleep tonight, we should go to bed now," he said wearily.

Ramborg fell asleep after a while. Simon slipped his arm out from under her neck, moved over to the very edge of the bed, and pulled the fur covers all the way up to his chin. His shirt was soaked through at the shoulder from her tears. He felt a bitter sympathy for his wife, but at the same time he realized with renewed bewilderment that he could no longer treat her as if she were a blind and inexperienced child. Now he had to acknowledge that Ramborg was a full-grown woman.

Gray light appeared in the windowpane; the May night was fading. He was dead tired, and tomorrow was the Sabbath. He wouldn't go to church in the morning, even though he might need to. He had once promised Lavrans that he would never miss a mass without an exceedingly good reason. But it hadn't helped him much to keep that promise during all these years, he thought bitterly. Tomorrow he was not going to ride to mass.

PART II

DEBTORS

CHAPTER 1

KRISTIN DID NOT hear a full account of what had happened between Erlend and Simon. Her husband told her and Bjørgulf what
Simon had said about his journey to Dyfrin, and he said that afterward they had exchanged words and ended up parting as foes. "I
can't tell you any more than that."

Erlend was rather pale, his expression firm and resolute. She
had seen him look that way only a few times before, in all the
years she had been married to him. She knew that this was something he would refuse to discuss any further.

She had never liked it when Erlend countered her questions
with that expression. God only knew she didn't consider herself
more than a simple woman; she would have preferred to avoid
taking responsibility for anything but her own children and her
household duties. And yet she had been forced to deal with so
many things that seemed to her more appropriate concerns for a
man to handle. But Erlend had thought it quite reasonable to let
them rest on her shoulders. So it didn't suit him to act so overbearing and to rebuff her when she wanted to know about things
that he had undertaken on his own that would affect the welfare
of them all.

She took this enmity between Erlend and Simon Darre greatly
to heart. Ramborg was her only sister. And when she thought
about losing Simon's companionship, she realized for the first time
how fond she had become of this man and how much gratitude
she owed him. His loyal friendship had been the best support she
had in her difficult situation.

She knew that now people would be talking about this all over
the countryside: that the folks of Jørundgaard had quarreled with
Simon of Formo too. Simon and Ramborg were liked and respected by everyone. But most people regarded Kristin, her hus-

121

band, and her sons with suspicion and ill will; this was something she had noticed long ago. Now they would be so alone.

Kristin felt as if she would sink into the earth from sorrow and shame on that first Sunday when she arrived at the green in front of the church and saw Simon standing a short distance away, among a group of farmers. He greeted her and her family with a nod, but it was the first time he didn't come over to shake hands and talk with them.

Ramborg did come over to her sister and took her hand. "It's dreadful that our husbands have fallen into discord, but you and I need not quarrel because of that." She stood on her toes to kiss Kristin so that everyone in the churchyard could see it. Kristin wasn't sure why, but she seemed to sense that Ramborg was not as sad as she might have been. She had never liked Erlend; God only knew whether she had set her husband against him, intentionally or not.

And yet Ramborg always came over to greet her sister whenever they met at church. Ulvhild asked in a loud voice why her aunt didn't come south to visit them anymore; then she ran over to Erlend, to cling to him and his oldest sons. Arngjerd stood quietly at her stepmother's side, took Kristin's hand, and looked embarrassed. Simon and Erlend, along with his sons, vigilantly avoided each other.

Kristin greatly missed her sister's children as well. She had grown fond of the two maidens. One day when Ramborg brought her son to mass, Kristin kissed Andres after the service and then burst into tears. She loved this tiny, frail boy so dearly. She couldn't help it, but now that she no longer had any small children of her own, it was a comfort to her to look after this little nephew from Formo and pamper him whenever his parents brought him along to Jørundgaard.

From Gaute she learned a little more about the matter because he told her what words were spoken between Erlend and Simon on that night when they met at Skindfeld-Gudrun's hut. The longer Kristin thought about it, the more it seemed to her that Erlend was most at fault. She had felt bitter toward Simon because he ought to have known his kinsman well enough to realize that Erlend would not have betrayed and deceived his brother in any dishonorable way, no matter how many strange things he might do out of recklessness or on impulse. And whenever Erlend saw what he had done, he usually behaved like a skittish stallion that has torn its reins loose and become wild with fright at what is dragging along behind.

But Erlend never seemed to understand that sometimes other people needed to protect their own interests in the face of the mischief that he had such a rare talent for stirring up. Then Erlend would fail to guard his tongue or watch how he behaved. She remembered from her own experience, back when she was still young and tender; time after time she had felt as if he were trampling on her heart with his reckless behavior. He had driven away his own brother. Even before Gunnulf entered the monastery, he had withdrawn from them, and she knew that Erlend was to blame. He had so often offended his pious and worthy brother, even though Gunnulf had never done anything but good for Erlend, as far as she knew. Now he had pushed Simon away, and when she wanted to know what had caused this animosity between him and their only friend, Erlend merely gave her a stubborn look and said he couldn't tell her.

She could see that he had told Naakkve more.

Kristin felt dismayed and uneasy when she noticed that Erlend and her eldest son would fall silent or change the topic of their conversation as soon as she came near, and this was not a rare occurrence.

Gaute and Lavrans and Munan kept closer to their mother than Nikulaus had ever done, and she had always talked more to them than to him. And yet she still felt that of all her children, her firstborn son was in some sense closest to her heart. After she had returned to live at Jørundgaard, memories of the time when she bore this son under her heart and gave birth to him became strangely vivid and alive. For she noticed in so many ways that the people of Sil had not forgotten the sins of her youth. It was almost as if they felt she had tarnished the honor of the entire region when she, daughter of the man who was regarded as their chieftain, had gone astray. They had not forgiven her, or the fact that she and Erlend had added mockery to Lavrans's sorrow and shame when they fooled him into giving away a seduced maiden with the grandest wedding that had ever been seen in Gudbrandsdal.

Kristin didn't know whether Erlend realized that people had begun gossiping about these old subjects again. If he did, he probably paid them no mind. He considered her neighbors no more than homespun farmers and fools, every one of them. And he taught his sons to think the same. It pained her soul to know that these people who had wished her so well back when she was Lavrans Bjørgulfsøn's pretty daughter, the rose of the northern valley, now despised Erlend Nikulaussøn and his wife and judged them harshly. She didn't plead with them; she didn't weep because she had become a stranger among them. But it hurt nevertheless. And it seemed as if even the steep mountains surrounding the valley that had sheltered her childhood now looked differently at her and her home: black with menace and stone-gray with a fierce determination to subdue her.

Once she had wept bitterly. Erlend knew about it, and he had had little patience with her back then. When he discovered that she had walked alone for many months with the burden of his child under her frightened, sorrowful heart, he did not take her in his arms and console her with tender and loving words. He was bitter and ashamed that it would come out how dishonorably he had acted toward Lavrans. But he hadn't thought about how much more difficult it would be for her on that day when she stood in disgrace before her proud and loving father.

And Erlend had not greeted his son with much joy when she finally brought the child into the light of life. That moment when her soul was released from endless anguish and dread and torment and she saw the hideous, shapeless fruit of her sin come alive under the fervent prayers of the priest and become the most beloved and healthy of children, then it felt as if her heart would melt with humble joy, and even the hot, defiant blood of her body turned to sweet, white, innocent milk. Yes, with God's help the boy would doubtless become a man, Erlend had said as she lay in bed, wanting him to rejoice with her over this precious treasure, which she could hardly bear to let out of her arms when the women wanted to tend to the child. He loved the children he had by Eline Ormsdatter—that much she had both seen and sensed—but when she

carried Naakkve over to Erlend and tried to place him in his father's arms, Erlend wrinkled his nose and asked what he was supposed to do with this infant who leaked from both ends. For years
Erlend would only grudgingly look at his eldest, lawfully born son,
unable to forget that Naakkve had come into the world at an in-
opportune time. And yet the boy was such a handsome and good
and promising child that any father would rejoice to see such a son
grow up to succeed him.

From the time he was quite little, Naakkve loved his father so
dearly that it was wondrous to behold. His whole small, fair face
would light up like the sun whenever his father took him on his
knee for a moment and spoke a few words to him or he was allowed to hold his father's hand to cross the courtyard. Steadfastly
Naakkve had courted his father's favor during that time when
Erlend was more fond of all his other children than the eldest.
Bjørgulf was his father's favorite when the boys were small, and
occasionally Erlend would take his sons along to the armory when
he went up there. That was where all the armor and weapons were
kept that were not in daily use at Husaby. While his father talked
and bantered with Bjørgulf, Naakkve would sit quietly on top of a
chest, simply breathing with happiness because he was allowed to
be there.

But as time passed and Bjørgulf's poor eyesight meant that he
could not accompany Erlend as readily as his other sons, and Bjørgulf also grew more taciturn and withdrawn, things changed.
Erlend began to seem almost a little embarrassed in the boy's presence. Kristin wondered whether Bjørgulf, in his heart, blamed his
father for destroying their well-being and taking his sons' future
with him when he fell—and whether Erlend knew or guessed as
much. However that might be, Bjørgulf was the only one of Erlend's sons who did not seem to look up to him with blind love
and boundless pride at calling him Father.

One morning the two smallest boys noticed that Erlend was
reading from the prayer book and fasting on bread and water.
They asked him why he was doing this since it wasn't a fast day.
Erlend replied that it was because of his sins. Kristin knew that
these fast days were part of the penance that had been imposed
upon Erlend for breaking his marriage vows with Sunniva Olavsdatter, and she knew that her oldest sons were aware of this.

Naakkve and Gaute seemed untroubled by it, but she happened to glance at Bjørgulf at that moment. The boy was sitting at the table, squinting nearsightedly at his bowl of food and chuckling to himself. Kristin had seen Gunnulf smile that way several times when Erlend was being most boastful. She didn't like it.

Now it was Naakkve whom Erlend always wanted to take along. And the youth seemed to come alive, as if all his roots were attached to his father. Naakkve served his father the way a young page serves his lord and chieftain. He took care of his father's horse himself and kept his harnesswork and weapons in order. He fastened Erlend's spurs on his feet and brought his hat and cape when Erlend was going out. He filled his father's goblet and served him slices of meat at the table, sitting on the bench just to the right of Erlend's seat. Erlend jested a bit over the boy's chivalrous and noble manners, but he was pleased, and he commanded more and more of Naakkve's attention.

Kristin saw that Erlend had now completely forgotten how she had struggled and begged to win from him a scrap of fatherly love for this child. And Naakkve had forgotten the time when she was the one he turned to, seeking solace from all his ills and advice for all his troubles when he was little. He had always been a loving son toward his mother, and he still was in many ways, but she felt that the older the boy became, the farther away he moved from her and her concerns. Naakkve lacked all sense for what she had to cope with. He was never disobliging when she gave him a task to do, but he was oddly awkward and clumsy at anything that might be called farm work. He did the chores without interest or desire and never finished anything. His mother thought that in many ways he was not unlike his deceased half brother, Orm Erlendssøn; he also resembled him in appearance. But Naakkve was strong and healthy, a lively dancer and sportsman, an excellent bowman and tolerably skilled in the use of other weapons, a good horseman and a superb skier. Kristin spoke about this one day to Ulf Haldorssøn, Naakkve's foster father.

Ulf said, "No one has lost more from Erlend's folly than that boy. There is not another youth growing up in Norway today who would make a more splendid horseman and chieftain than Naakkve."

But Kristin saw that Naakkve never gave a thought to what his father had ruined for him.

At that time there was once again great unrest in Norway, and rumors were flying all through the valleys, some of them reasonable and some of them completely unlikely. The noblemen in the south and west of the kingdom as well as in the uplands had grown exceedingly discontented with the rule of King Magnus. It was said they had even threatened to take up arms, rally the peasantry, and force Lord Magnus Eirikssøn to rule in accordance with their wishes and advice; otherwise they would proclaim his cousin, the young Jon Haftorssøn of Sudrheim, their king. His mother, Lady Agnes, was the daughter of the blessed King Haakon Haalegg. Not much was heard from Jon himself, but his brother Sigurd was supposed to be in the vanguard of the entire enterprise, and Bjarne, Erling Vidkunssøn's young son, was also part of it. People said that Sigurd had promised that if Jon became king, he would take one of Bjarne's sisters as his queen because the maidens of Giske were also descended from the ancient Norwegian kings. Sir Ivar Ogmundssøn, who had formerly been one of King Magnus's most ardent supporters, was now said to have joined forces with these young noblemen, as had many others among the wealthiest and most highborn of men. People said that Erling Vidkunssøn himself and the bishop of Bjørgvin stood behind the effort.

Kristin paid little mind to these rumors; she thought bitterly that she and her family were commoners now and the affairs of the realm no longer concerned them. And yet she had talked about this a bit with Simon Andressøn during the previous fall, and she also knew that he had spoken of it to Erlend. But she saw that Simon was loath to discuss such things—partly, no doubt, because he disapproved of his brothers getting involved in such dangerous matters. And Gyrd, at any rate, was being led along by his wife's kinsmen. But Simon also feared that it wouldn't be pleasant for Erlend to hear such talk since he had been born to take his place among men who counseled the rulers of Norway, but now misfortune had shut him out from the company of his peers.

And yet Kristin saw that Erlend spoke of these matters with his sons. One day she heard Naakkve say, "But if these men win out against King Magnus, then surely they can't be so cowardly, Father, that they wouldn't take up your case and force the king to make amends with you."

Erlend laughed.

His son continued, "You were the first to show the way to these men and remind them that it was never the custom among Norwegian nobles in the past to sit back calmly and tolerate injustice from their kings. It cost you your ancestral estates and your position as sheriff. The men who supported you escaped without a scratch. You alone have paid the price for all of them."

"Yes, and that's all the more reason why they would want to forget me," said Erlend with a laugh. "And the archbishopric has acquired Husaby against a loan. I don't think the gentlemen of the council will urge impoverished King Magnus to redeem it."

"The king is your kinsman, as are Sigurd Haftorssøn and most of the other men," replied Naakkve vehemently. "Not without shame can they desert the man who carried his shield with honor to the borderlands of the north and cleared Finnmark and the Gandvik coast[1] of the enemies of God and the Crown. Then they would indeed be miserable cowards."

Erlend gave a whistle. "Son, one thing I can tell you. I don't know how this venture of the Haftorssøns will end, but I would wager my own neck they don't dare show Lord Magnus the naked blade of a Norwegian sword. Talk and compromise are what I think will result, with not a single arrow fired. And those fellows won't exert themselves for my sake, because they know me and realize that I'm not as squeamish about honed steel as some of the others.

"Kinsmen you say . . . Yes, they're your third cousins, both Magnus and those sons of Haftor. I remember them from the time I served at King Haakon's court. It was fortunate that my kinswoman Lady Agnes was the daughter of a king; otherwise she might have found herself out on the wharves, pulling in fish, if a woman like your mother, out of pious mercy, didn't hire her to help out in the cowshed. More than once I've wiped the snouts of those Haftorssøns when they had to appear before their grandfather, and they came racing into the hall as snot-nosed as if they had just crept from their mother's lap. And if I gave them a swat out of loving kinship, to teach them some proper manners, they would shriek like stuck pigs. I hear they've made men of these Sudrheim changelings at last. But if you expect to receive the help of kinsmen from those quarters, you'd be looking for solace in the backside of a dog."

Later Kristin said to Erlend, "Naakkve is so young, my dear husband. Don't you think it's unwise to speak so openly about such matters with him?"

"You speak so gently, my dear wife," replied Erlend with a smile, "that I see you wish to rebuke me. When I was Naakkve's age, I was headed north to Vargøy for the first time. If Lady Inge-bjørg had remained loyal to me," he exclaimed vehemently, "I would have sent Naakkve and Gaute to serve her. In Denmark there might have been a future for two intrepid adventurers skilled with weapons."

"When I gave birth to these children," said Kristin bitterly, "I didn't think that our sons would seek their living in a foreign land."

"You know I didn't intend that either," said Erlend. "But man proposes, God disposes."

Then Kristin told herself that it wasn't simply that she felt a stab in her heart every time she noticed that Erlend and her sons, now that they were getting older, acted as if their concerns were beyond the comprehension of a woman. But she feared Erlend's reckless tongue; he never remembered that his sons were little more than children.

And yet as young as the boys were—Nikulaus was now seventeen winters old, Bjørgulf would be sixteen, and Gaute would turn fifteen in the fall—all three had a certain way with women that made their mother uneasy.

Admittedly nothing had happened that she could point to. They didn't run after women, they were never coarse or discourteous in speech, and they didn't like it when the servant men told vulgar stories or brought filthy rumors back to the manor. But Erlend too had always been very chivalrous and seemly; she had seen him blush at words over which both her father and Simon laughed heartily. But at the time she had vaguely felt that the other two laughed the way peasants laugh at tales about the Devil, while learned men, who know better his ferocious cunning, have little affection for such jests.

Even Erlend could not be called guilty of the sin of running after women; only people who didn't know the man would think he had loose ways, meaning that he had lured women to himself and then deliberately led them astray. She never denied that Erlend had had his way with her without resorting to seductive arts and without using deceit or force. And she was certain that it was not Erlend who had done the seducing in the case of the two married women with whom he had sinned. But when loose women approached him with bold and provocative manners, she had seen him turn into an inquisitive youth; an air of concealed and impetuous frivolity would come over the man.

With anguish she thought she could see that the sons of Erlend took after their father in this regard. They always forgot to think about how others would judge them before they acted, although afterward they would take what was said to heart. And when women greeted them with smiles and gentleness, they didn't become shy or sullen or awkward, as did most young boys their age. They would smile back and talk and behave as freely and easily as if they had been at the king's court and were familiar with royal customs. Kristin feared they would get mixed up in some misfortune or trouble out of sheer innocence. She thought the wealthy wives and daughters, as well as the poor servingwomen, were all much too flirtatious with these handsome boys. But like other young men, they would grow furious afterward if anyone teased them about a woman. Frida Styrkaarsdatter was particularly fond of doing this. She was a foolish woman, in spite of her age; she wasn't much younger than her mistress, and she had given birth to two bastard children. She had had difficulty even finding the father of the younger child. But Kristin had offered the poor thing a protective hand. Because Frida had nursed Bjørgulf and Skule with such care and affection, the mistress was quite indulgent toward this serving maid, even though she was annoyed that the woman was always talking to the boys about young maidens.

Kristin now thought it would be best if she could marry off her sons at a young age, but she knew this wouldn't be easy. The men whose daughters would be equal matches for Naakkve and Bjørgulf by birth and blood would not think her sons wealthy enough. And the condemnation and royal enmity their father had brought down upon himself would stand in the way if the boys tried to improve their lot through service with greater noblemen. With bitterness she thought about the days when Erlend and Erling Vidkunssøn had spoken of a marriage between Naakkve and one of the lord's daughters.

She knew of one or another young maiden now growing up in the valleys who might be suitable: wealthy and of good lineage, although for several generations their forefathers had refrained from serving at the king's court and had stayed home in their parishes. But she couldn't bear the thought that Erlend might be refused if they should make an offer to one of these landowners. In this situation Simon Darre would have been the best spokesman, but now Erlend had deprived them of his help.

She didn't think any of her sons had a desire to serve the Church, except perhaps Gaute or Lavrans. But Lavrans was still so young. And Gaute was the only one of the boys who gave her any real help with the estate.

Storms and snow had wreaked havoc with the fences that year, and the snowfall before Holy Cross Day had delayed the repairs, so the workers had to press hard to finish in time. For this reason, Kristin sent Naakkve and Bjørgulf off one day to mend the fence around a field up near the main road.

In midafternoon Kristin went out to see how the boys were handling the unaccustomed chore. Bjørgulf was working over by the lane leading to the manor; she stopped for a while to talk with him. Then she continued northward. There she saw Naakkve leaning over the fence and talking to a woman on horseback who had stopped at the side of the road, right next to the rails. He stroked the horse and then grabbed the girl's ankle, moving his hand, as if carelessly, up her leg under her clothing.

The maiden was the first to notice Kristin. She blushed and said something to Naakkve. Quickly he pulled his hand away and looked a little abashed. The girl was about to ride off, but Kristin called out a greeting and then talked to the maiden for a moment, asking about her kinswoman. The young girl was the niece of the mistress of Ulvsvold and had recently arrived for a visit. Kristin pretended that she hadn't seen anything, talking to Naakkve about the fence after the maiden had gone.

Not long after, Kristin happened to stay at Ulvsvold for two weeks' time because the mistress gave birth to a child and was then quite ill. Kristin was both her neighbor and considered the most capable healer in the region. Naakkve often came over with messages and queries for his mother, and the niece, Eyvor Haakonsdatter, would always find the opportunity to meet and talk with him. Kristin wasn't pleased by this; she had taken a disliking to the maiden and didn't find her beautiful, although she had heard that most men did. She was happy on the day she learned that Eyvor had returned home to Raumsdal.

But she didn't think Naakkve had been particularly fond of Eyvor, especially when she heard that Frida kept chattering about the daughter at Loptsgaard, Aasta Audunsdatter, and teasing Naakkve about her.

One day Kristin was in the brewhouse, boiling a juniper decoction, when she heard Frida once again carrying on about Aasta. Naakkve was with Gaute and their father outside behind the courtyard. They were building a boat that they wanted to take up to the small fishing lake in the mountains. Erlend was a moderately good boatbuilder. Naakkve grew cross, and then Gaute began to tease him too: Aasta might be a suitable match.

"Ask for her hand yourself if that's what you think," said his brother heatedly.

"No, I don't want her," replied Gaute, "because I've heard that red hair and pine forests thrive on meager soil. But you think that red hair is pretty."

"That saying can't be used about women, my son," said Erlend with a laugh. "Those with red hair usually have soft white skin."

Frida laughed uproariously, but Kristin grew angry. She thought this talk too frivolous for such young boys. She also remembered that Sunniva Olavsdatter had red hair, although her friends called it golden.

Then Gaute said, "You should be glad I didn't say anything; I didn't dare, for fear of sin. On the vigil night of Whitsunday you sat with Aasta in the grain tithe barn all the time we were dancing on the church hill. So you must be fond of her."

Naakkve was about to fall upon his brother, but at that moment Kristin came outside. After Gaute had left, she asked her other son, "What was that Gaute said about you and Aasta Audunsdatter?"

"I don't think anything was said that you didn't hear, Mother," replied the boy. His face was red, and he frowned angrily.

Annoyed, Kristin said, "It's unseemly that you young people can't hold a vigil night without dancing and leaping about between services. We never used to do that when I was a maiden."

"But you've told us yourself, Mother, that back when you were young, our grandfather used to sing while the people danced on the church hill."

"Well, not those kinds of ballads and not such wild dancing," said his mother. "And we children stayed properly with our parents; we didn't go off two by two and sit in the barn."

Naakkve was about to make an angry retort. Then Kristin happened to glance at Erlend. He was smiling so slyly as he eyed the plank he was about to cut with an axe. Indignant and dismayed, she went back inside the brewhouse.

But she thought a good deal about what she had heard. Aasta Audunsdatter was not a poor match; Loptsgaard was a wealthy estate, and there were three daughters, but no son. And Ingebjørg, Aasta's mother, belonged to an exceedingly good lineage.

She had never thought that one day the people of Jørundgaard might call Audun Torbergssøn kinsman. But he had suffered a stroke this past winter, and everyone thought he had little time left to live. The girl was seemly and charming in manner, and clever, or so Kristin had heard. If Naakkve had great affection for the maiden, there was no reason to oppose this marriage. They would still have to wait for two more years to hold the wedding, as young as Aasta and Naakkve both were, but then she would gladly welcome Aasta as her son's wife.

On a fine day in the middle of the summer Sira Solmund's sister came to see Kristin to borrow something. The women were standing outside the house to say their farewells when the priest's sister said, "Well, that Eyvor Haakonsdatter!" Her father had driven her from his estate because she was with child, so she had sought refuge at Ulvsvold.

Naakkve had been up in the loft; now he stopped on the lowest step. When his mother caught a glimpse of his face, she was suddenly so overcome that she could hardly feel her own legs beneath her. The boy was crimson all the way up to his ears as he walked away toward the main house.

But Kristin soon understood from the other woman's gossip that things must have been such with Eyvor long before she came to their parish for the first time in the spring. My poor, innocent boy, thought Kristin, sighing with relief. He must be ashamed that he thought well of the girl.

A few nights later Kristin was alone in bed because Erlend had gone out fishing. As far as she knew, Naakkve and Gaute had gone along with him. But she was awakened when Naakkve touched her and whispered that he needed to talk to her. He climbed up and sat at the foot of her bed.

"Mother, I've been out to talk with that poor woman Eyvor tonight. I was sure they were lying about her; I was so certain that I would have held a glowing piece of iron in my hand to prove that she was lying—that magpie from Romundgaard."

Kristin lay still and waited. Naakkve tried to speak firmly, but suddenly his voice threatened to break with emotion and distress.

"She was on her way to matins on the last day of Christmas. She was alone, and the road from their manor passes through the woods for a long stretch. There she met two men. It was still dark. She doesn't know who they were, maybe foresters from the mountains. In the end she couldn't defend herself any longer, the poor young child. She didn't dare tell her troubles to anyone. When her mother and father discovered her misfortune, they drove her from home, with slaps and curses as they pulled her hair. When she told me all this, Mother, she wept so hard that it would have melted a rock in the hills." Naakkve abruptly fell silent, breathing heavily.

Kristin said she thought it the worst misfortune that those villains had escaped. She hoped that God's justice would find them and that for their deeds they might suffer their just deserts on the executioner's block.

Then Naakkve began to talk about Eyvor's father, how rich he was and how he was related to several respected families. Eyvor intended to send the child away to be raised in another parish. Gudmund Darre's wife had given birth to a bastard child by a priest, and there sat Sigrid Andresdatter at Kruke, a good and hon-

ored woman. A man would have to be both hardhearted and unfair to pronounce Eyvor despoiled because against her will she had
been forced to suffer such shame and misfortune; surely she was
still fit to be the wife of an honorable man.

Kristin pitied the girl and cursed her assailants, and in her heart
she gave thanks and exulted over what good luck it was that
Naakkve would not come of age for three more years. Then she
told him gently to bear in mind that he should be careful not to
seek out Eyvor in her chamber late at night, as he had just done,
or to show himself at Ulvsvold unless he had tasks for the
landowner's servants. Otherwise he might unwittingly cause people to gossip even worse about the unfortunate child. It was all
well and good to say that those who claimed to doubt Eyvor's
word and refused to believe she had landed in this misfortune
without blame, wouldn't find him weak in the arms. All the same,
it would be painful for the poor girl if there was more talk.

Three weeks later Eyvor's father came to take his daughter
home for a betrothal banquet and wedding. She was to marry a
good farmer's son from her parish. At first both fathers had op-
posed the marriage because they were feuding over several sections
of land. In the winter the men had reached an agreement, and the
two young people were about to be betrothed, but suddenly Eyvor
had refused. She had set her heart on another man. Afterward she
realized it was too late for her to reject her first suitor. In the meantime she went to visit her aunt in Sil, no doubt thinking that there
she would receive help in concealing her shame, because she
wanted to marry this new man. But when Hillebjørg of Ulvsvold
saw what condition the girl was in, she sent her back to her parents. The rumors were true enough—her father was furious and
had struck his daughter several times, and she had indeed fled to
Ulvsvold—but now he had come to an agreement with her first
suitor, and Eyvor would have to settle for the man, no matter how
little she liked it.

Kristin saw that Naakkve took this greatly to heart. For days he
went around without saying a word, and his mother felt so sorry
for him that she hardly dared cast a glance in his direction. If he
met his mother's eye, he would turn bright red and look so
ashamed that it cut Kristin to the heart.

Whenever the servants at Jørundgaard started talking about

these events, their mistress would tell them sharply to hold their tongues. That filthy story and that wretched woman were not to be mentioned in her house. Frida was astonished. So many times she had heard Kristin Lavransdatter speak with forbearance and offer help with both hands to a maiden who had fallen into such misfortune. Frida herself had twice found salvation in the compassion of her mistress. But the few words Kristin said about Eyvor Haakonsdatter were as vile as anything a woman might say about another.

Erlend laughed when she told him how badly Naakkve had been fooled. It was one evening when she was sitting out on the green, spinning, and her husband came over and stretched out on the grass at her side.

"No misfortune has come of it," said Erlend. "Rather, it seems to me the boy has paid a small price to learn that a man shouldn't trust a woman."

"Is that so?" said his wife. Her voice quivered with stifled indignation.

"Yes," said Erlend, smiling. "Now you, when I first met you, I thought you were such a gentle maiden that you would hardly even take a bite out of a slice of cheese. As pliable as a silk ribbon and as mild as a dove. But you certainly fooled me, Kristin."

"How do you think things would have gone for all of us if I had been that soft and gentle?" she asked.

"No . . ." Erlend took her hands, and she had to stop working. He looked up at her with a radiant smile. Then he laid his head in her lap. "No, I didn't know, my sweet, what good fortune God was granting me when He set you in my path, Kristin."

But because she constantly had to restrain herself in order to hide her despair at Erlend's perpetual nonchalance, her anger would sometimes overwhelm her when she had to reprimand her sons. Her fists would turn harsh, and her words fierce. Ivar and Skule felt the brunt of it.

They were at the worst age, their thirteenth year, and so wild and willful that Kristin often wondered in utter despair whether any mother in Norway had ever given birth to such rogues. They were handsome, as all her children were, with black, silky soft, and curly hair, blue eyes beneath black brows, and lean, finely shaped faces. They were quite tall for their age, but still narrow-shouldered, with long, spare limbs. Their joints stood out like knots on a sprig of grain. They looked so much alike that no one outside their home could tell them apart, and in the countryside people called them the Jørundgaard swords—but it wasn't meant as a title of honor. Simon had first given them this name in jest because Erlend had presented each of them with a sword, and they never let these small swords out of their grasp except when they were in church. Kristin wasn't pleased with this gift, or with the fact that they were always rushing around with axes, spears, and bows. She feared it would land these hot-tempered boys in some kind of trouble. But Erlend said curtly that they were old enough now to become accustomed to carrying weapons.

She lived in constant fear for these twin sons of hers. When she didn't know where they were, she would secretly wring her hands and implore the Virgin Mary and Saint Olav to lead them back home, alive and unharmed. They went through mountain passes and up steep cliffs where no one had ever traveled before. They plundered eagles' nests and came home with hideous yellow-eyed fledglings hissing inside their tunics. They climbed among the boulders along the Laag and north in the gorge where the river plunged from one waterfall to the next. Once Ivar was nearly dragged to his death by his stirrups; he was trying to ride a half-tame young stallion, and God only knew how the boys had managed to put a saddle on the animal. And by chance, out of simple curiosity, they had ventured into the Finn's hut in Toldstad Forest. They had learned a few words of the Sami language from their father, and when they used them to greet the Finnish witch, she welcomed them with food and drink. They had eaten until they were bursting, even though it was a fast day. Kristin had always strictly enjoined that when the grown-ups were fasting, the children should make do with a small portion of food they didn't care for; it was what her own parents had accustomed her to when she was a child. For once Erlend also took his sons sternly to task. He burned all the tidbits that the Finnish woman had given the boys as provisions, and he strictly forbade them ever to approach even the outskirts of the woods where the Finns lived. And yet it amused him to hear about the boys' adventure. Later he would often tell Ivar and Skule about his travels up north and what he had observed of the ways of those people. And he would talk to the boys in that ugly and heathen language of theirs.

Otherwise Erlend almost never chastised his children, and whenever Kristin complained about the wild behavior of the twins, Erlend would dismiss it with a jest. At home on the estate they got into a great deal of mischief, although they could make themselves useful if they had to; they weren't clumsy-handed like Naakkve. But occasionally, when their mother had given them some chore to do and she went out to see how it was going, she would find the tools lying on the ground and the boys would be watching their father, who might be showing them how seafaring men tied knots.

When Lavrans Bjørgulfsøn painted tar crosses over the door to the livestock stalls or in other such places, he used to add a few flourishes with the brush: drawing a circle around the cross or painting a stroke through each of its arms. One day the twins decided to use one of these old crosses as a target. Kristin was beside herself with fury and despair at such unchristian behavior, but Erlend came to the children's defense. They were so young; they shouldn't be expected to think about the holiness of the cross every time they saw it painted above the door of a shed or on the back of a cow. The boys would be told to go up to the cross on the church hill, kneel down, and kiss it as they said five *Pater nosters* and fifteen *Ave Marias*. It wasn't necessary to call in Sira Solmund for such a reason. But this time Kristin had the support of Bjørgulf and Naakkve. The priest was summoned, and he sprinkled holy water on the wall and reprimanded the two young sinners with great severity.

They fed oxen and goats the heads of snakes to make them more vicious. They teased Munan because he was still clinging to his mother's skirts, and Gaute because he was the one they fought with most often. Otherwise the sons of Erlend stuck together with the greatest brotherly affection. But sometimes Gaute would give them a thrashing if they were too rough. Trying to talk some sense into them was like talking to a wall. And if their mother grew angry, they would stand there stiffly, their fists clenched, as they scowled at her with flashing eyes beneath frowning brows, their faces fiery red with rage. Kristin thought about what Gunnulf had said about Erlend: He had flung his knife at their father and raised his hand against him many times when he was a child. Then she would strike the twins, and strike them hard, because she was frightened. How would things end up for these children of hers if they weren't tamed in time?

Simon Darre was the only one who had ever had any power over the two wild boys. They loved their uncle, and they always complied whenever he chided them, in a friendly and calm manner. But now that they didn't see him anymore, Kristin hadn't noticed that they missed him. Dejected, she thought how faithless a child's heart could be.

But secretly, in her own heart, she knew that she was actually proudest of these two. If only she could break their terrible defiant and wild behavior, she thought that none of their brothers would make more promising men than they would. They were healthy, with good physical abilities; they were fearless, honest, generous, and kind toward all the poor. And more than once they had shown an alacrity and resourcefulness that seemed to her far beyond what might be expected of such young boys.

One evening during the hay harvesting Kristin was up late in the cookhouse when Munan came rushing in, screaming that the old goat shed was on fire. There were no men at home on the manor. Some were in the smithy, sharpening their scythes; some had gone north to the bridge where the young people usually gathered on summer evenings. Kristin grabbed a couple of buckets and set off running, calling to her maids to follow her.

The goat shed was a little old building with a roof that reached all the way down to the ground. It stood in the narrow passageway between the farmyard and the courtyard of the estate, right across from the stable and with other houses built close on either side. Kristin ran onto the gallery of the hearth house and found a broadaxe and a fire hook, but as she rounded the corner of the stable, she didn't see any fire, just a cloud of smoke billowing out of a hole in the roof of the goat shed. Ivar was sitting up on the ridge, hacking at the roof; Skule and Lavrans were inside, pulling down patches of the thatching and then stomping and trampling out the fire. Now they were joined by Erlend, Ulf, and the men who had been in the smithy. Munan had run over to warn them; so the fire was put out in short order. And yet the most terrible of misfortunes might easily have occurred. It was a sultry, still evening, but with occasional gusts of wind from the south, and if the fire had engulfed the goat shed, all the buildings at the north end of the courtyard—the stable, storerooms, and living quarters—would certainly have burned with it.

Ivar and Skule had been up on the stable roof. They had snared a hawk and were going to hang it from the gable when they caught a whiff of fire and saw smoke coming from the roof below them. They leaped to the ground at once, and with the small axes they were carrying they began chopping at the smoldering sod while they sent off Lavrans and Munan, who were playing nearby—one to find hooks and the other to get their mother. Fortunately the rafters and beams in the roof were quite rotten, but it was clear that this time the twins had saved their mother's estate by instantly setting about tearing down the burning roof and not wasting time by first running to get help from the grown-ups.

It was hard to understand how the fire had started, except that Gaute had passed that way an hour before, carrying embers to the smithy, and he admitted that the container had not been covered. A spark had probably flown up onto the tinder-dry sod roof.

But less was said about this than about the quick-wittedness of the twins and Lavrans when Ulf later imposed a fire watch and all the servants kept him company during the night while Kristin had strong ale and mead carried out to them. All three boys had been singed on their hands and feet; their shoes were so burned that they split into pieces. Young Lavrans was only nine years old, so it was hard for him to bear the pain patiently for very long, but from the start he was the proudest of the lot, walking around with his hands wrapped up and taking in the praise of the manor servants.

That night Erlend took his wife in his arms. "My Kristin, my Kristin . . . Don't complain so much about your children. Can't you see, my dear, what good breeding there is in our sons? You always treat these two hearty boys as if you thought their path would lead between the gallows and the execution block. Now it seems to me that you should enjoy some pleasure after all the pain and suffering and toil you've borne through all the years when you constantly carried a child under your belt, with another child at your breast and one on your arm. Back then you would talk of nothing else but those little imps, and now that they've grown up to be both sensible and manly, you walk among them as if you were deaf and dumb, hardly even answering when they speak to you. God help me, but it's as if you love them less now that you no longer have to worry for their sake and these big, handsome sons of ours can give you both help and joy."

Kristin didn't trust herself to answer with a single word.

But she lay in bed, unable to sleep. And toward morning she carefully stepped over her slumbering husband and walked barefoot over to the shuttered peephole, which she opened.

The sky was a hazy gray, and the air was cool. Far off to the south, where the mountains merged and closed off the valley, rain was sweeping over the plateaus. Kristin stood there for a moment, looking out. It was always so hot and stuffy in this loft above the new storeroom where they slept in the summertime. The trace of moisture in the air brought the strong, sweet scent of hay to her. Outside a bird or two chittered faintly in their sleep in the summer night.

Kristin rummaged around for her flint and lit a candle stump. She crept over to where Ivar and Skule were sleeping on a bench. She shone the light on them and touched their cheeks with the back of her hand. They both had a slight fever. Softly she said an *Ave Maria* and made the sign of the cross over them. The gallows and the execution block . . . to think that Erlend could jest about such things . . . he who had come so close. . . .

Lavrans whimpered and murmured in his sleep. Kristin stood bending over her two youngest sons, who were bedded down on a small bench at the foot of their parents' bed. Lavrans was hot and flushed and tossed back and forth but did not wake up when she touched him.

Gaute lay with his milk-white arms behind his head, under his long flaxen hair. He had thrown off all the bedclothes. He was so hot-blooded that he always slept naked, and his skin was such a dazzling white. The tan color of his face, neck, and hands stood out in sharp contrast. Kristin pulled the blanket up around his waist.

It was difficult for her to be angry with Gaute; he looked so much like her father. She hadn't said much to him about the calamity he had nearly brought upon them. As clever and level-headed as the boy was, she thought that doubtless he would learn from the incident and not forget it.

Naakkve and Bjørgulf slept in the other bed up in the loft. Kristin stood there longer, shining the light on the two sleeping young men. Black down already shadowed their childish, soft pink lips. Naakkve's foot was sticking out from the covers, slender, with a high instep, a deep arch over the sole, and not very clean. And yet, she thought, it wasn't long ago that the foot of this man was so small that she could wrap her fingers around it, and she had crushed it to her breast and raised it to her lips, nibbling on each tiny toe, for they were as rosy and sweet as the blossoms on a bil-berry twig.

It was probably true that she didn't pay enough heed to what God had granted her as her lot. The memory of those days when she was carrying Naakkve and the visions of terror she had wres-tled with . . . it could pass with fiery heat through her soul. She had been delivered the way a person wakes up to the blessed light of day after terrifying dreams with the oppressive weight of the mare[2] on her breast. But other women had awakened to see that the unhappiness of the day was worse than the very worst they had dreamed. And yet, whenever she saw a cripple or someone who was deformed, Kristin would feel heartsick at the reminder of her own fear for her unborn child. Then she would humble herself before God and Holy Olav with a burning fervor; she would has-ten to do good, striving to force tears of true remorse from her eyes as she prayed. But each time she would feel that unthawed discontent in her heart, the fresh surge would cool, and the sobs would seep out of her soul like water in sand. Then she consoled herself that she didn't have the gift of piety she had once hoped would be her inheritance from her father. She was hard and sinful, but surely she was no worse than most people, and like most peo-ple, she would have to bear the fiery blaze of that other world be-fore her heart could be melted and cleansed.

And yet sometimes she longed to be different. When she looked at the seven handsome sons sitting at her table or when she made her way up to church on Sabbath mornings as the bells tolled, call-ing so agreeably to joy and God's peace, and she saw the flock of straight-backed, well-dressed young boys, her sons, climbing the hillside ahead of her . . . She didn't know of any other woman who had given birth to so many children and had never experienced what it was like to lose one. All of them were handsome and healthy, without a flaw in their physical or mental capacities, although Bjørgulf's sight was poor. She wished she could forget her sorrows and be gentle and grateful, fearing and loving God as her father had done. She remembered her father had said that the person who recalls his sins with a humble spirit and bows before the cross of the Lord need never bow his head beneath any earthly unhappiness or injustice.

Kristin blew out the candle, pinched the wick, and returned the stump to its place between the uppermost logs in the wall. She went back over to the peephole. It was already daylight outside, but gray and dead. On the lower rooftops, upon which she gazed, the dirty, sun-bleached grass stirred faintly from a gust of wind; a little, rustling sound passed through the leaves of the birches across from the roof of the high loft building.

She looked down at her hands, holding on to the sill of the peephole. They were rough and worn; her arms were tanned all the way up to her elbows, and her muscles were swollen and as hard as wood. In her youth the children had sucked the blood and milk from her until every trace of maidenly smoothness and fresh plumpness had been sapped from her body. Now each day of toil stripped away a little more of the remnants of beauty that had distinguished her as the daughter, wife, and mother of men with noble blood. The slender white hands, the pale, soft arms, the fair complexion, which she had carefully shielded from sunburn with linen kerchiefs and protected with specially brewed cleansing concoctions . . . She had long ago grown indifferent to whether the sun shone directly on her face, sweaty from work, and turned it as brown as that of a poor peasant woman.

Her hair was the only thing she had left of her girlish beauty. It was just as luxuriant and brown, even though she seldom found time to wash or tend to it. The heavy, tangled braid that hung down her back hadn't been undone in three days.

Kristin pulled it forward over her shoulder, undid the plait, and shook out her hair, which still enveloped her like a cloak and reached below her knees. She took a comb from her chest, and shivering now and then, she sat in her shift beneath the peephole, open to the coolness of the morning, and gently combed out her tangled tresses.

When she was done with her hair and had rebraided it in a

tight, heavy rope, she felt a little better. Then she cautiously lifted
the sleeping Munan into her arms, placed him next to the wall in
her husband's bed, and then crawled in between them. She held
her youngest child in her arms, rested his head against her shoulder, and fell asleep.

She slept late the next morning. Erlend and the boys were already
up when she awakened. "I think you've been suckling at your
mother's breast when nobody's looking," said Erlend when he saw
Munan lying next to his mother. The boy grew cross, ran outside,
and crept across the gallery, out onto a carved beam atop the posts
holding up the gallery. He would prove he was a man. "Run!"
shouted Naakkve from down in the courtyard. He caught his little
brother in his arms, turned him upside down, and tossed him to
Bjørgulf. The two older boys wrestled with him until he was
laughing and shrieking at the same time.

But the following day when Munan cried because his fingers
had been stung by the recoil of the bowstring, the twins rolled him
up in a coverlet and carried him over to their mother's bed; in his
mouth they stuffed a piece of bread so big that the boy nearly
choked.

ERLEND'S HOUSE PRIEST at Husaby had taught his three oldest sons their lessons. They were not very diligent pupils, but all three learned quickly, and their mother, who had been raised with this kind of book learning, kept an eye on them so that the knowledge they gained was not altogether paltry.

During the year that Bjørgulf and Naakkve spent with Sira Eiliv at the monastery on Tautra, they had eagerly suckled at the breasts of Lady Wisdom, as the priest expressed it. Their teacher was an exceedingly old monk who had devoted his life with the zeal of a bee to gleaning knowledge from all the books he came across, both in Latin and in Old Norse. Sira Eiliv was himself a lover of wisdom, but during his years at Husaby he had had little opportunity to follow his inclination for bookish pursuits. For him the time spent with Aslak, the teacher, was like pasture grazing for starved cattle. And the two young boys, who kept close to their own priest while staying with the monks, followed the learned conversations of the men with their mouths agape. Then Brother Aslak and Sira Eiliv found joy in feeding these two young minds with the most delectable honey from the monastery's book treasures, which Brother Aslak had supplemented with many copied versions and excerpts of the most magnificent books. Soon the boys grew so clever that the monk seldom had to speak to them in Norwegian, and when their parents came to get them, both could answer the priest in Latin, fluently and correctly.

Afterward the brothers kept up what they had learned. There were many books at Jørundgaard. Lavrans had owned five. Two of them had been inherited by Ramborg when his estate was settled, but she had never wanted to learn to read, and Simon was not so practiced with written words that he had any desire to read for his own amusement, although he could decipher a letter and compose one himself. So' he asked Kristin to keep the books until his children were older. After they were married, Erlend gave Kristin three books that had belonged to his parents. She had received another book as a gift from Gunnulf Nikulaussøn. He had had it copied for his brother's wife from a book about Holy Olav and his miracles, several other saint legends, and the missive the Franciscan monks of Oslo had sent to the pope about Brother Edvin Rikardssøn, seeking to have him recognized as a saint. And finally, Naakkve had been given a prayer book by Sira Eiliv when they parted. Naakkve often read to his brother. He read fluently and well, with a slight lilt to his voice, the way Brother Aslak had taught him; he was most fond of the books in Latin—his own prayer book and one that had belonged to Lavrans Bjørgulfsøn. But his greatest treasure was a big, exceptionally splendid book that had been part of the family inheritance ever since the days of the ancestor who was his namesake, Bishop Nikulaus Arnessøn.

Kristin wanted her younger sons also to acquire learning that would be fitting for men of their birth. But it was difficult to know how this might be done. Sira Eirik was much too old, and Sira Solmund could read only from those books that he used for the church service. Much of what he read he didn't fully understand. On some evenings Lavrans found it amusing to sit with Naakkve and let his brother show him how to form the letters on his wax tablet, but the other three had absolutely no desire to learn such skills. One day Kristin took out a Norwegian book and asked Gaute to see if he could remember anything of what he had learned in his childhood from Sira Eiliv. But Gaute couldn't even manage to spell his way through three words, and when he came across the first symbol that stood for several letters, he closed the book with a laugh and said he didn't feel like playing that game anymore.

This was the reason that Sira Solmund came over to Jørundgaard one evening late in the summer and asked Nikulaus to accompany him home. A foreign knight had come from the Feast of Saint Olav in Nidaros and taken lodgings at Romundgaard, but he spoke no Norwegian. Nor did his soldiers or servants, while the guide who was escorting them spoke only a few words of their language. Sira Eirik was ill in bed. Could Naakkve come over and speak to the man in Latin?

Naakkve was not at all displeased to be asked to act as interpreter, but he feigned nonchalance and went with the priest. He returned home very late, in high spirits and quite drunk. He had been given wine, which the foreign knight had brought along and liberally poured for the priest and the deacon and Naakkve. His name was something like Sir Alland or Allart of Bekelar; he was from Flanders and was making a pilgrimage to various holy shrines in the northern countries. He was exceedingly friendly, and it had been no trouble to talk to him. Then Naakkve mentioned his request. From there the knight was headed for Oslo and then on to pilgrim sites in Denmark and Germany, and now he wanted Naakkve to come with him to be his interpreter, at least while he was in Norway. But he had also hinted that if the youth should accompany him out into the world, then Sir Allart was the man who could make his fortune. Where he came from, it seemed as if golden spurs and necklaces, heavy money pouches, and splendid weapons were simply waiting for a man like young Nikulaus Erlendssøn to come along and take them. Naakkve had replied that he was not yet of age and would need permission from his father. But Sir Allart had still pressed a gift upon him—he had expressly stated that it would in no way bind him—a knee-length, plum-blue silk tunic with silver bells on the points of the sleeves.

Erlend listened to him, saying hardly a word, with an oddly tense expression on his face. When Naakkve was finished, he sent Gaute to get the chest with his writing implements and at once set about composing a letter in Latin. Bjørgulf had to help him because Naakkve was in no condition to do much of anything and his father had sent him off to bed. In the letter Erlend invited the knight to his home on the following day, after prime[1] so they might discuss Sir Allart's offer to take the noble-born young man, Nikulaus Erlendssøn, into his service as his esquire. He asked the knight's forgiveness for returning his gift with the plea that Sir Allart might keep it until Nikulaus, with his father's consent, had been sworn into the man's service in accordance with such customs as prevailed among knights in all the lands.

Erlend dripped a little wax on the bottom of the letter and lightly pressed his small seal, the one on his ring, into it. Then he sent a servant boy off to Romundgaard at once with the letter and the silk tunic.

"Husband, surely you can't be thinking of sending your young son off to distant lands with an unknown foreigner," said Kristin, shivering.

"We shall see. . . ." Erlend smiled quite strangely. "But I don't think it's likely," he added when he noticed her distress. He smiled again and caressed her cheek.

At Erlend's request, Kristin had strewn the floor in the high loft with juniper and flowers, placed the best cushions on the benches, and set the table with a linen cloth and good food and drink in fine dishes and the precious silver-chased animal horns they had inherited from Lavrans. Erlend had shaved carefully, curled his hair, and dressed in a black, richly embroidered ankle-length robe made of foreign cloth. He went to meet his guest at the manor gate, and as they crossed the courtyard together, Kristin couldn't help thinking that her husband looked more like the French knights mentioned in the sagas than did the fat, fair-haired stranger in the colorful and resplendent garments made from velvet and sarcenet. She stood on the gallery of the high loft, beautifully attired and wearing a silk wimple. The Flemish man kissed her hand as she bade him *bienvenu*. She didn't exchange another word with him during all the hours he spent with them. She understood nothing of the men's conversation; nor did Sira Solmund, who had come with his guest. But the priest told the mistress that now he had assuredly made Naakkve's fortune. She neither agreed nor disagreed with him.

Erlend spoke a little French and could fluently speak the kind of German that mercenaries spoke; the discussion between him and the foreign knight flowed easily and courteously. But Kristin noticed that the Flemish man did not seem pleased as things progressed, although he strove to conceal his displeasure. Erlend had told his sons to wait over in the loft of the new storehouse until he sent word for them to join them, but they were not sent for.

Erlend and his wife escorted the knight and the priest to the gate. When their guests disappeared among the fields, Erlend turned to Kristin and said with that smile she found so distasteful, "I wouldn't let Naakkve leave the estate with that fellow even to go south to Breidin."

Ulf Haldorssøn came over to them. He and Erlend spoke a few words that Kristin couldn't hear, but Ulf swore fiercely and spat.

Erlend laughed and slapped the man on the shoulder. "Yes, if I'd been such a country dolt as the good farmers around here . . . But I've seen enough that I wouldn't let my fair young falcons out of my hands by selling them to the Devil. Sira Solmund had no idea, that blessed fool."

Kristin stood with her arms hanging at her sides, the color ebbing and rising in her face. Horror and shame overcame her, making her feel sick; her legs seemed to lose all strength. She had known about such things—as something endlessly remote—but that this unmentionable might venture as close as her own doorstep . . . It was like the last wave, threatening to overturn her storm-tossed, overloaded boat. Holy Mary, did she also need to fear *that* for her sons?

Erlend said with the same loathsome smile, "I already had my doubts last night. Sir Allart seemed to me a little too chivalrous from Naakkve's account. I know that it's not the custom among knights anywhere in the world to welcome a man who is to be taken into service by kissing him on the lips or by giving him costly presents before seeing proof of his abilities."

Shaking from head to toe, Kristin said, "Why did you ask me to strew the floor with roses and cover my table with linen cloths for such a—" And she uttered the worst of words.

Erlend frowned. He had picked up a stone and was keeping an eye on Munan's red cat, which was slithering on its stomach through the tall grass along the wall of the house, heading for the chickens near the stable door. Whoosh! He threw the stone. The cat streaked around the corner, and the flock of hens scattered. He turned to face his wife.

"I thought I could at least have a *look* at the man. If he had been a trustworthy fellow, then . . . But in that case I had to show the proper courtesy. I'm not Sir Allart's confessor. And you heard that he's planning to go to Oslo." Erlend laughed again. "Now it's possible that some of my true friends and dear kinsmen from the past may hear that we're not sitting up here at Jørundgaard shaking the lice from our rags or eating herring and oat *lefse*."

Bjørgulf had a headache and was lying in bed when Kristin came up to the loft at suppertime, and Naakkve said he didn't want to go over to the main house for the evening meal.

"You seem to me morose tonight, son," said his mother.

"How can you think that, Mother?" said Naakkve with a scornful smile. "The fact that I'm a worse fool than other men and it's easier to throw sand in my eyes . . . surely that's nothing to be morose about."

"Console yourself," said his father as they sat down at the table and Naakkve was still too quiet. "No doubt you'll go out into the world and have a chance to try your luck."

"That depends, Father," replied Naakkve in a low voice, as if he intended only Erlend to hear him, "whether Bjørgulf can go with me." Then he laughed softly. "But talk to Ivar and Skule about what you just said. They're merely waiting to reach the proper age before they set off."

Kristin stood up and put on her hooded cloak. She was going to go north to tend to the beggar at Ingebjørg's hut, she told them when they asked. The twins offered to go along and carry her sack, but she wanted to go alone.

The evenings were already quite dark, and north of the church the path passed through the woods and beneath the shadow of Hammer Ridge. There gusts of cold wind always issued from Rost Gorge, and the din of the river brought a trace of moisture to the air. Swarms of big white moths hovered and flitted under the trees, sometimes flying straight at her. The pale glow of the linen around her face and on her breast seemed to draw them in the dark. She swatted them away with her hand as she rushed upward, sliding on the slippery carpet of needles and stumbling over the writhing roots that sprawled across the path she was following.

A certain dream had haunted Kristin for many years. The first time she had it was on the night before Gaute was born, but occasionally she would still wake up, soaked with sweat, her heart hammering as if it would shatter in her chest, and she had dreamed the same thing.

She saw a meadow with flowers, a steep hill deep inside a pine forest that bordered the mound on three sides, dark and dense. At the foot of the slope a small lake mirrored the dim forest and the dappled green of the clearing. The sun was behind the trees; at the top of the hill the last long golden rays of evening light filtered through the boughs, and at the bottom of the lake sun-touched, gleaming clouds swam among the leaves of water lilies.

Halfway up the slope, standing deep in the avalanche of alpine catchflies and globeflowers and the pale green clouds of angelica, she saw her child. It must have been Naakkve the first time she had the dream; back then she had only two, and Bjørgulf was still in the cradle. Later she was never certain which of her children it might be. The little round, sunburned face under the fringe of yellow-brown hair seemed to her to resemble first one and then another of her sons, but the child was always between two and three years old and dressed in the kind of small dark yellow tunic that she usually sewed for her little boys as everyday attire, from homespun wool, dyed with lichen, and trimmed with red ribbon.

Sometimes she seemed to be on the other side of the lake. Or she might not be present at all when it happened, and yet she saw everything.

She saw her little son moving about, here and there, turning his face as he tugged at the flowers. And even though her heart felt the clutch of a dull anguish—a premonition of the evil about to occur—the dream always brought with it first a powerful, aching sweetness as she gazed at the lovely child there in the meadow.

Then she sees emerging from the darkness at the edge of the woods a furry bulk that is alive. It moves soundlessly, its tiny, vicious eyes smoldering. The bear reaches the top of the meadow and stands there, its head and shoulders swaying, as it considers the slope. Then it leaps. Kristin had never seen a bear alive, but she knew bears didn't leap that way. This is not a real bear. It runs like a cat; at the same moment it turns gray, and like a giant light-colored cat it flies with long, soft strides down the hill.

The mother is deathly frightened, but she can't reach the child to protect him; she can't make a sound of warning. Then the boy notices that *something* is there; he turns halfway and looks over his shoulder. With a horrifying, low-pitched cry of terror he tries to run downhill, lifting his legs high in the tall grass the way children do. And his mother hears the tiny crack of sap-filled stalks breaking as he runs through the profusion of blossoms. Now he stumbles over something in the grass, falls headlong, and in the next instant the beast is upon him with its back arched and its head lowered between its front paws. Then she wakes up.

And each time she would lie awake for hours before her attempts to reassure herself did any good. It was only a dream after all! She would draw into her arms her smallest child, who lay between herself and the wall, thinking that if it had been real, she could have done such and such: scared off the animal with a shriek or with a pole. And there was always the long, sharp knife that hung from her belt.

But just as she had convinced herself in this manner to calm down, it would sieze hold of her once again: the unbearable anguish of her dream as she stood powerless and watched her little son's pitiful, hopeless flight from the strong, ruthlessly swift, and hideous beast. Her blood felt as if it were boiling inside her, foaming so that it made her body swell, and her heart was about to burst, for it couldn't contain such a violent surge of blood.

Ingebjørg's hut lay up on Hammer Ridge, a short distance below the main road that led up to the heights. It had stood empty for many years, and the land had been leased to a man who had been allowed to clear space for a house nearby. An ill beggar who had been left behind by a procession of mendicants had now taken refuge inside. Kristin had sent food and clothing and medicine up to him when she heard of this, but she hadn't had time to visit him until now.

She saw that the poor man's life would soon be over. Kristin gave her sack to the beggar woman who was staying with him and then tended to the ill man, doing what little she could. When she heard that they had sent for the priest, she washed his face, hands, and feet so they would be clean to receive the last anointment.

The air was thick with smoke, and a terribly oppressive, foul smell filled the tiny room. When two women from the neighboring household came in, Kristin asked them to send word to Jørundgaard for anything they might need; then she bade them farewell and left. She suddenly had a strange, sick fear of meeting the priest with the *Corpus Domini*, so she took the first side path she encountered.

It was merely a cattle track, she soon realized. And it led her right into the wilderness. The fallen trees with their tangle of roots sticking up frightened her; she had to crawl over them in those places where she couldn't make her way around. Layers of moss slid out from under her feet when she clambered down over large rocks. Spiderwebs clung to her face, and branches swung at her and caught on her clothes. When she had to cross a small creek or she came to a marshy clearing in the woods, it was almost impossible to find a place where she could slip though the dense, wet thickets of leafy shrubs. And the loathsome white moths were everywhere, teeming beneath the trees in the darkness, swarming up in great clouds from the heath-covered mounds when she trod on them.

But at last she reached the flat rocks down by the Laag River. Here the pine forest thinned out because the trees had to twine their roots over barren rocks, and the forest floor was almost nothing but dry grayish-white reindeer moss, which crackled under her feet. Here and there a black, heath-covered mound was visible. The fragrance of pine needles was hotter and drier and sharper than higher up. Here all the branches of the trees always looked yellow-scorched from early spring on. The white moths continued to plague her.

The roar of the river drew her. She walked all the way over to the edge and looked down. Far below, the water shimmered white as it seethed and thundered over the rocks from one pool to the next.

The monotonous drone of the waterfalls resonated through her overwrought body and soul. It kept reminding her of something, of a time that was an eternity ago; even back then she realized that she would not have the strength to bear the fate she had chosen for herself. She had laid bare her protected, gentle girl's life to a ravaging, fleshly love; she had lived in anguish, anguish, anguish ever since—an unfree woman from the first moment she became a mother. She had given herself up to the world in her youth, and the more she squirmed and struggled against the bonds of the world, the more fiercely she felt herself imprisoned and fettered by them. She struggled to protect her sons with wings that were bound by the constraints of earthly care. She had striven to conceal her anguish and her inexpressible weakness from everyone, walking forward with her back erect and her face calm, holding her tongue, and fighting to ensure the welfare of her children in any way she could.

But always with that secret, breathless anguish: If things go badly for them, I won't be able to bear it. And deep in her heart she wailed at the memory of her father and mother. They had borne anguish and sorrow over their children, day after day, until their deaths; they had been able to carry this burden, and it was not because they loved their children any less but because they loved with a better kind of love.

Was this how she would see her struggle end? Had she conceived in her womb a flock of restless fledgling hawks that simply lay in her nest, waiting impatiently for the hour when their wings were strong enough to carry them beyond the most distant blue peaks? And their father would clap his hands and laugh: Fly, fly, my young birds.

They would take with them bloody threads from the roots of her heart when they flew off, and they wouldn't even know it. She would be left behind alone, and all the heartstrings, which had once bound her to this old home of hers, she had already sundered. That was how it would end, and she would be neither alive nor dead.

She turned on her heel, stumbling hastily across the pale, parched carpet of reindeer moss, with her cloak pulled tight around her because it was so unpleasant when it caught on the branches. At last she emerged onto the sparse meadow plains that lay slightly north of the farmers' banquet hall and the church. As she cut across the field, she caught sight of someone in the road. He called out: "Is that you, Kristin?" and she recognized her husband.

"You were gone a long time," said Erlend. "It's almost night, Kristin. I was starting to grow frightened."

"Were you frightened for me?" Her voice sounded more harsh and haughty than she had intended.

"Well, not exactly frightened . . . But I thought I would come out to meet you."

They barely spoke as they walked southward. All was quiet when they entered the courtyard. Some of the horses they kept on the manor were slowly moving along the walls of the main house, grazing, but all the servants had gone to bed.

Erlend headed straight for the storeroom loft, but Kristin turned toward the cookhouse. "I have to see to something," she replied to his query.

He stood leaning over the gallery railing, waiting for his wife, when he saw her come out of the cookhouse with a pine torch in her hand and go over to the hearth house. Erlend waited a moment and then ran down and followed her inside.

She had lit a candle and placed it on the table. Erlend felt an odd, cold shiver of fear pass through him when he saw her standing there with the lone candle in the empty house. Only the built-in furniture remained in the room, and the glow of the flame shimmered over the worn wood, unadorned and bare. The hearth was cold and swept clean, except for the torch, which had been tossed into it, still smoldering. They never used this building, Erlend and Kristin, and it must have been almost half a year since a fire had been lit inside. The air was strangely oppressive; missing was the vital blend of smells from people living there and coming and going; the smoke vent and doors had not been opened in all that time. The place also smelled of wool and hides; several rolled-up skins and sacks, which Kristin had taken from among the goods in the storeroom, were piled up on the empty bed that had belonged to Lavrans and Ragnfrid.

On the table lay a heap of small skeins of thread and yarn—linen and wool to be used for mending—which Kristin had set aside when she did the dyeing. She was going through them now, setting them in order.

Erlend sat down in the high seat at the end of the table. It seemed oddly spacious for the slender man, now that it had been stripped of its cushions and coverings. The two Olav warriors, with their helmets and shields bearing the sign of the cross, that Lavrans had carved into the armrests of the high seat scowled glumly and morosely under Erlend's slim tan hands. No man could carve foliage and animals more beautifully than Lavrans, but he had never been very skilled at capturing human likenesses.

The silence between them was so complete that not a sound was heard except for the hollow thudding out on the green, where the horses were plodding around in the summer night.

"Aren't you going to bed soon, Kristin?" he finally asked.

"Aren't you?"

"I thought I would wait for you," said her husband.

"I don't want to go yet. . . . I can't sleep."

After a moment he asked, "What is weighing so heavily on your heart, Kristin, that you don't think you'll be able to sleep?"

Kristin straightened up. She stood holding a skein of heather-green wool in her hands, tugging and pulling on it with her fingers.

"What was it you said to Naakkve today?" She swallowed a couple of times; her throat felt so parched. "Some piece of advice . . . He didn't think it was much good for him . . . but the two of you talked about Ivar and Skule. . . ."

"Oh . . . that!" Erlend gave a little smile. "I just told the boy . . . I do have a son-in-law, now that I think of it. Although Gerlak wouldn't be as eager to kiss my hands or carry my cape and sword as he used to be. But he has a ship on the sea and wealthy kin both in Bremen and in Lynn. Surely the man must realize that he's obliged to help his wife's brothers. I didn't stint on my gifts when I was a rich man and married my daughter to Ger-lak Tiedekenssøn."

Kristin did not reply.

At last Erlend exclaimed vehemently, "Jesus, Kristin, don't just stand there staring like that, as if you had turned to stone."

"I never thought, when we were first married, that our children would have to roam the world, begging food from the manors of strangers."

"No, and the Devil take me, I don't mean for them to beg! But if all seven of them have to grow their own food here on your estates, then it will be a peasant's diet, my Kristin. And I don't think my sons are suited to that. Ivar and Skule look like they'll turn out to be daredevils, and out in the world there is both wheat bread and cake for the man willing to slice his food with a sword."

"You intend your sons to become hired soldiers and merce-naries?"

"I hired on myself when I was young and served Earl Jacob. May God bless him, I say. I learned a few things back then that a man can never learn at home in this country, whether he's sitting in splendor in his high seat with a silver belt around his belly and swilling down ale or he's walking behind a plow and breathing in the farts of the farm horse. I lived a robust life in the earl's service; I say that even though I ended up with that stump chained to my foot when I was no older than Naakkve. But I was allowed to enjoy some of my youth."

"Silence!" Kristin's eyes grew dark. "Wouldn't you think it the most unbearable sorrow if your sons should be lured into such sin and misfortune?"

"Yes, may God protect them from that. But surely it shouldn't be necessary for them to copy all the follies of their father. It *is* possible, Kristin, to serve a noble lord without being saddled with such a burden."

"It is written that he who draws his sword shall lose his life by the sword, Erlend!"

"Yes, I've heard that said, my dear. And yet most of our forefathers, both yours and mine, Kristin, died peacefully and in a Christian manner in their beds, with the last rites and comfort for their souls. You only need think of your own father; he proved in his youth that he was a man who could use his sword."

"But that was during a war, Erlend, at the summons of the king to whom they had sworn allegiance; it was in order to protect their homeland that Father and the others took up their weapons. And yet Father said himself that it was not God's will that we should bear arms against each other—baptized Christian men."

"Yes, I know that. But the world has been this way ever since Adam and Eve ate from the tree—and that was before my time. It's not my fault that we're born with sin inside us."

"What shameful things you're saying!"

Erlend heatedly interrupted her. "Kristin, you know full well that I have never refused to atone and repent for my sins as best I could. It's true that I'm not a pious man. I saw too much in my childhood and youth. My father was such a dear friend of the great lords of the chapter.[2] They came and went at his house like gray pigs: Lord Eiliv, back when he was a priest, and Herr Sigvat Lande, and all the others, and they brought little else with them but quarrels and disputes. They were hardhearted and merciless toward their own bishop; they proved to be no more holy or peaceable even though each day they held the most sacred relics in their hands and lifted up God Himself in the bread and wine."

"Surely we are not to judge the priests. That's what Father always said: It's our obligation to bow before the priesthood and obey them, but their human behavior shall be judged by God alone."

"Yes, well . . ." Erlend hesitated. "I know he said that, and you've also said the same in the past. I know you're more pious than I can ever be. And yet, Kristin, I have difficulty accepting that this is the proper interpretation of God's words: that you should go about storing everything away and never forgetting. He had a long memory too, Lavrans did. No, I won't say anything about your father except that he was pious and noble, and you are too; I know that. But often when you speak so gently and sweetly, as if your mouth were full of honey, I fear that you're thinking mostly about old wrongs, and God will have to judge whether you're as pious in your heart as you are in words."

Suddenly Kristin fell forward, stretched out across the table with her face buried in her arms, and began shrieking. Erlend leaped to his feet. She lay there, weeping with raw, ragged sobs that shuddered down her back. Erlend put his arm around her shoulder.

"Kristin, what is it? What is it?" he repeated, sitting down next to her on the bench and trying to lift her head. "Kristin, don't weep like this. I think you must have lost your senses."

"I'm frightened!" She sat up, wringing her hands together in her lap. "I'm so frightened. Gentle Virgin Mary, help us all. I'm so frightened. What will become of my sons?"

"Yes, my Kristin . . . but you must get used to it. You can't keep hiding them under your skirts. Soon they'll be grown men, all our sons. And you're still acting like a bitch with pups." He sat with his legs crossed and his hands clasped around one knee, looking down at his wife with a weary expression. "You snap blindly at both friend and foe over anything that has to do with your offspring."

Abruptly she got to her feet and stood there for a moment, mutely wringing her hands. Then she began swiftly pacing the room. She didn't say a word, and Erlend sat in silence, watching her.

"Skule . . ." She stopped in front of her husband. "You gave your son an ill-fated name. But you insisted on it. You *wanted* the duke to rise up again in that child."

"It's a fine name, Kristin. Ill fated . . . that can mean many things. When I revived my great-grandfather through my son, I remembered that good fortune had deserted him, but he was still a king, and with better rights than the combmaker's descendants."

"You were certainly proud, you and Munan Baardsøn, that you were close kinsmen of King Haakon Haalegg."

"Yes, you know that Sverre's lineage gained royal blood from my father's aunt, Margret Skulesdatter."

For a long time both husband and wife stood staring into each other's eyes.

"Yes, I know what you're thinking, my fair wife." Erlend went back to the high seat and sat down. With his hands resting on the heads of the two warriors, he leaned forward slightly, giving her a cold and challenging smile. "But as you can see, my Kristin, it hasn't broken me to become a poor and friendless man. You should know that I have no fear that the lineage of my forefathers has fallen along with me from power and honor for all eternity. Good fortune has also deserted me; but if my plan had been carried out, my sons and I would now have positions and seats at the king's right hand, which we, his close kinsmen, are entitled to by birth. For me, no doubt, the game is over. But I see in my sons, Kristin, that they will attain the positions which are their birthright. You don't need to lament over them, and you must not try to bind them to this remote valley of yours. Let them freely make their own way. Then you might see, before you die, that they have once again won a foothold in their father's ancestral regions."

"Oh, how you can talk!" Hot, bitter tears rose up in his wife's eyes, but she brushed them aside and laughed, her mouth contorted. "You seem even more childish than the boys, Erlend! Sitting there and saying . . . when it was only today that Naakkve nearly won the kind of fortune that a Christian man can hardly speak of, if God hadn't saved us."

"Yes, and I was the one lucky enough to be God's instrument this time." Erlend shrugged his shoulders. Then he added in a somber voice, "Such things . . . you needn't fear, my Kristin. If this is what has frightened you from your wits, my poor wife!" He lowered his eyes and said almost timidly, "You should remember, Kristin, that your blessed father prayed for our children, just as he prayed for all of us, morning and night. And I firmly believe that salvation can be found for many things, for the worst of things, in such a good man's prayers of intercession." She noticed that her husband secretly made the sign of the cross on his own chest with his thumb.

But as distressed as she was, this only infuriated her more.

"Is that how you console yourself, Erlend, as you sit in my father's high seat? That your sons will be saved by his prayers, just as they are fed by his estates?"

Erlend grew pale. "Do you mean, Kristin, that I'm not worthy to sit in the high seat of Lavrans Bjørgulfsøn?"

His wife's lips moved, but not a word came.

Erlend rose to his feet. "Do you mean that? For if you do, then as surely as God is above us both, I will never sit here again.

"Answer me," he insisted when she remained standing in silence. A long shudder passed through his wife's body.

"He was . . . a better husband . . . the man who sat there before you." Her words were barely audible.

"Guard your tongue now, Kristin!" Erlend took a few steps toward her.

She straightened up with a start. "Go ahead and strike me. I've endured it before, and I can bear it now."

"I had no intention of . . . striking you." He stood leaning on the table. Again they stared at each other, and his face had that oddly unfamiliar calm she had seen only a few times before. Now it drove her into a rage. She knew she was in the right; what Erlend had said was foolish and irresponsible, but that expression of his made her feel as if she were utterly wrong.

She gazed at him, and feeling sick with anguish at her own words, she said, "I fear that it won't be *my* sons that will thrive once more among your lineage in Trøndelag."

Erlend turned blood red.

"You couldn't resist reminding me of Sunniva Olavsdatter, I see."

"I wasn't the one to mention her name. You did."

Erlend blushed even more.

"Haven't you ever thought, Kristin, that you weren't entirely without blame in that . . . misfortune? Do you remember that evening in Nidaros? I came and stood by your bed. I was terribly meek and sad about having grieved you, my wife. I came to beg your forgiveness for my wrong. You answered me by saying that I should go to bed where I had slept the night before."

"How could I know that you had slept with the wife of your kinsman?"

Erlend was silent for a moment. His face turned white and then red again. Abruptly he turned on his heel and left the room without a word.

Kristin didn't move. For a long time she stood there motionless, with her hands clasped under her chin, staring at the candle.

Suddenly she lifted her head and let out a long breath. For once he had been forced to listen.

Then she became aware of the sound of horse hooves out in the courtyard. She could tell from its gait that a horse was being led out of the stable. She crept over to the door and out onto the gallery and peered from behind the post.

The night had already turned a pale gray. Out in the courtyard stood Erlend and Ulf Haldorssøn. Erlend was holding his horse, and she saw that the animal was saddled and her husband was dressed for travel. The two men talked for a moment, but she couldn't make out a single word. Then Erlend swung himself up into the saddle and began riding north, at a walking pace, toward the manor gate. He didn't look back but seemed to be talking to Ulf, who was striding along next to the horse.

When they had disappeared between the fences, she tiptoed out, ran as soundlessly as she could up to the gate, and stood there listening. Now she could hear that Erlend had let Soten begin trotting along the main road.

A little later Ulf came walking back. He stopped abruptly when he caught sight of Kristin at the gate. For a moment they stood and stared at each other in the gray light. Ulf had bare feet in his shoes and was wearing a linen tunic under his cape.

"What is it?" his mistress asked heatedly.

"Surely you must know, for I have no idea."

"Where was he riding off to?" she asked.

"To Haugen." Ulf paused. "Erlend came in and woke me. He said he wanted to ride there tonight, and he seemed in a great hurry. He asked me to see to it that certain things were sent to him up there later on."

Kristin fell silent for a long time.

"He was angry?"

"He was calm." After a moment Ulf said quietly, "I fear, Kristin . . . I wonder if you might have said what should have been best left unspoken."

"Surely Erlend for once should be able to stand hearing me speak to him as if he were a sensible man," said Kristin vehemently.

They walked slowly down the hill. Ulf turned toward his own house, but she followed him.

"Ulf, kinsman," she implored him anxiously. "In the past you were the one who told me morning and night that for the sake of my sons I had to steel myself and speak to Erlend."

"Yes, but I've grown wiser over the years, Kristin. You haven't," he replied in the same tone of voice.

"You offer me such solace now," she said bitterly.

He placed his hand heavily on the woman's shoulder, but at first he didn't speak. As they stood there, it was so quiet they could both hear the endless roar of the river, which they usually didn't notice. Out across the countryside the roosters were crowing, and the cry of Kristin's own rooster echoed from the stable.

"Yes, I've had to learn to ration out the solace sparingly, Kristin. There's been a cruel shortage of it for several years now. We have to save it up because we don't know how long it might have to last."

She tore herself away from his hand. With her teeth biting her lower lip, she turned her face away. And then she fled back to the hearth house.

The morning was icy cold. She wrapped her cloak tightly around her and pulled the hood up over her head. With her dew-drenched shoes tucked up under her skirts and her crossed arms resting on her knees, she huddled at the edge of the cold hearth to think. Now and then a tremor passed over her face, but she did not cry.

She must have fallen asleep. She started up with an aching back, her body frozen through and stiff. The door stood ajar. She saw that sunlight filled the courtyard.

Kristin went out onto the gallery. The sun was already high;

from the fenced pasture below she could hear the bell of the horse that had gone lame. She looked toward the new storehouse. Then she noticed that Munan was standing up on the loft gallery, peering out from between the posts.

Her sons. It raced through her mind. What had they thought when they woke up and saw their parents' bed untouched?

She ran across the courtyard and up to the child. Munan was wearing only his shirt. As soon as his mother reached him, he put his hand in hers, as if he were afraid.

Inside the loft none of the boys was fully dressed; she realized that no one had woken them. All of them looked quickly at their mother and then glanced away. She picked up Munan's leggings and began helping him to put them on.

"Where's Father?" asked Lavrans in surprise.

"Your father rode north to Haugen early this morning," she replied. She saw that the older boys were listening as she said, "You know he's been talking about it so long, that he wanted to go up there to see to his manor."

The two youngest sons looked up into their mother's face with wide, atonished eyes, but the five older brothers hid their gaze from her as they left the loft.

CHAPTER 3

THE DAYS PASSED. At first Kristin wasn't worried. She didn't want to ponder over what Erlend might have meant by his behavior—fleeing from home like that in the middle of the night in a fit of rage—or how long he intended to stay north on his upland farm, punishing her with his absence. She was furious at her husband, but perhaps most furious because she couldn't deny that she too had been wrong and had said things she sincerely wished had not been said.

Certainly she had been wrong many times before, and in anger she had often spoken mean and vile words to her husband. But what offended her most bitterly was that Erlend would never offer to forget and forgive unless she first humbled herself and asked him meekly to do so. She didn't think she had let her temper get the better of her very often; couldn't he see that it was usually when she was tired and worn out with sorrows and anguish, which she had tried to bear alone? That was when she could easily lose mastery over her feelings. She thought Erlend might have remembered, after all the years of worry she had borne about the future of their sons, that during the past summer she had twice endured a terrible agony over Naakkve. Her eyes had been opened to the fact that after the burdens and toil of a young mother comes a new kind of fear and concern for the aging mother. Erlend's carefree chatter about having no fear for the future of his sons had angered her until she felt like a wild she-bear or like a bitch with pups. Erlend could go ahead and say that she was like a female dog with her children. She would always be alert and vigilant over them for as long as she had breath in her body.

If, for that reason, he chose to forget that she had stood by him every time it mattered, with all her strength, and that she had been both reasonable and fair, in spite of her anger, when he struck her and when he betrayed her with that hateful, loose woman from Lensvik, then she could do nothing to stop him. Even now, when she thought about it, she couldn't feel much anger or bitterness toward Erlend over the worst of the wrongs he had done her. Whenever she turned on him to complain about *that*, it was because she knew that he regretted it himself; he knew it was a great offense. But she had never been so angry with Erlend—nor was she now— that she didn't feel sorrow for the man himself when she remembered how he struck her or betrayed her, with everything that followed afterward. She always felt that with these outbursts of his unruly spirit he had sinned more against himself and the well-being of his own soul than he had against her.

What continued to vex her were all the small wounds he had caused her with his cruel nonchalance, his childish lack of patience, and even the wild and thoughtless kind of love he gave her whenever he showed that he did indeed love her. And during all those years when her heart was young and tender, when she realized that neither her health nor her strength of will would be sufficient—as she sat with her arms full of such defenseless little children—if their father, her husband, didn't show that he was both capable and loving enough to protect her and the young sons in her arms. It had been such torment to feel her body so weak, her mind so ignorant and inexperienced, and yet not dare rely on the wisdom and strength of her husband. She felt as if she had suffered deep wounds back then, which would never heal. Even the sweet pleasure of lifting up her infant, placing his loving mouth to her breast, and feeling his warm, soft little body in her arms was soured by fear and uneasiness. So small, so defenseless you are, and your father doesn't seem to remember that above all else he needs to keep you safe.

Now that her children had gained marrow in their bones and mettle in their spirits but still lacked the full wisdom of men, now he was luring them away from her. They were whirling away from her, both her husband and all her sons, with that strange, boyish playfulness which she seemed to have glimpsed in all the men she had ever met and in which a somber, fretful woman could never participate.

For her own sake then she felt only sorrow and anger when ever she thought about Erlend. But she grew fearful when she wondered what her sons were thinking.

Ulf had gone up to Dovre with two packhorses and taken Erlend the things he had sent for: clothing and a good many weapons, all four of his bows, sacks of arrowpoints and iron bolts, and three of his dogs. Munan and Lavrans wept loudly when Ulf took the small, short-haired female with the silky soft, drooping ears. It was a splendid foreign animal which the abbot of Holm had given to Erlend. That their father should own such a rare dog seemed, more than anything else, to elevate him above all other men in the eyes of the two young boys. And their father had promised that when the dog had pups, they would each be allowed to choose one from the litter.

When Ulf Haldorssøn returned, Kristin asked him whether Erlend had mentioned when he intended to come back home.

"No," said Ulf. "It looks like he means to settle in up there."

Ulf volunteered little else about his journey to Haugen. And Kristin had no desire to ask.

In the fall, when they moved from the new storeroom into other quarters, her oldest sons said that this winter they wanted to sleep upstairs in the high loft. Kristin granted them permission to do so; she would sleep alone with the two youngest boys in the main room below. On the first evening she said that now Lavrans could sleep in her bed as well.

The boy lay in bed, rolling around with delight and burrowing into the ticking. The children were used to having their beds made up on a bench, with leather sacks filled with straw and furs to wrap around them. But in the beds there was blue ticking to lie on and fine coverlets as well as furs, and their parents had white linen cases on their pillows.

"Is it just until Father comes home that I can sleep here?" asked Lavrans. "Then we'll have to move back to the bench, won't we, Mother?"

"Then you can sleep in the bed with Naakkve and Bjørgulf," replied his mother. "If the boys don't change their minds, that is, and move back downstairs when the weather turns cold." There was a little brick fireplace up in the loft, but it produced more smoke than heat, and the wind and cold were felt much more in the upper story.

As the fall wore on, an uncertain fear crept over Kristin; it grew from day to day, and the strain was difficult to bear. No one seemed to have heard from Erlend or seen him.

During the long, dark autumn nights she would lie awake, listening to the even breathing of the two little boys, noting the swirl of the wind around the corners of the house, and thinking about Erlend. If only he wasn't staying at that particular farm.

She hadn't been pleased when the two cousins had begun talking about Haugen. Munan Baardsøn was visiting them at the hostel in Oslo on one of the last evenings before their departure. Back then Munan had inherited sole ownership of the small manor of Haugen from his mother. Both he and Erlend had been quite drunk and boisterous, and while she sat there feeling tormented by their talk of that place of misfortune, Munan suddenly gave Erlend the farm—so that he wouldn't be entirely bereft of land in Norway. This happened amid much bantering and laughter; they even jested about the rumors that no one could live at Haugen because of the ghosts. The horror that Sir Munan Baardsøn had harbored in his heart ever since the violent death of his mother and her husband up there now seemed to have eased somewhat.

He ended up giving Erlend the deed and documents to Haugen. Kristin couldn't hide her displeasure that he had become the owner of that ignominious place.

But Erlend merely jested, "It's unlikely that either you or I will ever set foot in those buildings—if they're still standing, that is, and haven't collapsed. And surely neither Aunt Aashild nor Herr Bjørn will bring us the land rent themselves. So it shouldn't matter to us if it's true what people say, that they still haunt the place."

The year came to an end, and Kristin's thoughts were always circling around one thing: How was Erlend doing up north at Haugen? She grew so reticent that she barely spoke a word to her children or the servants except when she had to answer their questions. And they were reluctant to address their mistress unless it was absolutely necessary, for she gave such curt and impatient replies when they interrupted and disturbed her restless, anxious brooding. She was so unaware of this herself that when she finally noticed that the two youngest children had stopped asking her about their father or talking about him, she sighed and concluded that children forget so quickly. But she didn't realize how often she had scared them away with her impatient words when she told them to keep quiet and stop plaguing her.

To her oldest sons she said very little.

As long as the hard frost lasted, she could still tell strangers who passed by the manor and asked for her husband that he was up in the mountains trying his luck at hunting. But then a great snowfall descended upon both the countryside and the mountains during the first week of Advent.

Early in the morning on the day before Saint Lucia's Day, while it was still pitch-dark outside and the stars were bright, Kristin came out of the cowshed. She saw by the light of a pine torch stuck in a mound of snow that three of her sons were putting on their skis outside the door of the main house. And a short distance away stood Gaute's gelding with snowshoes under its feet and packs on its back. She guessed where they were headed, so she didn't dare say a word until she noticed that one of the boys was Bjørgulf; the other two were Naakkve and Gaute.

"Are you going out skiing, Bjørgulf? But it's going to be clear today, son!"

"As you can see, Mother, I am."

"Perhaps you'll all be home before the holy day?" she asked helplessly. Bjørgulf was a very poor skier. He couldn't tolerate the brilliance of the snow in his eyes and spent most of the winter indoors. But Naakkve replied that they might be gone for several days.

Kristin went home feeling fearful and uneasy. The twins were cross and sullen, so she realized that they had wanted to go along but their older brothers had refused to take them.

Early on the fifth day, around breakfast time, the three boys returned. They had left before dawn for Bjørgulf's sake, said Naakkve, in order to reach home before the sun came up. The two of them went straight up to the high loft; Bjørgulf looked dead tired. But Gaute carried the bags and packs into the house. He had two handsome pups for the small boys, who at once forgot all about their questions and grievances. Gaute seemed embarrassed but tried not to show it.

"And this," he said as he took something out of a sack, "this Father asked me to give to you."

Fourteen marten pelts, exceedingly beautiful. Kristin took them, greatly confused; she couldn't utter a single word in reply. There were far too many things she wanted to ask, but she was afraid of being overwhelmed if she opened even the smallest part of her heart. And Gaute was so young.

She could only manage to say, "They've already turned white, I see. Yes, we're deep into the winter half of the year now."

When Naakkve came downstairs and he and Gaute sat down to the porridge bowl, Kristin quickly told Frida that she would take food to Bjørgulf up in the loft herself. It occurred to her that she might be able to talk about things with the taciturn boy, who she knew was much more mature in spirit than his brothers.

He was lying in bed, holding a linen cloth over his eyes. His mother hung a kettle of water on the hook over the hearth, and while Bjørgulf propped himself up on his elbow to eat, she boiled a concoction of eyebright and celandine.

Kristin took away the empty food bowl, washed his red and swollen eyes with the concoction, and placed moist linen cloths over them. Then she finally gathered her courage to ask, "Didn't your father say anything about when he intends to come back home to us?"

"No."

"You always say so little, Bjørgulf," replied his mother after a moment.

"That seems to run in the family, Mother." After a pause he continued, "We met Simon and his men north of Rost Gorge. They were headed north with supplies."

"Did you speak to them?" she asked.

"No," he said with a laugh. "There seems to be some kind of sickness between us and our kinsmen that makes it impossible for friendship to thrive."

"Are you blaming me for that?" fumed his mother. "One minute you complain that we talk too little, and the next you say that we can't keep our friends."

Bjørgulf merely laughed again. Then he lifted himself up on his elbow, as if he were listening to his mother's breathing.

"In God's name, Mother, you mustn't cry now. I'm tired and dejected, unaccustomed as I am to traveling on skis. Pay no mind to whatever I say. Of course I know that you're not a woman who's fond of quarrels."

Kristin then left the loft at once. But she no longer dared, for any price, to ask this son what her children thought of these matters.

She would lie in bed, night after night, when the boys had gone up to the loft, listening and keeping watch. She wondered whether they talked to each other when they were alone up there. She could hear the thump of their boots as they dropped them to the floor, the clatter of their knife belts falling. She heard their voices but couldn't make out their words. They talked all at the same time, growing boisterous; it seemed to be half quarrel, half banter. One of the twins shouted loudly; then something was dragged across the floor, making dust sprinkle down from the ceiling into the main room. The gallery door crashed open with a bang, there was a stomping from outside on the gallery, and Ivar and Skule threatened and carried on as they pounded on the door. She heard Gaute's voice, loud and full of laughter. She could tell that he was standing just inside the door; he and the twins had been fighting again, and Gaute had ended up throwing the twins out. Finally she heard Naakkve's grown-up man's voice. He intervened, and the twins came back inside. For a little while longer their chatter and laughter reached her, and then the beds creaked overhead. Gradually silence fell. Then a steady drone interrupted by pauses could be heard—a drone like the sound of thunder deep inside the mountains.

Kristin smiled in the dark. Gaute snored whenever he was especially tired. Her father had done the same. Such similarities pleased her; the sons who took after Erlend in appearance were also like him in that they slept as soundlessly as birds. As she lay in bed, thinking about all the small likenesses that could be recognized in offspring, generation after generation, she had to smile to herself. The painful anguish in her heart loosened its grip for a moment, and the trance of sleep descended, tangling up all the threads of her thoughts as she sank down, first into well-being and then into oblivion.

They were young, she consoled herself. They probably didn't take it so hard.

But one day, shortly after New Year's, the curate Sira Solmund came to see Kristin at Jørundgaard. It was the first time he arrived uninvited, and Kristin welcomed him courteously, even though she had her suspicions at once. And it turned out just as she had thought: He felt it was his duty to inquire whether she and her husband had arbitrarily, and without Church consent, ended their marriage and, if so, which of the spouses was responsible for this unlawful act.

Kristin felt as if her eyes flitted restlessly, and she spoke too swiftly, using far too many words, as she explained to the priest that Erlend thought he should tend to his property up north in Dovre. It had been sorely neglected over the past few years, and the buildings were apparently in ruins. Considering that they had so many children, they needed to look after their welfare—and many other such matters. She gave much too detailed an account of the situation, so that even Sira Solmund, as dull-witted as he was, had to notice that she was feeling uncertain. She talked on and on about what an eager hunter Erlend was; surely the priest must know that. She showed him the marten pelts she had received from her husband, and in her confusion, before she realized it or could reconsider, she gave them to the priest.

Anger overtook her after Sira Solmund had gone. Erlend should have known that if he stayed away in this manner, their priest, being the kind of man he was, would show up to investigate the reason for his absence.

Sira Solmund was a little trifle of a man in appearance; it wasn't easy to guess his age, but he was supposedly about forty winters old. He was not very shrewd and apparently didn't possess an overabundance of learning, but he was an upright, pious, and moral priest. One of his sisters, an aging, childless widow and a wicked gossip, managed his meager household.

He wanted to be seen as a zealous servant of the Church, but he concerned himself mostly with paltry matters and common folk.

He had a timid disposition and was reluctant to meddle with the gentry or take up difficult questions, but once he did so, he grew quite fierce and stubborn.

In spite of this, he was well liked by his parishioners. On the one hand, people respected his quiet and honorable way of living; on the other hand, he was not nearly as avaricious or strict when it came to the rights of the Church or people's obligations as Sira Eirik had been. This was doubtless due to the fact that he was much less bold than the old priest.

But Sira Eirik had loved and respected every man and every child in all the surrounding villages. In the past people often grew angry when the priest strove, with unseemly greed, to secure the fortunes and wealth of the children he had conceived out of wedlock with his housekeeper. During the first years he lived in the parish, the people of Sil had a difficult time tolerating his imperious harshness toward anyone who overstepped the slightest dictate of Church law. He had been a soldier before he took his vows, and he had accompanied the pirate earl, Sir Alf of Tornberg, in his youth. This was all quite evident in his behavior.

But even back then the people had been proud of their priest, for he surpassed nearly all other parish priests in the realm in terms of knowledge, wisdom, physical strength, and courtly manners; he also had the loveliest singing voice. As the years passed and he had to endure the heavy trials God seemed to have placed on His servant because of his willfulness in his youth, Sira Eirik Kaaressøn grew so much in wisdom, piety, and righteousness that his name was now known and respected throughout the entire bishopric. When he journeyed to ecclesiastical meetings in the town of Hamar, he was honored as a father by all the other priests, and it was said that Bishop Halvard wanted to have him moved to a church which would have granted him a noble title and a seat in the cathedral chapter. But Sira Eirik supposedly requested to stay where he was; he gave his age as his excuse, and the fact that his sight had been failing him for many years.

On the main road at Sil, a little south of Formo, stood the beautiful cross carved from soapstone that Sira Eirik had paid to have erected where a rockslide on the slope had taken the lives of both his promising young sons forty years before. Older people in the

parish never passed that way without stopping to say a *Pater nos-*
ter and *Ave Maria* for the souls of Alf and Kaare.

The priest had married off his daughter with a dowry of property and cattle. He gave her to a handsome farmer's son of good
family from Viken. No one had any other thought but that Jon Fis
was a good lad. Six years later she had returned home to her father, starving, her health broken, wearing rags and full of lice,
holding a child by each hand, and with another one under her belt.
The people living in Sil back then all knew, although they never
mentioned it, that the children's father had been hanged as a thief
in Oslo. The sons of Jon didn't turn out well either, and now all
three of them were dead.

While his offspring were still alive, Sira Eirik had greedily
sought to adorn and honor his church with gifts. Now it was the
church that would doubtless acquire the majority of his fortune
and his precious books. The new Saint Olav and Saint Thomas
Church in Sil was much larger and more splendid than the old one
that had burned down, and Sira Eirik had endowed it with many
magnificent and costly adornments. He went to church every day
to say his prayers and to reflect, but now he only said mass for the
parishioners on high holy days.

It was Sira Solmund who now handled most of the other official
priestly duties. But when people had a heavy sorrow, or if their
souls were troubled by great difficulties or pangs of conscience,
they preferred to seek out their old parish priest, and they all felt
that they took home solace from a meeting with Sira Eirik.

One evening in early spring Kristin Lavransdatter went to Romundgaard and knocked on the door of Sira Eirik's house. She
didn't know how to bring up the subject she wanted to discuss, so
she talked about one thing and another after she had expressed her
greetings.

Finally the old man said a little impatiently, "Have you just
come here to bring me greetings, Kristin, and to see how I am? If
so, that is most kind of you. But it seems to me that you have
something on your mind, and if this is true, tell me about it now,
and don't waste time with idle talk."

Kristin clasped her hands in her lap and lowered her eyes. "I'm so unhappy, Sira Eirik, that my husband is living up there at Haugen."

"Surely the road isn't any longer," said the priest, "than that you can easily journey up there to talk to him and ask him to return home soon. He can't have so much to do up there on such a small one-man farm that he should need to stay any longer."

"I feel frightened when I think of him sitting alone up there in the winter nights," said Kristin, shivering.

"Erlend Nikulaussøn is old enough and strong enough to look out for himself."

"Sira Eirik . . . you know about everything that happened up there, back in the old days," whispered Kristin, her voice barely audible.

The priest turned his dim old eyes toward her; once they had been coal-black, sharp, and gleaming. He didn't say a word.

"Surely you must have heard what people say," she continued, speaking in the same low voice. "That the dead . . . still haunt the place."

"Do you mean you don't dare seek him out because of that? Or are you afraid the ghosts might break your husband's neck? If they haven't done it by now, Kristin, then no doubt they'll let him stay there in peace." The priest laughed harshly. "It's mostly just ignorance—heathen nonsense and superstition—when people start gossiping about ghosts and the return of dead men. I fear there are stern guards at the door, in that place where Herr Bjørn and Fru Aashild now find themselves."

"Sira Eirik," she whispered, her voice trembling, "do you believe there is no salvation for those two poor souls?"

"God forbid that I should dare judge the limits of His mercy. But I can't imagine that those two could have managed to settle their debts so quickly; all the slates the two of them have had a hand in carving have not yet been presented: her children, whom she abandoned, and the two of you, who took lessons from the wise woman. If I thought that it might help, so that some of the misdeeds she committed could be rectified . . . but since Erlend is living up there, God must not think it would be of any benefit for his aunt to reappear and warn him. For we know that it is through the grace of God and the compassion of Our Lady and the intercessionary prayers of the Church that a poor soul may be allowed to return to this world from the fires of purgatory if his sin is such that it can be absolved with the help of someone who is alive and in this manner shorten his time of torment. Such was the case with the wretched soul who moved the boundary between Hov and Jarpstad, or the farmer in Musudal with the false documents about the millstream. But souls cannot leave the fires of purgatory unless they have a lawful errand. It's mostly nonsense what people say about ghosts and phantoms or the mirages of the Devil, which disappear like smoke if you protect yourself with the sign of the cross and the name of the Lord."

"But what about the blessed ones who are with God, Sira Eirik?" she asked softly.

"You know quite well that the holy ones who are with God can be sent out to bring gifts and messages from Paradise."

"I once told you that I saw Brother Edvin Rikardssøn," she said in the same tone of voice.

"Yes, either it was a dream—and it might have been sent by God or one of his guardian angels—or else the monk is a holy man."

Shivering, Kristin whispered, "My father . . . Sira Eirik, I have prayed so often that I might be allowed to see his face one more time. I long so fervently to see him, Sira Eirik. And perhaps I might be able to tell from his expression what he wants me to do. If my father could give me advice in that way . . ." She had to bite her lip, and she used a corner of her wimple to brush away the tears that had welled up.

The priest shook his head.

"Pray for his soul, Kristin—although I'm convinced that Lavrans and your mother have long ago found solace with those from whom they sought comfort for all the sorrows they endured here on earth. And certainly Lavrans still holds you firmly in his love there too, but your prayers and the masses said for his soul will bind you and all the rest of us to him. How this occurs is one of the secret things that are difficult to fathom, but I have no doubt that this is a better way than if he should be disturbed in his peace to come here and appear before you."

Kristin had to sit still for a moment before she gained enough mastery over herself that she dared speak. But then she told the priest about everything that had happened between Erlend and her on the evening in the hearth house, repeating every word that was said, as best as she could remember.

The priest sat in silence for a long time after she was finished.

Then Kristin clapped her hands together harshly. "Sira Eirik! Do you think I was the one most at fault? Do you think I was so wrong that it wasn't a sin for Erlend to desert me and all our sons in this manner? Do you think it is fair for him to demand that I seek him out, fall to my knees, and take back the words I spoke in anger? Because I *know* that unless I do, he will never return home to us!"

"Do you think you need to call Lavrans back from the other world to ask his advice in this matter?" The priest stood up and placed his hand on the woman's shoulder. "The first time I saw you, Kristin, you were a tiny maiden. Lavrans made you stand between his knees as he crossed your little hands on your breast and told you to say the *Pater noster* for me. You repeated it in a lovely, clear voice, even though you didn't understand a single word. Later you learned the meaning of every prayer in our language; perhaps you've forgotten about that now.

"Have you forgotten that your father taught you and honored you and loved you? He honored the man before whom you are now afraid of humbling yourself. Or have you forgotten how splendid the feast was that he held for the two of you? And then you rode away from his manor like two thieves. Did you take with you Lavrans Bjørgulfsøn's esteem and honor?"

Sobbing, Kristin hid her face in her hands.

"Do you remember, Kristin? Did he ever demand that the two of you should fall to your knees before he thought he could take you back into his fatherly love? Do you think it too harsh a penance for your pride if you have to bow before a man whom you may not have wronged as much as you sinned against your father?"

"Jesus!" Kristin wept in utter despair. "Jesus, have mercy on me."

"I see that you at least remember his name," said the priest. "The name of the one your father strove to follow like a disciple and serve like a loyal knight." He touched the small crucifix that hung above them. "Free of sin, God's son died on the cross to atone for the sins we had committed against him.

"Go home now, Kristin, and think about what I have told you," said Sira Eirik after she had regained some measure of calm.

But during those very days a southerly gale set in with sleet and torrential rains; at times it was so fierce that people could barely cross their own courtyards without the risk of being swept away above all the rooftops; at least that was how it seemed. The roads through the countryside were completely impassable. The spring floods arrived so abruptly and turbulently that people had to move out of the estates that were most vulnerable. Kristin moved most of their belongings up into the loft of the new storehouse, and she was granted permission to put her livestock in Sira Eirik's springtime shed. The shed used at Jørundgaard in the spring was on the other side of the river. It was a dreadful toil in the storm; up in the meadows the snow was as soft as melted butter, and the animals were so wretched. Two of the best calves broke their legs as if they were tender stalks as they walked along.

On the day they moved the livestock Simon Darre suddenly appeared in the middle of the road with four of his servants. They set about lending a hand. In the wind and rain and all the tumult with the cattle that had to be prodded and the sheep and lambs that had to be carried, there was neither peace nor quiet for the kinsmen to talk. But after they returned to Jørundgaard in the evening and Kristin had seated Simon and his men in the main house—everyone who had helped out that day needed some warm ale—he spoke a few words with her. He asked her to go to Formo with the women and children, while he and two of his men would stay behind with Ulf and the boys. Kristin thanked him but said that she wanted to stay on her manor. Lavrans and Munan were already at Ulvsvold, and Jardtrud had gone to stay with Sira Solmund; she had become such good friends with the priest's sister.

Simon said, "People think it's strange, Kristin, that you two sisters never see each other. Ramborg won't be happy if I return home without you."

"I know it looks strange," she told him, "but I think it would look even stranger if we should visit my sister now, when the master of this estate is not home and people know that there's animosity between him and you."

Then Simon said no more, and soon after he and his men took their leave.

The week preceding Ascension Day arrived with a terrible storm, and on Tuesday word spread from farm to farm in the north of the region that the floods had now carried off the bridge up in Rost Gorge, which people crossed when they went up to the Høvring pastures. They began to fear for the big bridge south of the church. It was solidly built of the roughest timbers, with a high arch in the middle, and was supported underneath with thick posts that were sunk into the riverbed. But now the waters were flooding over the bridgeheads where they joined the banks, and beneath the vault of the bridge all kinds of debris that had been brought by the currents from the north were piling up. The Laag had now overflowed the low embankments on both shores, and in one place the water had accumulated across Jørundgaard's fields like in a cove, almost reaching the buildings. There was a hollow in the pastures and in the middle was the roof of the smithy, and the tops of the trees looked like little islands. The barn on the islet had already been swept away.

Very few people attended church from the farms on the east side of the river. They were afraid the bridge would be washed away and they wouldn't be able to get back home. But up on the other shore, on the slope beneath Laugarbru's barn, where there was some shelter from the storm, a dark cluster of people could be glimpsed through the gusts of snow. It was rumored that Sira Eirik had said he would carry the cross over the bridge and set it on the east bank of the river, even if no one dared follow him.

A squall of snow rushed toward the procession of people coming out of the church. The flakes formed slanting streaks in the air. Only a glimmer of the valley was visible: here and there a scrap of the darkening lake where the fields usually lay, the rush of clouds sweeping over the scree-covered slopes and the lobes of forest, and glimpses of the mountain peaks against the billowing clouds high overhead. The air was sated with the clamor of the river, rising and falling, with the roar from the forests, and with the howl of the wind. Occasionally a muffled crash could be heard, echoing the storm's fury from the mountains and the thunder of an avalanche of new snow.

The candles were blown out as soon as they were carried beyond the church gallery. That day fully grown young men had donned the white shirts of choirboys. The wind whipped at their garments. They walked along in a large group, carrying the banner with their hands, gripping the fabric so the wind wouldn't shred it to pieces as the procession leaned forward, struggling across the slope in the wind. But now and then, above the raging of the storm, the sound of Sira Eirik's resonant voice could be heard as he fought his way forward and sang:

Venite: revertamur ad Dominum; quia ipse cepit & sanabit nos: percutiet, & curabit nos, & vivemus in conspectu ejus. Sciemus sequemurque, ut cognoscamus Dominum. Alleluia.[1]

Kristin stopped, along with all the other women, when the procession reached the place where the water had overflowed the road, but the white-clad young boys, the deacons, and the priests were already up on the bridge, and almost all the men followed; the water came up to their knees.

The bridge shuddered and shook, and then the women noticed that an entire house was rushing from the north toward the bridge. It churned around and around in the current as it was carried along, partially shattered, with its timbers jutting out, but still managing to stay in one piece. The woman from Ulvsvold clung to Kristin Lavransdatter and moaned loudly; her husband's two nearly grown-up brothers were among the choirboys. Kristin screamed without words to the Virgin Mary, fixing her gaze on the group in the middle of the bridge where she could discern the white-clad figure of Naakkve among the men holding the banner. The women thought they could still hear Sira Eirik's voice, almost drowned out by the din.

He paused at the crest of the bridge and lifted the cross high up as the house struck. The bridge shuddered and swayed; to the people on both shores, it looked as if it had dipped slightly to the south. Then the procession moved on, disappearing behind the curved arch of the bridge and then reappearing on the opposite shore. The wreckage of the house had become tangled up in the heaps of other flotsam caught in the underpinnings of the bridge.

All of a sudden, like a miracle, silvery light began seeping from the windblown masses of clouds; a dull gleam like molten lead spread over the whole expanse of the swollen river. The haze lifted, the clouds scattered, the sun broke through, and as the procession came back over the bridge, the rays glittered on the cross. On the wet white alb of the priest, the crossed stripes of his stole shimmered a wondrous purple. The valley lay gilded and sparkling with moisture, as if at the bottom of a dark blue grotto, for the storm clouds had gathered around the mountain ridges and, brought low by the rays of the sun, had turned the heights black. The haze fled between the peaks, and the great crest above Formo reached up from the darkness, dazzling white with new snow.

She had seen Naakkve walk past. The drenched garments clung to the boys as they sang at the top of their lungs to the sunshine:

Salvator mundi, salva nos omnes. Kyrie, eleison, Christe, eleison, Christe, audi nos—.[2]

The priests with the cross had gone past; the group of farmers followed in their heavy, soaked clothing, but looking around them at the weather with amazed and shining faces as they took up the prayer's refrain: *Kyrie eleison!*

Suddenly she saw . . . She couldn't believe her own eyes, and now it was her turn to grab hold of the woman next to her for support. There was Erlend walking along in the procession; he was wearing a dripping wet coat made of reindeer hide with the hood pulled over his head. But it was him. His lips were slightly parted, and he was crying, *Kyrie eleison,* along with the others. He looked right at her as he walked past. She couldn't properly decipher the expression on his face, but it looked as if he wore a shadow of a smile.

Together with the other women, she joined the procession as it moved up the church hill, calling out with the others as the young boys sang the litany. She was unaware of anything except the wild pounding of her own heart.

During the mass she caught a glimpse of him only once. She

didn't dare stand in her customary place but hid in the darkness of the north nave.

As soon as the service was over, she rushed outdoors. She fled from her maids who had been in church. Outside, the countryside was steaming in the sunshine. Kristin raced home without noticing the sodden state of the road.

She spread a cloth over the table and set a full horn of mead before the master's high seat before she took time to exchange her wet clothes for her Sabbath finery: the dark blue, embroidered gown, silver belt, buckled shoes, and the wimple with the blue border. Then she knelt in the alcove. She couldn't think, she couldn't find the words she sought; over and over again she said the *Ave Maria*: Blessed Lady, dear Lord, son of the Virgin, you know what I want to say.

This went on for a long time. From her maids she heard that the men had gone back to the bridge; with broadaxes and hooks they were trying to remove the tangle of debris that had gotten caught. It was a matter of saving the bridge. The priests had also gone back after they had taken off their vestments.

It was well past midday when the men returned: Kristin's sons, Ulf Haldorssøn, and the three servants—an old man and two youths who had been given refuge on the manor.

Naakkve had already sat down at his place, to the right of the high seat. Suddenly he stood up, stepped forward, and rushed for the door.

Kristin softly called out his name.

A moment later he came back and sat down. The color came and went in his young face; he kept his eyes lowered, and now and then he had to bite his lip. His mother saw that he was struggling hard to master his feelings, but he managed to do so.

Finally the meal came to an end. Her sons, who were seated on the inner bench, rose to their feet and came around the end of the table past the vacant high seat, adjusting their belts as they usually did after they had put their knives back in their sheaths. Then they left the room.

When they had all gone, Kristin followed. In the sunshine, water was now streaming off all the eaves. There wasn't a soul in the courtyard except for Ulf; he was standing on the doorstep to his own house.

His face took on an oddly helpless expression when the mistress approached him. He didn't speak, and so she asked quietly, "Did you talk to him?"

"Only a few words. I saw that he and Naakkve talked."

After a moment he went on, "He was a little worried . . . about all of you . . . when the flooding got this bad. So he decided to head home to see how things were. Naakkve told him how you were handling everything.

"I don't know how he happened to hear about it . . . that you gave away the pelts he sent with Gaute in the fall. He was cross about that. Also when he heard that you had rushed home right after the mass; he thought you would have stayed to talk to him."

Kristin didn't say a word; she turned on her heel and went back inside.

That summer there were constant quarrels and strife between Ulf Haldorssøn and his wife. The son of Ulf's half brother, Haldor Jonssøn, had come to visit his kinsman in the spring, along with his wife; he had been married the year before. It was understood that Haldor would now lease the estate Ulf owned in Skaun and move there on turnover day.[3] But Jardtrud was angry because she thought Ulf had given his nephew conditions that were too good, and she saw that it was the men's intention to ensure for Haldor, perhaps through some kind of agreement, inheritance of the estate after his uncle's death.

Haldor had been Kristin's personal servant at Husaby, and she was very fond of the young man. She also liked his wife, who was a quiet and proper young woman. Shortly after Midsummer the couple had a son, and Kristin lent the wife her weaving house, where the mistresses of the estate used to reside whenever they gave birth. But Jardtrud took offense that Kristin herself should attend the woman as the foremost of the midwives, even though Jardtrud was young and quite inexperienced, unable to offer help with a birth or with caring for a newborn infant.

Kristin was the boy's godmother, and Ulf gave the christening banquet, but Jardtrud thought he lavished too much on it and put too many costly gifts in the cradle and in the mother's bed. To placate his wife somewhat, Ulf gave her several precious items from among his own possessions: a gilded cross on a chain, a fur-lined cape with a large silver clasp, a gold ring, and a silver brooch. But she saw that he refused to present her with a single parcel of land that he owned, aside from what he had given her when they married. Everything else would go to his half siblings if he himself had no offspring. Now Jardtrud lamented that her child had been still-born, and it seemed unlikely that she would have any more; she was ridiculed throughout the countryside because she talked about this to everyone.

Ulf had to ask Kristin to allow Haldor and Audhild to live in the hearth house after the young wife had gone to church for the first time after giving birth. Kristin gladly consented. She avoided Haldor because she was reminded of so many things that were painful to think about whenever she spoke with her former servant. But she talked a great deal with his wife, for Audhild wanted to help Kristin as much as she could. Toward the end of the summer the child fell gravely ill, and then Kristin stepped in to tend the boy for his young and inexperienced mother.

When the couple journeyed north in the fall, she missed them both, but she missed the child even more. She realized it was foolish, but in recent years she couldn't help feeling some measure of pain because she suddenly seemed to be barren—and yet she wasn't an old woman, not even forty.

It had helped to keep her thoughts off painful matters when she had the childish young wife and her infant to care for and advise. And even though she found it sad to see that Ulf Haldorssøn had not found greater happiness in his marriage, the state of affairs in the foreman's house had also served to divert her thoughts from other things.

After the way Erlend had behaved on Ascension Day, she hardly dared to speculate anymore about how the whole situation might end. The fact that he had appeared in the village and the church in full view of everyone and then had raced northward again without speaking a single word of greeting to his wife seemed to her so heartless that she felt as if she had at last grown completely indifferent toward him.

She had not exchanged a word with Simon Andressøn since the day of the spring floods when he came to help her. She would greet him and often speak a few words to her sister at church. But she had no idea what they thought about her affairs or the fact that Erlend had gone away to Dovre.

On the Sunday before Saint Bartholomew's Day, Sir Gyrd of Dyfrin came to church with the people from Formo. Simon looked immensely happy as he went inside for mass at his brother's side. And Ramborg came over to Kristin after the service, eagerly whispering that she was with child again and expected to give birth around the Feast of the Virgin Mary in the spring.

"Kristin, sister, can't you come home and celebrate with us today?"

Kristin shook her head sadly, patted the young woman's pale cheek, and prayed that God might bring the parents joy. But she said that she couldn't go to Formo.

After the falling-out with his brother-in-law, Simon tried to make himself believe that it was for the best. His position was such that he didn't need to ask how people might judge his actions in everything; he had helped Erlend and Kristin when it mattered, and the assistance he could offer them here in the parish was not so important that he should allow it to make his own life more complicated.

But when he heard that Erlend had left Jørundgaard, it was impossible for Simon to sustain the stubborn, melancholy calm he had striven to display. It was useless to tell himself that no one fully understood what lay behind Erlend's absence; people chattered so much but knew so little. Even so, he couldn't get himself mixed up in this matter. But he was still uneasy. At times he wondered whether he ought to seek out Erlend at Haugen and take back the words he had said when they parted; then he could see about finding some way to return order to the affairs of his brother-in-law and his wife's sister. But Simon never got any farther than thinking about this.

He didn't think anyone could tell from looking at him that his heart was uneasy. He lived as he always had, running his farm and managing his properties; he was merry and drank boldly in the company of friends; he went up to the mountains to hunt when he had time and spoiled his children when he was home. And never was an unkind word spoken between him and his wife. For the servants of the manor it must have looked as if the friendship between Ramborg and him was now better than it had ever been, since his wife was more even-tempered and calm, never exhibiting those fits of capriciousness and childish anger over petty matters. But secretly Simon felt awkward and uncertain in his wife's company; he could no longer make himself treat her as if she were still half a child, teasing and pampering her. He didn't know how he should treat her anymore.

Neither did he know how to take it when she told him one evening that she was again with child.

"I suppose you're not particularly happy about it, are you?" he finally said, stroking her hand.

"But surely *you* are happy, aren't you?" Ramborg pressed close to him, half crying and half laughing. He laughed, a little embarrassed, as he pulled her into his arms.

"I'll be sensible this time, Simon; I won't behave the way I did before. But you must *stay* with me, do you hear me? Even if all your brothers-in-law and all your brothers were to be led off to the gallows, one after the other, with their hands bound, you mustn't leave me!"

Simon laughed sadly. "Where would I go, my Ramborg? Geirmund, that poor creature, isn't likely to get mixed up in any weighty matters, and he's the only one left among my friends and kinsmen that I haven't quarreled with yet."

"Oh . . ." Ramborg laughed too as her tears fell. "That enmity will last only until they need a helping hand and you think you can offer it. I know you too well by now, my husband."

Two weeks later Gyrd Andressøn unexpectedly arrived at the manor. The Dyfrin knight had brought only a single man as an escort.

The meeting between the brothers took place with few words spoken. Sir Gyrd explained that he hadn't seen his sister and brother-in-law at Kruke in all these years, and so he had decided to come north to visit them. Since he was in the valley, Sigrid felt he should also visit Formo. "And I thought, brother, that surely you couldn't be so angry with me that you wouldn't offer me and my servant food and lodging until tomorrow."

"You know I will," said Simon as he stood looking down, his face dark red. "It was . . . noble of you, Gyrd, to come to see me."

The brothers walked through the fields after they had eaten. The grain was starting to turn pale on the slopes facing the sun, down by the river. The weather was so beautiful. The Laag now glittered gently enough, visible as little white flashes amid the alder trees. Big, glossy clouds drifted across the summer sky; sunshine filled the entire basin of the valley, and the mountain on the other side looked light blue and green in the shimmer of heat and the fleeting shadows of the clouds.

A pounding sound came from the pasture behind them as the horses trampled across the dry hillside; the herd came rushing through the alder thickets. Simon leaned over the fence. "Foal, foal . . . Bronstein's getting old, isn't he?" he said as Gyrd's horse poked his head over the rail and nudged his shoulder.

"Eighteen winters." Gyrd stroked the horse. "I thought, kinsman, that this matter . . . It wouldn't be right if it should end the friendship between you and me," he said without looking at his brother.

"It has grieved me every single day," replied Simon softly. "Thank you for coming, Gyrd."

They continued walking along the fence—Gyrd first, with Simon plodding behind. Finally they sank down on the edge of a little yellow-scorched stony embankment. A strong, sweet fragrance came from the small mounds of hay that were scattered about, where the scythe had scraped together short stalks of hay mixed with flowers between the piles of stones. Gyrd spoke of the reconciliation between King Magnus and the Haftorssøns and their followers.

After a moment Simon asked, "Do you think it's out of the question that any of these kinsmen of Erlend Nikulaussøn would be willing to attempt to win full reconciliation for him and clemency from the king?"

"There is not much *I* can do," said Gyrd Darre. "And they have few kind words to say of him, Simon, those who might be able to do something. Oh, I have little desire to talk of this matter *now*. I thought he was a bold and splendid fellow, but the others think he brought his plans to such a bad end. But I'd rather not talk of this now; I know you're so fond of that brother-in-law of yours."

Simon sat gazing out across the silvery white brilliance of the crowns of the trees on the hillside and the sparkling gleam of the river. Surprised, he thought that yes, in a way it was true, what Gyrd had said.

"Except that right now we are foes, Erlend and I," he said. "It's been a long time since we last spoke."

"It seems to me that you've grown quite quarrelsome over the years, Simon," said Gyrd with a laugh.

After a moment he continued, "Haven't you ever thought of moving away from these valleys? We kinsmen could support each other more if we lived closer to each other."

"How can you even think of such a thing? Formo is my ancestral estate . . ."

"Aasmund of Eiken owns part of the manor through inherited rights. And I know that he would not be unwilling to exchange one ancestral property for another. He hasn't yet given up the idea that if he could win your Arngjerd for his Grunde on the terms that he mentioned . . ."

Simon shook his head. "The lineage of our father's mother has resided on this estate ever since Norway was a heathen land. And it is here that I intend for Andres to live when I'm gone. I don't think you have your wits about you, brother. How could I give up Formo!"

"No, that's understandable." Gyrd blushed a little. "I merely thought that perhaps . . . Most of your kinsmen are at Raumarike, along with the friends from your youth; perhaps you might find that you'd thrive better there."

"I'm thriving *here*." Simon had also turned red. "This is the place where I can give the boy a secure seat." He looked at Gyrd, and his brother's fine, furrowed face took on an embarrassed expression. Gyrd's hair was now almost white, but his body was still just as slender and lithe as ever. He shifted rather uneasily; several stones rolled out from the pile of rocks and tumbled down the slope and into the grain.

"Are you going to send the whole scree down into my field?" asked Simon in a stern voice as he laughed. Gyrd leaped to his feet, light and agile, reaching out a hand to his brother, who moved more slowly.

Simon gripped his brother's hand for a moment after he got to his feet. Then he placed his arm around his brother's shoulder. Gyrd did the same, and with their arms loosely resting around each other's shoulders, the brothers slowly walked over the hills toward the manor.

They sat together in the Sæmund house that night; Simon would share a bed with his brother. They had said their evening prayers, but they wanted to empty the ale keg before they went to bed.

"*Benedictus tu in muliebris . . . mulieribus . . .* Do you remember that?" Simon laughed suddenly.

"Yes. It cost me a few blows across the back before Sira Magnus wrung our grandmother's misteachings out of my head." Gyrd smiled at the memory. "And he had a devilishly hard hand too. Do you remember, brother, that time when he sat and scratched the calves of his legs, and he had lifted up the hem of his robe? You whispered to me that if you had had such misshapen calves as Magnus Ketilssøn, you would have become a priest too and always worn full-length surcoats."

Simon smiled. Suddenly he seemed to *see* the boyish face of his brother, about to burst with stifled laughter, his eyes pitifully miserable. They weren't very old back then, and Sira Magnus was cruelly hard-handed whenever he had to reprimand them.

Gyrd had not been terribly clever when they were children. And it wasn't because Gyrd was a particularly wise man that Simon loved him now. But he felt warm with gratitude and tenderness toward his brother as he sat there: for every day of their kinship during almost forty years and for Gyrd, just the way he was—the most loyal and forthright of men.

It seemed to Simon that winning back his brother Gyrd was like gaining a firm foundation for at least one foot. And for such a long time his life had been so unreasonably disjointed and complicated.

He felt a warmth inside every time he thought about Gyrd, who had come to him to make amends for something that Simon himself had provoked when he rode to his brother's estate in anger and with curses. His heart overflowed with gratitude; he had to thank more than Gyrd.

A man such as Lavrans . . . He knew quite well how he would have handled such an event. He could follow his father-in-law as far as he was able, by giving out alms and the like. But he wasn't capable of such things as true contrition or contemplation of the

wounds of the Lord, unless he stared zealously at the crucifix—
and that was not what Lavrans had intended. Simon couldn't
bring forth tears of remorse; he hadn't wept more than two or
three times since he was a child, and never when he needed to
most, those times when he had committed the worst of sins: with
Arngjerd's mother while he was a married man and that killing the
previous year. And yet he had felt great regret; he thought that he
always sincerely regretted his sins, taking pains to confess and to
atone as the priest commanded. He was always diligent in saying
his prayers and saw to it that he gave the proper tithes and abun-
dant alms—with particular generosity in honor of the apostle Saint
Simon, Saint Olav, Saint Michael, and the Virgin Mary. Otherwise
he was content with what Sira Eirik had said: that salvation was to
be found in the cross alone and how a man faced or fought with
the Fiend was something for God to decide and not the man himself.

But now he felt an urge to show his gratitude to the holy ones
with greater fervor. His mother had told him that he was supposedly born on the birthday of the Virgin Mary. He decided that he
wanted to show the Lord's Mother his veneration with a prayer he
was not usually accustomed to saying. He had once had a beautiful prayer copied out, back when he was at the royal court, and he
took out the small piece of parchment.

Now, much later, he feared that it was probably intended more
as an appeal to King Haakon than for the sake of God or Mary
that he had acquired these small epistles with prayers and learned
them while he was among the king's retainers. All the young men
did so, for the king was in the habit of quizzing the pages about
what they knew of such useful knowledge when he lay in bed at
night, unable to sleep.

Oh yes . . . that was so long ago. The king's bedchamber in the
stone hall of the Oslo palace. On the little table next to his bed
burned a single candle; the light fell across the finely etched, faded,
and aging face of the man, resting above the red silken quilts.
When the priest had finished reading aloud and taken his leave, the
king often picked up the book himself and lay in bed, reading with
the heavy volume resting against his propped-up knees. On two
footstools over by the brick fireplace sat the pages; Simon nearly
always had the watch with Gunstein Ingasøn. It was pleasant in

the chamber. The fire burned brightly, giving heat without smoke, and the room seemed so snug with the cross-beamed ceiling and the walls always covered with tapestries. But they would grow sleepy from sitting there in that fashion, first listening to the priest read and then waiting for the king to fall asleep, as he rarely did until close to midnight. When he was sleeping, they were allowed to take turns keeping guard and napping on the bench between the fireplace and the door to the royal Council hall.

Occasionally the king would converse with them; this didn't happen often, but when it did, he was inexpressibly kind and charming. Or he would read aloud from the book a sentence or a few stanzas of a verse that he thought the young men might find useful or beneficial to hear.

One night Simon was awakened by King Haakon calling for him in pitch-darkness. The candle had burned out. Feeling wretched with shame, Simon blew some life into the embers and lit a new candle. The king lay in bed, smiling secretively.

"Does that Gunstein always snore so terribly?"

"Yes, my Lord."

"You share a bed with him in the dormitory, don't you? It might be deemed reasonable if you asked for another bedfellow for a while who makes less noise when he sleeps."

"Thank you, my Lord, but it doesn't bother me, Your Majesty!"

"Surely you must wake up, Simon, when that thunder explodes right next to your ear—don't you?"

"Yes, Your Grace, but then I give him a shove and turn him over a bit."

The king laughed. "I wonder whether you young men realize that being able to sleep so soundly is one of God's great gifts. When you reach my age, Simon my friend, perhaps you will remember my words."

That seemed endlessly far away—still clear, but not as if he were the same man, sitting here now, who had once been that young page.

One day at the beginning of Advent, when Kristin was almost alone on the estate—her sons were bringing home firewood and moss—she was surprised to see Simon Darre come riding into the courtyard. He had come to invite her and her sons to be their guests during Christmas.

"You know quite well, Simon, that we can't do that," she said somberly. "We can still be friends in our hearts, you and Ramborg and I, but as you know, it's not always possible for us to determine what we must do."

"Surely you don't mean that you're going to take this so far that you won't come to your only sister when she has to lie down to give birth."

Kristin prayed that all would go well and bring both of them joy. "But I can't tell you with certainty that I will come."

"Everyone will think it remarkably strange," admonished Simon. "You have a reputation for being the best midwife, and she's your sister, and the two of you are the mistresses of the largest estates in the northern part of the region."

"Quite a few children have been brought into the world on the great manors around here over the past few years, but I've never been asked to come. It's no longer the custom, Simon, for a birth to be considered improperly attended if the mistress of Jørund-gaard is not in the room." She saw that he was greatly distressed by her words, and so she continued, "Give my greetings to Ram-borg, and tell her that I will come to help her when it's time; but I cannot come to your Christmas feast, Simon."

But on the eighth day of the Christmas season she met Simon as he came to mass without Ramborg. No, she was feeling fine, he said, but she needed to rest and gather her strength, for the next day he was taking her and the children south to Dyfrin. The weather was so good for traveling by sleigh, and since Gyrd had invited them, and Ramborg was so keen on going, well . . .

ON THE DAY after Saint Paal's Day, Simon Darre rode north across Lake Mjøsa, accompanied by two men. A bitter frost had set in, but he didn't think he could stay away from home any longer; the sleighs would have to follow later, as soon as the cold had let up a bit.

At Hamar he met a friend, Vigleik Paalssøn of Fagaberg, and they continued on together. When they reached Lillehammer, they rested for a while at a farm where ale was served. As they sat and drank, several drunken fur peddlers began brawling in the room. Finally Simon stood up, stepped into the thick of things and separated them, but in doing so, he received a knife wound in his right forearm. It was little more than a scratch, so he paid it no mind, although the proprietress of the alehouse insisted on being allowed to bind a cloth around it.

He rode home with Vigleik and stayed the night at his manor. The men shared a bed, and toward morning Simon was awakened because the other man was thrashing in his sleep. Several times Vigleik called out his name, and so Simon woke him up to ask what was wrong.

Vigleik couldn't remember his dream properly. "But it was loathsome, and you were in it. One thing I do remember: Simon Reidarssøn stood in this room and asked you to leave with him. I saw him so clearly that I could have counted every single freckle on his face."

"I wish you could sell me that dream," said Simon, half in jest and half seriously. Simon Reidarssøn was his uncle's son, and they had been good friends when they were growing up, but the other Simon had died at the age of thirteen.

In the morning when the men sat down to eat, Vigleik noticed that Simon hadn't buttoned the sleeve of his tunic around his right wrist. The flesh was red and swollen all the way down to the back of his hand. He mentioned it, but Simon merely laughed.

A little later, when his friend begged him to stay on a few more days and to wait there for his wife—Vigleik couldn't forget his dream—Simon Andressøn replied, almost indignantly, "Surely you haven't had such a bad dream about me that I should keep to my bed because of a mere louse bite?"

Around sunset Simon and his men rode down to Lake Losna. It had been the most beautiful day; now the towering blue and white peaks turned gold and crimson in the twilight, while along the river the groves, heavy with rime, stood furry gray in the shadows. The men had excellent horses and a brisk ride ahead of them across the long lake; tiny bits of ice sprayed up, ringing and clinking beneath the hooves of the horses. A biting wind blew hard against them. Simon was freezing, but in spite of the cold, strange nauseating waves of heat kept washing over him, followed by icy spells that seemed to seep all the way into the marrow of his spine. Now and then he noticed that his tongue was swollen and felt oddly thick at the back of his throat. Even before they had crossed the lake he had to stop and ask one of his men to help him fasten his cape so it would support his right arm.

The servants had heard Vigleik Paalssøn recounting his dream; now they wanted their master to show them his wound. But Simon said it was nothing; it merely stung a bit. "I may have to get used to being left-handed for a few days."

But later that night, when the moon had risen and they were riding high along the ridge north of the lake, Simon realized that his arm might turn out to be rather troublesome after all. It ached all the way up to his armpit, the jolting of the horse caused him great pain, and the blood was hammering in his wounded limb. His head was pounding too, and spasms were shooting up from the back of his neck. He was hot and then cold by turn.

The winter road passed high up along the slope, partway through forest and partway across white fields. Simon gazed at everything: The full moon was sailing brightly in the pale blue sky, having driven all the stars far away; only a few larger ones still dared wander in the distant heavens. The white fields glittered and sparkled; the shadows fell short and jagged across the snow; inside the woods the uncertain light lay in splotches and stripes among the firs, heavy with snow. Simon saw all this.

But at the same time he saw quite clearly a meadow with tufts of ash-brown grass in the sunlight of early spring. Several small spruce trees had sprung up here and there at the edge of the field; they glowed green like velvet in the sun. He recognized this place; it was the pasture near his home at Dyfrin. The alder woods stood beyond the field with its tree trunks a springtime shiny gray and the tops brown with blossoms. Behind stretched the long, low Raumarike ridges, shimmering blue but still speckled white with snow. They were walking down toward the alder thicket, he and Simon Reidarssøn, carrying fishing gear and pike spears. They were on their way to the lake, which lay dark gray with patches of thawing ice, to fish at the open end. His dead cousin walked at his side; he saw his playmate's curly hair sticking out from his cap, reddish in the spring sunlight; he could see every freckle on the boy's face. The other Simon stuck out his lower lip and blew—phew, phew—whenever he thought his namesake was speaking gibberish. They jumped over meandering rivulets and leaped from mound to mound across the trickling snow water in the grassy meadow. The bottom was covered with moss; under the water it churned and frothed a lively green.

He was fully aware of everything around him; the whole time he saw the road passing up one hill and down another, through the woods and over white fields in the glittering moonlight. He saw the slumbering clusters of houses beneath snow-laden roofs casting shadows across the fields; he saw the band of fog hovering over the river in the bottom of the valley. He knew that it was Jon who was riding right behind him and who moved up alongside him whenever they entered open clearings, and yet he happened to call the man Simon several times. He knew it was wrong, but he couldn't help himself, even though he noticed that his servants grew alarmed.

"We must manage to reach the monks at Roaldstad tonight, men," he said once when his mind had cleared.

The men tried to dissuade him; instead they should see about finding lodgings as soon as possible, and they mentioned the nearest parsonage. But their master clung to his plan.

"It will be hard on the horses, Simon." The two men exchanged a glance.

But Simon merely laughed. They would have to manage it for once. He thought about the arduous miles. Pain shot through his whole body as he jolted in the saddle. But he wanted to go home because now he knew that he was fated to die.

Even though his heart was alternately freezing and burning in the winter night, at the same time he felt the mild spring sunshine of the pasture back home, while he and the dead boy kept walking and walking toward the alder thicket.

For brief moments the image would vanish and his head would clear, except that it ached so dreadfully. He asked one of his men to cut open the sleeve on his wounded arm. His face turned white and the sweat poured down when Jon Daalk cautiously slit open his vest and shirt from his wrist up to his shoulder, but he managed to support the swollen limb himself with his left hand. After a while the pain began to ease.

Then the men started discussing whether they should see about sending word back south to Dyfrin once they reached Roaldstad. But Simon had his objections. He didn't want to worry his wife with such a message when it might be unnecessary; a sleigh ride in this bitter cold would be ill advised. Perhaps, when they were home at Formo . . . They should wait and see. He tried to smile at Sigurd to cheer up the young servant, who looked quite frightened and distressed.

"But you can send word to Kristin at Jørundgaard as soon as we reach home. She's so skilled at healing." His tongue felt as thick and stiff as wood as he spoke.

Kiss me, Kristin, my betrothed! At first she would think he was speaking in delirium. No, Kristin. Then she would be surprised.

Erlend had understood. Ramborg had understood. But Kristin . . . She sat there with her sorrow and rancor, and yet as angry and bitter as she now felt toward that man Erlend, she still had no thoughts for anyone else but him. You've never cherished me enough, Kristin, my beloved, that you might consider how difficult it would be for me when I had to be a brother to the woman who was once meant to be my wife.

He hadn't realized it himself back then, when he parted from her outside the convent gate in Oslo: that he would continue to think about her in this way. That he would end up feeling as if nothing he had acquired afterward in life were an equal replacement for what he had lost back then. For the maiden who had been promised to him in his youth.

She would hear this before he died. She would give him one kiss.

I am the one who loved you and who loves you still.

He had once heard those words, and he had never been able to forget them. They were from the Virgin Mary's book of miracles, a saga about a nun who fled from her convent with a knight. The Virgin saved them in the end and forgave them in spite of their sin. If it was a sin that he said this to his wife's sister before he died, then God's Mother would grant him forgiveness for this as well. He had so seldom troubled her by asking for anything. . . .

I didn't believe it myself back then: that I would never feel truly happy or merry again . . .

"No, Simon, it's too great a burden for Sokka if she has to carry both of us . . . considering how far she has had to travel tonight," he said to the person who had climbed up behind him on the horse and was supporting him. "I can see that it's you, Sigurd, but I thought it was someone else."

Toward morning they reached the pilgrims' hostel, and the two monks who were in charge tended to the ill man. After he had revived a little under their care and the feverish daze had abated, Simon Andressøn insisted on borrowing a sleigh to continue northward.

The roads were in good condition; they changed horses along the way, journeyed all night, and arrived at Formo the following morning, at dawn. Simon had lain and dozed under all the covers that someone had spread over him. He felt so weighted down— sometimes he felt as if he were being crushed under heavy boulders—and his head ached terribly. Now and then he seemed to slip away. Then the pain would begin raging inside him again; it felt as if his body were swelling up more and more, growing unimaginably big and about to burst. There was a constant throbbing in his arm.

He tried to walk from the sleigh to the house, with his good arm around Jon's shoulder and Sigurd walking behind to support him. Simon sensed that the faces of the men were gray and grimy with weariness; they had spent two nights in a row in the saddle. He wanted to say something to them about it, but his tongue refused to obey him. He stumbled over the threshold and fell full length into the room—with a roar of pain as his swollen and misshapen arm struck against something. The sweat poured off him as he choked back the moans that rose up as he was undressed and helped into bed.

Not long afterward he noticed that Kristin Lavransdatter was standing next to the fireplace, grinding something with a pestle in a wooden bowl. The sound kept thudding right through his head. She poured something from a small pot into a goblet and added several drops from a glass vial that she took out of a chest. Then she emptied the crushed substance from the bowl into the pot and set it next to the fire. Such a quiet and competent manner she had.

She came over to the bed with the goblet in her hand. She walked with such ease. She was just as straight-backed and lovely as she had been as a maiden—this slender woman with the thin, somber face beneath the linen wimple. The back of his neck was also swollen, and it hurt when she slipped one arm under his shoulders to lift him up. She supported his head against her breast as she held the goblet to his lips with her left hand.

Simon smiled a little, and as she cautiously let his head slip back down to the pillow, he seized hold of her hand with his good one. Her fine, slim woman's hand was no longer soft or white.

"I suppose you can't sew silk with these fingers of yours anymore," said Simon. "But they're good and light—and how pleasantly cool your hand is, Kristin." He placed it on his forehead. Kristin remained standing there until she felt her palm grow warm; then she removed it and gently pressed her other hand against his burning brow, up along the hairline.

"Your arm has a nasty wound, Simon," she said, "but with God's help it will mend."

"I'm afraid that you won't be able to heal me, Kristin, no matter how skilled you are with medicines," said Simon. But his expression was almost cheerful. The potion began to take effect; he felt the pain much less. But his eyes felt so strange, as if he had no control over them. He thought he must be lying there with each eye squinting in opposite directions.

"No doubt things will go with me as they must," he said in the same tone of voice.

Kristin went back to her pots; she spread a paste on some linen cloths and then came over and wrapped the hot bandages around his arm, from the tips of his fingers all the way around his back and across his chest, where the swelling splayed out in red stripes from his armpit. It hurt at first, but soon the discomfort eased. She spread a woolen blanket on top and placed soft down pillows under his arm. Simon asked her what she had put on the bandages.

"Oh, various things—mostly comfrey and swallowwort," said Kristin. "If only it was summer, I could have picked them fresh from my herb garden. But I had a plentiful supply; thanks be to God I haven't needed them earlier this winter."

"What was it you once told me about swallowwort? You heard it from the abbess when you were at the convent . . . something about the name."

"Do you mean that in all languages it has a name that means 'swallow,' all the way from the Greek sea up to the northern lands?"

"Yes, because it blossoms everywhere when the swallows awake from their winter slumber." Simon pressed his lips together more firmly. By then he would have been in the ground for a long time.

"I want my resting place to be here, at the church, if I should die, Kristin," he said. "I'm such a rich man by now that someday Andres will most likely possess considerable power here at Formo. I wonder if Ramborg will have a son after I'm gone, in the spring. I would have liked to live long enough to see two sons on my estate."

Kristin told him she had sent word south to Dyfrin that he was gravely ill—with Gaute, who had ridden off that morning.

"You didn't send that child off alone, did you?" asked Simon with alarm.

There was no one at hand whom she thought could manage to keep up with Gaute riding Rauden, she told him. Simon said it would surely be a difficult journey for Ramborg; if only she wouldn't travel any faster than she could bear. "But I would like to see my children . . ."

Sometime later he began talking about his children again. He mentioned Arngjerd, wondering whether he might have been wrong not to accept the offer from the people of Eiken. But the man seemed too old to him, and he had been afraid that Grunde could turn out to be violent when he was drunk. He had always wanted to place Arngjerd in the most secure of circumstances. Now it would be Gyrd and Gudmund who would decide on her marriage. "Tell my brothers, Kristin, that I sent them my greetings and that they should tend to this matter with care. If you would take her back to Jørundgaard for a while, I would be most grateful, as I lie in my grave. And if Ramborg should remarry before Arngjerd's place is assured, then you must take her in, Kristin. You mustn't think that Ramborg has been anything but kind toward her, but if she should end up with both a stepmother and a stepfather, I'm afraid she would be regarded more as a servant girl than a . . . You remember that I was married to Halfrid when I became her father."

Kristin gently placed her hand on top of Simon's and promised she would do all she could for the maiden. She remembered everything she had seen of how difficult they were situated, those children who had a nobleman for a father and were conceived in adultery. Orm and Margret and Ulf Haldorssøn. She stroked Simon's hand over and over.

"It's not certain that you will die this time, you know, brother-in-law," she said with a little smile. A glimmer of the sweet and tender smile of a maiden could still pass over her thin, stern woman's face. You sweet, young Kristin.

Simon's fever was not as high that evening, and he said the pain was less. When Kristin changed the bandage on his arm, it was not as swollen, but his skin was darker, and when she cautiously pressed it, the marks from her fingers stayed for a moment.

Kristin sent the servants off to bed. She allowed Jon Daalk, who insisted on keeping watch over his master, to lie down on a bench in the room. She moved the chest with the carved back over next to the bed and sat down, leaning against the corner. Simon dozed and slept. Once when he woke up, he noticed that she had found a spindle. She was sitting erect, having stuck the distaff with the wool under her left arm, and her fingers were twining the yarn as the spindle dropped lower and lower beside her long, slender lap. Then she rolled up the yarn and began spinning again as the spindle dropped. He fell asleep watching her.

When he awoke again, toward morning, she was sitting in the same position, spinning. The light from the candle, which she had placed so the bed hangings would shield him, fell directly on her face. It was so pale and still. Her full, soft lips were narrow and pressed tight; she was sitting with her eyes lowered as she spun. She couldn't see that he was lying awake and staring at her in the shadow of the bed hangings. She looked so full of despair that Simon felt as if his heart were bleeding inside him as he lay there looking at her.

She stood up and went over to tend the fire. Without a sound. When she came back, she peeked behind the bed hangings and met his open eyes in the dark.

"How are you feeling now, Simon?" she asked gently.

"I feel fine . . . now."

But he seemed to notice that it felt tender under his left arm too, and under his chin when he moved his head. No, it must be just something he imagined.

Oh, she would never think that she had lost anything by rejecting his love; for that matter, he might as well tell her about it. It wasn't possible for *that* to make her any more melancholy. He wanted to say it to her before he died—at least once: I have loved you all these years.

His fever rose again. And his left arm was hurting after all.

"You must try to sleep some more, Simon. Perhaps you will soon feel better," she said softly.

"I've slept a great deal tonight." He began talking about his children again: the three he had and loved so dearly and the one who was still unborn. Then he fell silent; the pain returned much worse. "Lie down for a while, Kristin. Surely Jon can sit with me for a time if you think it necessary for someone to keep watch."

In the morning, when she took off the bandage, Simon replied calmly to her desperate expression: "Oh no, Kristin, there was already too much festering and poison in my arm, and I was chilled through before I came into your hands. I told you that I didn't think you could heal me. Don't be so sad about it, Kristin."

"You shouldn't have made such a long journey," she said faintly.

"No man lives longer than he is meant to live," replied Simon in the same voice. "I wanted to come home. There are things we must discuss: how everything is to be arranged after I'm gone."

He chuckled. "All fires burn out sooner or later."

Kristin gazed at him, her eyes shiny with tears. He had always had so many proverbs on his lips. She looked down at his flushed red face. The heavy cheeks and the folds under his chin seemed to have sunk, lying in deep furrows. His eyes seemed both dull and glistening, but then clarity and intent returned to them. He looked up at her with the steady, searching glance that had been the most constant expression in his small, sharp, steel-gray eyes.

When daylight filled the room, Kristin saw that Simon's face had grown pinched around the nose. A white streak stretched downward on either side to the corners of his mouth.

She walked over to the little glass-paned window and stood there, swallowing her tears. A golden-green light sparkled and gleamed in the thick coating of frost on the window. Outside, it was no doubt as beautiful a day as the whole week had been.

It was the mark of death. . . . She knew that.

She went back and slid her hand under the coverlet. His ankles were swollen all the way up to his calves.

"Do you want me—do you want me to send for Sira Eirik now?" she asked in a low voice.

"Yes, tonight," replied Simon.

He had to speak of it *before* he confessed and received the last rites. Afterward he must try to turn his thoughts in another direction.

"It's odd that you should be the one who will probably have to tend to my body," said Simon. "And I'm afraid I won't be a particularly handsome corpse."

Kristin forced back a sob. She moved away to prepare another soothing potion.

But Simon said, "I don't like these potions of yours, Kristin. They make my thoughts so muddled."

After a while he asked her to give him a little all the same. "But don't put so much in it that it will make me drowsy. I have to talk to you about something."

He took a sip and then lay waiting for the pain to ease enough that he would have the strength to talk to her clearly and calmly.

"Don't you want us to bring Sira Eirik to you, so he can speak the words that might give you comfort?"

"Yes, soon. But there is something I must say to you first."

He lay in silence for a while. Then he said, "Tell Erlend Niku-laussøn that the words I spoke to him the last time we parted—those words I have regretted every day since. I behaved in a petty and unmanly fashion toward my brother-in-law that night. Give him my greetings and tell him . . . beg him to forgive me."

Kristin sat with her head bowed. Simon saw that she had turned blood red under her wimple.

"You will give this message to your husband, won't you?" he asked.

She gave a small nod.

Then Simon went on. "If Erlend doesn't come to my funeral, you must seek him out, Kristin, and tell him this."

Kristin sat mutely, her face dark red.

"You wouldn't refuse to do what I ask of you, now that I'm about to die, would you?" asked Simon Andressøn.

"No," she whispered. "I will . . . do it."

"It's not good for your sons, Kristin, that there is enmity between their father and mother," Simon continued. "I wonder whether you've noticed how much it torments them. It's hard for those lively boys, knowing that their parents are the subject of gossip in the countryside."

Kristin replied in a harsh, low voice, "Erlend left our sons—not I. First my sons lost their foothold in the regions where they were born into noble lineage and property. If they now have to bear having gossip spread about them here in the valley, which is my home, I am not to blame."

Simon lay in silence for a moment. Then he said, "I haven't forgotten that, Kristin. There is much you have a right to complain about. Erlend has managed poorly for his children. But you must remember, if that plan of his had been carried out, his sons would now be well provided for, and he himself would be among the most powerful knights in the realm. The man who fails in such a venture is called a traitor to his king, but if he succeeds, people speak quite differently. Half of Norway thought as Erlend did back then: that we were poorly served by sharing a king with the Swedes and that the son of Knut Porse was probably made of stronger stuff than that coddled boy, if we could have won over Prince Haakon in his tender years. Many men stood behind Erlend at the time and tugged on the rope along with him; my own brothers did so, and many others who are now called good knights and men with coats of arms. Erlend alone had to fall. And back then, Kristin, your husband showed that he was a splendid and courageous man, even though he may have acted otherwise, both before and since."

Kristin sat in silence, trembling.

"I think, Kristin, that if this is the reason you've said bitter words to your husband, then you must take them back. You should be able to do it, Kristin. Once you held firmly enough to Erlend; you refused to listen to a word of truth about his behavior toward you when he acted in a way I never thought an honorable man would act, much less a highborn gentleman and a chivalrous retainer of the king. Do you remember where I found the two of you in Oslo? You could forgive Erlend for *that*, both at the time and later on."

Kristin replied quietly, "I had cast my lot with his by then. What would have become of me afterward if I had parted my life from Erlend's?"

"Look at me, Kristin," said Simon Darre, "and answer me truthfully. If I had held your father to his promise and chosen to take you as you were . . . If I had told you that I would never remind you of your shame, but I would not release you . . . What would you have done then?"

"I don't know."

Simon laughed harshly. "If I had forced you to celebrate a wedding with me, you would never have taken me willingly into your arms, Kristin, my fair one."

Now her face turned white. She sat with her eyes lowered and did not reply.

He laughed again. "I don't think you would have embraced me tenderly when I climbed into your bridal bed."

"I think I would have taken my knife to bed with me," she whispered in a stifled voice.

"I see you know the ballad about Knut of Borg," said Simon with a bitter smile. "I haven't heard that such a thing ever happened, but God only knows whether *you* might have done it!"

Some time later he went on, "It's also unheard of among Christian people for married folks to part ways of their own free will, as you two have done, without lawful cause and the consent of the bishop. Aren't you ashamed? You trampled on everyone, defied everyone in order to be together. When Erlend was in mortal danger, you thought of nothing but how to save him, and he thought much more about you than about his seven sons or his reputation and property. But whenever you can have each other in peace and security, you're no longer capable of maintaining calm and decency. Discord and discontent reigned between you at Husaby too—I saw it myself, Kristin.

"I tell you, for the sake of your sons, that you must seek reconciliation with your husband. If you are even the slightest bit at fault, then surely it's easier for you to offer Erlend your hand," he said in a somewhat gentler tone.

"It's easier for you than for Erlend Nikulaussøn, sitting up there at Haugen in poverty," he repeated.

"It's not easy for me," she whispered. "I think I've shown that I can do something for my children. I've struggled and struggled for them. . . ."

"That is true," said Simon. Then he asked, "Do you remember that day when we met on the road to Nidaros? You were sitting in the grass, nursing Naakkve."

Kristin nodded.

"Could you have done for that child at your breast what my sister did for her son? Given him away to those who were better able to provide for him?"

Kristin shook her head.

"But ask his father to forget what you may have said to him in anger . . . Do you mean that you're unable to do that for him and your six other fair sons? To tell your husband that the young lads need him to come home to them, to his own manor?"

"I will do as you ask, Simon," said Kristin softly. After a moment she continued, "You have used harsh words to tell me this.

In the past you've also chastised me more sternly than any other man has."

"Yes, but now I can assure this will be the last time." His voice had that teasing, merry ring to it that it used to have. "No, don't weep like that, Kristin. But remember, my sister, that you have made this promise to a dying man." Once again the old, mirthful glint came into his eyes.

"You know, Kristin . . . it's happened to me before that I learned you weren't to be counted on!

"Hush now, my dear," he implored a little later. He had been lying there listening to her piteous, broken sobs. "You should know that I remember you were also a good and loyal sister. We will remain friends to the end, my Kristin."

Toward evening he asked them to send for the priest. Sira Eirik came, heard his confession, and gave him the last oil and viaticum. He took leave of his servants and the sons of Erlend, the five who were home; Kristin had sent Naakkve to Kruke. Simon had asked to see Kristin's children, to bid them farewell.

On that night Kristin again kept vigil over the dying man. Toward morning she dozed off for a moment. She woke up to a strange sound; Simon lay there, moaning softly. It distressed her greatly when she heard this—that *he* should complain, as quietly and pitifully as a miserable, abandoned child, when he thought no one would hear him. She leaned down and kissed his face many times. She noticed that his breath and his whole body smelled sickly and of death. But when daylight came, she saw that his eyes were lively and clear and steadfast.

She could see that he suffered terrible pain when Jon and Sigurd lifted him up in a sheet while she changed his bed, making it as soft and comfortable as she could. He had refused any food for more than a day, but he was very thirsty.

After she had gotten him settled, he asked her to make the sign of the cross over him, saying, "Now I can't move my left arm anymore either."

But whenever we make the sign of the cross over ourselves or over anything that we want to protect with the cross, then we must remember how the cross was made sacred and what it means, and remember that with the suffering and death of the Lord, this symbol was given honor and power.

Simon remembered that he had once heard this read aloud. He wasn't used to thinking about much when he made the sign of the cross over his breast or his houses or possessions. He felt ill prepared and not ready to take leave of this earthly home; he had to console himself that he had prepared himself as best he could in the time he had, through confession, and he had been given the last rites. Ramborg . . . But she was so young; perhaps she would be much happier with a different man. His children . . . May God protect them. And Gyrd would look out for their welfare with loyalty and wisdom. And so he would have to put his trust in God, who judges a man not according to his worth but through His mercy.

Later that day Sigrid Andresdatter and Geirmund of Kruke arrived. Simon then asked Kristin to leave and take some rest, now that she had been keeping watch and tending to him for such a long time. "And soon it will be quite vexing to be around me," he said with a little smile. At that she broke into loud sobs for a moment; then she leaned down and once again kissed his wretched body, which was already starting to decay.

Simon lay in bed quietly. The fever and pain were now much less. He lay there thinking that it couldn't be much longer before he would be released.

He was surprised that he had spoken to Kristin as he had. It was not what he had intended to say to her. But he had not been able to speak of anything else. There were moments when he felt almost annoyed by this.

But surely the festering would soon reach his heart. A man's heart is the first thing to come alive in his mother's womb and the last thing to fall silent. Surely it would soon fall silent inside him.

That night his mind rambled. Several times he screamed loudly, and it was terrible to hear. Other times he lay there, laughing softly and saying his own name, or so Kristin thought. But Sigrid, who sat bending over him, whispered to her that he seemed to be talking about a boy, their cousin, who had been his good friend when they were children. Around midnight he grew calm and seemed to sleep. Then Sigrid persuaded Kristin to lie down for a while in the other bed in the room.

She was awakened by a commotion in the room. It was shortly

before daybreak, and then she heard that the death struggle had begun. Simon had lost his voice, but he still recognized her; she could tell by his eyes. Then it was as if a piece of steel had broken inside them; they rolled up under his eyelids. But for a moment he lay there, still alive, a rattling sound in his throat. The priest had come, and he said the prayers for the dying. The two women sat next to the bed and the entire household was in the room. Just before midday Simon finally breathed his last.

The next day Gyrd Darre came riding into the courtyard at Formo. He had ridden a horse to exhaustion along the way. Down at Breiden he had learned of his brother's death, so at first he seemed quite composed. But when his sister, weeping, threw her arms around his neck, he pulled her close and began to sob like a child himself.

He told them that Ramborg Lavransdatter was at Dyfrin with a newborn son. When Gaute Erlendssøn brought them the message, she had shrieked at once that she knew this would be the death of Simon. Then she fell to the floor with birth pains. The child was born six weeks early, but they hoped he would live.

A magnificent funeral feast was held in Simon Andressøn's honor, and he was buried right next to the cross at the Olav Church. People in the parish were pleased that he had chosen his resting place there. The ancient Formo lineage, which had died out with Simon Sæmundssøn on the male side, had been mighty and grand. Astrid Simonsdatter had made a wealthy marriage; her sons had borne the title of knight and sat on the royal Council, but they had seldom come home to their mother's ancestral manor. When her grandson decided to settle on the estate, people thought it was almost as if the old lineage had been revived. They soon forgot to think of Simon Andressøn as a stranger, and they felt great sorrow that he had died so young, for he was only forty-two winters old.

CHAPTER 5

WEEK AFTER WEEK passed, and Kristin prepared herself in her heart to take the dead man's message to Erlend. There was no doubt that she would do it, but it seemed to her a difficult task. In the meantime so much had to be done at home on the estates. She went about arguing with herself about postponing it.

At Whitsuntide, Ramborg Lavransdatter arrived at Formo. She had left her children behind at Dyfrin. They were well, she said when Kristin asked about them. The two maidens had wept bitterly and mourned their father. Andres was too young to understand. The youngest, Simon Simonssøn, was thriving, and they hoped he would grow up to be big and strong.

Ramborg went to church to visit her husband's grave a couple of times; otherwise she never left her manor. But Kristin went south to see her as often as she could. She now sincerely wished that she had known her sister better. The widow looked like such a child in her mourning garb. Her body seemed fragile and only half grown in the heavy, dark blue gown; the little triangle of her face was yellow and thin, framed by the linen bands beneath the black woolen veil, which fell in stiff folds from the crown of her head almost to the hem of her skirts. And she had dark circles under her big eyes, the coal-black pupils wide and always staring.

During the hay harvest there was a week's time when Kristin couldn't get away to see her sister. From the harvesters she heard that a guest was visiting Ramborg at Formo: Jammælt Halvardssøn. Kristin remembered that Simon had mentioned this man; he owned an exceedingly large estate not far from Dyfrin, and he and Simon had been friends since childhood.

A week into the harvest the rains came. Then Kristin rode over to see her sister. Kristin sat talking about the terrible weather and about the hay and then asked how things were going at Formo.

All of a sudden Ramborg said, "Jon will have to manage things here; I'm heading south in a few days, Kristin."

"Yes, you must be longing for your children, poor dear," said Kristin.

Ramborg stood up and paced the floor.

"I'm going to tell you something that will surprise you," the young woman said after a moment. "You and your sons will soon be invited to a betrothal feast at Dyfrin. I said yes to Jammælt before he left here, and Gyrd will hold the wedding."

Kristin sat without saying a word. Her sister stood staring at her, pale and dark-eyed.

Finally the older sister spoke, "I see that you won't be left a widow for very long after Simon's death. I thought you mourned him so grievously. But you can make your own decisions now."

Ramborg did not reply. After a moment Kristin asked, "Does Gyrd Darre know that you intend to marry again so soon?"

"Yes." Ramborg began pacing again. "Helga advises me to do so. Jammælt is rich." She laughed. "And Gyrd is such a clever man that he must have seen long ago that our life was so wretched together, Simon's and mine."

"What are you saying! No one else has ever noticed that your life together was wretched," Kristin said after a pause. "I don't think anyone has ever seen anything but friendship and goodwill between the two of you. Simon indulged you in every way, gave you everything you wished for, always kept in mind your youth, and took care that you should enjoy it and be spared toil and travail. He loved his children and showed you every day that he was grateful to you for giving birth to the two of them."

Ramborg smiled scornfully.

Kristin continued fiercely, "If you have any cause to think that your life wasn't good together, then surely Simon is not to blame."

"No," said Ramborg. "I will bear the blame—if *you* do not dare."

Kristin sat there, dumbfounded.

"I don't think you know what you're saying, sister," she replied at last.

"Yes, I do," said Ramborg. "But I can believe that *you* might not know. You've had so little thought for Simon that I'm convinced this may be new to you. You considered him good enough to turn to whenever you needed a helper who would gladly have carried red-hot iron for your sake. But never did you give any thought to Simon Andressøn or ask what it might have cost him. I was allowed to enjoy my youth, yes. With joy and gentleness Simon would lift me up into the saddle and send me off to feasts and merriment; with equal joy and gentleness he would welcome me when I came back home. He would pat me the way he patted his dog or his horse. He never missed me while I was gone."

Kristin was on her feet; she stood quietly next to the table. Ramborg was wringing her hands so the knuckles cracked, pacing back and forth in the room.

"Jammælt . . ." she said in a calmer voice. "I've known for years how he thought of me. I saw it even while his wife was still alive. Not that he ever gave himself away in word or deed—you mustn't think that! He grieved for Simon too and came to me often to console me—that much is true. It was Helga who said to both of us that now it would be fitting if we . . .

"And I don't know what I should wait for. I will never find more consolation or any less than I feel right now. I want to try living with a man who has been silently thinking of *me* for years on end. I know all too well what it feels like to live with a man who is silently thinking about someone else."

Kristin didn't move. Ramborg stopped in front of her, with her eyes flashing. "You know what I say is true!"

Kristin left the room without a word, her head bowed. As she stood in the rain outside in the courtyard, waiting for the servant to bring her horse, Ramborg appeared in the doorway. She stared at her sister with dark and hateful eyes.

Not until the next day did Kristin remember what she had promised Simon if Ramborg should marry again. She rode back to Formo. This was not an easy thing for her to do. And the worst of it was that she knew there was nothing she could say that would give her sister any help or solace. This marriage to Jammælt of Ælin seemed to her a rash decision when Ramborg was in such a state of mind. But Kristin realized that it would do no good for her to object.

Ramborg was sullen and morose and answered her sister curtly. Under no circumstances would she allow her stepdaughter to go to

Jørundgaard. "Things at your estate are not such that I would think it advisable to send a young maiden over there." Kristin replied meekly that Ramborg might be right about that, but she had promised Simon to make the offer.

"If Simon, in his feverish daze, didn't realize that he was offending me when he made this request of you, then surely you should realize that you offend me by mentioning it," said Ramborg, and Kristin had to return home without accomplishing her goal.

The next morning promised good weather. But when her sons came in for breakfast, Kristin told them they would have to bring in the hay without her. She had a mind to set off on a journey, and she might be gone several days.

"I'm thinking of going north to Dovre to find your father," she said. "I intend to ask him to forget the discord that has existed between the two of us, to ask him when he will come home to us."

Her sons blushed; they didn't dare look up, but she could tell they were glad. She pulled Munan into her arms and bent her face down to look at him. "You probably don't even remember your father, do you, little one?"

The boy nodded mutely with sparkling eyes. One by one the other sons cast a glance at their mother. Her face looked younger and more beautiful than they had seen it in many years.

She came out to the courtyard some time later, dressed for travel in her church attire: a black woolen gown trimmed with blue and silver at the neck and sleeves and a black, sleeveless hooded cloak since it was high summer. Naakkve and Gaute had saddled her horse as well as their own; they wanted to go with their mother. She didn't voice any objections. But she said little to her sons as they rode north across Rost Gorge and up toward Dovre. For the most part she was silent and preoccupied; if she spoke to the young lads, it was about other things, not about where they were going.

When they had gone so far that they could look up the slope and glimpse the rooftops of Haugen against the horizon, she asked the boys to turn back.

"You know full well that your father and I have much to talk about, and we would rather discuss things while we're alone."

The brothers nodded; they said goodbye to their mother and turned their horses around.

The wind from the mountains blew cool and fresh against her hot cheeks as she came over the last sharp rise. The sun gilded the small gray buildings, which cast long shadows across the courtyard. The grain was just about to form ears up there; it stood so lovely in the small fields, glistening and swaying in the wind. Tall crimson fireweed in bloom fluttered from all the heaps of stones and up on the crags; here and there the hay had been piled up in stacks. But there wasn't a trace of life on the farm—not even a dog to greet her or give warning.

Kristin unsaddled her horse and led it over to the water trough. She didn't want to let it roam loose, so she took it over to the stable. The sun shone through a big hole in the roof; the sod hung in strips between the beams. And there was no sign that a horse had stood there for quite some time. Kristin tended to the animal and then went back out to the courtyard.

She looked in the cowshed. It was dark and desolate; she could tell by the smell that it must have stood empty for a long time.

Several animal hides were stretched out to dry on the wall of the house; a swarm of blue flies buzzed up into the air as she approached. Near the north gable, earth had been piled up and sod spread over it, so the timbers were completely hidden. He must have done that to keep in the heat.

She fully expected the house to be locked, but the door opened when she touched the handle. Erlend hadn't even latched the door to his dwelling.

An unbearable stench met her as she stepped inside: the rank and pungent smell of hides and a stable. The first feeling that came over her as she stood in his house was a deep remorse and pity. This place seemed to her more like an animal's lair.

Oh yes, yes, yes, Simon—you were right!

It was a small house, but it had been beautifully and carefully built. The fireplace even had a brick chimney so that it wouldn't fill the room with smoke, as the hearths did in the high loft room back home. But when she tried to open the damper to air out the foul smell a bit, she saw that the chimney had been closed off with

several flat rocks. The glass pane in the window facing the gallery
was broken and stuffed with rags. The room had a wooden floor,
but it was so filthy that the floorboards were barely visible. There
were no cushions on the benches, but weapons, hides, and old
clothing were strewn about everywhere. Scraps of food littered the
dirty table. And the flies buzzed high and low.

She gave a start and stood there trembling, unable to breathe,
her heart pounding. In that bed over there, in the bed where that
thing had lain when she was here last . . . Something was lying
there now, covered with a length of homespun. She wasn't sure
what she thought. . . .

Then she clenched her teeth and forced herself to go over and
lift up the cloth. It was only Erlend's armor, with his helmet and
shield. They were lying on the bare boards of the bed, covered up.

She glanced at the other bed. That's where they had found
Bjørn and Aashild. That's where Erlend now slept. No doubt she
too would sleep there in the night.

How must it have been for him to live in this house, to sleep
here? Once again all her other feelings were drowned in pity. She
went over to the bed; it hadn't been cleaned in a long time. The
straw under the hide sheet had been pressed down until it was
quite hard. There was nothing else but a few sheepskin blankets
and a couple of pillows covered with homespun, so filthy that they
stank. Dust and dirt scattered as she touched the bedding. Erlend's
bed was no better than that of a stableboy in a stall.

Erlend, who could never have enough splendor around him. Erlend, who would put on silk shirts, velvet, and fine furs if he could
find the slightest excuse to do so; who resented having to let his
children wear handwoven homespun on workdays; and who had
never liked it when she nursed them herself or lent her maids a
hand with the housework—like a leaseholder's wife, he said.

Jesus, but he had brought this upon himself.

No, I won't say a word. I will take back everything I said, Simon. You were right. He must not stay here . . . the father of my
sons. I will offer him my hand and my lips and ask his forgiveness.

This isn't easy, Simon. But you were right. She remembered his
sharp gray eyes, his gaze just as steadfast, almost to the very end.
In that wretched body which had begun to decay, his pure, bright

spirit had shone from his eyes until his soul was drawn home, the way a blade is pulled back. She knew it was as Ramborg had said. He had loved her all these years.

Every single day in the months since his death she couldn't help thinking about him, and now she saw that she had realized it even before Ramborg spoke. During this time she had been forced to mull over all the memories she had of him, for as far back as she had known Simon Darre. In all these years she had carried false memories of this man who had once been her betrothed; she had tampered with these memories the way a corrupt ruler tampers with the coin and mixes impure ore with the silver. When he released her and took upon himself the blame for the breach of promise, she told herself, and believed it, that Simon Andressøn had turned away from her with contempt as soon as he realized that her honor had been disgraced. She had forgotten that when he let her go, on that day in the nuns' garden, he was certainly not thinking that she was no longer innocent or pure. Even back then he was willing to bear the shame for her inconstant and disobedient disposition; all he asked was that her father should be told that he was not the one who sought to break the agreement.

And there was something else she now knew. When he had learned the worst about her, he stood up to redeem for her a scrap of honor in the eyes of the world. If she could have given her heart to him then, Simon would have still taken her as his wife before the church door, and he would have tried to live with her so she would never feel that he concealed a memory of her shame.

But she still knew that she could never have loved him. She could never have loved Simon Andressøn. And yet . . . Everything that had enraged her about Erlend because he didn't have particular traits—those were the traits that Simon did possess. But she was a pitiful woman who couldn't help complaining.

Simon had given selflessly to the one he loved; no doubt she had believed that she did the same.

But when she received his gifts, without thought or thanks, Simon had merely smiled. Now she realized that he had often been melancholy when they were together. She now knew that he had concealed sorrow behind his strangely impassive demeanor. Then he would toss out some impertinent jest and push it aside, as ready as ever to protect and to help and to give.

She herself had raged, storing away and brooding over every grief, whenever she offered her gifts and Erlend paid them no mind.

Here, in this very room, she had stood and pronounced such bold words: "I was the one who took the wrong path, and I won't complain about Erlend even if it leads me out over the scree." That was what she had said to the woman whom she drove to her death in order to make room for her own love.

Kristin moaned aloud, clasped her hands before her breast, and stood there, rocking back and forth. Yes, she had said so proudly that she would not complain about Erlend Nikulaussøn if he grew tired of her, betrayed her, or even left her.

Yes, but if *that* was what Erlend had done . . . She thought she *would* have been able to stand it. If he had betrayed her once, and that had been the end of it. But he hadn't betrayed her; he had merely failed her again and again and made her life full of anguish and uncertainty. No, he had never betrayed her, nor had he ever made her feel secure. And she could see no end to it all. Here she stood now, about to beg him to come back, to fill her goblet each day with uncertainty and unrest, with expectations, with longings and fear and hope that would be shattered.

She felt now as if he had worn her out. She had neither the youth nor the courage to live with him any longer, and she would probably never grow so old that Erlend couldn't play with her heart. Not young enough to have the strength to live with him; not old enough to have patience with him. She had become a miserable woman; no doubt that was what she had always been. Simon was right.

Simon . . . and her father. They had held on to their loyal love for her, even as she trampled on them for the sake of this man whom she no longer had the strength to endure.

Oh, Simon. I know that never for a minute did you wish vengeance upon me. But I wonder, Simon, if you know in your grave, that now you have been avenged after all.

No, she couldn't bear it any longer; she would have to find something to do. She made up the bed and looked for a dishrag and broom, but they were not to be found anywhere. She glanced into the alcove; now she understood why it smelled like a stable. Erlend had made a stall for his horse in there. But it had been mucked out and cleaned. His saddle and harness, which hung on the wall, were well cared for and oiled, with all the torn pieces mended.

Compassion once more washed away all other thoughts. Did he keep Soten inside because he couldn't bear to be alone in the house?

Kristin heard a sound out on the gallery. She stepped over to the window. It was covered with dust and cobwebs, but she thought she caught a glimpse of a woman. She pulled the rag from the hole and peeked out. A woman was setting down a pail of milk and a small cheese out there. She was middle-aged and lame and wore ugly, tattered clothes. Kristin herself was hardly aware of how much easier she breathed.

She tidied up the room as best she could. She found the inscription that Bjørn Gunnarssøn had carved into a timber of the wall. It was in Latin, so she couldn't decipher the whole thing, but he called himself both *Dominus* and *Miles*, and she read the name of his ancestral estate in Elve County, which he had lost because of Aashild Gautesdatter. In the midst of the splendid carvings on the high seat was his coat of arms with its unicorn and water lilies.

A short time later Kristin heard a horse somewhere outside. She went over to the entryway and peered out.

From the leafy forest across from the farm a tall black stallion emerged, pulling a load of firewood. Erlend walked alongside to guide him. A dog was perched on top of the wood, and several more dogs were running around the sled.

Soten, the Castilian, strained against the harness and pulled the sledful of wood across the grassy courtyard. One of the dogs began barking as it crossed the green. Erlend, who had begun to unfasten the harnesses, noticed from all the dogs that something must be wrong. He took his axe from the load of wood and walked toward the house.

Kristin fled back inside, letting the door fall shut behind her. She crept over to the fireplace and stood there, trembling and waiting.

Erlend stepped inside with his axe in hand and the dogs milling around him on the threshold. They found the intruder at once and began barking furiously.

The first thing she noticed was the rush of blood that flooded his face, so youthful and red. The quick tremor on his fine, soft lips, and his big, deep-set eyes beneath the shadow of his brows. The sight of him took her breath away. No doubt she saw the old stubble of beard on the lower half of his face, and she saw that his disheveled hair was iron gray. But the color that came and went so swiftly in his cheeks, the way it had when they were young . . . He was just as young and handsome; it was as if nothing had been able to break him.

He was poorly clad. His blue shirt was filthy and tattered; over it he wore a leather vest, scratched and scraped and torn around the eyelets, but it fit snugly and followed pliantly the graceful, strong movements of his body. His tight leather hose was torn at one knee, and the seam was split on the back of the other leg. And yet he had never looked more like the descendant of chieftains and noblemen than he did now. With such calm dignity he carried his slender body with the wide, rather sloping shoulders and the long, elegant limbs. He stood there, his weight resting slightly on one foot, one hand stuck in the belt around his slim waist, the other holding the axe at his side.

He had called the dogs back, and now he stood staring at her, turning red and pale and not saying a word. For a good long time they both were silent. Finally the man spoke, his voice a little uncertain. "So you've come here, Kristin?"

"I wanted to see how you were doing up here," she replied.

"Well, now you've seen it." He glanced around the room. "You can see that I'm tolerably comfortable here; it's good that you happened to come by on a day when everything was tidied up so nicely." He noticed the shadow of a smile on her face. "Or perhaps you're the one who has been cleaning up," he said, laughing softly.

Erlend put down his axe and sat on the outer bench with his back leaning against the table. All of a sudden he grew somber. "You're standing there so . . . there's nothing wrong back home, is there? At Jørundgaard, I mean? With the boys?"

"No." Now she had the chance to present her purpose. "Our sons are thriving and show great promise. But they long so much for you, Erlend. It was my intention . . . I've come here, husband, to ask you to return home to us. We all miss you." She lowered her eyes.

"You look well, Kristin." Erlend gazed at her with a little smile.

Kristin stood there, red-faced, as if he had struck a blow to her ear.

"That's not why—"

"No, I know it's not because you think you're too young and fresh to be left a widow," Erlend said when she broke off. "I don't think any good would come of it if I returned home, Kristin," he added in a more serious tone. "In your hands everything is flourishing at Jørundgaard; I know that. You have good fortune with all your undertakings. And I am quite content with my situation here."

"The boys aren't happy that we . . . are quarreling," she replied softly.

"Oh . . ." Erlend hesitated. "They're so young. I don't think they take it so hard that they won't forget about it when it's time for them to leave their childhood behind. I might as well tell you," he added with a little smile, "that I see them from time to time."

She knew about this, but she felt humiliated by his words, and it seemed as if that was his intention, since he thought she didn't know. Her sons had never realized that she knew. But she replied somberly, "Then you also know that many things at Jørundgaard are not as they should be."

"We never talk about such matters," he said with the same smile. "We go hunting together. But you must be hungry and thirsty." He jumped up. "And here you stand . . . No, sit down in the high seat, Kristin. Yes, sit there, my dear. I won't crowd in next to you."

He brought in the milk and cheese and found some bread, butter, and dried meat. Kristin was hungry and quite thirsty, but she had trouble swallowing her food. Erlend ate in a hasty and careless manner, as had always been his custom when not among guests, and he was soon finished.

He talked about himself. The people who lived at the foot of the hill worked his land and brought him milk and a little food; otherwise he went into the mountains to hunt and fish. But then he mentioned that he was actually thinking about leaving the country, to seek service with some foreign warlord.

"Oh no, Erlend!"

He gave her a swift, searching glance. But she said no more. The light was growing dim in the room. Her face and wimple shone white against the dark wall. Erlend stood up and stoked the fire in the hearth. Then he straddled the outer bench and turned to face her; the red glow of the fire flickered over his body.

To think that he would even consider such a thing. He was almost as old as her father had been when he died. But it was all too likely that he would do it one day: take off on some whim, in search of new adventures.

"Don't you think it's enough?" said his wife heatedly. "Enough that you fled the village, leaving me and your sons behind? Do you have to flee the country to leave us too?"

"If I'd known what you thought of me, Kristin," said Erlend gravely, "I would have left *your* estate much sooner! But I now see that you've had to bear a great deal because of me."

"You know quite well, Erlend . . . You say *my* estate, but you have the rights of a husband over all that is mine." She herself could hear how weak her voice sounded.

"Yes," replied Erlend. "But I know I was a poor master over what I owned myself." He fell silent for a moment. "Naakkve . . . I remember the time before he was born, and you spoke of the child you were carrying, who would take my high seat after me. I now see, Kristin, that it was hard for you. It's best if things stay as they are. And I'm content with my life up here."

Kristin shuddered as she glanced around at the room in the fading light. Shadows now filled every cranny, and the glow from the flames danced.

"I don't understand," she said, on the verge of collapse, "how you can bear this house. You have nothing to occupy your time, and you're all alone. I think you could at least take on a workman."

"You mean that I should run the farm myself?" Erlend laughed. "Oh no, Kristin, you know I'm ill suited to be a farmer. I can never sit still."

"Sit still . . . But surely you're sitting still here . . . during the long winter."

Erlend smiled to himself; his eyes had an odd, remote look to them.

"Yes, in some sense you're right. When I don't have to think about anything but whatever happens to cross my mind and can come and go as I like. And you know that I've always been the kind of person who can fall asleep if there's nothing to keep watch over; I sleep like a hibernating bear whenever the weather isn't good enough to go into the mountains."

"Aren't you ever afraid to be here alone?" whispered Kristin.

At first he gave her a look of incomprehension. Then he laughed. "Because people say this place is haunted? I've never noticed anything. Sometimes I've wished that my kinsman Bjørn would pay me a visit. Do you remember that he once said he didn't think I'd be able to stand to feel the edge of a blade at my throat? I'd like to tell him now that I wasn't particularly frightened when I had the rope around my neck."

A long shiver rippled through Kristin's body. She sat without saying a word.

Erlend stood up. "It must be time for us to go to bed now, Kristin."

Stiff and cold, she watched Erlend remove the coverlet from his armor, spread it over the bed, and tuck it around the dirty pillows. "This is the best I have," he said.

"Erlend!" She clasped her hands under her breast. She searched for something to say, to win a little more time; she was so frightened. Then she remembered the promise she had made.

"Erlend, I have a message to give you. Simon asked me, when he was near the end, to bring you his greetings. Every single day he regretted the words he spoke to you when you last parted. 'Unmanly' he called them, and he asked you to forgive him."

"Simon." Erlend was standing with one hand on the bedpost; he lowered his eyes. "He's the one man I would least like to be reminded of."

"I don't know what came between the two of you," said Kristin. She thought Erlend's words remarkably heartless. "But it would be strange, and unlike Simon, if things were as he said, that he did not treat you justly. Surely he wasn't entirely to blame if this is true."

Erlend shook his head. "He stood by me like a brother when I was in need," he said in a low voice. "And I accepted his help and his friendship, and I never realized that it had always been difficult for him to tolerate me.

"It seems to me that it would have been easier to live in the old days, when two fellows like us could have fought a duel, meeting out on the islet to let the test of weapons decide who would win the fair maiden."

He picked up an old cape from the bench and slung it over his arm.

"Perhaps you'd like to keep the dogs inside with you to-night?"

Kristin had stood up.

"Where are you going, Erlend?"

"Out to the barn to sleep."

"No!"

Erlend stopped, standing there slender and straight-backed and young in the red glow from the dying embers in the fireplace.

"I don't dare sleep alone in this room. I don't dare."

"Do you dare sleep in my arms then?" She caught a glimpse of his smile in the darkness, and she grew faint. "Aren't you afraid that I might crush you to death, Kristin?"

"If only you would." She fell into his arms.

When she woke up, she could see from the windowpane that it was daylight outdoors. Something was weighing down her breast; Erlend was sleeping with his head on her shoulder. He had placed his arm across her body and was gripping her left arm with his hand.

She looked at her husband's iron-gray hair. She looked at her own small, withered breasts. Above and below them she could see the high, curved arch of her ribs under the thin covering of skin. A kind of terror seized hold of her as one memory after another from the night before rose up. In this room . . . the two of them, at their age . . . Horror and shame overwhelmed her as she saw the patches of red on her worn mother arms, on her shriveled bosom. Abruptly she grabbed the blanket to cover herself.

Erlend awoke, raised himself up on one elbow, and stared down at her face. His eyes were coal-black after his slumber.

"I thought . . ." He threw himself down beside her again; a

deep, wild tremor rushed through her at the sound of joy and anguish in his voice. "I thought I was dreaming again."

She opened her lips to his mouth and wrapped her arms around his neck. Never, never had it felt so blessed.

Later that afternoon, when the sunshine was already golden and the shadows lay stretched out across the green courtyard, they set off to get water from the creek. Erlend was carrying the two large buckets. Kristin walked at his side, lithe, straight-backed, and slender. Her wimple had slipped back and lay around her shoulders; her uncovered hair was a gleaming brown in the sun. She could feel it herself as she closed her eyes and lifted her face to the light. Her cheeks had turned red; the features of her face had softened. Each time she glanced over at him she would lower her gaze, overwhelmed, when she saw in Erlend's face how young she was.

Erlend decided that he wanted to bathe. As he walked farther down, Kristin sat on the thick carpet of grass, leaning her back against a rock. The murmuring and gurgling of the mountain stream lulled her into a doze; now and then, when mosquitoes or flies touched her skin, she would open her eyes briefly and swat them away with her hand. Down among the willow thickets, near the deep pool, she caught sight of Erlend's white body. He was standing with one foot up on a rock, scrubbing himself with tufts of grass. Then she closed her eyes again and smiled, weary but happy. She was just as powerless against him as ever.

Her husband came back and threw himself down on the grass in front of her, his hair wet, his red lips cold from the water as he pressed them to her hand. He had shaved and put on a better shirt, although it was not particularly grand either. Laughing, he pointed to his armpit, where the fabric was torn.

"You could have brought me a shirt when you finally decided to come north."

"I'll start sewing a shirt for you as soon as I get home, Erlend," she replied with a smile, caressing his forehead with her hand.

He grabbed hold of it. "Never will you leave here again, my Kristin."

She merely smiled without replying. Erlend pushed himself away so that he could lie down on his stomach. Under the bushes, in a damp, shady spot, grew a cluster of small, white, star-shaped flowers. Their petals had blue veins like a woman's breast, and in the center of each blossom sat a tiny brownish-blue bud. Erlend picked every one of them.

"You who are so clever about such things, Kristin—surely you must know what these flowers are called."

"They're called Friggja grass. No, Erlend . . ." She blushed and pushed away his hand as he tried to slip the flowers into her bodice.

Erlend laughed and gently bit the white petals, one after the other. Then he put all the flowers into her open hands and closed her fingers around them.

"Do you remember when we walked in the garden at Hofvin Hospice, and you gave me a rose?"

Kristin slowly shook her head as she gave him a little smile. "No. But you took a rose from my hand."

"And you let me take it. Just as you let me take you, Kristin. As gentle and pious as a rose. Later on you sometimes scratched me bloody, my sweet." He flung himself into her lap and put his arms around her waist. "Last night, Kristin . . . it did no good. You weren't allowed to sit there demurely and wait."

Kristin bent her head and hid her face against his shoulder.

On the fourth day they had taken refuge up in the birch woods among the foothills across from the farm, for on that day the tenant was bringing in the hay. Without discussing it, Kristin and Erlend had agreed that no one needed to know that she was visiting him. He went down to the buildings a few times to get food and drink, but she stayed among the alpine birches, sitting in the heather. From where they sat, they could see the man and woman toiling to carry home the hay bundles on their backs.

"Do you remember," asked Erlend, "the time you promised me that if I ended up on a smallholder's farm in the mountains, you would come and keep house for me? You wanted to have two cows and some sheep."

Kristin laughed a little and tugged at his hair. "What do you think our boys would think about that, Erlend? If their mother ran away and left them behind in that manner?"

"I think they would be happy to manage Jørundgaard on their own," said Erlend, laughing. "They're old enough now. Gaute is a capable farmer, even as young as he is. And Naakkve is almost a man."

"Oh no . . ." Kristin laughed softly. "It's probably true that he thinks so himself. Well, no doubt all five of them do. But he's still lacking a man's wisdom, that boy."

"If he takes after his father, it's possible that he might acquire it late, or perhaps never at all," replied Erlend. He gave a sly smile. "You think you can hide your children under the hem of your cloak, Kristin. Naakkve fathered a son this summer—you didn't know about that, did you?"

"No!" Kristin sat there, red-faced and horror-stricken.

"Yes, it was stillborn, and the boy is apparently careful not to go over there anymore. It was the widow of Paal's son, here at Haugsbrekken. She said it was his, and I suppose he wasn't without blame, no matter how things stood. Yes, we're getting to be so old, you and I—"

"How can you talk that way after your son has brought upon himself such dishonor and trouble!" It pierced her heart that her husband could speak so nonchalantly and that it seemed to amuse him that she hadn't known anything about it.

"Well, what do you want me to say?" asked Erlend in the same tone of voice. "The boy is eighteen winters old. You can see for yourself that it does little good for you to treat your sons as if they were children. When you move up here with me, we'll have to see about finding him a wife."

"Do you think it will be easy for us to find a suitable match for Naakkve? No, husband, after this I think you must realize that you need to come back home with me and lend a hand with the boys."

Vehemently Erlend propped himself up on his elbow. "I won't do that, Kristin. I'm a stranger here and will always be one in your parish. No one remembers anything about me except that I was condemned as a traitor and betrayer of the king. Didn't you ever think, during the years I've lived here at Jørundgaard, that my presence was an uneasy one? Back home in Skaun I was accustomed to a position of some importance among the people. Even during those days in my youth, when gossip flew about my evil ways and I was banned from the Church, I was still Erlend Niku-laussøn of Husaby! Then came the time, Kristin, when I had the joy of showing the people of the northern regions that I was not entirely debased from the honor of my ancestors. No, I tell you! Here on this little farm I'm a free man; no one glares at my footprints or talks behind my back. Do you hear me, Kristin, my only love? Stay with me! You will never have cause to regret it. Life here is better than it ever was at Husaby. I don't know why it is, Kristin, but I've never been so happy or lighthearted—not as a child or ever since. It was hell while Eline lived with me at Husaby, and you and I were never truly happy together there either. And yet the Almighty God knows that I have loved you every hour and every day that I've known you. I think that manor was cursed; Mother was tormented to death there, and my father was always an unhappy man. But here life is good, Kristin—if only you would stay with me. Kristin . . . As truly as God died on the cross for us, I love you as much today as on that evening when you slept under my cape, the night of Saint Margareta's Day. I sat and looked at you, such a pure and fresh and young and untouched flower you were!"

Kristin said quietly, "Do you remember, Erlend, that you prayed on that night that I would never weep a single tear for your sake?"

"Yes, and God and all the saints in Heaven know that I meant it! It's true that things turned out differently—as surely they must. That's what always happens while we live in this world. But I loved you, both when I treated you badly and when I treated you well. Stay here, Kristin!"

"Haven't you ever thought that it would be difficult for our sons?" she asked in the same quiet voice. "To have people talk about their father, as you admit? All seven of them can't very well run off to the mountains to escape the parish gossip."

Erlend lowered his eyes. "They're young," he said. "Handsome and intrepid boys. They'll figure out how to make their own way. But the two of us, Kristin . . . We don't have many years left before we'll be old. Do you want to squander the time you have remaining when you are beautiful and healthy and meant to rejoice in life? Kristin?"

She looked down to avoid the wild glint in his eyes. After a moment she said, "Have you forgotten, Erlend, that two of our sons are still children? What would you think of me if I left Lavrans and Munan behind?"

"Then you can bring them up here, unless Lavrans would rather stay with his brothers. He's not a little boy anymore. Is Munan still so handsome?" he asked, smiling.

"Yes," said Kristin, "he's a lovely child."

Then they sat in silence for a long time. When they spoke again, it was of other matters.

She woke up in the gray light of dawn the next day, as she had every morning up there. She lay in bed listening to the horses plodding around outside the house. She had her arms wrapped around Erlend's head. The other mornings, when she woke up in the early gray hour, she had been seized by the same anguish and shame as the first time; she had fought to subdue those feelings. The two of them were a married couple who had quarreled and now reconciled; nothing could benefit the children more than that their father and mother became friends once again.

But on this morning she lay there, struggling to remember her sons. For she felt as if she had been bewitched; Erlend had spirited her away and brought her up here, straight from the woods of Gerdarud, where he had taken her into his arms the first time. They were so young; it couldn't be true that she had already borne this man seven sons. She was the mother of tall, grown-up men. But she felt as if she had been lying here in his arms and merely dreamed about those long years they had spent together as husband and wife at Husaby. All his impetuous words resounded and enticed her; dizzy with fear, she felt as if Erlend had swept away her sevenfold burden of responsibility. This is the way it must feel when the young mare is unsaddled up in the mountain pasture. The packs and saddle and bridle are removed, and the wind and air of the mountain plateau stream against her; she is free to graze the fine grass on the heights, free to run as far as she likes across all the slopes.

But at the same time she was already yearning, with a sweet and willing sense of longing, to bear a new burden. She was yearning with a faint, tender giddiness for the one who would now live nearest her heart for nine long months. She had been certain of it, from the first morning she woke up here in Erlend's arms. Her barrenness had left her, along with the harsh, dry, gasping heat in her heart. She was hiding Erlend's child in her womb, and with a strangely gentle feeling of impatience, her soul was reaching out toward the hour when the infant would be brought into the light.

My big sons no longer need me, she thought. They think I'm unreasonable, that I nag them. We'll just be in their way, the little child and I. No, I can't leave here; we must stay here with Erlend. I can't leave.

But when they sat down together to eat breakfast, she mentioned nevertheless that she would have to return home to her children.

It was Lavrans and Munan she was thinking of. They were old enough now that she was embarrassed to imagine them living up here with Erlend and herself, perhaps looking with astonishment at their parents who had become so youthful. But those two couldn't be without her.

Erlend sat and stared at her as she talked about going home. At last he gave her a fleeting smile. "Well . . . if that's what you want, then you must go."

He wanted to accompany her for part of the journey. He rode all the way through Rost Gorge and up to Sil, until they could see a little of the church roof above the tops of the spruce trees. Then he said goodbye. He smiled to the very end, slyly confident.

"You know now, Kristin, that whether you come at night or by day, whether I have to wait for you a short time or a long time, I will welcome you as if you were the Queen of Heaven come down from the clouds to my farm."

She laughed. "I don't dare speak as grandly as that. But you must now realize, my love, that there will be great joy at your manor on the day the master returns to his own home."

He shook his head and chuckled. Smiling, they took leave of each other; smiling, Erlend leaned over as they sat on their horses, side by side, and kissed her many times, and between each kiss, he looked at her with his laughing eyes.

"So we'll see," he said finally, "which of us is more stubborn, my fair Kristin. This is not the last time we will meet; you and I both know that!" As she rode past the church, she gave a little shudder. She felt as if she were returning home from inside the mountain. As if Erlend were the mountain king himself and could not come past the church and the cross on the hill.

She pulled in the reins; she had a great urge to turn around and ride after him.

Then she looked out across the green slopes, down at her beautiful estate with the meadows and fields and the glistening curve of the river winding through the valley. The mountains rose up in a blue shimmer of heat. The sky was filled with billowing summer clouds. It was madness. There, with his sons, was where he belonged. He was no mountain knight; he was a Christian man, no matter how full he was of wild ideas and foolish whims. Her lawful husband, with whom she had endured both good and bad—beloved, beloved, no matter how sorely he had tormented her with his unpredictable impulses. She would have to be forbearing, since she could not live without him; she would have to strive to bear the anguish and uncertainty as best she could. She didn't think it would be long before he followed her—now that they had been together once again.

SHE TOLD HER sons that their father had to take care of a few things at Haugen before he moved home. No doubt he would come south early in the fall.

She went about her estate, looking young, her cheeks flushed, her face soft and gentle, moving more quickly about her work, although she didn't manage to accomplish nearly as much as she used to with her usual quiet and measured manner. She no longer chastised her sons sharply, as had been her custom whenever they did something wrong or failed to satisfy her demands properly. Now she spoke to them in a jesting manner or let it pass without saying a word.

Lavrans now wanted to sleep with his older brothers up in the loft.

"Yes, I suppose you should be counted among the grown-up boys too, my son." She ran her fingers through the boy's thick, golden-brown hair and pulled him close; he was already so tall that he came up to the middle of her breast. "What about you, Munan? Can you stand to have your mother treat you as a child for a while longer?" In the evenings, after the boy had gone to bed in the main room, he liked to have his mother sit on the bed and pamper him a bit. He would lie there with his head in her lap, chattering more childishly than he allowed himself to do during the day when his brothers could hear him. They would talk about when his father was coming home.

Then he would move over next to the wall, and his mother would spread the covers over him. Kristin would light a candle, pick up her sons' clothes that needed mending, and sit down to sew.

She pulled out the brooch pinned to her bodice and put her hand inside to touch her breasts. They were as round and firm as a young woman's. She pushed up her sleeve all the way to the shoulder and looked at her bare arm in the light. It had grown whiter and fuller. Then she stood up and took a few steps, noticing how softly she walked in her soft slippers. She ran her hands down over her slim hips; they were no longer sharp and dry like a man's. The blood coursed through her body the way sap flows through the trees in the spring. It was youth that was sprouting inside her.

She went to the brewhouse with Frida to pour warm water over the grain for the Christmas malt. Frida had neglected to tend to it in time, and the grain had lain there, swelling until it was completely dry. But Kristin didn't scold the maid; with a slight smile she listened to Frida's excuses. This was the first time that Kristin had failed to take care of it herself.

By Christmas she would have Erlend back home with her. When she sent word to him, he would have to return at once. The man wasn't so rash that he would refuse to relent this time; he had to realize that she couldn't possibly move up to Haugen, far from everyone, when she was no longer walking alone. But she would wait a little more before she sent word—even though it was certain enough—perhaps until she felt some sign of life. The second autumn that they lived at Jørundgaard, she had strayed from the road, as people called a miscarriage. But she had quickly taken solace. She was not afraid that it would happen again this time; it couldn't possibly. And yet . . .

She felt as if she had to wrap her entire body protectively around this tiny, fragile life she carried under her heart, the way a person cups her hands like a shield around a little, newly lit flame.

One day late in the fall Ivar and Skule came and told her they wanted to ride up to see their father. It was fine weather up in the mountains, and they wanted to ask if they could stay with him and go hunting during these days of bare frost.

Naakkve and Bjørgulf were sitting at the chessboard. They paused to listen.

"I don't know," said Kristin. She hadn't given any thought to who should carry her message. She looked at her two half-grown sons. She realized it was foolish, but she couldn't manage to speak of it to them. She could tell them to take Lavrans along and then ask him to talk to his father alone. He was so young that he wouldn't think it strange. And yet . . .

"Your father will soon be coming home," she said. "You might end up delaying him. And soon I'll be sending word to him myself."

The twins sulked. Naakkve looked up from the chess game and said curtly, "Do as our mother says, boys."

During Christmas she sent Naakkve north to Erlend. "You must tell him, son, that I am longing for him so greatly, as all of you must be too!" She didn't mention the other news that had come about; she thought it likely that this grown lad would have noticed it. He would have to decide for himself whether he would speak of it to his father.

Naakkve returned without having seen his father. Erlend had gone to Raumsdal. He must have received word that his daughter and her husband were about to move to Bjørgvin, and that Margret wanted to meet with her father at Veøy.

That was reasonable enough. Kristin lay awake at night, now and then stroking Munan's face as he slept at her side. She was sad that Erlend didn't come for Christmas. But it was reasonable that he should want to see his daughter while he had the chance. She wiped away her tears as they slid down her cheeks. She was so quick to weep, just as she had been when she was young.

Just after Christmas, Sira Eirik died. Kristin had visited him at Romundgaard several times during the fall after he had taken to his bed, and she attended his funeral. Otherwise she never went out among people. She thought it a great loss that their old parish priest was gone.

At the funeral she heard that someone had met Erlend north at Lesja. He was on his way home to his farm. Surely he would come soon.

Several days later she sat on the bench under the little window, breathing on her hand mirror, which she had taken out, and rubbing it shiny so she could study her face.

She had been as suntanned as a peasant woman during the past few years, but now all trace of the sun had vanished. Her skin was white, with round, bright red roses on her cheeks, like in a painting. Her face had not been so lovely since she was a young maiden. Kristin sat and held her breath with wondrous joy.

At last they would have a daughter, as Erlend had wished for so dearly, if it turned out as the wise women said. Magnhild. They would have to break with custom this time and name her after his mother.

Part of a fairy tale she had once heard drifted through her mind. Seven sons who were driven high into the wilderness as outlaws because of an unborn little sister. Then she laughed at herself; she didn't understand why she happened to think about that now.

She took from her sewing chest a shirt of the finest white linen, which she worked on whenever she was alone. She pulled out threads from the neckband and stitched birds and beasts on the loosely woven backing; it was years since she had done such fine embroidery. If only Erlend would come *now*, while it was still making her look beautiful: young and straight-backed, blushing and thriving.

Just after Saint Gregor's Day the weather turned so lovely that it was almost like spring. The snow began to melt, gleaming like silver; there were already bare brown patches on the slopes facing south, and the mountains rose up from the blue haze.

Gaute was standing outside in the courtyard, repairing a sleigh that had fallen apart. Naakkve was leaning against the wall of the woodshed, watching his brother work. At that moment Kristin came from the cookhouse, carrying with both hands a large trough full of newly baked wheat bread.

Gaute glanced up at his mother. Then he threw the axe and wheel hubs into the sleigh, ran after her, and took the trough from her; he carried it over to the storehouse.

Kristin had stopped where she was, her cheeks red. When Gaute came back, she went over to her sons. "I think the two of you should ride up to your father in the next few days. Tell him that he is sorely needed here at home to take over the management from me. I have so little strength now, and I will be in bed in the middle of the spring farm work."

The young boys listened to her, and they too blushed, but she could see that they were full of joy. Naakkve said, feigning non-

chalance, "We might as well ride up there today, around midafternoon prayers. What do you think, brother?"

On the following day around noon Kristin heard horsemen out in
the courtyard. It was Naakkve and Gaute; they were alone. They
stood next to their horses, their eyes on the ground, not saying a
word.

"What did your father say?" their mother asked.

Gaute stood leaning on his spear. He kept his eyes downcast.

Then Naakkve spoke. "Father asked us to tell you that he has
been waiting for you to come to him every day this winter. And he
said that you would be no less welcome than you were last time
you saw him."

The color came and went in Kristin's face.

"Didn't you mention to your father . . . that things are such
with me that . . . it won't be long before I have another child?"

Gaute replied without looking up, "Father didn't seem to think
that was any reason . . . that you shouldn't be able to move to
Haugen."

Kristin stood there for a moment. "What did he say?" she then
asked, her voice low and sharp.

Naakkve didn't want to speak. Gaute lifted his hand slightly,
casting a swift and beseeching glance at his brother. Then the older
son spoke after all. "Father asked us to tell you this: You knew
when the child was conceived how rich a man he was. And if he
hasn't grown any richer since, he hasn't grown any poorer either."

Kristin turned away from her sons and slowly walked back toward the main house. Heavy and weary, she sat down on the
bench under the window from which the spring sun had already
melted the ice and frost.

It *was* true. She had begged to sleep in his arms—at first. But it
wasn't kind of him to remind her of that now. She thought it
wasn't kind of Erlend to send her such a reply with their sons.

The spring weather held on. The wind blew from the south, and
the rain lasted for a week. The river rose, becoming swollen and
thunderous. It roared and rushed down the slopes; the snow
plunged down the mountainsides. And then the sunshine returned.

Kristin was standing outside behind the buildings in the grayish blue of the evening. A great chorus of birdsong came from the thicket down in the field. Gaute and the twins had gone up to the mountain pastures; they were in search of blackcock. In the morning the clamor of the birds' mating dance on the mountain slopes could be heard all the way down at the manor.

She clasped her hands under her breast. There was so little time left; she had to bear these last days with patience. She too had doubtless been stubborn and difficult to live with quite often. Unreasonable in her worries about the children . . . For too long, as Erlend had said. Yet it seemed to her that he was being harsh now. But the day would soon arrive when he would have to come to her; surely he knew that too.

It was sunny and rainy by turns. One afternoon her sons called to her. All seven of them were standing out in the courtyard along with all the servants. Above the valley stretched three rainbows. The innermost one ended at the buildings of Formo; it was unbroken, with brilliant colors. The two outer ones were fainter and faded away at the top.

Even as they stood there, staring at this astonishing fair omen, the sky grew dark and overcast. From the south a blizzard of snow swept in. It began snowing so hard that soon the whole world had turned white.

That evening Kristin told Munan the story about King Snjo and his pretty white daughter, whose name was Mjøll, and about King Harald Luva, who was brought up by the Dovre giant inside the mountain north of Dovre. She thought with sorrow and remorse that it was years since she had sat and told stories to her children in this fashion. She felt sorry that she had offered Lavrans and Munan so little pleasure of this kind. And they would soon be big boys. While the others had been small, back home at Husaby, she had spent the evenings telling them stories—often, so often.

She saw that her older sons were listening too. She blushed bright red and came to a stop. Munan asked her to tell them more. Naakkve stood up and moved closer.

"Do you remember, Mother, the story about Torstein Uksafot and the trolls of Høiland Forest? Tell us that one!"

As she talked, a memory came back to her. They had lain down to rest and to have something to eat in the birch grove down by the river: her father and the hay harvesters, both men and women. Her father was lying on his stomach; she was sitting astride him, on the small of his back, and kicking him in the flanks with her heels. It was a hot day, and she had been given permission to go barefoot, just like the grown-up women. Her father was reeling off the members of the Høiland troll lineage: Jernskjold married Skjoldvor; their daughters were Skjolddis and Skjoldgjerd, whom Torstein Uksafot killed. Skjoldgjerd had been married to Skjold-ketil, and their sons were Skjoldbjørn and Skjoldhedin and Valskjold, who wed Skjoldskjessa; they gave birth to Skjoldulf and Skjoldorm. Skjoldulf won Skjoldkatla, and together they conceived Skjold and Skjoldketil . . .

No, he had already used that name, cried Kolbjørn, laughing. For Lavrans had boasted that he would teach them two dozen troll names, but he hadn't even made it through the first dozen. Lavrans laughed too. "Well, you have to understand that even trolls revive the names of their ancestors!" But the workers refused to give in; they fined him a drink of mead for them all. And you shall have it, said the master. In the evening, after they went back home. But they wanted to have it at once, and finally Tordis was sent off to get the mead.

They stood in a circle and passed the big drinking horn around. Then they picked up their scythes and rakes and went back to the hay harvesting. Kristin was sent home with the empty horn. She carried it in front of her in both hands as she ran barefoot through the sunshine on the green path, up toward the manor. Now and then she would stop, whenever a few drops of mead had collected in the curve of the horn. Then she would tilt it over her little face and lick the gilded rim inside and out, as well as her fingers, tasting the sweetness.

Kristin Lavransdatter sat still, staring straight ahead. Father! She remembered a tremor passing over his face, a paleness, the way a forest slope grows pale whenever a stormy gust turns the leaves of the trees upside down. An edge of cold, sharp derision in his voice, a gleam in his gray eyes, like the glint of a half-drawn sword. A brief moment, and then it would vanish—into cheerful, good-humored jest when he was young, but becoming more often a quiet, slightly melancholy gentleness as he grew older. Something other than deep, tender sweetness had resided in her father's heart.

She had learned to understand it over the years. Her father's marvelous gentleness was not because he lacked a keen enough perception of the faults and wretchedness of others; it came from his constant searching of his own heart before God, crushing it in repentance over his own failings.

No, Father, I will not be impatient. I too have sinned greatly toward my husband.

On the evening of Holy Cross Day Kristin was sitting at the table with her house servants and seemed much the same as usual. But when her sons had gone up to the high loft to sleep, she quietly called Ulf Haldorssøn to her side. She asked him to go down to Isrid at the farm and ask her to come up to her mistress in the old weaving room.

Ulf said, "You must send word to Ranveig at Ulvsvold and to Haldis, the priest's sister, Kristin. It would be most fitting if you sent for Astrid and Ingebjørg of Loptsgaard to take charge of the room."

"There's no time for that," said Kristin. "I felt the first pangs just before midafternoon prayers. Do as I say, Ulf. I want only my own maids and Isrid at my side."

"Kristin," said Ulf somberly, "don't you see what vile gossip may come of this if you creep into hiding tonight."

Kristin let her arms fall heavily onto the table. She closed her eyes.

"Then let them talk, whoever wants to talk! I can't *bear* to see the eyes of those other women around me tonight."

The next morning her big sons sat in silence, their eyes lowered, as Munan talked on and on about the little brother he had seen in his mother's arms over in the weaving room. Finally Bjørgulf said that he didn't need to talk anymore about *that*.

Kristin lay in bed, merely listening; she felt as if she never slept so soundly that she wasn't listening and waiting.

She got out of bed on the eighth day, but the women who were with her could tell that she wasn't well. She was freezing, and then waves of heat would wash over her. On one day the milk would pour from her breasts and soak her clothes; the next day she didn't have enough to give the child his fill. But she refused to go back to bed. She never let the child out of her arms; she never put him in the cradle. At night she would take him to bed with her; in the daytime she carried him around, sitting at the hearth with him, sitting on her bed, listening and waiting and staring at her son, although at times she didn't seem to see him or to hear that he was crying. Then she would abruptly wake up. She would hold the boy in her arms and walk back and forth in the room with him. With her cheek pressed against his, she would hum softly to him, then sit down and place him to her breast, and sit there staring at him as she had before, her face as hard as stone.

One day when the boy was almost six weeks old, and the mother had not yet taken a single step across the threshold of the weaving room, Ulf Haldorssøn and Skule came in. They were dressed for travel.

"We're riding north to Haugen now, Kristin," said Ulf. "There has to be an end to this matter."

Kristin sat mute and motionless, with the boy at her breast. At first she didn't seem to comprehend. All of a sudden she jumped up, her face flushed blood red. "Do as you like. If you're longing for your proper master, I won't hold you back. It would be best if you drew your earnings now; then you won't need to come back here for them later."

Ulf began cursing fiercely. Then he looked at the woman standing there with the infant clutched to her bosom. He pressed his lips together and fell silent.

But Skule took a step forward. "Yes, Mother, I'm riding up to see Father now. If you're forgetting that Ulf has been a foster father to all of us children, then you should at least remember that you can't command and rule me as if I were a servant or an infant."

"Can't I?" Kristin struck him a blow to the ear so the boy staggered. "I think I can command and rule all of you as long as I give you food and clothing. Get out!" she shrieked, stomping her foot.

Skule was furious. But Ulf said quietly, "It's better this way, my boy, better for her to be unreasonable and angry than to see her sitting and staring as if she had lost her wits to grief."

Gunhild, her maid, came running after them. They were to come at once to see her mistress in the weaving room. She wanted to talk to them and to all her sons. In a curt, sharp voice, Kristin asked Ulf to ride down to Breidin to speak with a man who had leased two cows from her. He should take the twins along with him, and there was no need to return home until the next day. She sent Naakkve and Gaute up to the mountain pastures. She wanted them to go to Illmanddal to see to the horse paddock there. And on their way up they were to stop by to see Bjørn, the tar-burner and Isrid's son, and ask him to come to Jørundgaard that evening. It would do no good for them to object since tomorrow was the Sabbath.

The next morning, as the bells were ringing, the mistress left Jørundgaard, accompanied by Bjørn and Isrid, who carried the child. She had given them good and proper clothing, but for this first church visit after the birth Kristin herself was adorned with so much gold that everyone could see she was the mistress and the other two her servants.

Defiant and proud, she faced the indignant astonishment she felt directed at her from everyone on the church green. Oh yes, in the past she had come to church quite differently on such an occasion, accompanied by the most noble of women. Sira Solmund looked at her with unkind eyes as she stood before the church door with a taper in her hand, but he received her in his customary fashion.

Isrid had retreated into childhood by now and understood very little; Bjørn was an odd and taciturn man, who never interfered in anyone else's affairs. These two were the godmother and godfather.

Isrid told the priest the child's name. He gave a start. He hesitated. Then he pronounced it so loudly that it was heard by the people standing in the nave.

"Erlend. In the name of the Father, the Son, and the Holy Spirit . . ."

A shudder seemed to pass through the entire assembled congregation. And Kristin felt a wild, vindictive joy.

The child had looked quite strong when he was born. But from the very first week Kristin thought she could tell that he was not going to thrive. She herself had felt, at the moment she gave birth, that her heart was collapsing like an extinguished ember. When Isrid showed her the newborn son, she imagined that the spark of life had only an uncertain hold on this child. But she pushed this thought aside; an unspeakable number of times she had already felt as if her heart would break. And the child was plenty big and did not look weak.

But her uneasiness over the boy grew from day to day. He whimpered constantly and had a poor appetite. She often had to struggle for a long time before she could get him to take her breast. When she had finally enticed him to suckle, he would fall asleep almost at once. She couldn't see that he was getting any bigger.

With inexpressible anguish and heartache she thought she saw that from the day he was baptized and received his father's name, little Erlend began to weaken more quickly.

None of her children, no, none of them had she loved as she did this little unfortunate boy. None of them had she conceived in such sweet and wild joy; none had she carried with such happy anticipation. She thought back on the past nine months; in the end she had fought with all her life to hold on to hope and belief. She couldn't bear to lose this child, but neither could she bear to save him.

Almighty God, merciful Queen, Holy Olav. She could feel that this time it would do her no good to fling herself down and beg for her child's life.

Forgive us our sins, as we forgive those who have sinned against us.

She went to church every Sabbath, as was her custom. She kissed the doorpost, sprinkled herself with holy water, sank to her knees before the ancient crucifix above the choir. The Savior gazed down, sorrowful and gentle in his death throes. Christ died to save his murderers. Holy Olav stands before him, perpetually praying for intercession for those who drove him into exile and killed him.

As we forgive those who have sinned against us.

Blessed Mary, my child is dying!

Don't you know, Kristin, that I would rather have carried his cross and suffered his death myself than stand under my son's cross and watch him die? But since I knew that this had to happen to save the sinners, I consented in my heart. I consented when my son prayed: Father, forgive them, for they know not what they do.

As we forgive those who have sinned against us . . .

What you scream in your heart does not become a prayer until you have said your *Pater noster* without deceit.

Forgive us our sins . . . Do you remember how many times your sins were forgiven? Look at your sons over there on the men's side. Look at him standing in front, like the chieftain of that handsome group of youths. The fruit of your sin . . . For nearly twenty years you have seen God grant him greater looks, wisdom, and manliness. See His mercy. Where is your own mercy toward your youngest son back home?

Do you remember your father? Do you remember Simon Darre?

But deep in her heart Kristin felt that she had not forgiven Erlend. She could not, because she would not. She held on to her bowl of love, refusing to let it go, even though it now contained only these last, bitter dregs. The moment when she left Erlend behind, no longer thinking of him even with this corrosive bitterness, then everything that had been between them would be over.

So she stood there during mass and knew that it would be of no benefit to her. She tried to pray: Holy Olav, help me. Work a miracle on my heart so that I might say my prayer without deceit and think of Erlend with God-fearing peace in my soul. But she knew that she did not want this prayer to be heard. Then she felt that it was useless for her to pray to be allowed to keep the child. Young Erlend was on loan from God. Only on one condition could she keep him, and she refused to accept that condition. And it was useless to lie to Saint Olav. . . .

So she kept watch over the ill child. Her tears spilled out; she wept without a sound and without moving. Her face was as gray and stony as ever, although gradually the whites of her eyes and her eyelids turned blood red. If anyone came near her, she would quickly wipe her face and simply sit there, stiff and mute.

And yet it took so little to thaw her heart. If one of her big sons came in, cast a glance at the tiny child, and spoke a few kind and sympathetic words to him, then Kristin could hardly keep from bursting into loud sobs. If she could have talked to her grown-up sons about her anguish over the infant, she knew her heart would have melted. But they had grown shy around her now. Ever since that day when they came home and learned what name she had given their youngest brother, the boys seemed to have drawn closer together and stood so far away from her.

But one day, when Naakkve was looking at the child, he said, "Mother, give me permission . . . to seek out Father and tell him how things stand with the boy."

"It will no longer do any good," replied his mother in despair.

Munan didn't understand. He brought his playthings to the little brother, rejoiced when he was allowed to hold him, and thought he had made the child smile. Munan talked about when his father would come home and wondered what he would think of the new son. Kristin sat in silence, her face gray, and let her soul be torn apart by the boy's chatter.

The infant was now thin and wrinkled like an old man; his eyes were unnaturally big and clear. And yet he had begun to smile at his mother; she would moan softly whenever she saw this. Kristin caressed his small, thin limbs, held his feet in her hands. Never would this child lie there and reach with surprise for the sweet, strange, pale pink shapes that flailed in the air above him, which he didn't recognize as his own legs. Never would these tiny feet walk on the earth.

After she had sat through all the arduous days of the week and kept watch over the dying child, then she would think as she dressed for church that surely she was humble enough now. She had forgiven Erlend; she no longer cared about him. If only she might keep her sweetest, her most precious possession, then she would gladly forgive the man.

But when she stood before the cross, whispering her *Pater nos-ter,* and she came to the words *sicut et nos dimittibus debitoribus nostris,* then she would feel her heart harden, the way a hand clenches into a fist to strike. No!

Without hope, her soul aching, she would weep, for she could not *make* herself do it.

And so Erlend Erlendssøn died on the day before the Feast of Mary Magdalena, a little less than three months old.

CHAPTER 7

THAT AUTUMN BISHOP Halvard came north through the valley on an official church visit. He arrived in Sil on the day before Saint Matthew's Day. It had been more than two years since the bishop had come that far north, so there were many children who were to be confirmed this time. Munan Erlendssøn was among them; he was now eight years old.

Kristin asked Ulf Haldorssøn to present the child to the bishop; she didn't have a single friend in her home parish whom she could ask to do this. Ulf seemed pleased by her request. And so, when the church bells rang, the three of them walked up the hill: Kristin, Ulf, and the boy. Her other sons had been to the earlier mass—all of them except for Lavrans, who was in bed with a fever. They didn't want to attend this mass because it would be so crowded in the church.

As they walked past the foreman's house, Kristin noticed that many strange horses were tied to the fence outside. Farther along the road they were overtaken by Jardtrud, who was riding with a large entourage and raced past them. Ulf pretended not to see his wife and her kinsmen.

Kristin knew that Ulf had not set foot inside his own house since just after New Year's. Things had apparently gotten worse than usual between him and his wife, and afterward he had moved his clothes chest and his weapons up to the high loft, where he now lived with the boys. Once, in early spring, Kristin had mentioned that it was wrong for there to be such discord between him and his wife. Then he had looked at her and laughed, and she said no more.

The weather was sunny and beautiful. High over the valley the sky was blue between the peaks. The yellow foliage of the birch-covered slopes was beginning to thin out, and in the countryside

most of the grain had been cut, although a few acres of pale barley
still swayed near the farms, and the second crop of hay stood
green and wet with dew in the meadows. There were throngs of
people at the church, and a great neighing and whinneying of stal-
lions, because the church stables were full and many had been
forced to tie up their horses outside.

A muted, rancorous uneasiness passed through the crowd as
Kristin and her escort moved forward. A young man slapped his
thigh and laughed but was fiercely hushed by his elders. Kristin
walked with measured steps and erect bearing across the green and
then entered the cemetery. She paused for a moment at her child's
grave and at that of Simon Andressøn. A flat gray stone had been
placed on top of it, and on the stone was etched the likeness of a
man wearing a helmet and coat of mail, leaning his hands on a big,
triangular shield with his coat of arms. Around the edge of the
stone were chiseled the words:

*In pace. Simon Armiger. Proles Dom. Andreae Filii Gud-
mundi Militis Pater Noster.*

Ulf was standing outside the south door; he had left his sword
in the gallery.

At that moment Jardtrud entered the cemetery in the company
of four men: her two brothers and two old farmers. One of them
was Kolbein Jonssøn, who had been Lavrans Bjørgulfsøn's arms
bearer for many years. They walked toward the priest's entrance
south of the choir.

Ulf Haldorssøn raced over to block their way. Kristin heard
them speaking rapidly and vehemently; Ulf was trying to prevent
his wife and her escorts from going any farther. People in the
churchyard drew nearer; Kristin too moved closer. Then Ulf
jumped up onto the stone foundation on which the gallery rested,
leaned in, and pulled out the first axe he could reach. When one of
Jardtrud's brothers tried to pull it out of his hand, Ulf leaped forward and swung the axe in the air. The blow fell on the man's
shoulder, and then people came running and seized hold of Ulf. He
struggled to free himself. Kristin saw that his face was dark red,
contorted, and desperate.

Then Sira Solmund and a cleric from the bishop's party appeared in the priest's doorway. They exchanged a few words with the farmers. Three men who bore the white shields of the bishop took Ulf away at once, leading him out of the cemetery, while his wife and her escorts followed the two priests into the church.

Kristin approached the group of farmers. "What is it?" she asked sharply. "Why did they take Ulf away?"

"Surely you saw that he struck a man in the cemetery," replied one of them, his voice equally sharp. Everyone moved away from her so that she was left standing alone with her son at the church door.

Kristin thought she understood. Ulf's wife wanted to present a complaint against him to the bishop. By losing mastery of his feelings and breaching the sanctity of the cemetery, he had placed himself in a difficult position. When an unfamiliar deacon came to the door and peered outside, she went over to him, told him her name, and asked whether she might be taken to the bishop.

Inside the church all the sacred objects had been set out, but the candles on the altars were not yet lit. A little sunshine fell through the round windows high overhead and streamed between the dark brown pillars. Many of the congregation had already entered the nave and were sitting on the benches along the wall. In front of the bishop's seat in the choir stood a small group of people: Jardtrud Herbrandsdatter and her two brothers—Geirulv with his arm bandaged—Kolbein Jonssøn, Sigurd Geitung, and Tore Borghildssøn. Behind and on either side of the bishop's carved chair stood two young priests from Hamar, several other men from the bishop's party, and Sira Solmund.

All of them stared as the mistress of Jørundgaard stepped forward and courtsied deeply before the bishop.

Lord Halvard was a tall, stout man with an exceedingly venerable appearance. Beneath the red silk cap his hair gleamed snow-white at his temples, and his full, oval face was a blazing red. He had a strong, crooked nose and heavy jowls, and his mouth was as narrow as a slit, almost without lips, as it cut through his closely trimmed, grayish-white beard. But his bushy eyebrows were still dark above his glittering, coal-black eyes.

"May God be with you, Kristin Lavransdatter," said Lord Halvard. He gave the woman a penetrating look from under his heavy eyebrows. With one of his large, pale old man's hands he grasped the gold cross hanging on his chest; in the other hand, which rested on the lap of his dark violet robes, he held a wax tablet.

"What brings you to seek me out here, Mistress Kristin?" the bishop asked. "Don't you think it would be more fitting if you waited until the afternoon and came to see me at Romundgaard to tell me what is in your heart?"

"Jardtrud Herbrandsdatter has sought you out here, Reverend Father," replied Kristin. "Ulf Haldorssøn has now been in the service of my husband for thirty-five years; he has always been our loyal friend and helper and a good kinsman. I thought I might be able to help him in some way."

Jardtrud uttered a low cry of scorn or indignation. Everyone else stared at Kristin: the parishioners with bitterness, the bishop's party with intent curiosity. Lord Halvard cast a sharp glance around before he said to Kristin, "Are things such that you would venture to defend Ulf Haldorssøn? Surely you must know—" As she attempted to answer, he quickly added, raising one hand, "No one has the right to demand testimony from you in this matter—other than your husband—unless your conscience forces you to speak. Consider it carefully, before you—"

"I was mostly thinking, Lord Bishop, that Ulf let his temper get the better of him, and he took up arms at church; I thought I might aid him in this matter by offering to pay a guarantee. Or," she said with great effort, "my husband will certainly do all he can to help his friend and kinsman in this case."

The bishop turned impatiently to those standing nearby, who all seemed to be seized by strong emotions. "That woman doesn't need to be here. Her spokesman can wait over in the nave. Go over there, all of you, while I speak to the mistress. And send the parishioners outside for the time being, and Jardtrud Herbrandsdatter along with them."

One of the young priests had been busy laying out the bishop's vestments. Now he carefully set the miter with the gold cross on top of the spread-out folds of the cope and went over to speak to the people in the nave. The others followed him. The congregation, along with Jardtrud, left the church, and the verger closed the doors.

"You mentioned your husband," said the bishop, looking at

Kristin with the same expression as before. "Is it true that last summer you sought to be reconciled with him?"

"Yes, my Lord."

"But you were not reconciled?"

"My Lord, forgive me for saying this, but . . . I have no complaints about my husband. I sought you out to speak of this matter regarding Ulf Haldorssøn."

"Did your husband know you were carrying a child?" asked Lord Halvard. He seemed angered by her objection.

"Yes, my Lord," she replied in a low voice.

"How did Erlend Nikulaussøn receive the news?" asked the bishop.

Kristin stood twisting a corner of her wimple between her fingers, her eyes on the floor.

"Did he refuse to be reconciled with you when he heard about this?"

"My Lord, forgive me . . ." Kristin had turned bright red. "Whether my husband Erlend acted one way or another toward me . . . if it would help Ulf's case for him to come here, then I know that Erlend would hasten to his side."

The bishop frowned as he looked at her. "Do you mean out of friendship for this man, Ulf? Or, now that the matter has come to light, will Erlend after all agree to acknowledge the child you gave birth to this spring?"

Kristin lifted her head and stared at the bishop with wide eyes and parted lips. For the first time she began to understand what his words signified.

Lord Halvard gave her a somber look. "It's true, mistress, that no one other than your husband has the right to bring charges against you for this. But surely you must realize that he will bring upon both you and himself a great sin if he takes on the paternity of another man's child in order to protect Ulf. It would be better for all of you, if you have sinned, to confess and repent of this sin."

The color came and went in Kristin's face. "Has someone said that my husband wouldn't . . . that it was not his child?"

The bishop reluctantly replied, "Would you have me believe, Kristin, that you had no idea what people have been saying about you and your overseer?"

"No, I didn't." She straightened up, standing with her head tilted back slightly, her face white under the folds of her wimple. "I pray you, my Reverend Lord and Father—if people have been whispering rumors about me behind my back, then ask them to repeat them to my face!"

"No names have been mentioned," replied the bishop. "That is against the law. But Jardtrud Herbrandsdatter has asked permission to leave her husband and go home with her kinsmen because she accuses him of keeping company with another woman, a married woman, and conceiving a child with her."

For a moment both of them fell silent. Then Kristin repeated, "My Lord, I beg you to show me such mercy that you would demand these men to speak so that I might hear them, to say that *I* am supposed to be this woman."

Bishop Halvard gave her a sharp and piercing look. Then he waved his hand, and the men in the nave approached and stood around his chair. Lord Halvard spoke: "You good men of Sil have come to me today at an inconvenient time, bringing a complaint which by rights should have been presented first to my plenipotentiary. I have acceded to this because I know that you cannot be fully knowledgeable of the law. But now this woman, Mistress Kristin Lavransdatter of Jørundgaard, has come to me with an odd request. She begs me to ask you if you dare say to her face what people have been saying in the parish: that her husband, Erlend Nikulaussøn, is not the father of the child she gave birth to this spring."

Sira Solmund replied, "It has been said on every estate and in every hovel throughout the countryside that the child was conceived in adultery and with blood guilt, by the mistress and her overseer. And it seems to us hardly credible that she did not know of this rumor herself."

The bishop was about to speak, but Kristin said, in a loud and firm voice, "So help me Almighty God, the Virgin Mary, Saint Olav, and the archbishop Saint Thomas, I did not know this lie was being said about us."

"Then it's hard to understand why you felt such a need to conceal the fact that you were with child," said the priest. "You hid from everyone and barely came out of your house all winter."

"It's been a long time since I had any friends among the farmers of this parish; I've had so little to do with anyone here over the past few years. And yet I didn't know until now that everyone seems to be my foe. But I came to church on every Sabbath," she said.

"Yes, and you wrapped yourself up in cloaks and dressed so that no one might see you were growing big under your belt."

"As any woman would do; surely any woman would want to look decent in the company of other people," replied Kristin curtly.

The priest continued, "If the child was your husband's, as you say, then surely you wouldn't have tended to the infant so poorly that you caused him to die of neglect."

One of the young priests from Hamar quickly stepped forward and caught hold of Kristin. A moment later she stood as she had before, pale and straight-backed. She thanked the priest with a nod of her head.

Sira Solmund vehemently declared, "That's what the serving-women at Jørundgaard said. My sister, who has been to the manor, witnessed it herself. The mistress went about with her breasts bursting with milk, so that her clothing was soaked through. But any woman who saw the boy's body can testify that he died of starvation."

Bishop Halvard put up his hand. "That's enough, Sira Solmund. We will keep to the matter at hand, which is whether Jardtrud Herbrandsdatter had any other basis for her claims when she brought her case against her husband than that she had heard rumors, which the mistress here says are lies. And whether Kristin can dispute these rumors. Surely no one would claim that she laid hands on the child . . ."

But Kristin stood there, her face pale, and did not speak.

The bishop said to the parish priest, "But you, Sira Solmund, it was your duty to speak to this woman and let her know what was being said. Haven't you done so?"

The priest blushed. "I have said heartfelt prayers for this woman, that she might willingly give up her stubborn ways and seek remorse and repentance. Her father was not *my* friend," said the priest heatedly. "And yet I know that Lavrans of Jørundgaard was a righteous man and a firm believer. No doubt he might have deserved better, but this daughter of his has brought shame after shame upon him. She was barely a grown maiden before her loose ways caused two boys here in the parish to die. Then she broke her promise and betrothal to a fine and splendid knight's son, whom her father had chosen to be her husband, and forced her own will, using dishonorable means, to win this man, who you, my Lord, know full well was condemned as a traitor and betrayer of the Crown. But I thought that at last her heart would have to soften when she saw how she was hated and scorned—she and all her family—and with the worst of reputations, living there at Jørundgaard, where her father and Ragnfrid Ivarsdatter had enjoyed the respect and love of everyone.

"But it was too much when she brought her son here today to be confirmed, and that man was supposed to present the boy to you when the whole parish knows that she lives with him in both adultery and blood guilt."

The bishop gestured for the other man to be silent.

"How closely related is Ulf Haldorssøn to your husband?" he asked Kristin.

"Ulf's rightful father was Sir Baard Petersøn of Hestnes. He had the same mother as his half brother Gaute Erlendssøn of Skogheim, who was Erlend Nikulaussøn's maternal grandfather."

Lord Halvard turned impatiently to Sira Solmund, "There is no blood guilt; her mother-in-law and Ulf are cousins. It would be a breach of kinship ties and a grave sin if it were true, but you need not make it any worse than that."

"Ulf Haldorssøn is godfather to this woman's eldest son," said Sira Solmund.

The bishop looked at her, and Kristin answered, "Yes, my Lord."

Lord Halvard sat in silence for a while.

"May God help you, Kristin Lavransdatter," he said sorrowfully. "I knew your father in the past; I was his guest at Jørundgaard in my youth. I remember that you were a lovely, innocent child. If Lavrans Bjørgulfsøn had been alive, this would never have happened. Think of your father, Kristin. For his sake, you must put aside this shame and cleanse yourself, if you can."

In a flash the memory came back to her; she recognized the

bishop. A winter's day at sunset . . . a red, rearing colt in the court-yard and a priest with a fringe of black hair around his flaming red face. Hanging on to the halter, splattered with froth, he was trying to tame the wild animal and climb on to its back without a saddle. Groups of drunken, laughing Christmas guests were crowding around, her father among them, red-faced from liquor and the cold, shouting loudly and merrily.

She turned toward Kolbein Jonssøn.

"Kolbein! You who have known me ever since I wore a child's cap, you who knew me and my sisters back home with my father and mother . . . I know that you were so fond of my father that you . . . Kolbein, do you believe such a thing of me?"

The farmer Kolbein looked at her, his face stern and sorrowful. "Fond of your father, you say . . . Yes, we who were his men, poor servants and commoners who loved Lavrans of Jørundgaard and thought he was the kind of man that God wanted a chieftain to be . . .

"Don't ask us, Kristin Lavransdatter, we who saw how your father loved you and how you rewarded his love, what we think you might be capable of doing!"

Kristin bowed her head to her breast. The bishop couldn't get another word out of her; she would no longer answer his questions.

Then Lord Halvard stood up. Next to the high altar was a small door which led to the enclosed section of the gallery behind the apse of the choir. Part of it was used as the sacristy, and part of it was furnished with several little hatches through which the lepers could receive the Host when they stood out there and listened to the mass, separated from the rest of the congregation. But no one in the parish had suffered from leprosy for many years.

"Perhaps it would be best if you waited out there, Kristin, until everyone has come inside for the service. I want to talk to you later, but in the meantime you may go home to your family."

Kristin curtsied before the bishop. "I would rather go home now, venerable Lord, with your permission."

"As you please, Mistress Lavransdatter. May God protect you, Kristin. If you are guilty, then they will plead your defense: God Himself and His martyrs who are the lords of the church here: Saint Olav and Saint Thomas, who died for the sake of righteousness."

Kristin curtsied once more before the bishop. Then she went through the priest's door out into the cemetery.

A small boy wearing a new red tunic stood there all alone, his bearing stiff and erect. Munan tilted his pale child's face up toward his mother for a moment, his eyes big and frightened.

Her sons . . . She hadn't thought about them before. In a flash she saw her flock of boys: the way they had stood at the periphery of her life during the past years, crowding together like a herd of horses in a thunderstorm, alert and wary, far away from her as she struggled through the final death throes of her love. What had they understood, what had they thought, what had they endured as she wrestled with her passion? What would become of them now?

She held Munan's small, scrubbed fist in her hand. The child stared straight ahead; his lips quivered slightly, but he held his head high.

Hand in hand Kristin Lavransdatter and her son walked across the churchyard and out onto the hillside. She thought about her sons, and she felt as if she would break down and collapse on the ground. The throngs of people moved toward the church door, as the bells rang from the nearby bell tower.

She had once heard a saga about a murdered man who couldn't fall to the ground because he had so many spears in his body. She couldn't fall as she walked along because of all the eyes piercing through her.

Mother and child entered the high loft room. Her sons were huddled around Bjørgulf, who was sitting at the table. Naakkve straightened up and stood over his brothers, with one hand on the shoulder of the half-blind boy. Kristin looked at the narrow, dark, blue-eyed visage of her firstborn son, with the soft, downy black beard around his mouth.

"You know about it?" she asked calmly, walking over to the group.

"Yes." Naakkve spoke for all of them. "Gunhild was at church."

Kristin paused for a moment. The other boys turned back to

their eldest brother, until their mother asked, "Did any of you know that such things were being said in the countryside—about Ulf and me?"

Then Ivar Erlendssøn abruptly turned to face her. "Don't you think you would have heard the clamor of our actions if we had? I know *I* couldn't have sat still and let my mother be branded an adulteress—not even if I knew it was true that she *was!*"

Kristin gazed at them sorrowfully. "I wonder, my sons, what you must have thought about everything that has happened here over the last few years."

The boys stood in silence. Then Bjørgulf lifted his face and looked up at his mother with his failing eyes. "Jesus Christus, Mother, what were we supposed to think? This past year and all the other years before that! Do you think it was easy for us to figure out what to think?"

Naakkve said, "Oh yes, Mother. I know I should have talked to you, but you behaved in such a way that made it impossible for us. And when you let our youngest brother be baptized as if you wanted to call our father a dead man—" He broke off, gesturing vehemently.

Bjørgulf continued. "You and Father thought of nothing else but your quarrel. Not about the fact that we had grown up to be men in the meantime. You never paid any heed to anyone who happened to come between your weapons and was dealt bloody wounds."

He had leaped to his feet. Naakkve placed a hand on his shoulder. Kristin saw it was true: The two were grown men. She felt as if she were standing naked before them; she had shamelessly revealed herself to her children.

This was what they had seen most as they grew up: that their parents were getting old, that their youthful ardor was pitifully ill suited to them, and that they had not been able to age with honor and dignity.

Then the voice of a child cut through the silence. Munan shrieked in wild despair, "Mother! Are they coming to take you prisoner, Mother? Are they coming to take Mother away from us now?"

He threw his arms around her and buried his face against her waist. Kristin pulled him close, sank down onto a bench, and gathered the little boy into her arms. She tried to console him. "Little son, little son, you mustn't cry."

"No one can take Mother away from us." Gaute came over and touched his little brother. "Don't cry. They can't do anything to her. You must get hold of yourself, Munan. Rest assured that we will protect our mother, my boy!"

Kristin sat holding the child tightly in her arms; she felt as if he had saved her with his tears.

Then Lavrans spoke, sitting up in bed with the flush of fever on his cheeks. "Well, what are you going to do, brothers?"

"When the mass is over," said Naakkve, "we'll go over to the parsonage and offer to pay a guarantee for our foster father. That's the first thing we'll do. Do you agree, my lads?"

Bjørgulf, Gaute, Ivar, and Skule assented.

Kristin said, "Ulf raised a weapon against a man in the cemetery. And I must do something to clear both his name and mine from these rumors. These are such serious matters, boys, that I think you young men must seek someone else's counsel to decide what should be done."

"Who should we ask for advice?" said Naakkve, a little scornfully.

"Sir Sigurd of Sundbu is my cousin," replied his mother hesitantly.

"Since that has never occurred to him before," said the young man in the same tone of voice, "I don't think it fitting for the sons of Erlend to go begging to him now, when we're in need. What do you say, brothers? Even if we're not legally of age, we can still wield our weapons with skill, all five of us."

"Boys," said Kristin, "using weapons will get you nowhere in this matter."

"You must let us decide that, Mother," replied Naakkve curtly. "But now, Mother, I think you should let us eat. And sit down in your usual place—for the servants' sake," he said, as if he could command her.

She could hardly eat a thing. She sat and pondered . . . She didn't dare ask whether they would now send word to their father. And she wondered how this case would be handled. She knew little of the law in such matters; no doubt she would have to refute the rumors by swearing an oath along with either five or eleven others.[1] If so, it would probably take place at the church of Ullinsyn in Vaagaa. She had kinsmen there on nearly every large estate, from her mother's lineage. If her oath failed, and she had to stand before their eyes without being able to clear herself of this shameful charge . . . It would bring shame upon her father. He had been an outsider here in the valley. But he had known how to assert himself; everyone had respected him. Whenever Lavrans Bjørgulfsøn took up a matter at a *ting* or a meeting, he had always won full support. Still, she knew it was on him that her shame would fall. She suddenly realized how alone her father had stood; in spite of everything, he was alone and a stranger among the people here every time she heaped upon him one more burden of sorrow and shame and disgrace.

She didn't think she could ever feel this way anymore; again and again she had thought her heart would burst into bloody pieces, and now, once again, it felt as if it would break.

Gaute went out to the gallery and looked north. "People are leaving the church," he said. "Shall we wait until they've gone some distance away?"

"No," replied Naakkve. "Let them see that the sons of Erlend are coming. We should get ready now, lads. We had better wear our steel helmets."

Only Naakkve owned proper armor. He left the coat of mail behind, but he put on his helmet and picked up his shield, his sword, and a long lance. Bjørgulf and Gaute put on the old iron hats that boys wore when they practiced sword fighting, while Ivar and Skule had to be content with the small steel caps that peasant soldiers still wore. Their mother looked at them. She had such a shattered feeling in her breast.

"It seems to me ill advised, my sons, for you to arm yourselves in this fashion to go over to the parsonage," she said uneasily. "You shouldn't forget about the peace of the Sabbath and the presence of the bishop."

Naakkve replied, "Honor has grown scarce here at Jørundgaard, Mother. We have to pay dearly for whatever we can get."

"Not you, Bjørgulf," pleaded their mother fearfully, for the weak-sighted boy had picked up a big battleaxe. "Remember that you can't see well, son!"

"Oh, I can see as far as I need to," said Bjørgulf, weighing the axe in his hand.

Gaute went over to young Lavrans's bed and took down their grandfather's great sword, which the boy always insisted on keeping on the wall above his bed. He drew the blade from its scabbard and looked at it.

"You must lend me your sword, kinsman. I think our grandfather would be pleased if we took it along on this venture."

Kristin wrung her hands as she sat there. She felt as if she would scream—with terror and the utmost dread, but also with a power that was stronger than either her torment or her fear. The way she had screamed when she gave birth to these men. Wound after countless wound she had endured in this life, but now she knew that they all had healed; the scars were as tender as raw flesh, but she knew that she would not bleed to death. Never had she felt more alive than she did now.

Blossoms and leaves had been stripped away from her, but she had not been cut down, nor had she fallen. For the first time since she had given birth to the children of Erlend Nikulaussøn, she completely forgot about the father and saw only her sons.

But the sons did not look at their mother, who sat there, pale, with strained and frightened eyes. Munan was still on her lap; he hadn't let go of her even for a moment. The five boys left the loft.

Kristin stood up and stepped out onto the gallery. They emerged from behind the buildings and walked swiftly along the path toward Romundgaard between the pale, swaying acres of barley. Their steel caps and iron hats gleamed dully, but the sun glittered on Naakkve's lance and on the spearpoints of the twins. She stood staring after the five young men. She was mother to them all.

Back inside she collapsed before the chest over which the picture of Mary hung. Sobs tore her apart. Munan began to cry too, and weeping, he crept close to his mother. Lavrans leaped out of bed and threw himself to his knees on the other side of her. She put her arms around both her youngest sons.

Ever since the infant had died, she had wondered why she should pray. Hard, cold, and heavy as stone, she had felt as if she were falling into the gaping maw of Hell. Now the prayers burst from her lips of their own volition; without any conscious will, her soul streamed toward Mary, maiden and mother, the Queen of Heaven and earth, with cries of anguish and gratitude and praise. Mary, Mary, I have so much—I still have endless treasures that can be plundered from me. Merciful Mother, take them into your protection!

There were many people in the courtyard of Romundgaard. When the sons of Erlend arrived, several farmers asked them what they wanted.

"We want nothing from you . . . yet," said Naakkve, smiling slyly. "We have business with the bishop today, Magnus. Later my brothers and I may decide that we want to have a few words with the rest of you too. But today you have no need to fear us."

There was a great deal of shouting and commotion. Sira Solmund came out and tried to forbid the boys to stay, but then several farmers took up their cause and said they should be allowed to make inquiries about this charge against their mother. The bishop's men came out and told the sons of Erlend they would have to leave because food was being served and no one had time to listen to them. But the farmers were not pleased by this.

"What is it, good folks?" thundered a voice overhead. No one had noticed that Lord Halvard himself had come out onto the loft gallery. Now he was standing there in his violet robes, with the red silk cap on his white hair, tall and stout and looking like a chieftain. "Who are these young men?"

He was told that they were Kristin's sons from Jørundgaard.

"Are you the oldest?" the bishop asked Naakkve. "Then I will talk to you. But the others must wait here in the courtyard in the meantime."

Naakkve climbed the steps to the high loft and followed the bishop into the room. Lord Halvard sat down in the high seat and looked at the young man standing before him, leaning on his lance.

"What is your name?"

"Nikulaus Erlendssøn, my Lord."

"Do you think you need to be so well armed, Nikulaus Erlendssøn, in order to speak to your bishop?" asked the other man with a little smile.

Nikulaus blushed bright red. He went over to the corner, put down his weapons and cape, and came back. He stood before the bishop, bareheaded, his face lowered, with one hand clasping the wrist of the other, his bearing easy and free, but seemly and respectful.

Lord Halvard thought that this young man had been taught courtly and noble manners. And he couldn't have been a child when his father lost his riches and honorable position; he must certainly remember the time when he was considered the heir of Husaby. He was a handsome lad as well; the bishop felt great compassion for him.

"Were those your brothers, all those young men who were with you? How many of you are there, you sons of Erlend?"

"There are seven of us still living, my Lord."

"So many young lives involved in this." The bishop gave an involuntary sigh. "Sit down, Nikulaus. I suppose you want to talk to me about these rumors that have come forth about your mother and her overseer?"

"Thank you, Your Grace, but I would prefer to stand."

The bishop looked thoughtfully at the youth. Then he said slowly, "I must tell you, Nikulaus, that I find it difficult to believe that what has been said about Kristin Lavransdatter is true. And no one other than her husband has the right to accuse her of adultery. But then there is the matter of the kinship between your father and this man Ulf and the fact that he is your godfather. Jardtrud has presented her complaint in such a manner that there is much to indicate a lack of honor on your mother's part. Do you know whether it's true what she says: that the man often struck her and that he has shunned her bed for almost a year?"

"Ulf and Jardtrud did not live well together; our foster father was no longer young when he married, and he can be rather stubborn and hot-tempered. Toward myself and my brothers, and toward our father and mother, he has always been the most loyal kinsman and friend. That is the first request I intended to make of you, kind sir: If it is at all possible, that you would release Ulf as a free man against payment of a guarantee."

"You are not yet of lawful age?" asked the bishop.

"No, my Lord. But our mother is willing to pay whatever guarantee you might demand."

The bishop shook his head.

"But my father will do the same, I'm certain of that. It's my intention to ride straight from here to see him, to tell him what has happened. If you would grant him an audience tomorrow . . ."

The bishop rested his chin on his hand and sat there stroking his beard with his thumb, making a faint scraping sound.

"Sit down, Nikulaus," he said, "and we'll be able to talk better." Naakkve bowed politely and sat down. "So then it's true that Ulf has refused to live with his wife?" he continued as if he just happened to remember it.

"Yes, my Lord. As far as I know . . ."

The bishop couldn't help smiling, and then the young man smiled a little too.

"Ulf has been sleeping in the loft with all of us brothers since Christmas."

The bishop sat in silence for a moment. "What about food? Where does he eat?"

"He had his wife pack provisions for him whenever he went into the woods or left the estate." Naakkve's expression grew a little uncertain. "There were some quarrels about that. Mother thought it best for him to take his meals with us, as he did before he was married. Ulf didn't want to do that because he said people would talk if he changed the terms of the agreement which he and Father made when he set up his own household, about the goods that he would be given from the estate. And he didn't think it was right for Mother to provide food for him again without some deductions in what he had been granted. But it was arranged as Mother wanted, and Ulf began taking his meals with us again. The other part was to be figured out later."

"Hmm . . . Otherwise your mother has a reputation for keeping a close eye on her property, and she is an exceedingly enterprising and frugal woman."

"Not with food," said Naakkve eagerly. "Anyone will tell you that—any man or woman who has ever served on our estate. Mother is the most generous of women when it comes to food. In that regard she's no different now from when we were rich. She's never happier than when she can set some special dish on the table, and she makes such an abundance that every servant, right down to the goatherd and the beggar, receives his share of the good food."

"Hmm . . ." The bishop sat lost in thought. "You mentioned that you wanted to seek out your father?"

"Yes, my Lord. Surely that must be the reasonable thing to do?" When the bishop didn't reply, he continued. "We spoke to Father this winter, my brother Gaute and I. We also told him that Mother was with child. But we saw no sign, nor did we hear a single word from his lips, that might indicate he had doubts that Mother had not been as faithful as gold to him or that he was surprised. But Father has never felt at ease in Sil; he wanted to live on his own farm in Dovre, and Mother was up there for a while this summer. He was angry because she refused to stay and keep house for him. He wanted her to let Gaute and me manage Jørundgaard while she moved to Haugen."

Bishop Halvard kept rubbing his beard as he studied the young man.

No matter what sort of man Erlend Nikulaussøn might be, surely he wouldn't have been contemptible enough to accuse his wife of adultery before their young sons.

In spite of everything that seemed to speak against Kristin Lavransdatter, he just didn't believe it. He thought she was telling the truth when she denied knowledge of the suspicions about her and Ulf Haldorssøn. And yet he remembered that this woman had been weak before, when desires of the flesh had beckoned; with loathsome deceit she and this man with whom she now lived in discord had managed to win Lavrans's consent.

When the talk turned to the death of the child, he saw at once that her conscience troubled her. But even if she had neglected her child, she could not be brought before a court of law for that reason. She would have to repent before God, in accordance with the strictures of her confessor. And the child might still be her husband's even if she had cared for it poorly. She couldn't possibly be glad to be burdened with another infant, now that she was no longer young and had been abandoned by her husband, with seven sons already, and in much more meager circumstances than was their birthright. It would be unreasonable to expect that she could have had much love for that child.

He didn't think she was an unfaithful wife, although only God knew what he had heard and experienced in the forty years he had been a priest and listened to confessions. But he believed her.

And yet there was only one way in which he could interpret Erlend Nikulaussøn's behavior in this matter. He had refused to seek out his wife while she was with child, or after the birth, or when the infant died. He must have thought that he was not the father.

What now remained to find out was how the man would act. Whether he would stand up and defend his wife all the same, for the sake of his seven sons, as an honorable man would do. Or whether, now that these rumors were being openly discussed, he would bring charges against her. Based on what the bishop had heard about Erlend of Husaby, he wasn't sure he could count on the man not to do this.

"Who are your mother's closest kinsmen?" he asked.

"Jammælt Halvardssøn of Ælin is married to her sister, the widow of Simon Darre of Formo. She also has two cousins: Ketil Aasmundssøn of Skog and his sister, Ragna, who is married to Sigurd Kyrning. Ivar Gjesling of Ringheim and his brother, Haavard Trondssøn, are the sons of her mother's brother. But all of them live far away."

"What about Sir Sigurd Eldjarn of Sundbu? He and your mother are cousins. In a case like this the knight must step forward to defend his kinswoman, Nikulaus! You must seek him out this very day and tell him about this, my friend!"

Naakkve replied reluctantly, "Honorable Lord, there has been little kinship between him and us. And I don't think, my Lord, that it would benefit Mother's case if this man came to her defense. Erlend Eldjarn's lineage is not well liked here in the villages. Nothing harmed my father more in the eyes of the people than the fact that the Gjeslings had joined him in the plot that cost us Husaby, while they lost Sundbu."

"Yes, Erlend Eldjarn . . ." The bishop laughed a little. "Yes, he had a talent for disagreeing with people; he quarreled with all his kinsmen up here in the north. Your maternal grandfather, who was a pious man and not afraid to give in if it meant strengthening the peace and harmony among kin—even he couldn't manage any better. He and Erlend Eldjarn were the bitterest of foes."

"Yes." Naakkve couldn't help chuckling. "And it wasn't over anything important either: two embroidered sheets and a blue-hemmed towel. Altogether they weren't worth more than two marks. But my grandmother had impressed upon her husband that he must make sure to acquire these things when her father's estate was settled, and Gudrun Ivarsdatter had also spoken of them to her own husband. Erlend Eldjarn finally seized them and hid them away in his traveling bag, but Lavrans took them out again. He felt he had the most right to these things, for it was Ragnfrid who had made them as a young maiden, while she was living at home at Sundbu. When Erlend became aware of this, he struck my grandfather in the face, and then Grandfather threw him to the floor three times and shook him like a pelt. After that they never spoke again, and it was all because of those scraps of fabric; Mother has them at home in her chest."

The bishop laughed heartily. He knew this story well, which had amused everyone greatly when it occurred: that the husbands of the daughters of Ivar should be so eager to please their wives. But he had achieved what he intended: The features of the young man's face had thawed into a smile, and the wary, anguished expression had been driven from his handsome blue-gray eyes for a moment. Then Lord Halvard laughed even louder.

"Oh yes, Nikulaus, they did speak to each other one more time, and I was present. It was in Oslo, at the Christmas banquet, the year before Queen Eufemia died. My blessed Lord King Haakon was talking to Lavrans; he had come south to bring his greetings to his lord and to pledge his loyal service. The king told him that this enmity between the husbands of two sisters was unchristian and the behavior of petty men. Lavrans went over to where Erlend Eldjarn was standing with several other royal retainers and asked him in a friendly manner to forgive him for losing his temper; he said he would send the things to Fru Gudrun with loving greetings from her brother and sister. Erlend replied that he would agree to reconcile if Lavrans would accept the blame before the men standing there and admit that he had acted like a thief and a robber with regard to the inheritance of their father-in-law. Lavrans turned on his heel and walked away—and *that*, I believe, was the last time Ivar Gjesling's sons-in-law ever met on this earth," concluded the bishop, laughing loudly.

"But listen to me, Nikulaus Erlendssøn," he said, placing the palms of his hands together. "I don't know whether it would be wise to make such haste to bring your father here or to set this Ulf Haldorssøn free. It seems to me that your mother *must* clear her name since there has been so much talk that she has sinned. But as matters now stand, do you think it would be easy for Kristin to find the women willing to swear the oath along with her?"

Nikulaus looked up at the bishop; his eyes grew uncertain and fearful.

"But wait a few days, Nikulaus! Your father and Ulf are strangers in the region and not well liked. Kristin and Jardtrud both are from here in the valley, but Jardtrud is from much farther south, while your mother is one of their own. And I've noticed that Lavrans Bjørgulfsøn has not been forgotten by the people. It looks as if they mostly had intended to chastise her because she seemed to them a bad daughter. And yet already I can see that many realize the father would be poorly served by raising such an outcry against his child. They are remorseful and repentant, and soon there will be nothing they wish for more than that Kristin should be able to clear her name. And perhaps Jardtrud will have scant evidence to present when she has a look inside her bag. But it's another matter if her husband goes around turning people against him."

"My Lord," said Naakkve, looking up at the bishop, "forgive me for saying this, but I find this difficult to accept. That we should do nothing for our foster father and that we should not bring our father to stand at Mother's side."

"Nevertheless, my son," said Bishop Halvard, "I beg you to take my advice. Let us not hasten to summon Erlend Nikulaussøn here. But I will write a letter to Sir Sigurd of Sundbu, asking him to come see me at once. What's that?" He stood up and went out on the gallery.

Against the wall of the building stood Gaute and Bjørgulf Erlendssøn, and several of the bishop's men were threatening them with weapons. Bjørgulf struck a man to the ground with a blow of his axe as the bishop and Naakkve came outside. Gaute defended himself with his sword. Some farmers seized hold of Ivar and Skule, while others led away the wounded man. Sira Solmund stood off to the side, bleeding from his mouth and nose.

"Halt!" shouted Lord Halvard. "Throw down your weapons,

you sons of Erlend." He went down to the courtyard and approached the young men, who obeyed at once. "What is the meaning of this?"

Sira Solmund stepped forward, bowed, and said, "I can tell you, Reverend Father, that Gaute Erlendssøn has broken the peace of the Sabbath and struck me, his parish priest, as you can see!"

Then a middle-aged farmer stepped forward, greeted the bishop, and said, "Reverend Father, the boy was sorely provoked. This priest spoke of his mother in such a way that it would be difficult to expect Gaute to listen peaceably."

"Keep silent, priest. I cannot listen to more than one of you at a time," said Lord Halvard impatiently. "Speak, Olav Trondssøn."

Olav Trondssøn said, "The priest tried to rankle the sons of Erlend, but Bjørgulf and Gaute countered his words, calmly enough. Gaute also said what we all know is true: that Kristin was with her husband at Dovre for a time this past summer, and that's when he was conceived, the poor infant who has stirred up all this trouble. But then the priest said the people of Jørundgaard have always had so much book learning—no doubt she knew the story of King David and Bathsheba—but Erlend Nikulaussøn might have been just as cunning as Uriah the knight."[2]

The bishop's face turned as purple as his robes; his black eyes flashed. He looked at Sira Solmund for a moment, but he did not speak to him.

"Surely you must know, Gaute Erlendssøn, that with this deed you have brought the ban of the Church upon your head," he said. Then he ordered the sons of Erlend to be escorted home to Jørundgaard; he sent along two of his men and four farmers, whom the bishop selected from among the most honorable and sensible, to keep guard over them.

"You must go with them as well, Nikulaus," he told Naakkve. "But stay calm. Your brothers have not helped your mother, but I realize they were sorely vexed."

In his heart the bishop of Hamar didn't think that Kristin's sons had harmed her case. He saw that there were already many who held a different opinion of the mistress of Jørundgaard than they had in the morning, when she caused the goblet to overflow by coming to church with Ulf Haldorssøn so that he might be godfather to her son. One of them was Kolbein Jonssøn, so Lord Halvard put him in charge of the guards.

Naakkve was the first to enter the high loft where Kristin was sitting on the bed with Lavrans, holding Munan on her lap. He told her what had happened but put great weight on the fact that the bishop considered her innocent and also thought the younger brothers had been greatly provoked to react as violently as they had. He counseled his mother not to seek out the bishop herself.

Then the four brothers were escorted into the room. Their mother stared at them; she was pale, with an odd look in her eye. In the midst of her deep despair and anguish, she felt again the strange swelling of her heart, as if it might burst. And yet she said calmly to Gaute, "Ill advised was your behavior, son, and you brought little honor to the sword of Lavrans Bjørgulfsøn by drawing it against a crowd of farmers who stood there gnawing on rumors."

"First I drew it against the bishop's armed men," said Gaute indignantly. "But it's true it did little honor to our grandfather that we had to bear arms against anyone for such a reason."

Kristin looked at her son. Then she had to turn away. As much as his words pained her, she had to smile too—like when a child bites his mother's nipple with his first teeth, she thought.

"Mother," said Naakkve, "now I think it best if you go, and take Munan with you. You mustn't leave him alone even for a moment until he is calmer," he said quietly. "Keep him indoors so he doesn't see that his brothers are under guard."

Kristin stood up. "My sons, if you don't think me undeserving, then I would ask that you kiss me before I leave."

Naakkve, Bjørgulf, Ivar, and Skule went over and kissed her. The one who had been banned gave his mother a sorrowful look; when she held out her hand to him, he took a fold of her sleeve and kissed it. Kristin saw that all of them, except for Gaute, were now taller than she was. She straightened up Lavrans's bed a bit, and then she left with Munan.

There were four buildings with lofts at Jørundgaard: the high loft house, the new storeroom—which had been the summer quarters during Kristin's childhood, before Lavrans built the large house—the old storeroom, and the salt shed, which also had a loft. That's where the servingwomen slept in the summer.

Kristin went up to the loft above the new storeroom with Munan. The two of them had slept there ever since the death of the infant. She was pacing back and forth when Frida and Gunhild brought the evening porridge. Kristin asked Frida to see to it that the guardsmen were given ale and food. The maid replied that she had already done so—at Naakkve's bidding—but the men had said they would not accept anything from Kristin since they were at her manor for such a purpose. They had received food and drink from somewhere else.

"Even so, you must have a keg of foreign ale brought to them."

Gunhild, the younger maid, was red-eyed from weeping. "None of the house servants believes this of you, Kristin Lavransdatter; surely you must know that. We always said that we knew it was a lie."

"So you have heard this gossip before?" said her mistress. "It would have been better if you had mentioned it to me."

"We didn't dare because of Ulf," said Frida.

And Gunhild said as she wept, "He warned us to keep it from you. I often thought that I should mention it and beg you to be more wary . . . when you would sit and talk to Ulf until late into the night."

"Ulf . . . so he has known about this?" asked Kristin softly.

"Jardtrud has accused him of it for a long time; that was apparently always the reason that he struck her. One evening during Christmas, about the time when you were growing heavy, we were sitting and drinking with them in the foreman's house. Solveig and Øivind were there too, along with several people from south in the parish. Suddenly Jardtrud said that he was the one who had caused it. Ulf hit her with his belt so the buckle drew blood. Since then Jardtrud has gone around saying that Ulf did not deny it with a single word."

"And ever since people have been talking about this in the countryside?" asked the mistress.

"Yes. But those of us who are your servants have always denied it," said Gunhild in tears.

To calm Munan, Kristin had to lie down next to the boy and take him in her arms, but she did not undress, and she did not sleep that night.

In the meantime, up in the high loft, young Lavrans had gotten out of bed and put on his clothes. Toward evening, when Naakkve went downstairs to help tend to the livestock, the boy went out to the stable. He saddled the red gelding that belonged to Gaute; it was the best horse except for the stallion, which he didn't trust himself to ride.

Several of the men standing guard on the estate came out and asked the boy where he was headed.

"I didn't know that I was a prisoner too," replied young Lavrans. "But I don't need to hide it from you. Surely you wouldn't refuse to allow me to ride to Sundbu to bring back the knight to defend his kinswoman."

"It will soon be dark, my boy," said Kolbein Jonssøn. "We can't let this child ride across Vaage Gorge at night. We must speak to his mother."

"No, don't do that," said Lavrans. His lips quivered. "The purpose of my journey is such that I will trust in God and the Virgin Mary to keep watch over me, if my mother is without blame. And if not, then it makes little difference—" He broke off, for he was close to tears.

The man stood in silence for a moment. Kolbein gazed at the handsome, fair-haired child. "Go on then, and may God be with you, Lavrans Erlendssøn," he said, and was about to help the boy into the saddle.

But Lavrans led the horse forward so the men had to step aside. At the big boulder near the manor gate, he climbed up and then flung himself onto the back of Raud. Then he galloped westward, along the road to Vaagaa.

LAVRANS HAD RIDDEN his horse into a lather by the time he reached the spot where he knew a path led up through the scree and steep cliffs that rise up everywhere on the north side of Silsaa valley. He knew he had to make it to the heights before dark. He didn't know these mountains between Vaagaa, Sil, and Dovre, but the gelding had grazed here one summer, and he had carried Gaute to Haugen many times, although along different paths. Young Lavrans leaned forward and patted the neck of his horse.

"You must find the way to Haugen, Raud, my son. You must carry me to Father tonight, my horse."

As soon as he reached the crest of the mountains and was once again sitting in the saddle, darkness fell quickly. He rode through a marshy hollow; an endless progression of narrow ridges was silhouetted against the ever-darkening sky. There were groves of birches on the valley slopes, and their trunks shone white. Wet clusters of leaves constantly brushed against the horse's chest and the boy's face. Stones were dislodged by the animal's hooves and rolled down into the creek at the bottom of the incline. Raud found his way in the dark, up and down the hillsides, and the trickling of the creek sounded first close and then far away. Once some beast bayed into the mountain night, but Lavrans couldn't tell what it was. And the wind rushed and sang, first stronger, then fainter.

The child held his spear along the neck of his horse, so that the tip pointed forward between the animal's ears. This was bear country, this valley here. He wondered when it would end. Very softly he began to hum into the darkness: *"Kyrie eleison, Christe eleison, Kyrie eleison, Christe eleison."*

Raud splashed through the shallow crossing of a mountain stream. The sky became even more star-strewn all around; the

mountain peaks looked more distant against the blackness of the
night, and the wind sang with a different tone in the vast space.
The boy let the horse choose his own path as he hummed as much
as he could remember of the hymn, "*Jesus Redemptor omnium—
Tu lumen et splendor patris*," interspersed with "*Kyrie eleison*."
Now he could see by the stars that they were riding almost due
south, but he didn't dare do anything but trust the horse and let
him lead. They were riding over rocky slopes with reindeer moss
gleaming palely on the stones beneath him. Raud paused for a moment, panting and peering into the night. Lavrans saw that the sky
was growing lighter in the east; clouds were billowing up, edged
with silver underneath. His horse moved on, now headed directly
toward the rising moon. It must be about an hour before midnight,
as far as the boy could tell.

When the moon slipped free of the crests off in the distance,
new snow gleamed atop the domes and rounded summits, and
drifting wisps of fog turned the passes and peaks white. Lavrans
recognized where he was in the mountains. He was on the mossy
plateau beneath the Blue Domes.

Soon afterward he found a path leading down into the valley.
And three hours later Raud limped into the courtyard of Haugen,
which was white with moonlight.

When Erland opened the door, the boy collapsed on the floor of
the gallery in a deep faint.

Some time later Lavrans woke up in bed, lying between filthy,
rank-smelling fur covers. Light shone from a pine torch that had
been stuck in a crack in the wall nearby. His father was standing
over him, moistening his face with something. His father was only
half dressed, and the boy noticed in the flickering light that his hair
was completely gray.

"Mother . . ." said young Lavrans, looking up.

Erlend turned away so his son wouldn't see his face. "Yes,"
he said after a moment, almost inaudibly. "Is your mother—has
she . . . is your mother . . . ill?"

"You must come home at once, Father, and save her. Now
they're accusing her of the worst of things. They've taken Ulf and
her and my brothers captive, Father!"

Erlend touched the boy's hot face and hands; his fever had
flared up again. "What are you saying?" But Lavrans sat up and

gave a fairly coherent account of everything that had taken place back home the day before. His father listened in silence, but halfway through the boy's story he began to finish getting dressed. He pulled on his boots and fastened his spurs. Then he went to get some milk and food and brought them over to the child.

"But you can't stay here alone in this house, my son. I will take you over to Aslaug, north of here in Brekken, before I ride home."

"Father." Lavrans grabbed his arm. "No, I want to go home with you."

"You're ill, little son," said Erlend, and the boy couldn't recall ever hearing such a tender tone in his father's voice.

"No, Father . . . I want to go home with you—to Mother. I want to go home to my mother. . . ." Now he was weeping like a small child.

"But Raud is limping, my boy." Erlend took his son on his lap, but he could not console the child. "And you're so tired. . . ." Finally he said, "Well, well . . . Soten can surely carry both of us."

After he had led out the stallion, put Raud inside, and tended to the animal, he said, "You must make sure to remember that someone comes north to take care of your horse . . . and my things."

"Are you going to stay home now, Father?" asked Lavrans joyfully.

Erlend gazed straight ahead. "I don't know. But I have a feeling I won't be back here again."

"Shouldn't you be better armed, Father?" the boy asked, for aside from his sword Erlend had picked up only a small, lightweight axe and was now about to leave the house. "Aren't you even going to take your shield?"

Erlend looked at his shield. The oxhide was so scratched and torn that the red lion against the white field had almost disappeared. He put it back down and spread the covers over it again.

"I'm armed well enough to drive a horde of farmers from my manor," he said. He went outside, closed the door to the house, mounted his horse, and helped the boy climb up behind him.

The sky was growing more and more overcast. By the time they had come partway down the slope, where the forest was quite dense, they were riding in darkness. Erlend noticed that his son was so tired that he could hardly hold on. Then he let Lavrans sit in front of him, and he held the boy in his arms. The young, fair-haired head rested against his chest; of all the children, Lavrans was most like his mother. Erlend kissed the top of his head as he straightened the hood on the boy's cape.

"Did your mother grieve greatly when the infant died this summer?" he asked once, quite softly.

Young Lavrans replied, "She didn't cry after he died. But she has gone up to the cemetery gate every night since. Gaute and Naakkve usually follow her when she leaves, but they haven't dared speak to her, and they don't dare let Mother see that they've been keeping watch over her."

A little later Erlend said, "She didn't cry? I remember back when your mother was young, and she wept as readily as the dew drips from goat willow reeds along the creek. She was so gentle and tender, Kristin, whenever she was with people whom she knew wished her well. Later on she had to learn to be harder, and most often I was the one to blame."

"Gunhild and Frida say that in all the days our youngest brother lived," continued Lavrans, "she cried every minute when she thought no one would see her."

"May God help me," said Erlend in a low voice. "I've been a foolish man."

They rode through the valley floor, with the curve of the river at their backs. Erlend wrapped his cape around the boy as best he could. Lavrans dozed and kept threatening to fall asleep. He sensed that his father's body smelled like that of a poor man. He had a vague memory from his early childhood, while they were living at Husaby, when his father would come from the bathhouse on Saturdays and he would have several little balls in his hands. They smelled so good, and the delicate, sweet scent would cling to his palms and to his clothing during the whole Sabbath.

Erlend rode steadily and briskly. Down on the moors it was pitch-dark. Without thinking about it, he knew at every moment where he was; he recognized the changing sound of the river's clamor, as the Laag rushed through rapids and plunged over falls. Their path took them across flat stretches, where the sparks flew from the horse's hooves. Soten ran with confidence and ease among the writhing roots of pine trees, where the road passed through thick forest; there was a soft gurgling and rushing sound as he raced across small green plains where a meandering rivulet from the mountains streamed across. By daybreak he would be home, and that would be a fitting hour.

The whole time Erlend was doubtless thinking about that moon-blue wintry night long ago when he drove a sleigh down through this very valley. Bjørn Gunnarssøn sat in back, holding a dead woman in his arms. But the memory was pale and distant, just as everything the child had told him seemed distant and unreal: all that had happened down in the village and those mad rumors about Kristin. Somehow his mind refused to grasp it. After he arrived, there would surely be time enough to think about what he should do. Nothing seemed real except the feeling of strain and fear—now that he would soon see Kristin.

He had waited and waited for her. He had never doubted that one day she would come to him—up until he heard what name she had given the child.

Stepping out of the church into the gray light were those people who had been to early mass to hear one of the priests from Hamar preach. The ones who emerged first saw Erlend Nikulaussøn ride past toward home, and they told the others. Some uneasiness and a great deal of talk arose; people headed down the slope and stood in groups at the place where the lane to Jørundgaard diverged from the main road.

Erlend rode into the courtyard as the waning moon sank behind the rim of clouds and the mountain ridge, pale in the dawn light.

Outside the foreman's house stood a group of people: Jardtrud's kinsmen and her friends who had stayed with her overnight. At the sound of horse hooves in the courtyard the men who had been keeping guard in the room under the high loft came outside.

Erlend reined in his horse. He gazed down at the farmers and said in a loud, mocking voice, "Is there a feast being held on my estate and I know nothing about it? Or why are you good folks gathered here at this early hour?"

Angry, dark looks met him from all sides. Erlend sat tall and slender astride the long-legged foreign stallion. Before, Soten's mane had been clipped short, but now it was thick and uncut. The horse was ungroomed and had gray hairs on his head, but his eyes glittered dangerously, and he stomped and shifted uneasily, laying his ears back and tossing his small, elegant head so that flecks of lather sprinkled his neck and shoulders and the rider. The harness-work had once been red and the saddle inlaid with gold; now they were worn and broken and mended. And the man was dressed almost like a beggar. His hair, which billowed from under a simple black woolen hat, was grayish white; a gray stubble grew on his pale, furrowed face with the big nose. But he sat erect, and he was smiling arrogantly down at the crowd of farmers. He looked young, in spite of everything, and like a chieftain. Fierce hatred surged toward this outsider, who sat there, holding his head high and uncowed—after all the grief and shame and misery he had brought upon those whom these people considered their own chieftains.

And yet the farmer who was the first to answer Erlend spoke with restraint. "I see you have found your son, Erlend, so I think you must know that we have not gathered here for any feast. And it seems strange you would jest about such a matter."

Erlend looked down at the child, who was still asleep. His voice grew more gentle.

"The boy is ill; surely you must see that. The news he brought me from here in the parish seemed so unbelievable that I thought he must be speaking in a feverish daze.

"And some of it is nonsense, after all, I see." Erlend frowned as he glanced at the stable door. Ulf Haldorssøn and two other men—one of them his brother-in-law—were at that moment leading out several horses.

Ulf let go of his horse and strode swiftly toward his master.

"Have you finally come, Erlend? And there's the boy—praise be to Christ and the Virgin Mary! His mother doesn't know he was missing. We were about to go out to look for him. The bishop released me on my sworn oath when he heard the child had set off alone for Vaagaa. How is Lavrans?" he asked anxiously.

"Thank God you've found the boy," said Jardtrud, weeping. She had come out into the courtyard.

"Are you here, Jardtrud?" said Erlend. "That will be the first thing I see to: that you leave my estate, you and your cohorts. First we'll drive off this gossiping woman, and then anyone else who has spread lies about my wife will be fined."

"That cannot be done, Erlend," said Ulf Haldorssøn. "Jardtrud is my lawful wife. I don't think either she or I has any desire to stay together, but she will not leave my house until I have placed in the hands of my brothers-in-law her livestock, dowry, betrothal gifts, and wedding gifts."

"Am I not the master of this estate?" asked Erlend, furious.

"You will have to ask Kristin Lavransdatter about that," said Ulf. "Here she comes."

The mistress was standing on the gallery of the new storeroom. Now she slowly came down the stairs. Without thinking, she pulled her wimple forward—it had slipped back off her head—and she smoothed her church gown, which she had worn since the day before. But her face was as motionless as stone.

Erlend rode forward to meet her, at a walking pace. Bending down a bit, he stared with fearful confusion at his wife's gray, dead face.

"Kristin," he implored. "My Kristin. I've come home to you."

She didn't seem to hear or see him. Then Lavrans, who was sitting in his father's arms and had gradually woken up, slid down to the ground. The moment his feet touched the grass, the boy collapsed and he lay in a heap.

A tremor passed over his mother's face. She leaned down and lifted the big boy in her arms, pressing his head against her throat, as if he were a little child. But his long legs hung down limply in front of her.

"Kristin, my dearest love," begged Erlend in despair. "Oh, Kristin, I know I've come to you much too late . . ."

Again a tremor passed over his wife's face.

"It's not too late," she said, her voice low and harsh. She stared down at her son, who lay in a swoon in her arms. "Our last child is already in the ground, and now it's Lavrans's turn. Gaute has been banished by the Church, and our other sons . . . But the two of us still own much that can be ruined, Erlend!"

She turned away from him and began walking across the courtyard with the child. Erlend rode after her, keeping his horse at her side.

"Kristin—Jesus, what can I do for you? Kristin, don't you want me to stay with you now?"

"I don't need you to do anything more for me," said his wife in the same tone of voice. "You cannot help me, whether you stay here or you throw yourself into the Laag."

Erlend's sons had come out onto the gallery of the high loft. Now Gaute ran down and raced toward his mother, trying to stop her.

"Mother," he begged. Then she gave him a look, and he halted in bewilderment.

Several farmers were standing at the bottom of the loft stairs.

"Move aside, men," said the mistress, trying to pass them with her burden.

Soten tossed his head and danced uneasily; Erlend turned the horse halfway around, and Kolbein Jonssøn grabbed the bridle. Kristin hadn't seen what was happening; now she turned to look over her shoulder.

"Let go of the horse, Kolbein. If he wants to ride off, then let him."

Kolbein took a firmer grip and replied, "Don't you see, Kristin, that it's time for the master to stay home on his estate? You at least should realize it," he said to Erlend.

But Erlend struck the man over the hand and urged the stallion forward, so the old man fell. A couple of other men leaped forward.

Erlend shouted, "Get away from here! You have nothing to do with matters concerning me or my wife—and I'm not the master. I refuse to bind myself to a manor like a calf to the stall. I may not own this estate, but neither does this estate own me!"

Kristin turned to face her husband and screamed, "Go ahead and ride off! Ride, ride like the Devil to Hell. That's where you've driven me and cast off everything you've ever owned or been given—"

What occurred next happened so fast that no one properly foresaw it or could prevent it. Tore Borghildssøn and another man grabbed her by the arms. "Kristin, you mustn't speak that way to your husband."

Erlend rode up close to them.

"Do you dare to lay hands on my wife?" He swung his axe and struck at Tore Borghildssøn. The blow fell between his shoulder blades, and the man sank to the ground. Erlend lifted his axe again, but as he raised up in the stirrups, a man ran a spear through him, and it pierced his groin. It was the son of Tore Borghildssøn who did this.

Soten reared up and kicked with his front hooves. Erlend pressed his knees against the animal's sides and leaned forward as he pulled on the reins with his left hand and again raised his axe. But almost at once he lost one of his stirrups, and the blood gushed down over his left thigh. Several arrows and spears whistled across the courtyard. Ulf and Erlend's sons rushed into the throng with axes raised and swords drawn. Then a man stabbed the stallion Erlend was riding, and the animal fell to his knees, whinnying so wildly and shrilly that the horses in the stable replied.

Erlend stood up, his legs straddling the animal. He put his hand on Bjørgulf's shoulder and stepped off. Gaute came up and grabbed his father under the other arm.

"Kill him," he said, meaning the horse, which had now rolled onto his side and lay with his neck stretched out, blood frothing around his jaw, and his mighty hooves flailing. Ulf Haldorssøn complied.

The farmers had retreated. Two men carried Tore Borghildssøn over to the foreman's house, and one of the bishop's men led away his companion, who was wounded.

Kristin had put Lavrans down, since he had now regained his wits; they stood there, clinging to each other. She didn't seem to understand what had taken place; it had all happened so fast.

Her sons began helping their father toward the high loft house, but Erlend said, "I don't want to go in there. I don't want to die where Lavrans died."

Kristin ran forward and threw her arms around her husband's neck. Her frozen face shattered, contorted with sobs, the way ice is splintered when struck by a stone. "Erlend, Erlend!"

Erlend bent his head down so his cheek touched hers, and he stood in that manner for a moment.

"Help me up into the old storeroom, boys," he said. "I want to lie down there."

Hastily Kristin and her sons made up the bed in the old loft and helped Erlend undress. Kristin bandaged his wounds. The blood was gushing in spurts from the gash of the spear in his groin, and he had an arrow wound on the lower left side of his chest, but it was not bleeding much.

Erlend stroked his wife's head. "I'm afraid you won't be able to heal me, my Kristin."

She looked up, despairing. A great shudder passed through her body. She remembered that Simon had said the same thing, and this seemed to her the worst omen, that Erlend should speak the same words.

He lay in bed, supported with pillows and cushions, and with his left leg raised to stop the blood flowing from his groin wound. Kristin sat leaning over him. Then he took her hand. "Do you remember the first night we slept together in this bed, my sweet? I didn't know then that you were already carrying a secret sorrow for which I was to blame. And that was not the first sorrow you had to bear for my sake, Kristin."

She held his hand in both of hers. His skin was cracked, with dirt ingrained around his small, grooved fingernails and in the creases of every joint of his long fingers. Kristin lifted his hand to her breast and then to her lips; her tears streamed over it.

"Your lips are so hot," said Erlend softly. "I waited and waited for you . . . I longed so terribly . . . Finally I thought I should give in; I should come down here to you, but then I heard . . . I thought, when I heard that he had died, that now it would be too late for me to come to you."

Sobbing, Kristin replied, "I was still waiting for you, Erlend. I thought that someday you would have to come to the boy's grave."

"But then you would not have welcomed me as your friend," said Erlend. "And God knows you had no reason to do so either. As sweet and lovely as you are, my Kristin," he whispered, closing his eyes.

She sobbed quietly, in great distress.

"Now nothing remains," said her husband in the same tone as before, "except for us to try to forgive each other as a Christian husband and wife, if you can . . ."

"Erlend, Erlend . . ." She leaned over him and kissed his white face. "You shouldn't talk so much, my Erlend."

"I think I must make haste to say what I have to say," replied her husband. "Where is Naakkve?" he asked uneasily.

He was told that the night before, as soon as Naakkve heard that his younger brother was headed for Sundbu, he had set off after him as fast as his horse would go. He must be quite distraught by now, since he hadn't found the child. Erlend sighed, his hands fumbling restlessly on the coverlet.

His six sons stepped up to the bed.

"No, I haven't handled things well for you, my sons," said their father. He began to cough, in a strange and cautious manner. Bloody froth seeped out of his lips. Kristin wiped it away with her wimple.

Erlend lay quietly for a moment. "Now you must forgive me, if you can. Never forget, my fine boys, that your mother has striven on your behalf every day, during all the years that she and I have lived together. Never has there been any enmity between us except that for which I was to blame because I paid too little mind to your well-being. But she has loved you more than her own life."

"We won't forget," replied Gaute, weeping, "that you, Father, seemed to us all our days the most courageous of men and the noblest of chieftains. We were proud to be called your sons—no less so when fortune forsook you than during your days of prosperity."

"You say this because you understand so little," said Erlend. He gave a brittle, sputtering laugh. "But do not cause your mother the sorrow of taking after me; she has had enough to struggle with since she married me."

"Erlend, Erlend," sobbed Kristin.

The sons kissed their father's hand and cheek; weeping, they turned away and sat down against the wall. Gaute put his arm around Munan's shoulder and pulled the boy close; the twins sat hand in hand. Erlend again placed his hand in Kristin's. His was cold. Then she pulled the covers all the way up to his chin but sat holding his hand in her own under the blankets.

"Erlend," she said, weeping. "May God have mercy on us—we must send word to the priest for you."

"Yes," said Erlend faintly. "Someone must ride up to Dovre to bring Sira Guttorm, my parish priest."

"Erlend, he won't get here in time," she said in horror.

"Yes, he will," said Erlend vehemently. "If God will grant me . . .

For I refuse to receive the last rites from that priest who has been spreading gossip about you."

"Erlend—in the name of Jesus—you must not talk that way."

Ulf Haldorssøn stepped forward and bent over the dying man. "I will ride to Dovre, Erlend."

"Do you remember, Ulf," said Erlend, his voice beginning to sound weak and confused, "the time we left Hestnes, you and I?" He laughed a bit. "And I promised that all my days I would stand by you as your loyal kinsman . . . God save me, kinsman . . . Of the two of us, it was most often you and not I who showed the loyalty of kin, my friend Ulf. I give you . . . thanks . . . for that, kinsman."

Ulf leaned down and kissed the man's bloody lips. "I thank you too, Erlend Nikulaussøn."

He lit a candle, placed it near the deathbed, and left the room.

Erlend's eyes had closed again. Kristin sat staring at his white face; now and then she caressed it with her hand. She thought she could see that he was sinking toward death.

"Erlend," she implored him softly. "In the name of Jesus, let us send word to Sira Solmund for you. God is God, no matter what priest brings Him to us."

"No!" Her husband sat up in bed so that the covers slid down his naked, sallow body. The bandages across his breast and stomach were once again colored with bright red splotches from the fresh blood pouring out. "I am a sinful man. May God bestow on me the grace of His mercy, as much as He will grant me, but I know . . ." He fell back against the pillows and whispered almost inaudibly, "I will not live long enough to be . . . so old . . . and so pious . . . that I can bear . . . to sit calmly in the same room with someone who has told lies about you."

"Erlend, Erlend—think of your soul!"

The man shook his head on the pillows. His eyelids had fallen shut again.

"Erlend!" She clasped her hands; she screamed loudly, in the utmost distress. "Erlend, don't you understand that after the way you have acted toward me, this *has* to be said!"

Erlend opened his big eyes. His lips were pale blue, but a remnant of his youthful smile flickered across his ravaged face.

"Kiss me, Kristin," he whispered. There was a trace of laughter in his voice. "Surely there has been too much else between you and me—besides Christendom and marriage—for it to be possible for us to . . . take leave of each other . . . as a Christian husband and wife."

She called and called his name, but he lay with closed eyes, his face as pale as newly split wood beneath his gray hair. A little blood seeped from the corners of his mouth; she wiped it away, whispering entreaties. When she moved, she could feel her clothes were cold and sticky, wet with the blood that had spattered her when she helped him inside and put him to bed. Now and then a faint gurgling came from Erlend's chest, and he seemed to have trouble breathing; but he did not move again, nor was he aware of anything more as he surely and steadily sank into the torpor of death.

The loft door was abruptly thrown open. Naakkve came rushing in; he flung himself down beside the bed and seized his father's hand as he called his name.

Behind him came a tall, stout gentleman wearing a traveling cape. He bowed to Kristin.

"If I had known, my kinswoman, that you were in need of the help of your kin . . ." Then he broke off as he saw that the man was dying. He crossed himself and went over to the farthest corner of the room. Quietly the Sundbu knight began saying the prayer for the dying, but Kristin seemed not to have even noticed Sir Sigurd's arrival.

Naakkve was on his knees, bending over the bed. "Father! Father! Don't you know me anymore, Father?" He pressed his face against Erlend's hand, which Kristin was holding. The young man's tears and kisses showered the hands of both his parents.

Kristin pushed her son's head aside a little—as if she were suddenly half awake.

"You're disturbing us," she said impatiently. "Go away."

Naakkve straightened up as he knelt there. "Go? But, Mother . . ."

"Yes. Go sit down with your brothers over there."

Naakkve lifted his young face—wet with tears, contorted with grief—but his mother's eyes saw nothing. Then he went over to the bench where his six brothers were already sitting. Kristin paid no attention; she simply stared, with wild eyes, at Erlend's face, which now shone snow-white in the light of the candle.

A short time later the door was opened again. Bearing candles and ringing a silver bell, deacons and a priest followed Bishop Halvard into the loft. Ulf Haldorssøn entered last. Erlend's sons and Sir Sigurd stood up and then fell to their knees before the body of the Lord. But Kristin merely raised her head, and for a moment she turned her tear-filled eyes, seeing nothing, toward those who had arrived. Then she lay back down, the way she was before, stretched out across Erlend's corpse.

PART III

THE CROSS

CHAPTER 1

ALL FIRES BURN out sooner or later.

There came a time when these words spoken by Simon Darre resounded once more in Kristin's heart.

It was the summer of the fourth year after Erlend Nikulaussøn's death, and of the seven sons, only Gaute and Lavrans remained with their mother at Jørundgaard.

Two years before, the old smithy had burned down, and Gaute had built a new one north of the farm, up toward the main road. The old smithy had stood to the south of the buildings, down by the river in a low curve of land between Jørund's burial mound and several great heaps of rocks which had apparently been cleared from the fields long ago. Almost every year during the flood season the water would reach all the way up to the smithy.

Now there was nothing left on the site but the heavy, fire-scorched stones that showed where the threshold had been and the brick fireplace. Soft, slender blades of pale green grass were now sprouting from the dark, charred floor.

This year Kristin Lavransdatter had sown a field of flax near the site of the old smithy; Gaute had wanted to put grain in the acres closer to the manor, where the mistresses of Jørundgaard, since ancient times, had always planted flax and cultivated onions. And so Kristin often went out to the far fields to see to her flax. On Thursday evenings she would carry a gift of ale and food to the farmer in the mound.[1] On light summer evenings the lonely fireplace in the meadow looked at times like some ancient heathen altar as it was glimpsed through the grass, grayish white and streaked with soot. On hot summer days, under the baking sun, she would take her basket to the rock heaps at midday to pick raspberries or to gather the leaves of fireweed, which could be used to make cooling drinks for a fever.

283

The last notes of the church bells' noon greeting to the Mother of God died away in the light-sated air up among the peaks. The countryside seemed to be settling into sleep beneath the flood of white sunlight. Ever since the dew-soaked dawn, scythes had been ringing in the flowery meadows; the scrape of iron against whetstones and the shouting of voices could be heard from every farm, near and far. Now all the sounds of busy toiling fell away; it was time for the midday rest. Kristin sat down on a pile of stones and listened. Only the roar of the river could be heard now, and a slight rustling of the leaves in the grove, along with the faint rubbing and soft buzzing of flies over the meadow, and the clinking bell of a solitary cow somewhere off in the distance. A bird flapped its way, swift and mute, along the edge of the alder thicket; another flew up from a meadow tussock and with a harsh cry perched atop a thistle.

But the drifting blue shadows on the hillsides, the fair-weather clouds billowing up over the mountain ridges and melting into the blue summer sky, the glitter of the Laag's water beyond the trees, the white glint of sunlight on all the leaves—these things she noticed more as silent sounds, audible only to her inner ear, rather than as visible images. With her wimple pulled forward over her brow, Kristin sat and listened to the play of light and shadow across the valley.

All fires burn out sooner or later.

In the alder woods along the marshy riverbank, pockets of water sparkled in the darkness between the dense willow bushes. Star grass grew there, along with tufts of cotton grass and thick carpets of marshlocks with their dusty green, five-pointed leaves and reddish brown flowers. Kristin had picked an enormous pile of them. Many times she had pondered whether this herb might possess useful powers; she had dried it and boiled it and added it to ale and mead. But it didn't seem good for anything. And yet Kristin could never resist going out to the marsh and getting her shoes wet to gather the plant.

Now she stripped all the leaves from the stalks and plaited a wreath from the dark flowers. They had the color of both red wine and brown mead, and in the center, under the knot of red filaments, they were as moist as honey. Sometimes Kristin would plait a wreath for the picture of the Virgin Mary up in the high loft; she had heard from priests who had been to the southern lands that this was the custom there.

Otherwise she no longer had anyone to make wreaths for. Here in the valley the young men didn't wear wreaths on their heads when they went out to dance on the green. In some areas of Trøndelag the men who came home from the royal court had introduced the custom. Kristin thought this thick, dark red wreath would be well suited to Gaute's fair face and flaxen hair or Lavrans's nut-brown mane.

It was so long ago that she used to walk through the pasture above Husaby with the foster mothers and all her young sons on those long, fair-weather days in the summer. Then she and Frida couldn't make wreaths fast enough for all the impatient little children. She remembered when she still had Lavrans at her breast, but Ivar and Skule thought the infant should have a wreath too; the four-year-olds thought it should be made from very tiny flowers.

Now she had only grown-up children.

Young Lavrans was fifteen winters old; he couldn't yet be considered full-grown. But his mother had gradually realized that this son was in some ways more distant from her than all the other children. He didn't purposely shun her, as Bjørgulf had done, and he wasn't aloof, nor did he *seem* particularly taciturn, the way the blind boy was. But he was apparently much quieter by nature, although no one had noticed this when all the brothers were home. He was bright and lively, always seemed happy and kind, and everyone was fond of the charming child without thinking about the fact that Lavrans nearly always went about in silence and alone.

He was considered the handsomest of all the handsome sons of Kristin of Jørundgaard. Their mother always thought that the one she happened to be thinking about at the moment was the most handsome, but she too could see there was a radiance about Lavrans Erlendssøn. His light brown hair and apple-fresh cheeks seemed gilded, sated with sunshine; his big dark gray eyes seemed to be strewn with tiny yellow sparks. He looked much the way she had looked when she was young, with her fair coloring burnished tan by the sun. And he was tall and strong for his age, capable and diligent at any task he was given, obedient to his mother and older brothers, merry, good-natured, and companionable. And yet there was this odd sense of reserve about the boy.

During the winter evenings, when the servants gathered in the weaving room to pass the time with talk and banter as each person was occupied with some chore, Lavrans would sit there as if in a dream. Many a summer evening, when the daily work on the farm was done, Kristin would go out and sit with the boy as he lay on the green, chewing on a piece of resin or twirling a sprig of sorrel between his lips. She would look at his eyes as she spoke to him; he seemed to be shifting his attention back from far away. Then he would smile up at his mother's face and give her a proper and sensible reply. Often the two of them would sit together for hours on the hillside, talking comfortably and with ease. But as soon as she stood up to go inside, it seemed as if Lavrans would let his thoughts wander again.

She couldn't figure out what it was the boy was pondering so deeply. He was skilled enough in sports and the use of weapons, but he was much less zealous than her other sons had been about such things, and he never went out hunting alone, although he was pleased whenever Gaute asked him to go along on a hunt. And he never seemed to notice that women cast tender eyes on this fair young boy. He had no interest in book learning, and the youngest son paid little attention to all the older boys' talk of their plans to enter a monastery. Kristin couldn't see that the boy had given any thought to his future, other than that he would continue to stay there at home all his days and help Gaute with the farm work, as he did now.

Sometimes this strange, aloof creature reminded Kristin Lavransdatter a bit of his father. But Erlend's soft, languid manner had often given way to a boisterous wildness, and Lavrans had none of his father's quick, hot disposition. Erlend had never been far removed from what was going on around him.

Lavrans was now the youngest. Munan had long ago been laid to rest in the grave beside his father and little brother. He died early in the spring, the year after Erlend was killed.

After her husband's death the widow had behaved as if she neither heard nor saw a thing. Stronger than pain or sorrow was the feeling she had of a numbing chill and a dull lassitude in both her body and soul, as if she herself were bleeding to death from his mortal wounds.

Her whole life had resided in his arms ever since that thunder-laden midday hour in the barn at Skog when she gave herself to Erlend Nikulaussøn for the first time. Back then she was so young and inexperienced; she understood so little about what she was doing but strove to hide that she was close to tears because he was hurting her. She smiled, for she thought she was giving her lover the most precious of gifts. And whether or not it was a good gift, she had given him herself, completely and forever. Her maidenly life, which God had mercifully adorned with beauty and health when He allowed her to be born into secure and honorable cir-cumstances, which her parents had protected during all those years as they brought her up with the most loving strictness: With both hands she had given all this to Erlend, and ever since she had lived within his embrace.

So many times in the years that followed she had received his caresses, and stony and cold with anger, she had obediently com-plied with her husband's will, while she felt on the verge of col-lapse, ravaged by weariness. She had felt a sort of resentful pleasure when she looked at Erlend's lovely face and healthy, graceful body—at least *that* could no longer blind her to the man's faults. Yes, he was just as young and just as handsome; he could still overwhelm her with caresses that were as ardent as they had been in the days when she too was young. But *she* had aged, she thought, feeling a rush of triumphant pride. It was easy for some-one to stay young if he refused to learn, refused to adapt to his lot in life, and refused to fight to change his circumstances in accor-dance with his will.

And yet even when she received his kisses with her lips pressed tight, when she turned her whole being away from him in order to fight for the future of her sons, she sensed that she threw herself into this effort with the same fiery passion this man had once ig-nited in her blood. She thought the years had cooled her ardor be-cause she no longer felt desire whenever Erlend had that old glint in his eyes or that deep tone to his voice, which had made her swoon, helpless and powerless with joy, the first time she met him. But just as she had once longed to ease the heavy burden of separation and the anguish of her heart in her meetings with Erlend, she now felt a dull but fervent longing for a goal that would one day be reached when she, at long last, was a white-haired old woman and saw her sons well provided for and secure. Now it was for Erlend's sons that she endured the old fear of the uncertainty that lay ahead. And yet she was tormented with a longing that was like a hunger and a burning thirst—she must see her sons flourish.

And just as she had once given herself to Erlend, she later surrendered herself to the world that had sprung up around their life together. She threw herself into fulfilling every demand that had to be met; she lent a hand with every task that needed to be done in order to ensure the well-being of Erlend and his children. She began to understand that Erlend was always with her when she sat at Husaby and studied the documents in her husband's chest along with their priest, or when she talked to his leaseholders and laborers, or worked alongside her maids in the living quarters and cookhouse, or sat in the horse pasture with the foster mothers and kept an eye on her children on those lovely summer days. She came to realize that she turned her anger on Erlend whenever anything went wrong in the house and whenever the children disobeyed her will; but it was also toward him that her great joy streamed whenever they brought the hay in dry during the summer or had a good harvest of grain in the fall, or whenever her calves were thriving, and whenever she heard her boys shouting and laughing in the courtyard. The knowledge that she belonged to him blazed deep within her heart whenever she laid aside the last of the Sabbath clothes she had sewn for her seven sons and stood rejoicing over the pile of lovely, carefully stitched work she had done that winter. *He* was the one she was sick and tired of one spring evening when she walked home with her maids from the river. They had been washing wool from the last shearing, boiling water in a kettle on the shore and rinsing the wool in the current. And the mistress herself felt a great strain in her back, and her arms were coal-black with dung; the smell of sheep and dirty fat had soaked into her clothes until she thought her body would never be clean, even after three visits to the bathhouse.

But now that he was gone, it seemed to the widow that there was no purpose left to the restless toil of her life. *He* had been cut down, and so she had to die like a tree whose roots have been severed. The young shoots that had sprung up around her lap would now have to grow from their own roots. Each of them was old enough to decide his own fate. The thought flitted through Kristin's mind that if she had realized this before, back when Erlend mentioned it to her . . . Shadowy images of a life with Erlend up at his mountain farm passed through her mind: the two of them youthful again, with the little child between them. But she felt neither regret nor remorse. She had not been able to cut her life away from that of her sons; now death would soon separate them, for without Erlend she had no strength to live. All that had happened and would happen was meant to be. Everything happens as it is meant to be.

Her hair and her skin turned gray; she took little interest in bathing or tending to her clothes properly. At night she would lie in bed thinking about her life with Erlend; in the daytime she would walk about as if in a dream, never speaking to anyone unless addressed first, not seeming to hear even when her young sons spoke to her. This diligent and alert woman did not raise a hand to do any work. Love had always been behind her toil with earthly matters. Erlend had never given her much thanks for that; it was not the way he wanted to be loved. But she couldn't help it; it was her nature to love with great toil and care.

She seemed to be slipping toward the torpor of death. Then the scourge came to the countryside, flinging her sons onto their sickbeds, and the mother woke up.

The sickness was more dangerous for grown-ups than for children. Ivar was struck so hard that no one expected him to live. The youth acquired enormous strength in his fevered state; he bellowed and wanted to get out of bed to take up arms. His father's death seemed to be weighing on his mind. With great difficulty Naakkve and Bjørgulf managed to hold him down. Then it was Bjørgulf's turn to take to his bed. Lavrans lay with his face swollen beyond recognition with festering sores; his eyes glittered dully between narrow slits and looked as if they would be extinguished in a blaze of fever.

Kristin kept vigil in the loft with all three of them. Naakkve and Gaute had had the sickness as boys, and Skule was less ill than his brothers. Frida was taking care of him and Munan downstairs in the main room. No one thought there was any danger for Munan, but he had never been strong, and one evening when they thought he had already recovered, he suddenly fell into a faint. Frida had just enough time to warn his mother. Kristin ran downstairs, and a moment later Munan breathed his last in her arms.

The child's death aroused in her a new, wide-awake despair. Her wild grief over the infant who had died at his mother's breast had seemed red-tinged with the memory of all her crushed dreams of happiness. Back then the storm in her heart had kept her going. And the dire strain, which ended with her seeing her husband killed before her very eyes, left behind such a weariness in her soul that Kristin was convinced she would soon die of grief over Erlend. But that certainty had dulled the sharpness of her pain. She went about feeling the twilight and shadows growing all around her as she waited for the door to open for her in turn.

Over Munan's little body his mother stood alert and gray. This lovely, sweet little boy had been her youngest child for so many years, the last of her sons whom she still dared caress and laugh at when she ought to have been stern and somber, chastising him for his little misdeeds and careless acts. And he had been so loving and attached to his mother. It cut into her living flesh. As bound to life as she still was, it wasn't possible for a woman to die as easily as she had thought, after she had poured her life's blood into so many new young hearts.

In cold, sober despair she moved between the child who lay on his bier and her ill sons. Munan was laid out in the old storeroom, where first the infant and then his father had lain. Three bodies on her manor in less than a year. Her heart was withered with anguish, but rigid and mute, she waited for the next one to die; she expected it, like an inevitable fate. She had never fully understood what she had been given when God bestowed on her so many children. The worst of it was that in some ways she *had* understood. But she had thought more about the troubles, the pain, the anguish, and the strife—even though she had learned over and over again, from her yearning every time a child grew out of her arms, and from her joy every time a new one lay at her breast, that her happiness was inexpressibly greater than her struggles or pain. She had grumbled because the father of her children was such an unreliable man, who gave so little thought to the descendants who would come after him. She always forgot that he had been no different when she broke God's commandments and trampled on her own family in order to win him.

Now he had fallen from her side. And now she expected to see her sons die, one after the other. Perhaps in the end she would be left all alone, a childless mother.

There were so many things she had seen before to which she had given little thought, back when she viewed the world as if through the veil of Erlend's and her love. No doubt she had noticed how Naakkve took it seriously that he was the firstborn son and should be the leader and chieftain of his brothers. No doubt she had also seen that he was very fond of Munan. And yet she was greatly shaken, as if by something unexpected, when she saw his terrible grief at the death of his youngest brother.

But her other sons regained their health, although it took a long time. On Easter Day she was able to go to church with four sons, but Bjørgulf was still in bed, and Ivar was too weak to leave the house. Lavrans had grown quite tall while he was sick in bed, and in other ways it seemed as if the events of the past half year had carried him far beyond his years.

Kristin felt as if she were now an old woman. It seemed to her that a woman was young as long as she had little children sleeping in her arms at night, playing around her during the day, and demanding her care at all times. When a mother's children have grown away from her, then she becomes an old woman.

Her new brother-in-law, Jammælt Halvardssøn, said that the sons of Erlend were still quite young, and she herself was little more than forty years old. Surely she would soon decide to marry again; she needed a husband to help her manage her property and raise her younger sons. He mentioned several good men who he thought would be a noble match for Kristin; she should come to Ælin for a visit in the fall, and then he would see to it that she met these men, and afterward they could discuss the matter at greater length.

Kristin smiled wanly. It was true that she *wasn't* more than forty years old. If she had heard about another woman who had been widowed at such a young age, with so many half-grown children, she would have said the same as Jammælt: The woman should marry again and seek support from a new husband; she might even give him more children. But she herself would not.

It was just after Easter that Jammælt of Ælin came to Jørundgaard, and this was the second time that Kristin met her sister's new husband. She and her sons had not attended either the betrothal feast at Dyfrin or the wedding at Ælin. The two banquets had been held within a short time of each other during the spring when she was carrying her last child. As soon as Jammælt heard of the death of Erlend Nikulaussøn, he had rushed to Sil; in both word and deed he had helped his wife's sister and nephews. As best he could, he took care of everything that had to be done after the master's death, and he handled the case against the killers, since none of Erlend's sons had yet come of age. But back then Kristin had paid no heed to anything happening around her. Even the sentencing of Gudmund Toressøn, who was found to be the murderer of Erlend, seemed to make little impression on her.

This time she talked more with her brother-in-law, and he seemed to her a pleasant man. He was not young; he was the same age as Simon Darre. A calm and steadfast man, tall and stout, with a dark complexion and quite a handsome face, but rather stoop-shouldered. He and Gaute became good friends at once. Ever since their father's death Naakkve and Bjørgulf had grown closer to each other but had withdrawn from all the others. Ivar and Skule told their mother that they liked Jammælt, "but it seems to us that Ramborg could have shown Simon more respect by staying a widow a little longer; this new husband of hers is not his equal." Kristin saw that these two unruly sons of hers still remembered Simon Andressøn. They had allowed him to admonish them both with sharp words and mild jests, even though the two impatient boys refused to hear a word of chastisement from their own parents except with eyes flashing with anger and hands clenched into fists.

While Jammælt was at Jørundgaard, Munan Baardsøn also paid a visit to Kristin. There was now little remaining of the former Sir

Munan the Prancer. He had been a towering and imposing figure in the old days; back then he had carried his bulky body with some amount of grace, so that he seemed taller and more stately than he was. Now rheumatism had crippled him, and his flesh hung on his shriveled body; more than anything he resembled a little goblin, with a bald pate and a meager fringe of lank white hair at the back of his head. Once a thick blue-black beard had darkened his taut, full cheeks and jaw, but now an abundance of gray stubble grew in all the slack folds of his cheeks and throat, which he had a hard time shaving with his knife. He had grown bleary-eyed, he slobbered a bit, and he was terribly plagued by a weak stomach.

He had brought along his son Inge, whom people called Fluga, after his mother. He was already an old man. The father had offered this son a great deal of help in the world; he had found him a rich match and managed to get Bishop Halvard to take an interest in Inge. Munan had been married to the bishop's cousin Katrin. Lord Halvard wanted to help Inge become prosperous so that he wouldn't deplete the inheritance of Fru Katrin's children. The bishop had been given authority over the county of Hedemark, and he had then made Inge Munanssøn his envoy, so he now owned quite a few properties in Skaun and Ridabu. His mother had also bought a farm in those parts; she was now a most pious and charitable woman who had vowed to live a pure life until her death. "Well, she is neither aged nor infirm," said Munan crossly when Kristin laughed. He had doubtless wanted to arrange things so that Brynhild would move in with him and manage his household at his estate in Hamar, but she had refused.

He had so little joy in his old age, Sir Munan complained. His children were full of rancor. Those siblings who had the same mother had joined forces against the others, quarreling and squabbling with their half siblings. Worst of all was his youngest daughter; she had been born to one of his paramours while he was a married man, so she could be given no share of the inheritance. For that reason, she was trying to glean from him all that she could while he was still alive. She was a widow and had settled at Skogheim, the estate which was Sir Munan's only real home. Neither her father nor her siblings could roust her from the place. Munan was deathly afraid of her, but whenever he tried to run off to live with one of his other children, they would torment him with complaints about the greed and dishonest behavior of their other siblings. He felt most comfortable with his youngest, lawfully born daughter, who was a nun at Gimsøy. He liked to stay for a time in the convent's hostel, striving hard to better his soul with penances and prayers under the guidance of his daughter, but he didn't have the strength to stay there for long. Kristin wasn't convinced that Brynhild's sons were any kinder toward their father than his other children, but that was something that Munan Baardsøn refused to admit; he loved them more than all his other offspring.

As pitiful as this kinsman of hers now was, it was during the time spent with him that Kristin's stony grief first began to thaw. Sir Munan talked about Erlend day and night. When he wasn't lamenting over his own trials, he could talk of nothing else but his dead cousin, boasting of Erlend's exploits—particularly about his reckless youth. Erlend's wild boldness as soon as he made his way out into the world, away from his home at Husaby—where Fru Magnhild went about raging over his father while his father raged over his elder son—and away from Hestnes and Sir Baard, his pious, somber foster father. It might have seemed that Sir Munan's chatter would offer an odd sort of consolation for Erlend's grieving widow. But in his own way the knight had loved his young kinsman, and all his days he had thought Erlend surpassed every other man in appearance, courage—yes, even in good sense, although he had never wanted to use it, said Munan earnestly. And even though Kristin had to recall that it surely was not in Erlend's best interest that he had joined the king's retainers at the age of sixteen, with this cousin as his mentor and guide, nevertheless she had to smile with tender sorrow at Munan Baardsøn. He talked so that the spittle flew from his lips and the tears seeped from his old red-rimmed eyes, as he remembered Erlend's sparkling joy and spirit in those days of his youth, before he became tangled up in misfortune with Eline Ormsdatter and was branded for life.

Jammælt Halvardssøn, who was having a serious conversation with Gaute and Naakkve, cast a wondering glance at his sister-in-law. She was sitting on the bench against the wall with that loathsome old man and Ulf Haldorssøn, who Jammælt thought looked so sinister, but she was smiling as she talked to them and served them ale. He hadn't seen her smile before, but it suited her, and her little, low laugh was like that of a young maiden.

Jammælt said that it would be impossible for all six brothers to continue living on their mother's estate. It was not expected that any wealthy man of equal birth would give one of his kinswomen to Nikulaus in marriage if his five brothers settled there with him and perhaps continued to take their food from the manor after they married. And they ought to see about finding a wife for the young man; he was already twenty winters old and seemed to have a hardy disposition. For this reason Jammælt wanted to take Ivar and Skule home with him when he returned south; he would find some way to ensure their future. After Erlend Nikulaussøn had lost his life in such an unfortunate manner, it so happened that the great chieftains of the land suddenly remembered that the murdered man had been one of their peers—by birth and blood meant to surpass most of them, charming and magnanimous in many ways, and in battle a daring chieftain and skilled swordsman. But he had not had fortune on his side. Measures of the utmost severity had been levied against those men who had taken part in the murder of the landowner in his own courtyard. And Jammælt could report that many had asked him about Erlend's sons. He had met the men of Sudrheim during Christmas, and they had mentioned that these young boys were their kinsmen. Sir Jon had asked him to bring his greetings and say that he would receive and treat the sons of Erlend Nikulaussøn as his kin if any of them wanted to join his household. Jon Haftorssøn was now about to marry the maiden Elin, who was Erling Vidkunssøn's youngest daughter, and the young bride had asked whether the sons looked like their father. She remembered that Erlend had visited them in Bjørgvin when she was a child, and she had thought him to be the handsomest of men. And her brother, Bjarne Erlingssøn, had said that anything he could do for Erlend Nikulaussøn's sons, he would do with the most heartfelt joy.

Kristin sat and looked at her twin sons as Jammælt talked. They looked more and more like their father: Silky, fine soot-black hair clung smoothly to their heads, although it curled a bit across their brows and down the back of their slender tan necks. They had thin faces with long, jutting noses and delicate, small mouths with a knot of muscle at each corner. But their chins were blunter and broader and their eyes were darker than Erlend's. And above all else, his eyes were what had made Erlend so astoundingly handsome, his wife now thought. When he opened them in that lean, dark face beneath the pitch-black hair, they were so unexpectedly clear and light blue.

But now there was a glint of steely blue in the eyes of the young boys when Skule replied to his uncle. He was the one who usually spoke for both twins.

"We thank you for this fine offer, kinsman. But we have already spoken with Sir Munan and Inge and sought the advice of our older brothers, and we have come to an agreement with Inge and his father. These men are our closest kin of Father's lineage; we will go south with Inge and intend to stay at his estate this summer and for some time to come."

That evening the boys came downstairs to the main room to speak to Kristin after she had gone to bed.

"We hope that you will understand, Mother," said Ivar Erlendssøn.

"We refuse to beg for the help and friendship of kin from those men who sat in silence and watched our father wrongly suffer," added Skule.

Their mother nodded.

It seemed to her that her sons had acted properly. She realized that Jammælt was a sensible and fair-minded man, and his offer had been well intended, but she was pleased the boys were loyal to their father. And yet she could never have imagined that her sons would one day come to serve the son of Brynhild Fluga.

The twins left with Inge Fluga as soon as Ivar was strong enough to ride. It was very quiet at the manor after they were gone. Their mother remembered that at this time the year before, she lay in bed in the weaving room with a newborn child; it seemed to her like a dream. Such a short time ago she had felt so young, with her soul stirred up by the yearnings and sorrows of a young woman, by hopes and hatreds and love. Now her flock had shrunk to four sons, and in her soul the only thing stirring was an uneasiness

for the grown young men. In the silence that descended upon
Jørundgaard after the departure of the twins, her fear for Bjørgulf
flared up with bright flames.

When guests arrived, he and Naakkve moved to the old hearth
house. Bjørgulf would get out of bed in the daytime, but he had
still not been outdoors. With deep fear Kristin noticed that Bjørgulf was always sitting in the same spot; he never walked around,
he hardly moved at all when she came to see him. She knew that
his eyes had grown worse during his last illness. Naakkve was terribly quiet, but he had been that way ever since his father's death,
and he seemed to avoid his mother as much as he could.

Finally one day she gathered her courage and asked her eldest
son how things now stood with Bjørgulf's eyesight. For a while
Naakkve gave only evasive replies, but at last she demanded that
her son tell her the truth.

Naakkve said, "He can still make out strong light—" All at
once the young man's face lost all color; abruptly he turned away
and left the room.

Much later that day, after Kristin had wept until she was so
weary that she thought she could trust herself to speak calmly with
her son, she went over to the old house.

Bjørgulf was lying in bed. As soon as she came in and sat down
on the edge of his bed, she could tell by his face that he knew she
had spoken to Naakkve.

"Mother. You mustn't cry, Mother," he begged fearfully.

What she most wanted to do was to fling herself at her son,
gather him into her arms, and weep over him, grieving over his
harsh fate. But she merely slipped her hand into his under the coverlet.

"God is sorely testing your manhood, my son," she said
hoarsely.

Bjørgulf's expression changed, becoming firm and resolute. But
it took a moment before he could speak.

"I've known for a long time, Mother, that this was what I was
destined to endure. Even back when we were at Tautra . . . Brother
Aslak spoke to me about it and said that if things should go in
such a way . . .

"The way our Lord Jesus was tempted in the wilderness, he

said. He told me that the true wilderness for a Christian man's soul was when his sight and senses were blocked—then he would follow the footsteps of the Lord out of the wilderness, even if his body was still with his brothers or kinsmen. He read to me from the books of Saint Bernard about such things. And when a soul realizes that God has chosen him for such a difficult test of his manhood, then he shouldn't be afraid that he won't have the strength. God knows my soul better than the soul knows itself."

He continued to talk to his mother in this manner, consoling her with a wisdom and strength of spirit that seemed far beyond his years.

That evening Naakkve came to Kristin and asked to speak with her alone. Then he told her that he and Bjørgulf intended to enter the holy brotherhood and to take the vows of monks at Tautra.

Kristin was dismayed, but Naakkve kept on talking, quite calmly. They would wait until Gaute had come of age and could lawfully act on behalf of his mother and younger siblings. They wanted to enter the monastery with as much property as was befitting the sons of Erlend Nikulaussøn of Husaby, but they also wanted to ensure the welfare of their brothers. From their father the sons of Erlend had inherited nothing of value that was worth mentioning, but the three who were born before Gunnulf Nikulaussøn had entered the cloister owned several shares of estates in the north. He had made these gifts to his nephews when he dispersed his wealth, although most of what he hadn't given to the Church or for ecclesiastical use he had left to his brother. And since Naakkve and Bjørgulf would not demand their full share of the inheritance, it would be a great relief to Gaute, who would then become the head of the family and carry on the lineage, if the two of them were dead to the world, as Naakkve put it.

Kristin felt close to fainting. Never had she dreamed that Naakkve would consider a monk's life. But she did not protest; she was too overwhelmed. And she didn't dare try to dissuade her sons from such a noble and meaningful enterprise.

"Back when we were boys and were staying with the monks up there in the north, we promised each other that we would never be parted," said Naakkve.

His mother nodded; she knew that. But she had thought their

intention was for Bjørgulf to continue to live with Naakkve, even after the older boy was married.

It seemed to Kristin almost miraculous that Bjørgulf, as young as he was, could bear his misfortune in such a manly fashion. Whenever she spoke to him of it, during that spring, she heard nothing but god-fearing and courageous words from his lips. It seemed to her incomprehensible, but it must be because he had realized for many years that this would be the outcome of his failing eyesight, and he must have been preparing his soul ever since the time he had stayed with the monks.

But then she had to consider what a terrible burden this unfortunate child of hers had endured—while she had paid so little heed as she went about absorbed with her own concerns. Now, whenever she had a moment to herself, Kristin Lavransdatter would slip away and kneel down before the picture of the Virgin Mary up in the loft or before her altar in the north end of the church when it was open. Lamenting with all her heart, she would pray with humble tears for the Savior's gentle Mother to serve as Bjørgulf's mother in her stead and to offer him all that his earthly mother had left undone.

One summer night Kristin lay awake in bed. Naakkve and Bjørgulf had moved back into the high loft room, but Gaute was sleeping downstairs with Lavrans because Naakkve had said that the older brothers wanted to practice keeping vigil and praying. She was just about to fall asleep at last when she was awakened by someone walking quietly along the gallery of the loft. She heard a stumbling on the stairs and recognized the blind man's gait.

He must be going out on some errand, she thought, but all the same she got up and began looking for her clothes. Then she heard a door flung open upstairs, and someone raced down the steps, taking them two or three at a time.

Kristin ran to the entryway and out the door. The fog was so thick outside that only the buildings directly across the courtyard could be glimpsed. Up by the manor gate Bjørgulf was furiously struggling to free himself from his brother's grasp.

"Do you lose anything," cried the blind man, "if you're rid of me? Then you'll be released from all your oaths . . . and you won't have to be dead to this world."

Kristin couldn't hear what Naakkve said in reply. She ran bare-foot through the soaking wet grass. By this time Bjørgulf had pulled free; suddenly, as if struck down, he fell upon the boulder by the gate and began beating it with his fists.

Naakkve saw his mother and took a few swift steps in her di-rection. "Go inside, Mother. I can handle this best alone. You *must* go inside, I tell you," he whispered urgently, and then he turned around and went back to lean over his brother.

Their mother remained standing some distance away. The grass was drenched with moisture, water was dripping from all the eaves, and drops were trickling from every leaf; it had rained all day, but now the clouds had descended as a thick white fog. When her sons headed back after a while—Naakkve had taken Bjørgulf by the arm and was leading him—Kristin retreated to the entryway door.

She saw that Bjørgulf's face was bleeding; he must have hit him-self on the rock. Involuntarily Kristin pressed her hand to her lips and bit her own flesh.

On the stairs Bjørgulf tried once more to pull away from Naakkve. He threw himself against the wall and shouted, "I curse, I curse the day I was born!"

When she heard Naakkve shut the loft door behind them, Kristin crept upstairs and stood outside on the gallery. For a long time she could hear Bjørgulf's voice inside. He raged and shouted and swore; a few of his vehement words she could understand. Every once in a while she would hear Naakkve talking to him, but his voice was only a subdued murmur. Finally Bjørgulf began sob-bing, loudly and as if his heart would break.

Kristin stood trembling with cold and anguish. She was wearing only a cloak over her shift; she stood there so long that her loose, flowing hair became wet with the raw night air. At last there was silence in the loft.

Entering the main room downstairs, she went over to the bed where Gaute and Lavrans were sleeping. They hadn't heard any-thing. With tears streaming down her face, she reached out a hand in the dark and touched the two warm faces, listening to the boys' measured, healthy breathing. She now felt as if these two were all that she had left of her riches.

Shivering with cold, she climbed into her own bed. One of the dogs lying next to Gaute's bed came padding across the room and jumped up, circling around and then leaning against her feet. The dog was in the habit of doing this at night, and she didn't have the heart to chase him away, even though he was heavy and pressed on her legs so they would turn numb. But the dog had belonged to Erlend and was his favorite—a shaggy coal-black old bearhound. Tonight, thought Kristin, it was good to have him lying there, warming her frozen feet.

She didn't see Naakkve the next morning until at the breakfast table. Then he came in and sat down in the high seat, which had been his place since his father's death.

He didn't say a word during the meal, and he had dark circles under his eyes. His mother followed him when he went back outside.

"How is Bjørgulf now?" she asked in a low voice.

Naakkve continued to evade her eyes, but he replied in an equally low voice that Bjørgulf was asleep.

"Has . . . has he been this way before?" she whispered fearfully.

Naakkve nodded, turned away from her, and went back upstairs to his brother.

Naakkve watched over Bjørgulf night and day, and kept his mother away from him as much as possible. But Kristin saw that the two young men spent many hours struggling with each other.

It was Nikulaus Erlendssøn who was supposed to be the master of Jørundgaard now, but he had no time to tend to the managing of the estate. He also seemed to have as little interest and ability as his father had had. And so Kristin and Gaute saw to everything, for that summer Ulf Haldorssøn had left her too.

After the unfortunate events that ended with the killing of Erlend Nikulaussøn, Ulf's wife had gone home with her brothers. Ulf stayed on at Jørundgaard; he said he wanted to show everyone that he couldn't be driven away by gossip and lies. But he hinted that he had lived long enough at Jørundgaard; he thought he might head north to his own estate in Skaun as soon as enough time had passed so that no one could say he was fleeing from the rumors.

But then the bishop's plenipotentiary began making inquiries into the matter, to determine whether Ulf Haldorssøn had unlawfully spurned his wife. And so Ulf made preparations to leave; he went to get Jardtrud, and they were now setting off together for the north, before the autumn weather made the road through the mountains impassable. He told Gaute that he wanted to join forces with his half sister's husband, who was a swordsmith in Nidaros, and live there, but he would settle Jardtrud at Skjoldvirkstad, which his nephew would continue to manage for him.

On his last evening Kristin drank a toast to him with the gold-chased silver goblet her father had inherited from his paternal grandfather, Sir Ketil the Swede. She asked him to accept the goblet as a keepsake to remember her by. Then she slipped onto his finger a gold ring that had belonged to Erlend; he was to have it in his memory.

Ulf gave her a kiss to thank her. "It's customary among kinsmen," he said with a laugh. "You probably never imagined, Kristin, when we first met, and I was the servant who came to get you to escort you to my master, that we would part in this way."

Kristin turned bright red, for he was smiling at her with that old, mocking smile, but she thought she could see in his eyes that he was sad. Then she said, "All the same, Ulf, aren't you longing for Trøndelag—you who were born and raised in the north? Many a time I too have longed for the fjord, and I lived there only a few years." Ulf laughed again, and then she added quietly, "If I ever offended you in my youth, with my overbearing manner or . . . I didn't know that you were close kin, you and Erlend. But now you must forgive me!"

"No . . . but Erlend was not the one who refused to acknowledge our kinship. I was so insolent in my youth; since my father had ousted me from his lineage, I refused to beg—" He stood up abruptly and went over to where Bjørgulf was sitting on the bench. "You see, Bjørgulf, my foster son . . . your father . . . and Gunnulf, they treated me as a kinsman even back when we were boys—just the opposite of how my brothers and sisters at Hestnes behaved. Afterward . . . to others I never presented myself as Erlend's kinsman because I saw that in that way I could serve him better . . . as well as his wife and all of you, my foster sons. Do you understand?" he asked earnestly, placing his hand on Bjørgulf's face, hiding the extinguished eyes.

"I understand." Bjørgulf's reply was almost stifled behind the other man's fingers; he nodded under Ulf's hand.

"We understand, foster father." Nikulaus laid his hand heavily on Ulf's shoulder, and Gaute moved closer to the group.

Kristin felt strangely ill at ease. They seemed to be speaking of things that she could not comprehend. Then she too stepped over to the men as she said, "Be assured, Ulf, my kinsman, that all of us understand. Never have Erlend and I had a more loyal friend than you. May God bless you!"

The next day Ulf Haldorssøn set off for the north.

Over the course of the winter Bjørgulf seemed to settle down, as far as Kristin could tell. Once again he came to the table for meals with the servants of the house, he went with them to mass, and he willingly and gladly accepted the help and services that his mother so dearly wanted to offer him.

As time passed and Kristin never heard her sons make any mention of the monastery, she realized how unspeakably reluctant she was to give up her eldest son to the life of a monk.

She couldn't help admitting that a cloister would be the best place for Bjørgulf. But she didn't see how she could bear to lose Naakkve in that way. It must be true, after all, that her firstborn was somehow bound closer to her heart than her other sons.

Nor could she see that Naakkve was suited to be a monk. He did have a talent for learned games and a fondness for devotional practices; nevertheless, his mother didn't think he was particularly disposed toward spiritual matters. He didn't attend the parish church with any special zeal. He often missed the services, giving some meager excuse, and she knew that neither he nor Bjørgulf confessed to their parish priest anything but the most ordinary of sins. The new priest, Sira Dag Rolfssøn, was the son of Rolf of Blakarsarv, who had been married to Ragnfrid Ivarsdatter's cousin; for this reason he often visited his kinswoman's estate. He was a young man about thirty years old, well educated and a good cleric, but the two oldest sons never warmed to him. With Gaute, on the other hand, he soon became good friends.

Gaute was the only one of Erlend's sons who had made friends among the people of Sil. But none of the others had continued to be as much an outsider as Nikulaus was. He never had anything to do with the other youths. If he went to the places where young people gathered to dance or meet, he usually stood on the outskirts of the green to watch, asserting by his demeanor that he was too good to take part. But if he was so inclined, he might join in the games unasked, and then everyone saw that he was doing it to show off. He was vigorous, strong, and agile, and it was easy to provoke him to fight. But after he had defeated two or three of the most renowned opponents in the parish, people had to tolerate his presence. And if he wished to dance with a maiden, he paid no heed to her brothers or kinsmen but simply danced with the girl and walked and sat with her alone. No woman ever said no when Nikulaus Erlendssøn requested her company, which did not make people like him any better.

After his brother had gone blind, Naakkve seldom left his side, but if he went out in the evening, he acted no differently from before. For the most part he also gave up his long hunting expeditions, but that fall he had bought himself an exceedingly costly white falcon from the sheriff, and he was as eager as ever to practice his bowmanship and prowess in sports. Bjørgulf had taught himself to play chess blind, and the brothers would often spend an entire day at the chessboard; they were both the most zealous of players.

Then Kristin heard people talking about Naakkve and a young maiden, Tordis Gunnarsdatter from Skjenne. The following summer she was staying up in the mountain pastures. Many times Naakkve was away from home at night. Kristin found out that he had been with Tordis.

The mother's heart trembled and twisted and turned like an aspen leaf on its stem. Tordis belonged to an old and respected family; she herself was a good and innocent child. Naakkve couldn't possibly mean to dishonor her. If the two young people forgot themselves, then he would have to make the girl his wife. Sick with anguish and shame, Kristin realized nevertheless that she would not be overly aggrieved if this should happen. Only two years ago she would never have stood for it if Tordis Gunnarsdatter were to succeed her as the mistress of Jørundgaard. The maiden's grandfa-

ther was still alive and lived on his estate with four married sons;
she herself had many siblings. She would not be a wealthy bride.
And every woman of that lineage had given birth to at least one
witless child. The children were either exchanged at birth or possessed by the mountain spirits; no matter how they strove to
protect the women in childbed, neither baptism nor sacred incan-
tations seemed to help. There were now two old men at Skjenne
whom Sira Eirik had judged to be changelings, as well as two children who were deaf and mute. And the wood nymph had bewitched Tordis's oldest brother when he was seventeen. Otherwise
those belonging to the Skjenne lineage were a handsome lot, their
livestock flourished, and good fortune followed them, but they
were too numerous for their family to have any wealth.

God only knew whether Naakkve could have abandoned his resolve without sinning if he had already promised himself to the
service of the Virgin Mary. But a man always had to spend one
year as a young brother in the monastery before he was ordained;
he could withdraw voluntarily if he realized that he was not meant
to serve God in that way. And she had heard that the French
countess who was the mother of the great doctor of theology, the
friar Sir Thomas Aquinas, had locked her son in with a beautiful,
wanton woman in order to shake his resolve when he wanted to
retreat from the world. Kristin thought this was the vilest thing she
had ever heard, and yet when the woman died, she had reconciled
with God. So it must not be such a terrible sin if Kristin now imagined that she would open her arms to embrace Tordis of Skjenne as
the wife of her son.

In the autumn Jammælt Halvardssøn came to Formo, and he confirmed the rumors of great news that had also reached the valley.
In consultation with the highest leaders of the Church and Norway's Council of knights and noblemen, King Magnus Eirikssøn
had decided to divide his realms between the two sons he had fathered with his queen, Lady Blanche. At the meeting of nobles in
Vardberg, he had given the younger son, Prince Haakon, the title
of king of Norway. Both learned priests and laymen of the gentry
had sworn sacred oaths to defend the land under his hand. He was
supposed to be a handsome and promising three-year-old child,
and he was to be brought up in Norway with four foster mothers,

all the most highborn wives of knights, and with two spiritual and two worldly chieftains as his foster fathers when King Magnus and Queen Blanche were in Sweden. It was said that Sir Erling Vidkunssøn and the bishops of Bjørgvin and Oslo were behind this selection of a sovereign, and Bjarne Erlingssøn had presented the matter to the king; Lord Magnus loved Bjarne above all his other Norwegian men. Everyone expected the greatest benefits for the realm of Norway now that they would once again have a king who was reared and lived among them, who would protect the laws and rights and interests of the country instead of squandering his time, energies, and the wealth of the kingdom on incursions in other lands.

Kristin had heard about the selection of a king, just as she had heard about the discord with the German merchants in Bjørgvin and about the king's wars in Sweden and Denmark. But these events had touched her so little—like the echo of thunder from the mountains after a storm had passed over the countryside and was far away. No doubt her sons had discussed these matters with each other. Jammælt's account threw the sons of Erlend into a state of violent agitation. Bjørgulf sat with his forehead resting in his hand so he could hide his blind eyes. Gaute listened with his lips parted as his fingers tightly clenched the hilt of his dagger. Lavrans's breathing was swift and audible, and all of a sudden he turned away from his uncle and looked at Naakkve, sitting in the high seat. The oldest son's face was pale, and his eyes blazed.

"It has been the fate of many a man," said Naakkve, "that those who were his fiercest opponents in life found success on the road he had pointed out to them—but only after they had made him into fodder for the worms. After his mouth was stuffed with earth, the lesser men no longer shrank from affirming the truth of his words."

"That may well be, kinsman," said Jammælt in a placating tone. "You may be right about that. Your father was the first of all men to think of this way out of the foreign lands—with two brothers on the thrones, here and in Sweden. Erlend Nikulaussøn was a deep-thinking, wise, and magnanimous man. I see that. But take care what you now say, Nikulaus. Surely you wouldn't want your words to be spread as gossip that might harm Skule."

"Skule didn't ask my permission to do what he did," said Naakkve sharply.

"No, he probably didn't remember that you had come of age by now," replied Jammælt in the same tone as before. "And I didn't think about it either, so it was with my consent and blessing that he placed his hand on Bjarne's sword and swore allegiance."

"I think he did remember it, but the whelp knew I would never give my consent. And no doubt the Giske men needed this salve for their guilty consciences."

Skule Erlendssøn had joined Bjarne Erlingssøn as one of his loyal men. He had met the great chieftain when he was visiting his aunt at Ælin during Christmas, and Bjarne had explained to the boy that it was largely due to the intercession of Sir Erling and himself that Erlend had been granted his life. Without their support Simon Andressøn would never have been able to accomplish his mission with King Magnus. Ivar was still with Inge Fluga.

Kristin knew that what Bjarne Erlingssøn had said was not entirely untrue—it was in accordance with Simon's own account of his journey to Tunsberg—and yet during all these years she had always thought of Erling Vidkunssøn with great bitterness; it seemed to her that he should have been able to help her husband attain better terms if he had wished to do so. Bjarne hadn't been capable of much back then, as young as he was. But she wasn't pleased that Skule had joined up with this man, and in an odd way it took her breath away that the twins had acted on their own and had set off into the world. They were no more than children, she thought.

After Jammælt's visit the uneasiness of her mind grew so great that she hardly dared think at all. If it was true what the men said—that the prosperity and security of the people of the realm would increase beyond words if this small boy in Tunsberg Castle were now called Norway's king—then they could have been enjoying this turn of events for almost ten years if Erlend hadn't . . . No! She refused to think about *that* when she thought about the dead. But she couldn't help it because she knew that in her sons' eyes their father was magnificent and perfect, the most splendid warrior and chieftain, without faults or flaws. And she herself had thought, during all these years, that Erlend had been betrayed by his peers and wealthy kinsmen; her husband had suffered great in-

justice. But Naakkve went too far when he said that *they* had
made him into fodder for the worms. She too bore her own heavy
share of the blame, but it was mostly Erlend's folly and his desperate obstinacy that had brought about his wretched death.

But no . . . all the same, she wasn't pleased that Skule was now
in the service of Bjarne Erlingssøn.

Would she ever live to see the day when she was released from
the ceaseless torment of anguish and unrest? Oh Jesus, remember
the anguish and grief that your own mother bore for your sake;
have mercy on me, a mother, and give me comfort!

She felt uneasy even about Gaute. The boy had the makings of
the most capable of farmers, but he was so impetuous in his eager-
ness to restore prosperity to his lineage. Naakkve gave him free
rein, and Gaute had his hands in so many enterprises. With several other men of the parish he had now started up the old iron-
smelting sites in the mountains. And he sold off far too much; he
sold not only the goods from the land leases but also part of the
yield from his own estate. All her days Kristin had been used to
seeing full storerooms and stalls on her farm, and she grew a little
cross with Gaute when he frowned in disapproval at the rancid
butter and made fun of the ten-year-old bacon she had hung up.
But she wanted to know that on her manor there would never be a
shortage of food; she would never have to turn a poor man away
unaided if years of drought should strike the countryside. And
there would be nothing lacking when the time came for weddings
and christening feasts and banquets to be held once again on the
old estate.

Her ambitious hopes for her sons had been diminished. She
would be content if they would settle down here in her parish. She
could combine and exchange her properties in such a fashion that
three of them could live on their own estates. And Jørundgaard,
along with the portion of Laugarbru that lay on this side of the
river, could feed three leaseholders. They might not be circumstances fit for noblemen, but they wouldn't be poor folk either.
Peace reigned in the valley; here little was heard about all the unrest among chieftains of the land. If this should be perceived as a
decline in the power and prestige of their lineage . . . well, God
would be able to further the interests of their descendants if He

saw that it would be to their benefit. But surely it would be vain of her to hope that she might see them all gathered around her in this manner. It was unlikely they would settle down so easily, these sons of hers who had Erlend Nikulaussøn as their father.

During this time her soul found peace and solace whenever she let her thoughts dwell on the two children she had laid to rest up in the cemetery.

Every day, over the ensuing years, she had thought of them; as she watched children of the same age grow and thrive, she would wonder how her own would have looked by now.

As she went about her daily chores, just as diligent and hardworking as ever, but reticent and preoccupied, her dead children were always with her. In her dreams they grew older and flourished, and they turned out, in every way, to be exactly as she had wished. Munan was as loyal to his kinsmen as Naakkve, but he was as cheerful and talkative with his mother as Gaute was, and he never worried her with unwise impulses. He was as gentle and thoughtful as Lavrans, but Munan would tell his mother all the strange things he was pondering. He was as clever as Bjørgulf, but no misfortune clouded his way through life, so his wisdom held no bitterness. He was as self-reliant, strong, and bold as the twins, but not as unruly or stubborn.

And she recalled once more all the sweet, merry memories of the loving charm of her children when they were small every time she thought about little Erlend. He stood on her lap, waiting to be dressed. She put her hands around his chubby, naked body, and he reached up with his small hands and face and his whole precious body toward her face and her caresses. She taught him to walk. She had placed a folded cloth across his chest and up under his arms; he hung in this harness, as heavy as a sack, vigorously fumbling backward with his feet. Then he laughed until he was wriggling like a worm from laughter. She carried him in her arms out to the farmyard to see the calves and lambs, and he shrieked with joy at the sow with all her piglets. He leaned his head back and gaped at the doves perched in the stable hayloft. He ran to her in the tall grass around the heaps of stones, crying out at each berry he saw and eating them out of her hand so avidly that her palm was wet from his greedy little mouth.

All the joys of her children she remembered and relived in this dream life with her two little sons, and all her sorrows she forgot.

It was spring for the third time since Erlend had been laid in his grave. Kristin heard no more about Tordis and Naakkve. Neither did she hear anything about the cloister. And her hope grew; she couldn't help it. She was so reluctant to sacrifice her eldest son to the life of a monk.

Right before Saint Jon's Day, Ivar Erlendssøn came home to Jørundgaard. The twins had been young lads in their sixteenth year when they left home. Now Ivar was a grown man, almost eighteen years old, and his mother thought he had become so handsome and manly that she could hardly get her fill of looking at him.

On the first morning Kristin took breakfast up to Ivar as he lay in bed. Honey-baked wheat bread, *lefse,* and ale that she had tapped from the last keg of Christmas brew. She sat on the edge of his bed while he ate and drank, smiling at everything he said. She got up to look at his clothes, turning and fingering each garment; she rummaged through his traveling bag and weighed his new silver brooch in her slender reddish-brown hand; she drew his dagger out of its sheath and praised it, along with all his other possessions. Then she sat down on the bed again, looked at her son, and listened with a smile in her eyes and on her lips to everything the young man told her.

Then Ivar said, "I might as well tell you why I've come home, Mother. I've come to obtain Naakkve's consent for my marriage."

Overwhelmed, Kristin clasped her hands together. "My Ivar! As young as you are . . . Surely you haven't committed some folly!"

Ivar begged his mother to listen. She was a young widow, Signe Gamalsdatter of Rognheim in Fauskar. The estate was worth six marks in land taxes, and most of it was her sole property, which she had inherited through her only child. But she had become embroiled in a lawsuit with her husband's kinsmen, and Inge Fluga had tried to acquire all manner of unlawful benefits for himself if he was to help the widow win justice. Ivar had become indignant and had taken up the woman's defense, accompanying her to the bishop himself, for Lord Halvard had always shown Ivar a fatherly goodwill every time they had met. Inge Munanssøn's actions in the county could not bear close scrutiny, but he had been wise enough to stay on friendly terms with the nobles of the countryside, frightening the peasants into their mouseholes. And he had thrown sand in the bishop's eyes with his great cleverness. It was doubtless for Munan's sake that Lord Halvard had refrained from being too stern. But now things did not look good for Inge, so the cousins had parted with the gravest enmity when Ivar took his horse and rode off from Inge Fluga's manor. Then he had decided to pay a visit at Rognheim, in the south, before he left the region. That was at Eastertime, and he had been staying with Signe ever since, helping her on the estate in the springtime. Now they had agreed that he would marry her. *She* didn't think that Ivar Erlendssøn was too young to be her husband and protect her interests. And the bishop, as he had said, looked on him with favor. He was still much too young and lacking in learning for Lord Halvard to appoint him to any position, but Ivar was convinced that he would do well if he settled at Rognheim as a married man.

Kristin sat fidgeting with her keys in her lap. This was sensible talk. And Inge Fluga certainly deserved no better. But she wondered what that poor old man, Munan Baardsøn, would say about all this.

About the bride she learned that Signe was thirty winters old, from a lowborn and impoverished family, but her first husband had acquired much wealth so that she was now comfortably situated, and she was an honorable, kind, and diligent woman.

Nikulaus and Gaute accompanied Ivar south to have a look at the widow, but Kristin wanted to stay home with Bjørgulf. When her sons returned, Naakkve could tell his mother that Ivar was now betrothed to Signe Gamalsdatter. The wedding would be celebrated at Rognheim in the autumn.

Not long after his arrival back home Naakkve came to see his mother one evening as she sat sewing in the weaving room. He barred the door. Then he said that now that Gaute was twenty years old and Ivar would also come of age by marrying, he and Bjørgulf intended to journey north in the fall and ask to be accepted as novices at the monastery. Kristin said little; they spoke mainly about how they would arrange those things that her two oldest sons would want to take with them from their inheritance.

But a few days later men came to Jørundgaard with an invitation to a betrothal banquet: Aasmund of Skjenne was going to celebrate the betrothal of his daughter Tordis to a good farmer's son from Dovre.

That evening Naakkve came again to see his mother in the weaving room, and once again he barred the door behind him. He sat on the edge of the hearth, poking a twig into the embers. Kristin had lit a small fire since the nights were cold that summer.

"Nothing but feasts and carousing, my mother," he said with a little laugh. "The betrothal banquet at Rognheim and the celebration at Skjenne and then Ivar's wedding. When Tordis rides in her wedding procession, I doubt I'll be riding along; by that time I will have donned cloister garb."

Kristin didn't reply at once. But then, without looking up from her sewing—she was making a banquet tunic for Ivar—she said, "Many probably thought it would be a great sorrow for Tordis Gunnarsdatter if you became a monk."

"I once thought so myself," replied Naakkve.

Kristin let her sewing sink to her lap. She looked at her son; his face was impassive and calm. And he was so handsome. His dark hair brushed back from his white forehead, curling softly behind his ears and along the slender, tan stalk of his neck. His features were more regular than his father's; his face was broader and more solid, his nose not as big, and his mouth not as small. His clear blue eyes were lovely beneath the straight black brows. And yet he didn't *seem* as handsome as Erlend had been. It was his father's animal-like softness and languid charm, his air of inextinguishable youth that Naakkve did not possess.

Kristin picked up her work again, but she didn't go back to sewing. After a moment, as she looked down and tucked in a hem of the cloth with her needle, she said, "Do you realize, Naakkve, that I haven't voiced a single word of objection to your godly plans? I wouldn't dare do so. But you're young, and you know quite well—being more learned than I am—that it is written somewhere that it ill suits a man to turn around and look over his shoulder once he has set his hand to the plow."

Not a muscle moved in her son's face.

"I know that you've had these thoughts in mind for a long time," continued his mother. "Ever since you were children. But back then you didn't understand what you would be giving up. Now that you've reached the age of a man . . . Don't you think it would be advisable if you waited a while longer to see if you have the calling? *You* were born to take over this estate and become the head of your lineage."

"You dare to advise me now?" Naakkve took several deep breaths. He stood up. All of a sudden he slapped his hand to his breast and tore open his tunic and shirt so his mother could see his naked chest where his birthmark, the five little blood-red, fiery specks, shone amid the black hair.

"I suppose you thought I was too young to understand what you were sighing about with moans and tears whenever you kissed me here, back when I was a little lad. I may not have understood, but I could never forget the words you spoke.

"Mother, Mother . . . Have you forgotten that Father died the most wretched of deaths, unconfessed and unanointed? And *you* dare to dissuade us!

"I think Bjørgulf and I know what we're turning away from. It doesn't seem to me such a great sacrifice to give up this estate and marriage—or the kind of peace and happiness that you and Father had together during all the years I can remember."

Kristin put down her sewing. All that she and Erlend had lived through, both bad and good . . . A wealth of memories washed over her. This child understood so little what he was renouncing. With all his youthful fights, bold exploits, careless dealings, and games of love—he was no more than an innocent child.

Naakkve saw the tears well up in his mother's eyes; he shouted, "*Quid mihi et tibi est, mulier.*"[2] Kristin cringed, but her son spoke with violent agitation. "God did not say those words because he felt scorn for his mother. But he chastised her, that pure pearl without blemish or flaw, when she tried to counsel him on how to use the power that he had been given by his Father in Heaven and not by his mother's flesh. Mother, you must not advise me about this; do not venture to do so."

Kristin bent her head to her breast.

After a moment Naakkve said in a low voice, "Have you forgotten, Mother, that you pushed me away—" He paused, as if he didn't trust his own voice. But then he continued, "I wanted to kneel beside you at my father's deathbed, but you told me to go away. Don't you realize my heart wails in my chest whenever I think about that?"

Kristin whispered, almost inaudibly, "Is that why you've been so . . . cold . . . toward me during all these years I've been a widow?"

Her son was silent.

"I begin to understand . . . You've never forgiven me for that, have you, Naakkve?"

Naakkve looked away. "Sometimes . . . I have forgiven you, Mother," he said, his voice faint.

"But not very often . . . Oh, Naakkve, Naakkve!" she cried bitterly. "Do you think I loved Bjørgulf any less than you? I'm his mother. I'm mother to both of you! It was cruel of you to keep closing the door between him and me!"

Naakkve's pale face turned even whiter. "Yes, Mother, I closed the door. Cruel, you say. May Jesus comfort you, but you don't know . . ." His voice faded to a whisper, as if the boy's strength were spent. "I didn't think you should . . . We had to spare you."

He turned on his heel, went to the door, and unbarred it. But then he paused and stood there with his back to Kristin. Finally she softly called out his name. He came back and stood before her with his head bowed.

"Mother . . . I know this isn't . . . easy . . . for you."

She placed her hands on his shoulders. He hid his eyes from her gaze, but he bent down and kissed her on the wrist. Kristin recalled that his father had once done the same, but she couldn't remember when.

She stroked his sleeve, and then he lifted his hand and patted her on the cheek. They sat down again, both of them silent for a time.

"Mother," said Naakkve after a while, his voice steady and quiet, "do you still have the cross that my brother Orm left to you?"

"Yes," said Kristin. "He made me promise never to part with it."

"I think if Orm had known about it, he would have consented to letting me have it. I too will now be without inheritance or lineage."

Kristin pulled the little silver cross from her bodice. Naakkve accepted it; it was warm from his mother's breast. Respectfully he kissed the reliquary in the center of the cross, fastened the thin chain around his neck, and hid the cross inside his clothing.

"Do you remember your brother Orm?" asked his mother.

"I'm not sure. I think I do . . . but perhaps that's just because you always talked so much about him, back when I was little."

Naakkve sat before his mother for a while longer. Then he stood up. "Good night, Mother!"

"May God bless you, Naakkve. Good night!"

He left her. Kristin folded up the wedding tunic for Ivar, put away her sewing things, and covered the hearth.

"May God bless you, may God bless you, my Naakkve." Then she blew out the candle and left the old building.

Some time later Kristin happened to meet Tordis at a manor on the outskirts of the parish. The people there had fallen ill and hadn't been able to bring in the hay, so the brothers and sisters of the Olav guild had gone to lend them a hand. That evening Kristin accompanied the girl part of the way home. She walked along slowly, as an old woman does, and chatted; little by little she turned the conversation so that Tordis found herself telling Naakkve's mother all about what there had been between the two of them.

Yes, she had met with him in the paddock at home, and the summer before, when she was staying up in their mountain pastures, he had come to see her several times at night. But he had never tried to be too bold with her. She knew what people said about Naakkve, but he had never offended her, in either word or deed. But he had lain beside her on top of the bedcovers a few times, and they had talked. She once asked him if it was his intention to court her. He replied that he couldn't; he had promised himself to the service of the Virgin Mary. He told her the same thing in the spring, when they happened to speak to each other. And then she decided that she would no longer resist the wishes of her grandfather and father.

"It would have brought great sorrow upon both of you if he had broken his promise and you had defied your kinsmen," said Kristin. She stood leaning on her rake and looked at the young maiden. The child had a gentle, lovely round face, and a thick braid of the most beautiful fair hair. "God will surely bestow happiness on you, my Tordis. He seems a most intrepid and fine boy, your betrothed."

"Yes, I'm quite fond of Haavard," said the girl, and began to sob bitterly.

Kristin consoled her with words befitting the lips of an old and sensible woman. Inside, she moaned with longing; she so dearly wished she could have called this good, fresh child her daughter.

After Ivar's wedding she stayed at Rognheim for a while. Signe Gamalsdatter was not beautiful and looked both weary and old, but she was kind and gentle. She seemed to have a deep love for her young husband, and she welcomed his mother and brothers as if she thought them to be so high above her that she couldn't possibly honor or serve them well enough. For Kristin it was a new experience to have this woman go out of her way to anticipate her wishes and tend to her comfort. Not even when she was the wealthy mistress of Husaby, commanding dozens of servants, did anyone ever serve Kristin in a way that showed they were thinking of the mistress's ease or well-being. She had never spared herself when she bore the brunt of the work for the benefit of the whole household, and no one else ever thought of sparing her either. Signe's obliging concern for the welfare of her mother-in-law during the days she was at Rognheim did Kristin good. She soon grew so fond of Signe that almost as often as she prayed to God to grant Ivar happiness in his marriage, she also prayed that Signe might never have reason to regret that she had given herself and all her properties to such a young husband.

Right after Michaelmas Naakkve and Bjørgulf headed north for Trøndelag. The only thing she had heard since then was that they had arrived safely in Nidaros and had been accepted as novices by the brotherhood at Tautra.

And now Kristin had lived at Jørundgaard for almost a year with only two of her sons. But she was surprised it wasn't longer than that. On that day, the previous fall, when she had come riding past the church and looked down to see the slopes lying under a blanket of cold, raw fog so that she couldn't make out the buildings of her own estate—she had accompanied her two oldest sons as far as Dovre—then she had thought this was what someone must feel who is riding toward home and knows that the farm lying there is nothing but ashes and cold, charred timbers.

Now, whenever she took the old path home past the site of the smithy—and by now it was almost overgrown, with tufts of yellow bedstraw, bluebells, and sweet peas spilling over the borders of the lush meadow—it seemed almost as if she were looking at a picture of her own life: the weather-beaten, soot-covered old hearth that would never again be lit by a fire. The ground was strewn with bits of coal, but thin, short, gleaming tendrils of grass were springing up all over the abandoned site. And in the cracks of the old hearth blossomed fireweed, which sows its seeds everywhere, with its exquisite, long red tassels.

CHAPTER 2

SOMETIMES, AFTER KRISTIN had gone to bed, she would be awakened by people entering the courtyard on horseback. There would be a pounding on the door to the loft, and she would hear Gaute greet his guests loudly and joyously. The servants would have to get up and go out. There was a clattering and stomping overhead; Kristin could hear Ingrid's cross voice. Yes, she was a good child, that young maid, and she didn't let anyone get too forward with her. A roar of laughing young voices would greet her sharp and lively words. Frida shrieked; the poor thing, she never grew any wiser. She was not much younger than Kristin, and yet at times her mistress had to keep an eye on her.

Then Kristin would turn over in bed and go back to sleep.

Gaute was always up before dawn the next morning, as usual. He never stayed in bed any longer even if he had been up drinking ale the night before. But his guests wouldn't appear until breakfast time. Then they would stay at the manor all day; sometimes they had trade to discuss, sometimes it was merely a friendly visit. Gaute was most hospitable.

Kristin saw to it that Gaute's friends were offered the best of everything. She wasn't aware that she went about smiling quietly at the hum of youth and merry activity returning to her father's estate. But she seldom talked with the young men, and she saw little of them. What she did see was that Gaute was well liked and happy.

Gaute Erlendssøn was as much liked by commoners as by the wealthy landowners. The case against the men who killed Erlend had brought great misfortune upon their kin, and there were doubtless people on many manors and belonging to many lineages who vigilantly avoided meeting any of the Erlendssøns, but Gaute himself had not a single foe.

Sir Sigurd of Sundbu had taken a keen liking to his young kinsman. This cousin of hers, whom Kristin had never met until fate
led him to the deathbed of Erlend Nikulaussøn, had shown her the
greatest loyalty of a kinsman. He stayed at Jørundgaard almost
until Christmas and did everything he could to help the widow and
her fatherless young boys. The sons of Erlend displayed their gratitude in a noble and courteous manner, but only Gaute drew close
to him and had spent a great deal of time at Sundbu since then.

When this nephew of Ivar Gjesling eventually died, the estate
would pass out of the hands of his lineage; he was childless, and
the Haftorssøns were his closest descendants. Sir Sigurd was already quite an old man, and he had endured a terrible fate when
his young wife lost her wits during her first childbirth. For nearly
forty years now he had been married to this madwoman, but he
still went in almost daily to see how she was doing. She lived in
one of the best houses at Sundbu and had many maids to look after her. "Do you know me today, Gyrid?" her husband would ask.
Sometimes she didn't answer, but other times she said, "I know
you well. You're the prophet Isaiah who lives north at Brotveit, beneath Brotveit Peak." She always had a spindle at her side. When
she was feeling good, she would spin a fine, even yarn, but when
things were bad, she would unravel her own work and strew all
over the room the wool that her maids had carded. After Gaute
had told Kristin about this, she always welcomed her cousin with
the most heartfelt kindness when he came to visit. But she declined to go to Sundbu; she hadn't been there since the day of her
wedding.

Gaute Erlendssøn was much smaller in stature than Kristin's
other sons. Between his tall mother and lanky brothers he looked
almost short, but he was actually of average height. In general
Gaute seemed to have grown larger in all respects now that his
two older brothers and the twins, who were born after him, had
left. Beside them he had always been a quiet figure. People in the
region called him an exceedingly handsome man, and he did have
a lovely face. With his flaxen yellow hair and big gray eyes so
finely set beneath his brow, with his narrow, suitably full counte-
nance, fresh complexion, and beautiful mouth, he looked much
like his grandfather Lavrans. His head was handsomely set on his
shoulders, and his hands, which were well shaped and rather large,

were unusually strong. But the lower half of his body was a little too short, and he was quite bowlegged. For this reason he always wore his clothing long unless, for the sake of his work, he had to put on a short tunic—although at the time it was more and more thought to be elegant and courtly for men to have their banquet attire cut shorter than in the past. The farmers learned of this fashion from traveling noblemen who passed through the valley. But whenever Gaute Erlendssøn arrived at church or at a feast wearing his ankle-length embroidered green Sabbath surcoat, the silver belt around his waist and the great cape with the squirrel-skin lining thrown back over his shoulders, the people of the parish would turn pleased and gentle eyes on the young master of Jørundgaard. Gaute always carried a magnificent silver-chased axe Lavrans Bjørgulfsøn had inherited from his father-in-law, Ivar Gjesling. And everyone thought it splendid to see Gaute Erlendssøn following in the footsteps of his forefathers, even as young as he was, and keeping up the good farming traditions of the past, in his attire, demeanor, and the way he lived.

On horseback Gaute was the handsomest man anyone had ever seen. He was the boldest of riders, and people in the countryside boasted there wasn't a horse in all of Norway that Gaute couldn't manage to tame and ride. When he was in Bjørgvin the year before, he had purportedly mastered a young stallion that no man had ever been able to handle or ride; under Gaute's hands he was so submissive that he could be ridden without a saddle and with a maiden's ribbons as reins. But when Kristin asked her son about this story, he merely laughed and refused to talk about it.

Kristin knew that Gaute was reckless in his dealings with women, and this did not please her, but she thought it was mostly because the women treated the handsome young man much too kindly, and Gaute had an open and charming manner. Surely it was largely banter and foolishness; he didn't take such matters seriously or go about concealing things the way Naakkve had. He came and told his mother himself when he had conceived a child with a young girl over at Sundbu; that had happened two years ago. Kristin heard from Sir Sigurd that Gaute had generously provided the mother with a good dowry, befitting her position, and he wanted to bring the child to Jørundgaard after she had been weaned from her mother's breast. He seemed to be quite fond of his little daughter; he always went to see her whenever he was at Vaagaa. She was the loveliest child, Gaute proudly reported, and he had had her baptized Magnhild. Kristin agreed that since the boy had sinned, it was best if he brought the child home and became her loyal father. She looked forward with joy to having little Magnhild live with them. But then she died, only a year old. Gaute was greatly distressed when he heard the news, and Kristin thought it sad that she had never seen her little granddaughter.

Kristin had always had a difficult time reprimanding Gaute. He had been so miserable when he was little, and later he had continued to cling to his mother more than the other children had. Then there was the fact that he resembled her father. And he had been so steadfast and trustworthy as a child; with his somber and grownup manner he had walked at her side and often lent her a well-intentioned helping hand that he, in his childish innocence, thought would be of the greatest benefit to his mother. No, she had never been able to be stern with Gaute; when he did something wrong out of thoughtlessness or the natural ignorance of his years, he never needed more than a few gentle, admonishing words, so sensible and wise the boy was.

When Gaute was two years old, their house priest at Husaby, who had a particularly good understanding of childhood illnesses, advised that the boy be given mother's milk again, since no other measures had helped. The twins were newborns, and Frida, who was nursing Skule, had much more milk than the infant could consume. But the maid found the poor boy loathsome. Gaute looked terrible, with his big head and thin, wizened body; he could neither speak nor stand on his own. She was afraid he might be a changeling, even though the child had been healthy and fair-looking up until he fell ill at the age of ten months. All the same, Frida refused to put Gaute to her breast, and so Kristin had to nurse him herself, and he was allowed to suckle until he was four winters old.

Since then Frida had never liked Gaute; she was always scolding him, as much as she dared for fear of his mother. Frida now sat next to her mistress on the women's bench and carried her keys whenever Kristin was away from home. She said whatever she liked to the mistress and her family; Kristin showed her great forbearance and found the woman amusing, even though she was often annoyed with her too. Nevertheless, she always tried to make amends and smooth things over whenever Frida had done something wrong or spoken too coarsely. Now the maid had a hard time accepting that Gaute sat in the high seat and was to be master of the estate. She seemed to consider him no more than a foolish boy; she boasted about his brothers, especially Bjørgulf and Skule, whom she had nursed, while she mocked Gaute's short stature and crooked legs. Gaute took it with good humor.

"Well, you know, Frida, if I had nursed at your breast, I would have become a giant just like my brothers. But I had to be content with my mother's breast." And he smiled at Kristin.

Mother and son often went out walking in the evening. In many places the path across the fields was so narrow that Kristin had to walk behind Gaute. He would stroll along carrying the long-hafted axe, so manly that his mother had to smile behind his back. She had an impetuous, youthful desire to rush at him from behind and pull him to her, laughing and chattering with Gaute the way she had done occasionally when he was a child.

Sometimes they would go all the way down to the place on the riverbank where the washing was done and sit down to listen to the roar of the water rushing past, bright and roiling in the dusk. Usually they said very little to each other. But once in a while Gaute would ask his mother about the old days in the region and about her own lineage. Kristin would tell him what she had heard and seen in her childhood. His father and the years at Husaby were never mentioned on those nights.

"Mother, you're sitting here shivering," Gaute said one evening. "It's cold tonight."

"Yes, and I've grown stiff from sitting on this stone." Kristin stood up. "I'm getting to be an old woman, my Gaute!"

Walking back, she placed her hand on his shoulder for support.

Lavrans was sleeping like a rock in his bed. Kristin lit the little oil lamp; she felt like sitting up for a while to enjoy the sea calm in her own soul. And there was always some task to occupy her hands. Upstairs Gaute was clattering around with something; then she heard him climb into bed. Kristin straightened her back for a moment, smiling a bit at the tiny flame in the lamp. She moved her lips faintly, making the sign of the cross over her face and breast and in the air in front of her. Then she picked up her sewing again.

Bjørn, the old dog, stood up and shook himself, stretching out his front paws full length as he yawned. He padded across the floor to his mistress. As soon as she started petting him, he placed his front paws on her lap. When she spoke to him gently, the dog eagerly licked her face and hands as he wagged his tail. Then Bjørn slunk off again, turning his head to peer at Kristin. Guilt shone in his tiny eyes and was evident in his whole bulky, wiry-haired body, right down to the tip of his tail. Kristin smiled quietly and pretended not to notice; then the dog jumped up onto her bed and curled up at the foot.

After a while she blew out the lamp, pinched the spark off the wick, and tossed it into the oil. The light of the summer night was rising outside the little windowpane. Kristin said her last prayers of the day, silently undressed, and slipped into bed. She tucked the pillows comfortably under her breast and shoulders, and the old dog settled against her back. A moment later she fell asleep.

Bishop Halvard had assigned Sira Dag to the cleric's position in the parish, and from him Gaute had purchased the bishop's tithes for three years hence. He had also traded for hides and food in the region, sending the goods over the winter roads to Raumsdal and from there by ship to Bjørgvin in the spring. Kristin wasn't pleased with these ventures of her son; she herself had always sold her goods in Hamar, because both her father and Simon Andressøn had done so. But Gaute had formed some sort of trade partnership with his kinsman Gerlak Paus. And Gerlak was a clever merchant, with close ties to many of the richest German merchants in Bjørgvin.

Erlend's daughter Margret and her husband had come to Jørundgaard during the summer after Erlend's death. They presented great gifts to the church for his soul. When Margret was a young maiden back home at Husaby, there had been scant friendship between her and her stepmother, and she had cared little for her small half brothers. Now she was thirty years old, with no children from her marriage; now she showed her handsome, grown-up brothers the most loving sisterly affection. And she was the one who arranged the agreement between Gaute and her husband.

Margret was still beautiful, but she had grown so big and fat that Kristin didn't think she had ever seen such a stout woman. But there was all the more room for silver links on her belt, while a silver brooch as large as a small shield fit nicely between her enormous breasts. Her heavy body was always adorned like an altar with the costliest of fabrics and gilded metals. Gerlak Tiede-kenssøn seemed to have the greatest love for his wife.

A year earlier Gaute had visited his sister and brother-in-law in Bjørgvin during the spring meetings, and in the fall he traveled over the mountains with a herd of horses, which he sold in town. The journey turned out to be so profitable that Gaute swore he would do it again this autumn. Kristin thought he should be allowed to do as he wished. No doubt he had some of his father's lust for travel in his blood; surely he would settle down as he grew older. When his mother saw that he was aching to get away, she urged him to go. Last year he had been forced to come home through the mountains at the height of winter.

He set off on a beautiful sunny morning right after Saint Bartholomew's Day. It was the time for slaughtering the goats, and the whole manor smelled of cooked goat meat. Everyone had eaten his fill and was feeling content. All summer long they had tasted no fresh meat except on high holy days, but now they had their share of the pungent meat and the strong, fatty broth at both breakfast and supper for many days. Kristin was exhausted and elated after helping with the first big slaughtering of the year and making sausages. She stood on the main road and waved with a corner of her wimple at Gaute's entourage. It was a lovely sight: splendid horses and fresh young men riding along with glittering weapons and jangling harnesses. There was a great thundering as they rode across the high bridge. Gaute turned in his saddle and waved his hat, and Kristin waved back, giving a giddy little cry of joy and pride.

Just after Winter Day[1] rain and sleet swept in over the countryside, with storms and snow in the mountains. Kristin was a little uneasy, for Gaute had still not returned. But she was never as fearful for him as she had been for the others; she believed in the good fortune of this son.

A week later Kristin was coming out of the cowshed late one

evening when she caught sight of several horsemen up by the manor gate. The fog was billowing like white smoke around the lantern she carried; she began walking through the rain to meet the group of dark, fur-clad men. Could it be Gaute? It was unlikely that strangers would be arriving so late.

Then she saw that the rider in front was Sigurd of Sundbu. With the slight stiffness of an old man, he dismounted from his horse.

"Yes, I bring you news from Gaute, Kristin," he said after they had greeted each other. "He arrived at Sundbu yesterday."

It was so dark she couldn't make out his expression. But his voice sounded so strange. And when he walked toward the door of the main house, he told his men to go with Kristin's stableboy to the servants' quarters. She grew frightened when he said nothing more, but when they were alone in the room, she asked quite calmly, "What news do you bring, kinsman? Is he ill, since he hasn't come home with you?"

"No, Gaute is so well that I've never seen him look better. But his men were tired . . ."

He blew at the foam on the ale bowl that Kristin handed to him, then took a swallow and praised the brew.

"Good ale should be given to the one who brings good news," said the mistress with a smile.

"Well, I wonder what you'll say when you've heard all of my news," he remarked rather diffidently. "He did not return alone this time, your son . . ."

Kristin stood there waiting.

"He has brought along . . . well, she's the daughter of Helge of Hovland. He has apparently taken this—this maiden . . . taken her by force from her father."

Kristin still said nothing. But she sat down on the bench across from him. Her lips were narrow and pressed tight.

"Gaute asked me to come here; I suppose he was afraid you wouldn't be pleased. He asked me to tell you the news, and now I've done so," concluded Sir Sigurd faintly.

"You must tell me everything you know about this matter, Sigurd," said Kristin calmly.

Sir Sigurd did as she asked, in a vague and disjointed way, with a great deal of roundabout talk. He himself seemed to be quite horrified by Gaute's action. But from his account Kristin discerned that Gaute had met the maiden in Bjørgvin the year before. Her name was Jofrid, and no, she had not been abducted. But Gaute had probably realized that it would do no good to speak to the maiden's kinsmen about marriage. Helge of Hovland was a very wealthy man and belonged to the lineage known as Duk, with estates all over Voss. And then the Devil had tempted the two young people. . . . Sir Sigurd tugged at his clothing and scratched his head, as if he were swarming with lice.

Then, this past summer—when Kristin thought that Gaute was at Sundbu and was going to accompany Sir Sigurd into the mountain pastures to hunt for two vicious bears—he had actually journeyed over the heights and down to Sogn; Jofrid was staying there with a married sister. Helge had three daughters and no sons. Sigurd groaned in distress; yes, he had promised Gaute to keep silent about this. He knew the boy must be going to see a maiden, but he had never dreamed that Gaute was thinking of doing anything so foolish.

"Yes, my son is going to have to pay dearly for this," replied Kristin. Her face was impassive and calm.

Sigurd said that winter had now set in for good, and the roads were nearly impassable. After the men of Hovland had had time to think things over, perhaps they would see . . . It was best if Gaute won Jofrid with the consent of her kinsmen—now that she was already his.

"But what if they don't see things that way? And demand revenge for abducting a woman?"

Sir Sigurd squirmed and scratched even more.

"I suppose it's an unredeemable offense,"[2] he said quietly. "I'm not quite certain . . ."

Kristin did not reply.

Then Sir Sigurd continued, his voice imploring, "Gaute said . . . He expected that you would welcome them kindly. He said that surely you are not so old that you've forgotten . . . Well, he said that you won the husband you insisted on having—do you understand?"

Kristin nodded.

"She's the fairest child I have ever seen in my life, Kristin," said Sigurd fervently. Tears welled up in his eyes. "It's terrible that the

Devil has lured Gaute into this misdeed, but surely you will receive these two poor children with kindness, won't you?"

Kristin nodded again.

The countryside was sodden the next day, pallid and black under torrents of rain when Gaute rode into the courtyard around mid-afternoon prayers.

Kristin felt a cold sweat on her brow as she leaned against the doorway. There stood Gaute, lifting down from her horse a woman dressed in a hooded black cloak. She was small in build, barely reaching up to his shoulders. Gaute tried to take her hand to lead her forward, but she pushed him away and came to meet Kristin alone. Gaute busied himself talking to the servants and giving orders to the men who had accompanied him. Then he cast another glance at the two women standing in front of the door; Kristin was holding both hands of the newly arrived girl. Gaute rushed over to them with a joyful greeting on his lips. In the entryway Sir Sigurd put his arm around his shoulder and gave him a fatherly pat, huffing and puffing after the strain.

Kristin was taken by surprise when the girl lifted her face, so white and so lovely inside the drenched hood of her cloak. And she was so young and as small as a child.

Then the girl said, "I do not expect to be welcomed by you, Gaute's mother, but now all doors have been closed to me except this one. If you will tolerate my presence here on the manor, mistress, then I will never forget that I arrived here without property or honor, but with good intentions to serve you and Gaute, my lord."

Before she knew it, Kristin had taken the girl's hands and said, "May God forgive my son for what he has brought upon you, my fair child. Come in, Jofrid. May God help both of you, just as I will help you as best I can!"

A moment later she realized that she had offered much too warm a welcome to this woman, whom she did not know. But by then Jofrid had taken off her outer garments. Her heavy winter gown, which was a pale blue woven homespun, was dripping wet at the hem, and the rain had soaked right through her cloak to her shoulders. There was a gentle, sorrowful dignity about this child-like girl. She kept her small head with its dark tresses gracefully bowed; two thick pitch-black braids fell past her waist. Kristin kindly took Jofrid's hand and led her to the warmest place on the bench next to the hearth. "You must be freezing," she said.

Gaute came over and gave his mother a hearty embrace. "Mother, things will happen as they must. Have you ever seen as beautiful a maiden as my Jofrid? I had to have her, whatever it may cost me. And you must treat her with kindness, my dearest mother. . . ."

Jofrid Helgesdatter was indeed beautiful; Kristin could not stop looking at her. She was rather short, with wide shoulders and hips, but a soft and charming figure. And her skin was so delicate and pure that she was lovely even though her face was quite pale. The features of her face were short and broad, but the expansive, strong arc of her cheeks and chin gave it beauty, and her wide mouth had thin, rosy lips with small, even teeth that looked like a child's first teeth. When she raised her heavy eyelids, her clear gray-green eyes were like shining stars beneath the long black eyelashes. Black hair, light-colored eyes—Kristin had always thought that was the most beautiful combination, ever since she had seen Erlend for the first time. Most of her own handsome sons had that coloring.

Kristin showed Jofrid to a place on the women's bench next to her own. She sat there, graceful and shy, among all the servants she didn't know, eating little and blushing every time Gaute drank a toast to her during the meal.

He was bursting with pride and restless elation as he sat in the high seat. To honor her son's return home, Kristin had spread a cloth over the table that evening and set two wax tapers in the candlesticks made of gilded copper. Gaute and Sir Sigurd were constantly toasting each other, and the old gentleman grew more and more maudlin, putting his arm around Gaute's shoulder and promising to speak on his behalf to his wealthy kinsmen, yes, even to King Magnus himself. Surely he would be able to obtain for him reconciliation with the maiden's offended kin. Sigurd Eldjarn himself had not a single foe; it was his father's rancorous temperament and his own misfortune with his wife that had made him so alone.

In the end Gaute sprang to his feet with the drinking horn in his hand. How handsome he is, thought Kristin, and how like Father!

Her father had been the same way when he was beginning to feel drunk—so radiant with joy, straight-backed and lively.

"Things are now such between this woman, Jofrid Helgesdatter, and myself that today we celebrate our homecoming, and later we will celebrate our wedding, if God grants us such happiness. You, Sigurd, we thank for your steadfast kinship, and you, Mother, for welcoming us as I expected you would, with your loyal, motherly warmth. As we brothers have often discussed, you seem to us the most magnanimous of women and the most loving mother. Therefore I ask you to honor us by preparing our bridal bed in such a fine and beautiful manner that without shame I can invite Jofrid to sleep there beside me. And I ask you to accompany Jofrid up to the loft yourself, so that she might retire with as much seemliness as possible since she has neither a mother still alive nor any kinswomen here."

Sir Sigurd was now quite drunk, and he burst out laughing. "You slept together in my loft; if I didn't know better . . . I thought the two of you had already shared a bed before."

Gaute shook his golden hair impatiently. "Yes, kinsman, but this is the first night Jofrid will sleep in my arms on her own manor, God willing.

"But I beg you good people to drink and be merry tonight. Now you have seen the woman who will be my wife here at Jørundgaard. This woman and no other—I swear this before God, our Lord, and on my Christian faith. I expect all of you to respect her, both servants and maids, and I expect you, my men, to help me keep and protect her in a seemly manner, my boys."

During all the shouting and commotion that accompanied Gaute's speech, Kristin quietly left the table and whispered to Ingrid to follow her up to the loft.

Lavrans Bjørgulfsøn's magnificent loft room had fallen into disrepair over the years, after the sons of Erlend had moved in. Kristin hadn't wanted to give the reckless boys any but the coarsest and most essential of bedclothes and pieces of furniture, and she seldom had the room cleaned, for it wasn't worth the effort. Gaute and his friends tracked in filth and manure as quickly as she swept it out. There was an ingrained smell from men coming in and flinging themselves onto the beds, soaked and sweaty and muddy from the woods and the farmyard—a smell of the stables and leather garments and wet dogs.

Now Kristin and her maid quickly swept and cleaned as best they could. The mistress brought in fine bed coverlets, blankets, and cushions and burned some juniper. On a little table which she moved close to the bed she placed a silver goblet filled with the last of the wine in the house, a loaf of wheat bread, and a candle in an iron holder. This was as elegant as she could make things on such short notice.

Weapons hung on the timbered wall next to the alcove: Erlend's heavy two-handed sword and the smaller sword he used to carry, along with felling axes and broadaxes; Bjørgulf's and Naakkve's axes still hung there too. And the two small axes that the boys seldom used because they considered them too lightweight. But these were the tools that her father had used to carve and shape all manner of objects with such skill and care that afterward he only had to do the fine polishing with his gouge and knife. Kristin carried the axes into the alcove and put them inside Erlend's chest, where his bloody shirt lay, along with the axe he was holding in his hand when he received the mortal wound.

Laughing, Gaute invited Lavrans to light the way up to the loft for his bride. The boy was both embarrassed and proud. Kristin saw that Lavrans understood his brother's unlawful wedding was a dangerous game, but he was high-spirited and giddy from these strange events; with sparkling eyes he gazed at Gaute and his beautiful betrothed.

On the stairs up to the loft the candle went out. Jofrid said to Kristin, "Gaute should not have asked you to do this, even though he was drunk. Don't come any farther with me, mistress. Have no fear that I might forget I'm a fallen woman, cut off from the counsel of my kin."

"I'm not too good to serve you," said Kristin, "not until my son has atoned for his sin against you and you can rightly call me mother-in-law. Sit down and I'll comb your hair. Your hair is beautiful beyond compare, child."

But after the servants were asleep and Kristin was lying in bed, she once again felt a certain uneasiness. Without thinking, she had told this Jofrid more than she meant to . . . yet. But she was so young, and she showed so clearly that she didn't expect to be regarded as any better than what she was: a child who had fled from honor and obedience.

So that's the way it looked . . . when people let the bridal procession and homeward journey come before the wedding. Kristin sighed. Once she too had been willing to risk the same for Erlend, but she didn't know whether she would have dared if his mother had been living at Husaby. No, no, she wouldn't make things any worse for the child upstairs.

Sir Sigurd was still staggering around the room; he was to sleep with Lavrans. In a mawkish way, but with sincere intentions, he talked about the two young people; he would spare nothing to help them find a good outcome to this reckless venture.

The next day Jofrid showed Gaute's mother what she had brought along to the manor: two leather sacks with clothes and a little chest made of walrus tusk in which she kept her jewelry. As if she had read Kristin's thoughts, Jofrid said that these possessions belonged to her; they had been given to her for her own use, as gifts and inherited items, mostly from her mother. She had taken nothing from her father.

Full of sorrow, Kristin sat leaning her cheek on her hand. On that night, an eternity ago, when she had collected her gold in a chest to steal away from home . . . Most of what *she* had put inside were gifts from the parents she had secretly shamed and whom she was openly going to offend and distress.

But if these were Jofrid's own possessions and if her mother's inheritance was only jewelry, then she must come from an exceedingly wealthy home. Kristin estimated that the goods she saw before her were worth more than thirty marks in silver. The scarlet gown alone, with its white fur and silver clasps and the silk-lined hood that went with it, must have cost ten or twelve marks. It was all well and good if the maiden's father would agree to reconcile with Gaute, but her son could never be considered an equal match for this woman. And if Helge brought such harsh charges against Gaute, as he had the right and ability to do, things looked quite bleak indeed.

"My mother always wore this ring," said Jofrid. "If you will accept it, mistress, then I'll know that you don't judge me as sternly as a good and highborn woman might be expected to do."

"Oh, but then I might be tempted to take the place of your mother," said Kristin with a smile, putting the ring on her finger. It was a little silver ring set with a lovely white agate, and Kristin thought the child must consider it especially precious because it reminded her of her mother. "I expect I must give you a gift in return." She brought over her chest and took out the gold ring with sapphires. "Gaute's father put this ring in my bed after I brought his son into the world."

Jofrid accepted the ring by kissing Kristin's hand. "Otherwise I had thought of asking you for another gift . . . Mother. . . ." She smiled so charmingly. "Don't be afraid that Gaute has brought home a lazy or incapable woman. But I own no proper work dress. Give me an old gown of yours and allow me to lend you a hand; perhaps then you will soon grow to like me better than it is reasonable for me to expect right now."

And then Kristin had to show the young maiden everything she had in her chests, and Jofrid praised all of Kristin's lovely handiwork with such rapt attention that the older woman ended up giving her one thing after another: two linen sheets with silk-knotted embroidery, a blue-trimmed towel, a coverlet woven in four panels, and finally the long tapestry with the falcon hunt woven into it. "I don't want these things to leave this manor, but with the help of God and the Virgin Mary, this house will someday be yours." Then they both went over to the storehouses and stayed there for many hours, enjoying each other's company.

Kristin wanted to give Jofrid her green homespun gown with the black tufts woven into the fabric, but Jofrid thought it much too fine for a work dress. Poor thing, she was just trying to flatter her husband's mother, thought Kristin, hiding a smile. At last they found an old brown dress Jofrid thought would be suitable if she cut it shorter and sewed patches under the arms and on the elbows. She asked to borrow a scissors and sewing things at once, and then she sat down to sew. Kristin took up some mending as well, and the two women were still sitting there together when Gaute and Sir Sigurd came in for the evening meal.

KRISTIN HAD TO admit with all her heart that Jofrid was a woman who knew how to use her hands. *If* things went well, then Gaute was certainly fortunate; he would have a wife who was as hardworking and diligent as she was rich and beautiful. Kristin herself could not have found a more capable woman to succeed her at Jørundgaard, not if she had searched through all of Norway. One day she said—and afterward she wasn't sure what had happened to make the words spill from her lips—that on the day Jofrid Helgesdatter became Gaute's lawful wife, she would give her keys to the young woman and move out to the old house with Lavrans.

Afterward she thought she should have considered these words more carefully before she uttered them. There were already many instances when she had spoken of something too soon when she was talking with Jofrid.

But there was the fact that Jofrid was not well. Kristin had noticed it almost at once after the young girl arrived. And Kristin remembered the first winter she had spent at Husaby; *she* at least had been married, and her husband and father were bound by kinship, no matter what might happen to their friendship after the sin came to light. All the same, she had suffered so terribly from remorse and shame, and her heart had felt bitter toward Erlend. But she was already nineteen winters old back then, while Jofrid was barely seventeen. And here she was now, abducted and without rights, far from her home and among strangers, carrying Gaute's child under her heart. Kristin could not deny that Jofrid seemed to be stronger and braver than she herself had been.

But Jofrid hadn't breached the sanctity of the convent; she hadn't broken promises and betrothal vows; she hadn't betrayed her parents or lied to them or stolen their honor behind their backs. Even though these two young people had dared sin against the laws, constraints, and moral customs of the land, they needn't have *such* an anguished conscience. Kristin prayed fervently for a good outcome to Gaute's foolhardy deed, and she consoled herself that God, in His fairness, couldn't possibly deal Gaute and Jofrid any harsher circumstances than she and Erlend had been given. And *they* had been married; their child of sin had been born to share in a lawful inheritance from all his kinsmen.

Since neither Gaute nor Jofrid spoke of the matter, Kristin didn't want to mention it either, although she longed to have a talk with the inexperienced young woman. Jofrid should spare herself and enjoy her morning rest instead of getting up before everyone else on the manor. Kristin saw that it was Jofrid's desire to rise before her mother-in-law and to accomplish more than she did. But Jofrid was not the kind of person Kristin could offer either help or solicitude. The only thing she could do was silently take the heaviest work away from her and treat her as if she were the rightful young mistress on the estate, both when they were alone and in front of the servants.

Frida was furious at having to relinquish her place next to her mistress and give it to Gaute's . . . She used an odious word to describe Jofrid one day when she and Kristin were together in the cookhouse. For once Kristin struck her maid.

"How splendid to hear such words from you, an old nag lusting after men as you do!"

Frida wiped the blood from her nose and mouth.

"Aren't you supposed to be better than a poor man's offspring, daughters of great chieftains such as yourself and this Jofrid? You know with certainty that a bridal bed with silken sheets awaits you. You're the ones who must be shameless and lusting after men if you can't wait but have to run off into the woods with young lads and end up with wayside bastards—for shame, I say to you!"

"Hold your tongue now. Go out and wash yourself. You're standing there bleeding into the dough," said her mistress quite calmly.

Frida met Jofrid in the doorway. Kristin saw from the young woman's face that she must have heard the conversation with the maid.

"The poor thing's chatter is as foolish as she is. I can't send her away; she has no place to go." Jofrid smiled scornfully. Then Kristin said, "She was the foster mother for two of my sons."

"But she wasn't Gaute's foster mother," replied Jofrid. "She reminds us both of that fact as often as she can. Can't you marry her off?" she asked sharply.

Kristin had to laugh. "Don't you think I've tried? But all it took was for the man to have a few words with his future bride. . . ."

Kristin thought she should seize the opportunity to talk with Jofrid, to let her know that here she would meet with only maternal goodwill. But Jofrid looked angry and defiant.

In the meantime it was now clearly evident that Jofrid was not walking alone. One day she was going to clean some feathers for new mattresses. Kristin advised her to tie back her hair so it wouldn't be covered with down. Jofrid bound a linen cloth around her head.

"No doubt this is now more fitting than going bareheaded," she said with a little laugh.

"That may well be," said Kristin curtly.

And yet she wasn't pleased that Jofrid should jest about such a thing.

A few days later Kristin came out of the cookhouse and saw Jofrid cutting open several black grouse; there was blood spattered all over her arms. Horror-stricken, Kristin pushed her aside.

"Child, you mustn't do this bloody work *now*. Don't you know better than that?"

"Oh, surely you don't believe everything women say is true," said Jofrid skeptically.

Then Kristin told her about the marks of fire that Naakkve had received on his chest. She purposely spoke of it in such a way that Jofrid would understand she was not yet married when she looked at the burning church.

"I suppose you hadn't thought such a thing of me," she said quietly.

"Oh yes, Gaute has already told me: Your father had promised you to Simon Andressøn, but you ran off with Erlend Nikulaussøn to his aunt, and then Lavrans had to give his consent."

"It wasn't exactly like that; we didn't run off. Simon released me as soon as he realized that I was more fond of Erlend than of him, and then my father gave his consent—unwillingly, but he placed my hand in Erlend's. I was betrothed for a year. Does that seem worse to you?" asked Kristin, for Jofrid had turned bright red and gave her a look of horror.

The girl used her knife to scrape off the blood from her white arms.

"Yes," she said in a low but firm voice. "I would not have squandered my good reputation and honor needlessly. But I won't say anything of this to Gaute," she said quickly. "He thinks his father carried you off by force because he could not win you with entreaty."

No doubt what she said was true, thought Kristin.

As time passed and Kristin continued to ponder the matter, it seemed to her that the most honorable thing to do was for Gaute to send word to Helge of Hovland, to place his case in his hands and ask to be given Jofrid as his wife on such terms as her father decided to grant them. But whenever she spoke of this to Gaute, he would look dismayed and refuse to answer. Finally he asked his mother crossly whether she could get a letter over the mountains in the wintertime. No, she told him, but Sira Dag could surely send a letter to Nes and then onward along the coast; the priests always managed to get their letters through, even during the winter. Gaute said it would be too costly.

"Then it will not be with your wife that you have a child this spring," said his mother indignantly.

"Even so, the matter cannot be arranged so quickly," said Gaute. Kristin could see that he was quite angry.

A terrible, dark fear seized hold of her as time went on. She couldn't help noticing that Gaute's first ardent joy over Jofrid had vanished completely; he went about looking sullen and ill tempered. From the very start this matter of Gaute abducting his bride had seemed as bad as it could be, but his mother thought it would be much worse if afterward the man turned cowardly. If the two young people regretted their sin, that was all well and good, but she had an ugly suspicion that there was more of an unmanly fear in Gaute toward the man he had offended than any god-fearing remorse. Gaute—all her days she had thought the most highly of this son of hers; it couldn't be true what people said: that he was unreliable and dealt carelessly with women, that he was already tired of Jofrid, now that his bride had faded and grown heavy and the day was approaching when he would have to answer for his actions to her kinsmen.

She sought excuses for her son. If Jofrid had allowed herself to be seduced so easily . . . she who had never witnessed anything during her upbringing other than the seemly behavior of pious people . . . Kristin's sons had known from childhood that their own mother had sinned, that their father had conceived children with another man's wife during his youth, and that he had sinned with a married woman when they were nearly grown boys. Ulf Haldorssøn, their foster father, and Frida's frivolous chatter . . . Oh, it wasn't so strange that these young men should be weak in that way. Gaute would have to marry Jofrid, if he could win the consent of her kinsmen, and be grateful for it. But it would be a shame for Jofrid if she should now see that Gaute married her reluctantly and without desire.

One day during Lent Kristin and Jofrid were preparing sacks of provisions for the woodcutters. They pounded dried fish thin and flat, pressed butter into containers, and filled wooden casks with ale and milk. Kristin saw that Jofrid now found it terribly difficult to stand or walk for very long, but she merely grew annoyed if Kristin told her to sit down and rest. To appease her a little, Kristin happened to mention the story about the stallion that Gaute had supposedly tamed with a maiden's hair ribbon. "Surely it must have been yours?"

"No," said Jofrid crossly, turning crimson. But then she added, "The ribbon belonged to Aasa, my sister." She laughed and said, "Gaute courted her first, but when I came home, he couldn't decide which of us he liked best. But Aasa was the one he had expected to find visiting Dagrun last summer when he went to Sogn. And he was angry when I teased him about her; he swore by God and man that he was not the sort to come too close to the daughters of worthy men. He said there had been nothing between him and Aasa that would prevent him from sleeping without sin in my arms that night. I took him at his word." She laughed again. When she saw Kristin's expression, she nodded stubbornly.

"Yes, I want Gaute to be my husband, and he will be, you can count on that, Mother. I most often get what I want."

Kristin woke up to pitch-darkness. The cold bit at her cheeks and chin; when she pulled the blanket more snugly around her, she noticed there was frost on it from her breath. It had to be nearly morning, but she dreaded getting up and seeing the stars. She curled up under the covers to warm herself a little more. At that moment she remembered her dream.

She seemed to be lying in bed in the little house at Husaby, and she had just given birth to a child. She was holding him in her arms, wrapped in a lambskin, which had rolled up and fallen away from the infant's little dark red body. He was holding his tiny clenched hands over his face, with his knees tucked up to his belly and his feet crossed; now and then he would stir a bit. It didn't occur to her to wonder why the boy wasn't swaddled properly and why there were no other women with them in the room. Her heat was still enveloping the child as he lay close to her; through her arm she could feel a tug at the roots of her heart every time he stirred. Weariness and pain were still shrouding her like a darkness that was starting to fade as she lay there and gazed at her son, feeling her joy and love for him ceaselessly growing the way the rim of daylight grows brighter along the mountain crest.

But at the same time as she lay there in bed, she was also standing outside the house. Below her stretched the countryside, lit by the morning sun. It was an early spring day. She drank in the sharp, fresh air; the wind was icy cold, but it tasted of the faraway sea and of thawing snow. The ridges were bathed with morning sunlight on the opposite side of the valley, with snowless patches around the farms. Pale crusted snow shone like silver in all the clearings amid the dark green forests. The sky was swept clean, a bright yellow and pale blue with only a few dark, windblown clusters of clouds hovering high above. But it was cold. Where she was standing the snowdrift was still frozen hard after the night frost, and between the buildings lay cold shadows, for the sun was directly above the eastern ridge, behind the manor. And right in front of her, where the shadows ended, the morning wind was rippling through the pale year-old grass; it moved and shimmered, with clumps of ice shiny as steel still among the roots.

Oh . . . Oh . . . Against her will, a sigh of lament rose up from her breast. She still had Lavrans; she could hear the boy's even breathing from the other bed. And Gaute. He was asleep up in the loft with his paramour. Kristin sighed again, moved restlessly, and Erlend's old dog settled against her legs, which were tucked up underneath the bedclothes.

Now she could hear that Jofrid was up and walking across the floor. Kristin quickly got out of bed and stuck her feet into her fur-lined boots, putting on her homespun dress and fur jacket. In the dark she fumbled her way over to the hearth, crouched down to stir the ashes and blow on them, but there was not the slightest spark; the fire had died out in the night.

She pulled her flint out of the pouch on her belt, but the tinder must have gotten wet and then froze. Finally she gave up trying, picked up the ember pan, and went upstairs to borrow some coals from Jofrid.

A good fire was burning in the little fireplace, lighting up the room. In the glow of the flames Jofrid sat stitching the copper clasp more securely to Gaute's reindeer coat. Over in the dim light of the bed, Kristin caught a glimpse of the man's naked torso. Gaute slept without covers even in the most biting cold. He was sitting up and having something to eat in bed.

Jofrid got to her feet heavily, with a proprietary air. Wouldn't Mother like a drop of ale? She had heated up the morning drink for Gaute. And Mother should take along this pitcher for Lavrans; he was going out with Gaute to cut wood that day. It would be cold for the men.

Kristin involuntarily grimaced when she was back downstairs and lit the fire. Seeing Jofrid busy with domestic chores and Gaute sitting there, openly allowing his wife to serve him . . . and his paramour's concern for her unlawful husband—all this seemed to Kristin so loathsome and immodest.

Lavrans stayed out in the forest, but Gaute came home that night, worn out and hungry. The women sat at the table after the servants had left, keeping the master company while he drank.

Kristin saw that Jofrid was not feeling well that evening. She kept letting her sewing sink to her lap as spasms of pain flickered across her face.

"Are you in pain, Jofrid?" asked Kristin softly.

"Yes, a little. In my feet and legs," replied the girl. She had toiled all day long, as usual, refusing to spare herself. Now pain had overtaken her, and her legs had swollen up.

Suddenly little tears spilled out from her lowered eyes. Kristin had never seen a woman cry in such a strange fashion; without a sound, her teeth clenched tight, she sat there weeping clear, round tears. Kristin thought they looked as hard as pearls, trickling down the haggard brown-flecked face. Jofrid looked angry that she was forced to surrender; reluctantly she allowed Kristin to help her over to the bed.

Gaute followed. "Are you in pain, my Jofrid?" he asked awkwardly. His face was fiery red from the cold, and he looked genuinely unhappy as he watched his mother helping Jofrid get settled, taking off her shoes and socks and tending to her swollen feet and legs. "Are you in pain, my Jofrid?" he kept asking.

"Yes," said Jofrid, in a low voice, biting back her rage. "Do you think I'd behave this way if I wasn't?"

"Are you in pain, my Jofrid?" he repeated.

"Surely you can see for yourself. Don't stand there moping like a foolish boy!" Kristin turned to face her son, her eyes blazing. The dull knot of fear about how things would turn out, of impatience because she had to tolerate the disorderly life of these two on her estate, of gnawing doubt about her son's manliness—all these things erupted in a ferocious rage: "Are you such a simpleton that you think she might be feeling *good*? She can see that you're not man enough to venture over the mountains because it's windy and snowing. You know full well that soon she'll have to crawl on her knees, this poor woman, and writhe in the greatest of torments—and her child will be called a bastard, because you don't dare go to her father. You sit here in the house warming the bench, not daring to lift a finger to protect the wife you have or your child soon to be born. *Your* father was not so afraid of my father that he didn't dare seek him out, or so fainthearted that he refused to ski through the mountains in the wintertime. Shame on you, Gaute, and pity me who must live to see the day when I call my son a timid man, one of the sons that Erlend gave me!"

Gaute picked up the heavy carved chair with both hands and slammed it against the floor; he ran over to the table and swept everything off. Then he rushed to the door, giving one last kick to the chair. They heard him cursing as he climbed the stairs to the loft.

"Oh no, Mother. You were much too hard on Gaute." Jofrid propped herself up on her elbow. "You can't reasonably expect him to risk his life going into the mountains in the winter in order to seek out my father and find out whether he'll be allowed to marry his seduced bride, with no dowry other than the shift I wore when he took me away, or else be driven from the land as an outlaw."

Waves of anger were still washing through Kristin's heart. She replied proudly, "And yet I don't believe *my* son would think that way!"

"No," said Jofrid. "If he didn't have me to think for him . . ." When she saw Kristin's expression, laughter crept into her voice. "Dear Mother, I've had trouble enough trying to restrain Gaute. I refuse to let him commit any more follies for my sake and cause our children to lose the riches that I can expect to inherit from my kinsmen if Gaute can come to an agreement that will be the best and most honorable one for all of us."

"What do you mean by that?" asked Kristin.

"I mean that when my kinsmen seek out Gaute, Sir Sigurd will meet them, so they will see that Gaute is not without kin. He will have to bear paying full restitution, but then Father will allow him to marry me, and I will regain my right to an inheritance along with my sisters."

"So you are partially to blame," said Kristin, "for the child coming into the world before you are married?"

"If I could run away with Gaute, then . . . Surely no one would believe that he has placed a sword blade in bed between us all these nights."

"Didn't he ever seek out your kinsmen to ask for your hand in marriage?" asked Kristin.

"No, we knew it would have been futile, even if Gaute had been a much richer man than he is." Jofrid burst out laughing again. "Don't you see, Mother? Father thinks he knows better than any man how to trade horses. But a person would have to be more alert than my father is if he wanted to fool Gaute Erlendssøn in an exchange of horses."

Kristin couldn't help smiling, in spite of her ill temper.

"I don't know the law very well in such cases," she said somberly. "But I'm not certain, Jofrid, that it will be easy for Gaute to obtain what you would consider a good reconciliation. If Gaute is sentenced as an outlaw, and your father takes you back home and lets you suffer his wrath, or if he demands that you enter a convent to atone for your sins . . ."

"He can't send me to a convent without sending splendid gifts along with me, and it will be less costly and more honorable if he reconciles with Gaute and demands restitution. You see, then he won't have to give up any cattle when he marries me off. And because of his dislike for Olav, my sister's husband, I think I will share in the inheritance with my sisters. If not, then my kinsmen will have to see to this child's welfare too. And I know Father would think twice before he tried to take me back home to Hovland with a bastard child, to let me suffer his wrath—knowing *me* as he does.

"I don't know much about the law either, but I know Father, and I know Gaute. And now enough time has already passed that this proposal cannot be presented until I myself am delivered and healthy again. Then, Mother, you will not see me weeping! Oh no, I have no doubt that Gaute will have his reconciliation on such terms as—

"No, Mother . . . Gaute, who is a descendant of highborn men and kings . . . And you, who come from the best of lineages in Norway . . . If you have had to endure seeing your sons sink below the rank that was their birthright, then you will see prosperity regained for your descendants in the children that Gaute and I shall have."

Kristin sat in silence. It was indeed conceivable that things might happen as Jofrid wished; she realized that she hadn't needed to worry so much on her behalf. The girl's face was now quite gaunt; the rounded softness of her cheeks had wasted away, and it was easier to see what a large, strong jaw she had.

Jofrid yawned, pushed herself up into a sitting position, and looked around for her shoes. Kristin helped her to put them on. Jofrid thanked her and said, "Don't trouble Gaute anymore,

Mother. He finds it hard to bear that we won't be married before-hand, but I refuse to make my child poor even before he's born."

Two weeks later Jofrid gave birth to a big, fair son, and Gaute sent word to Sundbu the very same day. Sir Sigurd came at once to Jørundgaard, and he held Erlend Gautessøn when the boy was baptized. But as happy as Kristin Lavransdatter was with her grandson, it still angered her that Erlend's name should be given for the first time to a paramour's child.

"Your father risked more to give his son his birthright," she told Gaute one evening as he sat in the weaving room and watched her get the boy ready for the night. Jofrid was already sleeping sweetly in her bed. "His love for old Sir Nikulaus was somewhat strained, but even so, he would never have shown his father such disrespect as to name his son after him if he were not lawfully born."

"And Orm . . . he was named for his maternal grandfather, wasn't he?" said Gaute. "Yes, I know, Mother, those may not be the words most becoming a good son. But you should realize that my brothers and I all noticed that while our father was alive, you didn't think he was the proper example for us in many matters. And yet now you talk about him constantly, as if he had been a holy man, or close to it. You should know that we realize he wasn't. All of us would be proud if we ever attained Father's stature—or even reached to his shoulders. We remember that he was noble and courageous, foremost among men in terms of those qualities that suit a man best. But you can't make us believe he was the most submissive or seemly of men in a woman's chamber or the most capable of farmers.

"And yet no one need wish anything better for you, my Erlend, than that you should take after him!" He picked up his child, now properly swaddled, and touched his chin to the tiny red face framed by the light-colored wool cloth. "This gifted and promising boy, Erlend Gautessøn of Jørundgaard—you should tell your grandmother that *you* aren't afraid your father will fail you." He made the sign of the cross over the child and put him back in Kristin's arms, then went over to the bed and looked down at the slumbering young mother.

"My Jofrid is as well as she can be, you say? She looks pale, but

I suppose you must know best. Sleep well in here, and may God's peace be with you."

One month after the birth of the boy, Gaute held a splendid christening feast, and his kinsmen came from far away to attend the celebration. Kristin assumed that Gaute had asked them to come in order to counsel him on his position; it was now spring, and he could soon expect to hear news from Jofrid's kin.

Kristin had the joy of seeing Ivar and Skule come home together. And her cousins came to Jørundgaard too: Sigurd Kyrning, who was married to her uncle's daughter from Skog, Ivar Gjesling of Ringheim, and Haavard Trondssøn. She hadn't seen the Trondssøns since Erlend had brought misfortune down upon the men of Sundbu. Now they were older; they had always been carefree and reckless, but intrepid and magnanimous, and they hadn't changed much at all. They greeted the sons of Erlend and Sir Sigurd, who was their cousin and successor at Sundbu, with a free and open manner befitting kinsmen. The ale and mead flowed in rivers in honor of little Erlend. Gaute and Jofrid welcomed their guests as unrestrainedly as if they had been wed and the king himself had married them. Everyone was joyous, and no one seemed to consider that the honor of these two young people was still at stake. But Kristin learned that Jofrid had not forgotten.

"The more bold and swaggering they are when they meet my father, the more easily he will comply," she said. "And Olav Piper could never hide the fact that he would be pleased to sit on the same bench as men from the ancient lineages."

The only one who did not seem to feel quite comfortable in this gathering of kin was Sir Jammælt Halvardssøn. King Magnus had made him a knight at Christmas; Ramborg Lavransdatter was now the wife of a knight.

This time Sir Jammælt had brought his eldest son, Andres Simonssøn, along with him. Kristin had asked him to do so the last time Jammælt came north, for she had heard a rumor that there was supposedly something strange about the boy. Then she grew terribly frightened; she wondered whether some harm might have been done to his soul or body because of what she had done in his behalf when he was a child. But his stepfather said no, the boy was healthy and strong, as good as gold, and perhaps cleverer than most people. But it was true that he had second sight. Sometimes he seemed to drift away, and when he came back, he would often do peculiar things. Such as the year before. One day he took his silver spoon, the one Kristin had given to him at his birth, and a torn shirt that had belonged to his father, and he left the manor and went down to a bridge that stretches across the river along the main road near Ælin. There he sat for many hours, waiting. Eventually three poor people came walking across the bridge: an old beggar and a young woman holding an infant. Andres went over and gave the things to them, and then asked if he might carry the child for the woman. Back home everyone was desperate with anguish when Andres didn't appear for meals or by nightfall. They went out looking for him, and at last Jammælt heard that Andres had been seen far north in the next parish, in the company of a couple known as Krepp and Kraaka; he was carrying their infant. When Jammælt finally found the boy on the following day, Andres explained that he had heard a voice during mass on the previous Sunday while he was looking at the images painted on the front of the altar. It showed the Mother of God and Saint Joseph leaving the land of Egypt and carrying a child, and he wished that he had lived back then, for he would have asked to accompany them and carry the child for the Virgin Mary. Then he heard a voice, the gentlest and sweetest voice in the world, and it promised to show him a sign if he would go out to Bjerkheim Bridge on a certain day.

Otherwise Andres was reluctant to speak of his visions, because their parish priest had said they were partly imagined and partly due to a confused and muddled state of mind, and he frightened his mother out of her wits with his strange ways. But he talked to an old servant woman, an exceedingly pious woman, and to a friar who used to wander through the countryside during Lent and Advent. The boy would doubtless choose the spiritual life, so Simon Simonssøn was sure to be the one who would settle at Formo when the time came. He was a healthy and lively child who looked a great deal like his father, and he was Ramborg's favorite.

Ramborg and Jammælt had not yet had a child of their own. Kristin had heard from those who had seen Ramborg at Raumarike that she had grown quite fat and lazy. She kept company with the wealthiest and mightiest people in the south, but she never wanted to make the trip to her home valley, and Kristin hadn't seen her only sister since they parted on that day at Formo. But Kristin was convinced that Ramborg's resentment toward her remained unchanged. She got on well with Jammælt, and he tended to the well-being of his stepchildren with loving care. If he should die with no children of his own, he had arranged for the eldest son of the man who would inherit most of his property to marry Ulvhild Simonsdatter; in that way at least the daughter of Simon Darre would have some benefit from his inheritance. Arngjerd had married Grunde of Eiken the year after her father's death; Gyrd Darre and Jammælt had provided her with a rich dowry, as they knew Simon would have wanted. And Jammælt said she was well. Grunde appeared to let his wife guide him in all manner of things, and they already had three handsome children.

Kristin was strangely moved when she saw Simon and Ramborg's oldest son again. He was the living image of Lavrans Bjørgulfsøn, even more than Gaute. And over the past few years Kristin had given up her belief that Gaute might be anything like her father in temperament.

Andres Darre was now twelve years old, tall and slender, fair and lovely and rather quiet, although he seemed robust and cheerful enough, with good physical abilities and a hearty appetite, except that he refused to eat meat. There was something that set him apart from other boys, but Kristin couldn't say what it was, although she watched him closely. Andres became good friends with his aunt, but he never mentioned his visions, and he didn't have any of his spells while in Sil.

The four sons of Erlend seemed to enjoy being together on their mother's estate, but Kristin didn't manage to talk much with her sons. When they were discussing things among themselves, she felt as if their lives and well-being had now slipped beyond her view. The two who came from far away had left their childhood home behind, and the two who lived on the manor were on the verge of taking its management out of her hands. The gathering took place in the midst of the springtime shortages, and she saw that Gaute must have been making preparations for it by rationing the fodder more strictly than usual that winter; he had also borrowed fodder

from Sir Sigurd. But he had done all these things without consult-
ing her. And all the advice regarding Gaute's case was also presented without including her, even though she sat in the same
room with the men.

For this reason she was not surprised when Ivar came to her one
day and said that Lavrans would be leaving with him when he
went back to Rognheim.

Ivar Erlendssøn also told his mother on another day that he
thought she should move to Rognheim with him after Gaute was
married. "Signe is a more amenable daughter-in-law to live with, I
think. And it can't possibly be easy for you to give up your charge
of the household when you are used to running everything." But
otherwise he seemed to be fond of Jofrid—he and all the other
men. Only Sir Jammælt seemed to regard her with some coolness.

Kristin sat with her little grandson on her lap, thinking that it
wouldn't be easy no matter where she was. It was difficult getting
old. It seemed such a short time ago that she herself was the young
woman, when it was her fate that prompted the clamor of the
men's counsel and strife. Now she had been pushed into the back-
ground. Not long ago her own sons had been just like this little
boy. She recalled her dream about the newborn child. During
this time the thought of her own mother often came to her; she
couldn't remember her mother except as an aging and melancholy
woman. But she too had once been young, when she lay and
warmed herself with the heat of her own body; her mother's body
and soul had also been marked in her youth by carrying and giving
birth to her children. And doubtless she hadn't given it any more
thought than Kristin had when she sat with the sweet young life at
her breast—that as long as they both should live, each day would
take the child farther and farther away from her arms.

"After you had a child yourself, Kristin, I thought you would
understand," her mother had once said. Now she realized that her
mother's heart had been deeply etched with memories of her
daughter, memories of her thoughts about the child from before
she was born and from all the years the child could not remember,
memories of fears and hopes and dreams that children would
never know had been dreamed on their behalf, before it was their
own turn to fear and hope and dream in secret.

Finally the gathering of kinsmen split up, and some went to stay with Jammælt at Formo while others accompanied Sigurd over to Vaagaa. Then one day two of Gaute's leaseholders from the south of the valley came racing into the courtyard. The sheriff was on his way north to seek out Gaute at home, and the maiden's father and kinsmen were with him. Young Lavrans ran straight to the stable. The next evening it looked as if an army had gathered at Jørundgaard; all of Gaute's kinsmen were there along with their armed men, and his friends from the countryside had come as well.

Then Helge of Hovland arrived in a great procession to demand his rights from the man who had abducted his daughter. Kristin caught a glimpse of Helge Duk as he rode into the courtyard alongside Sir Paal Sørkvessøn, the sheriff himself. Jofrid's father was an older, tall, and stoop-backed man who looked quite ill; it was evident that he limped when he got off his horse. Her sister's husband, Olav Piper, was short, wide, and thickset; both his face and hair were red.

Gaute stepped forward to meet them, his posture erect and dignified, and behind him he had an entire phalanx of kinsmen and friends. They stood in a semicircle in front of the stairs to the high loft; in the middle were the two older gentlemen holding the rank of knight: Sir Sigurd and Sir Jammælt. Kristin and Jofrid watched the meeting from the entryway to the weaving room, but they couldn't hear what was said.

The men went up to the loft, and the two women retreated inside the weaving room. Neither of them felt like talking. Kristin sat down near the hearth; Jofrid paced the floor, holding her child in her arms. They continued in this way for a while; then Jofrid wrapped a blanket around the boy and left the room with him. An hour later Jammælt Halvardssøn came in to find his wife's sister sitting alone, and he told her what had happened.

Gaute had offered Helge Duk sixteen marks in gold for Jofrid's honor and for taking her by force. This was the same amount that Helge's brother had been given in restitution for the life of his son. Gaute would then wed Jofrid with her father's consent and provide all the proper betrothal and wedding gifts, but in return Helge would have to accept Gaute and Jofrid with full reconciliation so that she would be given the same dowry as her sisters and share with them in the inheritance. Sir Sigurd, on behalf of Gaute's kinsmen, offered a guarantee that he would keep to this agreement. Helge Duk seemed willing to accept this offer at once, but his sons-in-law—Olav Piper and Nerid Kaaressøn, who was betrothed to Aasa—voiced objections. They said Gaute must be the most arrogant of men if he dared to think he could set his own terms for his marriage to a maiden he had shamed while she was at her brother-in-law's manor and had then been taken by force. Or to demand that she be allowed to share the inheritance with her sisters.

It was easy to see, said Jammælt, that Gaute was not pleased he would have to haggle over the price for marrying a highborn maiden whom he had seduced and who had now given birth to his son. But it was also easy to see that he had learned his lessons and prayers by heart, so he didn't have to read them out of a book.

In the midst of the discussion, as friends on both sides attempted to mediate, Jofrid came into the room with the child in her arms. Then her father broke down and could no longer hold back his tears. And so the matter was decided as she wished.

It was clear that Gaute could never have paid such a fine, but Jofrid's dowry was set at the same amount, so things came out even. The result of the meeting was that Gaute won Jofrid but received little more than what she had brought in her sacks when she arrived at Jørundgaard. But he gave her documents for almost all that he owned as betrothal and wedding gifts, and his brothers gave their assent. One day he would acquire great riches from her—provided their marriage was not childless, said Ivar Gjesling with a laugh, and the other men laughed too. But Kristin blushed crimson because Jammælt sat there listening to all the coarse jests that were uttered.

The next day Gaute Erlendssøn was betrothed to Jofrid Helgesdatter, and afterward she went to church for the first time after the birth, honored as if she had been a married woman. Sira Dag said she was entitled to this. Then she went to Sundbu with the child and remained under Sir Sigurd's protection until the wedding.

It took place a month later, just after Saint Jon's Day, and it was both beautiful and grand. The following morning Kristin Lavransdatter, with great ceremony, gave her keys to her son, and Gaute then fastened the ring to his wife's belt.

Afterward Sir Sigurd Eldjarn held a great banquet at Sundbu, and there he and his cousins, the former Sundbu men, solemnly swore and sealed a vow of friendship. Sir Sigurd generously presented costly gifts from his estate, both to the Gjeslings and to all his guests, according to how close they were as kin or friends— drinking horns, eating vessels, jewelry, weapons, furs, and horses. People then judged that Gaute Erlendssøn had brought this matter of abducting his bride to the most honorable of ends.

CHAPTER 4

ONE SUMMER MORNING a year later Kristin was out on the gallery of the old hearth house, cleaning out several chests of tools that stood there. When she heard horses being led into the courtyard, she went to have a look, peering between the narrow pillars of the gallery. One of the servants was leading two horses, and Gaute had appeared in the stable doorway; the boy Erlend was sitting astride his father's shoulders. The bright little face looked over the top of the man's yellow hair, and Gaute was holding the boy's tiny hands clasped in his own big tan hands under his chin. He handed the child to a maid who came across the courtyard and then mounted his horse. But when Erlend screamed and reached for his father, Gaute took him back and set him in front of him on the saddle. At that moment Jofrid came out of the main house.

"Are you taking Erlend with you? Where are you headed?"

Gaute replied that he was going up to the mill; the river was threatening to carry it away. "And Erlend says he wants to go with his father."

"Have you lost your wits?" She quickly pulled the boy down, and Gaute roared with laughter.

"I think you actually believed I was going to take him along!"

"Yes." His wife laughed too. "You're always taking the poor boy everywhere. I think you'd do the same as the lynx: eat your own young before you'd let anyone else take him."

She lifted the child's hand to wave to Gaute as he rode off from the estate. Then she put the boy down on the grass and squatted down next to him for a moment to talk to him a bit before she continued on her way over to the new storeroom and up to the loft.

Kristin stood where she was, gazing at her grandson. The morning sun shone so brightly on the little child dressed in red. Young

351

Erlend twirled around in circles, staring down at the grass. Then he caught sight of a big pile of wood chips, and at once he busily began strewing them all around. Kristin laughed.

He was fifteen months old, but his parents thought he was ahead of his age, because he could walk and run and even say two or three words. Now he was heading straight for the little stream that ran through the lower part of the courtyard and became a gurgling creek whenever it rained in the mountains. Kristin ran over and picked him up in her arms.

"You mustn't. Your mother will be cross if you get wet."

The boy drew his lips into a pout; he was probably wondering whether to cry because he wasn't allowed to splash in the stream or to give in. Getting wet was quite a big sin for him. Jofrid was much too strict with him about such matters. But he looked so clever. Laughing, Kristin kissed the boy, put him down, and went back to the gallery. But she made little headway with her work; mostly she stood and looked out at the courtyard.

The morning sun glowed so gentle and lovely above the three storerooms across from her. Kristin felt as if she hadn't taken a good look at them for a long time. How splendid the buildings were with the pillars adorning their loft galleries and the elaborate carvings. The gilded weather vane on the crossed timbers of the gable of the new storeroom glittered against the blue haze covering the mountains in the distance. This year, after the wet spring, the grass was so fresh on the rooftops.

Kristin gave a little sigh, cast another glance at little Erlend, and then turned back to the chests.

Suddenly the wailing cry of a child pierced the air behind her. She threw down everything she was holding and rushed outside. Erlend was shrieking as he looked back and forth from his finger to a half-dead wasp lying in the grass. When his grandmother lifted him up to soothe him, he screamed even louder. And when she, amid much crying and complaining, put some damp earth and a cold green leaf on the sting, his wailing became quite dreadful.

Hushing and caressing him, Kristin carried the boy into her house, but he screamed as if he were in deadly pain—and then stopped short in the middle of a howl. He recognized the box and horn spoon that his grandmother was taking down from above the door. Kristin dipped pieces of *lefse* in honey and fed them to the child as she continued to soothe him, placing her cheek against his fair neck where the hair was still short and curly from the days when he lay in his cradle and rubbed his head against the pillow. And then Erlend forgot all about his sorrow and turned his face up toward Kristin, offering to pat and kiss her with sticky hands and lips.

As they sat there, Jofrid came into the room.

"Have you brought him indoors? You didn't need to do that, Mother. I was just upstairs in the loft."

Kristin mentioned what had happened to Erlend outside. "Didn't you hear him scream?"

Jofrid thanked her mother-in-law. "But now we won't trouble you anymore." And she picked up the child, who was now reaching out for his mother and wanted to go to her, and they left the room.

Kristin put away the honey box. Then she continued to sit there, with nothing to occupy her hands. The chests on the gallery could wait until Ingrid came in.

It had been intended that she would have Frida Styrkaarsdatter as her maid when she moved out to the old house. But then Frida married one of the servants who had come with Helge Duk, a lad young enough to be her son.

"It's the custom in our part of the country for our servants to listen to their masters when they're offered advice for their own good," said Jofrid when Kristin wondered how this marriage had come about.

"But here in this parish," said Kristin, "the commoners aren't accustomed to obeying us if we're unreasonable, nor do they follow our advice unless it's of equal benefit to them and to us. I'm giving you good advice, Jofrid; you should keep it in mind."

"What Mother says is true," added Gaute, but his voice was quite meek.

Even before he was married, Kristin had noticed that Gaute was very reluctant to speak against Jofrid. And he had become the most amenable of husbands.

Kristin didn't deny that Gaute could stand to listen to what his wife had to say about many things; she was more sensible, capable, and hardworking than most women. And she was no more loose in her ways than Kristin herself had been. She too had trampled on her duties as a daughter and sold her honor since she could not win the man she had set her heart on in any better way. After she had gotten what she wanted, she became the most honorable and faithful wife. Kristin could see that Jofrid had great love for her husband; she was proud of his handsome appearance and his esteemed lineage. Her sisters had married wealthy men, but it was best to look at their husbands at night, when the moon wasn't shining, and their ancestors weren't even worth mentioning, Jofrid said scornfully. She zealously tended to her husband's welfare and honor as she perceived it, and at home she indulged him as best she could. But if Gaute suggested that he might have a different opinion from his wife regarding even the smallest matter, Jofrid would first agree with such an expression that Gaute would begin to waver, and then she would bring him around to her point of view.

But Gaute was flourishing. No one could doubt that these two young people lived well together. Gaute loved his wife, and both of them were so proud of their son and loved him beyond all measure.

So everything should have been fine and good. If only Jofrid Helgesdatter hadn't been . . . well, she was stingy; Kristin couldn't find any other word for it. If she hadn't been stingy, Kristin wouldn't have felt annoyed that her daughter-in-law had such a desire to take charge.

During the grain harvest that very first autumn, right after Jofrid had returned to the estate as a married woman, Kristin could see that the servants were already discontented, although they seldom said anything. But the old mistress noticed it just the same.

Sometimes it had also happened in Kristin's day that the servants were forced to eat herring that was sour, or bacon as yellow and rancid as a resinous pine torch, or spoiled meat. But then everyone knew that their mistress was bound to make up for it with something particularly good at another meal: milk porridge or fresh cheese or good ale out of season. And if there was food that was about to go bad and had to be eaten, everyone simply felt as if Kristin's full storerooms were overflowing. If people were in need, the abundance at Jørundgaard offered security for everyone.

But now people were already uncertain whether Jofrid would prove to be generous with the food if there should be a shortage among the peasants.

This was what angered her mother-in-law, for she felt it diminished the honor of the manor and its owner.

It didn't trouble her as much that she had discovered firsthand, over the course of the year, that her daughter-in-law always saved the best for her own. On Saint Bartholomew's Day she received two goat carcasses instead of the four she should have been given. It was true that wolverines had ravaged the smaller livestock in the mountains the previous summer, and yet Kristin thought it petty to hold back from slaughtering two more goats on such a large estate. But she held her tongue. It was the same way with everything she was supposed to be given from the farm: the autumn slaughtering, grain and flour, fodder for her four cows and two horses. She received either smaller amounts or poor-quality goods. She saw that Gaute was both embarrassed and ashamed by this, but he didn't dare do anything for fear of his wife, and so he pretended not to notice.

Gaute was just as magnanimous as all of Erlend's sons. In his brothers Kristin had called it extravagance. But Gaute was a toiler, and frugal in his own way. As long as he had the best horses and dogs and a few good falcons, he would have been content to live like the smallholders of the valley. But whenever visitors came to the estate, he was a gracious host to all his guests and a generous man toward beggars—and thus a landowner after his mother's own heart. She felt this was the proper way of living for the gentry—those nobles who resided on the ancestral estates in their home districts. They should produce goods and squander nothing needlessly, but neither should they spare anything whenever love of God and His poor, or concern for furthering the honor of their lineage, demanded that goods should be handed out.

Now she saw that Jofrid liked Gaute's rich friends and highborn kinsmen best. And yet in this regard Gaute seemed less willing to comply with his wife's wishes; he tried to hold on to his old companions from his youth. His drinking cohorts, Jofrid called them, and Kristin now learned that Gaute had been much wilder than she knew. These friends never came to the manor uninvited after he was a married man. But as yet no poor supplicant had gone unaided by Gaute, although he gave fewer gifts if Jofrid was watching. Behind her back he dared to give more. But not much was allowed to take place behind her back.

And Kristin realized that Jofrid was jealous of her. She had possessed Gaute's friendship and trust so completely during all the years since he was a poor little child who was neither fully alive nor dead. Now she noticed that Jofrid wasn't pleased if Gaute sat down beside his mother to ask her advice or got her to talk about the way things were in the past. If the man stayed for long in the old house with his mother, Jofrid was certain to find an excuse to come over.

And she grew jealous if her mother-in-law paid too much attention to little Erlend.

Amid the short, trampled-down grass out in the courtyard grew several herbs with coarse, leathery dark leaves. Now, during the sunny days of midsummer, a little stalk had sprung up with tiny, delicate pale blue flowers in the center of each flattened rosette of leaves. Kristin thought the old outer leaves, scarred as they were by each time a servant's foot or a cow's hoof had crushed them, must love the sweet, bright blossoming shoot which sprang from its heart, just as she loved her son's son.

He seemed to her to be life from her life and flesh from her flesh, just as dear as her own children but even sweeter. Whenever she held him in her arms, she noticed that the boy's mother would keep a jealous eye on the two of them and would come to take him away as soon as she deemed it proper and then possessively put him to her breast, hugging him greedily. Then it occurred to Kristin Lavransdatter in a new way that the interpreters of God's words were right. Life on this earth was irredeemably tainted by strife; in this world, wherever people mingled, producing new descendants, allowing themselves to be drawn together by physical love and loving their own flesh, sorrows of the heart and broken expectations were bound to occur as surely as the frost appears in the autumn. Both life and death would separate friends in the end, as surely as the winter separates the tree from its leaves.

One evening, two weeks before Saint Olav's Day, a group of beggars happened to come to Jørundgaard and asked for lodgings for the night. Kristin was standing on the gallery of the old storeroom—it was now under her charge—and she heard Jofrid come out and tell the poor people that they would be given food, but she could not give them shelter. "There are many of us on this manor, and my mother-in-law lives here too; she owns half the buildings."

Anger flared up in the former mistress. Never before had any wayfarers been refused a night's lodging at Jørundgaard, and the sun was already touching the crest of the mountains. She ran downstairs and went over to Jofrid and the beggars.

"They may take shelter in my house, Jofrid, and I might as well be the one to give them food too. Here on this manor we have never refused lodging to a fellow Christian if he asked for it in the name of God."

"You must do as you please, Mother," replied Jofrid, her face blazing red.

When Kristin had a look at the beggars, she almost regretted her offer. It was not entirely without cause that the young wife had been unwilling to have these people on her estate overnight. Gaute and the servants had gone up to the hay meadows near Sil Lake and would not be home that evening. Jofrid was home alone with the parish's charity cases, two old people and two children, whose turn it was to stay at Jørundgaard, and Kristin had only her maid in the old house. Although Kristin was used to seeing all kinds of people among the wandering groups of beggars, she didn't like the looks of this lot. Four of them were big, strong young men; three of them had red hair and small, wild eyes. They seemed to be brothers. But the fourth one, whose nose had once been split open on both sides and who was missing his ears, sounded as if he might be a foreigner. There were also two old people. A short, bent old man with a greenish-yellow face, his hair and beard ravaged by dirt and age and his belly swollen as if with some illness. He walked on crutches, alongside an old woman wearing a wimple that was completely soaked with blood and pus, her neck and face covered with sores. Kristin shuddered at the thought of this woman getting near Erlend. All the same, for the sake of these two wretched old people, it was good that the group wouldn't have to wander through Hammer Ridge in the night.

The beggars behaved peaceably enough. Once the earless man tried to seize hold of Ingrid as she went back and forth to the table, but Bjørn got to his feet at once, barking and growling. Otherwise the group seemed despondent and weary; they had struggled much and gleaned little, they said in reply to the mistress's questions. Surely things would be better in Nidaros. The old woman was pleased when Kristin gave her a goat horn containing a soothing salve made from the purest lamb oil and the water of an infant. But she declined when Kristin offered to soak her wimple with warm water and give her a clean linen cloth; well, she would agree to accept the cloth.

Nevertheless, Kristin had her young maid, Ingrid, sleep on the side of the bed next to the wall. Several times during the night Bjørn growled, but otherwise everything was quiet. Shortly past midnight the dog ran over to the door and uttered a couple of short barks. Kristin heard horses in the courtyard and realized that Gaute had come home. She guessed that Jofrid must have sent word to him.

The next morning Kristin filled the sacks of the beggars generously, and they hadn't even passed the manor gate before she saw Jofrid and Gaute heading swiftly toward her house.

Kristin sat down and picked up her spindle. She greeted her children gently as they came in and asked Gaute about the hay. Jofrid sniffed; the guests had left a rank stench behind in the room. But her mother-in-law pretended not to notice. Gaute shifted his feet uneasily and seemed to have trouble telling her what the purpose of their visit might be.

Then Jofrid spoke. "There's something I think it would be best for us to talk about, Mother. I know that you feel I'm more tight-fisted than you deem proper for the mistress of Jørundgaard. I know that's what you think and that you also think I'm diminishing Gaute's honor by acting this way. Now I don't have to tell you I was fearful last night about taking in that lot because I was alone on the estate with my infant and a few charity cases; I saw that you realized this as soon as you had a look at your guests. But I've noticed before that you think I'm miserly with food and inhospitable toward the poor.

"That is not so, Mother, but Jørundgaard is no longer a grand estate belonging to a royal retainer and wealthy man as it was in the time of your father and mother. You were the child of a rich man and kept company with rich and powerful kinsmen; you made a wealthy marriage, and your husband took you away to even greater power and splendor than you had grown up with. No one can expect that you in your old age should fully understand how different Gaute's position is now, having lost his father's inheritance and sharing half of your father's wealth with many brothers. But *I* dare not forget that I brought little more to his estate than the child I carried under my bosom and a heavy debt for my friend to bear because I consented to his act of force against my kinsmen. Things may get better with time, but I'm obliged to pray to God that my father might have a long life. We are young, Gaute and I, and don't know how many children we are destined to have. You *must* believe, mother-in-law, that I have no other thought behind my actions than what is best for my husband and our children."

"I believe you, Jofrid." Kristin gazed somberly at the flushed face of her son's wife. "And I have never meddled in your charge of the household or denied that you're a capable woman and a good and loyal wife for my son. But you must let me manage my own affairs as I am used to doing. As you say, I'm an old woman and no longer able to learn new ways."

The young people saw that Kristin had no more to say to them, and a few minutes later they took their leave.

As usual, Kristin had to agree that Jofrid was right—at first. But after she thought it over, it seemed to her . . . No, all the same, there was no use in comparing Gaute's alms with her father's. Gifts for the souls of the poor and strangers who had died in the parish, marriage contributions to fatherless maidens, banquets on the feast days of her father's favorite saints, stipends for sinners and those who were ill who wanted to seek out Saint Olav. Even if Gaute had been much richer than he was, no one would have expected him to pay for such expenses. Gaute gave no more thought to his Creator than was necessary. He was generous and kindhearted, but Kristin had seen that her father had a reverence for the poor people he helped because Jesus had chosen the lot of a poor man when he assumed human form. And her father had loved hard toil and thought all handwork should be honored because Mary, the Mother of God, chose to do spinning to earn food for her family and herself, even though she was the daughter of rich parents and belonged to the lineage of kings and the foremost priests of the Holy Land.

Two days later, early in the morning, when Jofrid was only half dressed and Gaute was still in bed, Kristin came into their room. She was wearing a robe and cape of gray homespun, with a wide-brimmed black felt hat over her wimple and sturdy shoes on her feet. Gaute turned blood-red when he saw his mother dressed in such attire. Kristin said she wanted to go to Nidaros for the Feast of Saint Olav, and she asked her son to look after her chores while she was gone.

Gaute protested vigorously; she should at least borrow horses and men to escort her and take her maid along. But his words had little authority, as might be expected from a man lying naked in bed before his mother's eyes. Kristin felt such pity for his bewilderment that she came up with the idea that she had had a dream.

"And I long to see your brothers again—" But then she had to turn away. She had not yet dared express in her heart how much she yearned for and dreaded this reunion with her two oldest sons.

Gaute insisted on accompanying his mother part of the way. While he dressed and had something to eat, Kristin sat laughing and playing with little Erlend; he chattered on, alert and lively with the morning. She kissed Jofrid farewell, and she had never done that before. Out in the courtyard all the servants had gathered; Ingrid had told them that Mistress Kristin was going on a pilgrimage to Nidaros.

Kristin picked up the heavy iron-shod staff, and since she didn't want to ride, Gaute put her travel bag on his horse's back and let the animal walk on ahead.

Up on the church hill Kristin turned around and looked down at her estate. How lovely it looked in the dewy, sun-drenched morning. The river shone white. The servants were still standing there; she could make out Jofrid's light-colored gown and wimple, and the child like a red speck in her arms. Gaute saw that his mother's face turned pale with emotion.

The road led up through the woods beneath the shadow of Hammer Ridge. Kristin walked as easily as a young maiden. She and her son said very little to each other. After they had walked for two hours, they reached the place where the road turns north under Rost Peak and the whole Dovre countryside stretches below, to the north. Then Kristin said that Gaute should go no farther with her, but first she wanted to sit down and rest for a while.

Beneath them lay the valley with the pale green ribbon of the river cutting through it and the farms like small green patches on the forested slopes. But higher up, the moss-covered heights, brown and lichen-yellow, arched against the gray scree and bare peaks, flecked with snowdrifts. The shadows of the clouds drifted over the valley and plains, but in the north the mountains were so brightly lit; one mountainous shape after another had freed itself from the misty cloak and loomed blue, one beyond the other. And Kristin's yearning glided north with the cloud clusters to the long road she had before her and raced across the valley, in among the great barricading slopes and the steep, narrow paths through the wilds across the plateaus. A few more days and she would be on her way down through the beautiful green valleys of Trøndelag, following the current of the river toward the great fjord. She shuddered at the memory of the familiar villages along the sea, where she had spent her youth. Erlend's handsome figure appeared before her eyes, shifting in stance and demeanor, swift and indistinct, as if she were seeing him mirrored in a rippling stream. At last she would reach Feginsbrekka, at the marble cross, and Nidaros would be lying there at the mouth of the river, between the blue fjord and the green Strind: on the shore the magnificent light-colored church with its dizzying towers and golden weather vanes, with the blaze of the evening sun on the rose in the middle of its breast. And deep inside the fjord, beneath the blue peaks of Frosta, lay Tautra, low and dark like the back of a whale, with its church tower like a dorsal fin. Oh, Bjørgulf . . . oh, Naakkve.

But when she looked back over her shoulder, she could still catch a glimpse of her home mountain beneath Høvringen. It lay in shadow, but with an accustomed eye she could see where the pasture path wound through the woods. She knew the gray domes that rose up over the carpet of forest; they surrounded the old meadows belonging to the people of Sil.

The sound of a *lur* echoed from the hills: several shrill tones that died away and then reappeared. It sounded as if children were practicing blowing the horn. A distant clanging of bells, the rush of the river fading lazily away, and the deep sighs of the forest in the quiet, warm day. Kristin's heart trembled anxiously in the silence.

Homesickness urged her forward; homesickness drew her back toward the village and the manor. Pictures of everyday things teemed before her eyes: She saw herself leaping with the goats along the path through the sparse woods south of their mountain pasture. A cow had strayed into the marsh; the sun was shining brightly. When she paused for a moment to listen, she felt her own sweat stinging her skin. She saw the courtyard back home in swirling snow—a dingy white, stormy day seething toward a wild winter night. She was almost blown back into the entryway when she opened the door; the blizzard took her breath away, but there they came, those two snow-covered bundles, men wearing long fur coats: Ivar and Skule had come home. The tips of their skis sank deep into the great snowdrift that always formed across the courtyard when the wind blew from the northwest. Then there were always huge drifts in two parts of the courtyard. All of a sudden she felt herself longing with love for those two drifts that she and all the manor servants had cursed each winter; she felt as if she were condemned never to see them again.

Feelings of longing seemed to burst from her heart; they ran in all directions, like streams of blood, seeking out paths to all the places in the wide landscape where she had lived, to all her sons roaming through the world, to all her dead lying under the earth. She wondered: Had she turned cowardly? She had never felt this way before.

Then she noticed that Gaute was staring at her. She gave him a fleeting, rueful smile. It was time now for them to say goodbye and for her to continue on.

Gaute called to his horse, which had been grazing across the green hillside. He ran to get him and then came back, and they said farewell. Kristin already had her travel bag over her shoulder and her son was putting his foot into the stirrup when he turned around and took a few steps toward her.

"Mother!" For a moment she looked into the depths of his helpless, shame-filled eyes. "You haven't been . . . no doubt you haven't been very pleased the last few years. Mother, Jofrid means well; she has great respect for you. Even so, I should have told her more about the kind of woman you are and have been all your days."

"Why do you happen to think about this now, my Gaute?" His mother's voice was gentle and surprised. "I'm quite aware that I'm no longer young, and old people are supposed to be difficult to please; all the same, I haven't aged so much that I don't have the wits to understand you or your wife. It would trouble me greatly if Jofrid should think that it has been a thankless struggle, after all she has done to spare me work and worry. Do not think, my son, that I fail to see your wife's virtues or your own loyal love for your mother. If I haven't shown it as much as you might have expected, you must have forbearance and remember that's the way old people are."

Gaute stared at his mother, open-mouthed. "Mother . . ." Then he burst into tears and leaned against his horse, shaking with sobs.

But Kristin stood her ground; her voice revealed nothing except amazement and maternal kindness.

"My Gaute, you are young, and you've been my little lamb all your days, as your father used to say. But you must not carry on like this, son. Now you're the master back home, and a grown man. If I were setting off for Romaborg or Jorsal, well . . . But it's unlikely that I will encounter any great dangers on this journey. I will find others to keep me company, you know; if not before, then when I reach Toftar. From there groups of pilgrims leave every morning during this time."

"Mother, Mother, don't leave us! Now that we've taken all power and authority out of your hands, pushed you aside into a corner . . ."

Kristin shook her head with a little smile. "I'm afraid my children seem to think I have an overbearing desire to take charge."

Gaute turned to face her. She took one of his hands in hers and placed her other hand on his shoulder as she implored him to believe that she was not ungrateful toward him or Jofrid; she asked God to be with him. Then she turned him toward his horse, and with a laugh she gave him a thump between his shoulders for good luck.

She stood gazing after him until he disappeared beneath the cliff. How handsome he looked riding the big blue-black horse.

She felt so strange. She sensed everything around her with such unusual clarity: the sun-sated air, the hot fragrance of the pine forest, the chittering of tiny sparrows in the grass. At the same time she was looking inside herself, seeing pictures the way someone with a high fever may believe she is peering at inner images. Inside her there was an empty house, completely silent, dimly lit, and with a smell of desolation. The scene shifted: a tidal shore from which the sea had retreated far away; rounded, light-colored stones, heaps of dark, lifeless seaweed, all sorts of flotsam.

Then she shifted her travel bag to a more comfortable position, picked up her staff, and set off down toward the valley. If she was not meant to come back, then it was God's will and useless to be frightened. But more likely it was because she was old. . . . She made the sign of the cross and strode faster, longing just the same to reach the hillside where the road passed among farms.

Only for one short section of the public road was it possible to see the buildings of Haugen high on the mountain crest. Her heart began hammering at the mere thought.

As she had predicted, she met more pilgrims when she reached Toftar late in the day. The next morning she was joined by several others as they all set off into the mountains.

A priest and his servant, along with two women, his mother and sister, were on horseback, and they soon pulled far ahead of those on foot. Kristin felt a pang in her heart as she gazed after another woman riding between her two children.

In her group there were two older peasants from a little farm in Dovre. There were also two younger men from Oslo, laborers from the town, and a farmer with his daughter and son-in-law, both of them quite young. They were traveling with the young couple's child, a tiny maiden about eighteen months old, and they had a horse, which they took turns riding. These three were from a parish far to the south called Andabu; Kristin didn't know exactly where it lay. On the first evening Kristin offered to take a look at the child because she was incessantly crying and moaning; she looked so pitiful with her big, bald head and tiny, limp body. She couldn't yet talk or sit up on her own. The mother seemed

ashamed of her daughter. The next morning when Kristin offered
to carry the child for a while, she was left in her care, and the
other woman strode on ahead; she seemed a most neglectful
mother. But they were so young, both she and her husband, hardly
more than eighteen years old, and she must be weary of carrying
the heavy child, who was always whining and weeping. The
grandfather was an ugly, sullen, and cross middle-aged man, but
he was the one who had urged this journey to Nidaros with his
granddaughter, so he seemed to have some affection for her.
Kristin walked at the back of the group with him and the two
Franciscan monks, and it vexed her that the man from Andabu
never offered to let the monks borrow his horse. Anyone could see
that the younger monk was terribly ill.

The older one, Brother Arngrim, was a rotund little man with a
round, red, freckled face, alert brown eyes, and a fox-red fringe of
hair around his skull. He talked incessantly, mostly about the
poverty of their daily life—the friars of Skidan. The order had recently acquired an estate in that town, but they were so impoverished that they were barely able to keep up the services, and the
church they intended to erect would probably never be built. He
placed the blame on the wealthy nuns in Gimsøy, who persecuted
the poor friars with rancor and malice, and they had now brought
a lawsuit against them. He spoke effusively about all their worst
traits. Kristin wasn't pleased to hear the monk talk in this manner,
and she didn't believe his claims that the abbess had not been chosen in accordance with Church law or that the nuns slept through
their daily prayers, gossiped, and carried on unseemly conversations at the table in the refectory. Yes, he even said bluntly that
people thought one of the sisters had not remained pure. But
Kristin saw that Brother Arngrim was otherwise a good-hearted
and kindly man. He carried the ill child for long stretches of the
way whenever he saw that Kristin's arms were growing weary. If
the girl began to howl too fiercely, he would set off running across
the plain, with his robes lifted high so the juniper bushes scratched
his dark, hairy legs and the mud splashed up from the marshy hol-
lows, shouting and hollering for the mother to stop because the
child was thirsty. Then he would hurry back to the ill man, Brother
Torgils; toward him he was the most tender and loving father.

The sick monk made it impossible to reach Hjerdkinn that

night, but the two men from Dovre knew of a stone hut in a field a little to the south, near a lake, and so the pilgrims headed that way. The evening had turned cold. The shores of the lake were miry, and white mist swirled up from the marshes so the birch forest was dripping with dew. A slender crescent moon hung in the west above the mountain domes, almost as pale yellow and dull as the sky. More and more often Brother Torgils had to stop; he coughed so badly that it was terrible to hear. Brother Arngrim would support him and then wipe his face and mouth afterward, showing Kristin his hand with a shake of his head; it was bloody from the other man's spit.

They found the hut, but it had fallen in. Then they looked for a sheltered spot and made a fire. But the poor folks from the south hadn't expected that a night in the mountains would be so icy cold. Kristin pulled from her travel bag the cape Gaute had urged her to take because it was especially lightweight and warm, made from bought fabric and lined with beaver fur. When she wrapped it around Brother Torgils, he whispered—he was so hoarse that he could barely manage to speak—that the child should be allowed to lie next to him. And so she was placed beside him. She fretted, and the monk coughed, but now and then they both slept for a while.

Part of the night Kristin kept watch and tended the fire along with one of the Dovre men and Brother Arngrim. The pale yellow glimmer moved northward—the mountain lake lay white and still; fish rose up, rippling the surface—but beneath the towering dome on the opposite side, the water mirrored a deep blackness. Once they heard a hideous snarling shriek from the far shore; the monk cringed and grabbed the other two by the arm. Kristin and the farmer thought it must be some beast; then they heard stones falling, as if someone were walking across the scree over there, and another cry, like the coarse voice of a man. The monk began praying loudly: *"Jesus Kristus, Soter,"* Kristin heard. And *"vicit leo de tribu Juda."*[1] Then they heard a door slam somewhere on the slope.

The gray light of dawn began rising. The scree on the other side and the clusters of birch trees emerged. Then the other Dovre farmer and the man from Oslo relieved them. The last thing Kristin thought about before she fell asleep next to the fire was that if they made such little progress during the day—and she would have to give the friars a gift of money when they parted—then she would soon have to beg food from the farms when they reached Gauldal.

The sun was already high and the morning wind was darkening the lake with small swells when the frozen pilgrims gathered around Brother Arngrim as he said the morning prayers. Brother Torgils sat huddled on the ground, his teeth chattering, and tried to keep from coughing while he murmured along. When Kristin looked at the two ash-gray monk's cowls lit by the morning sun, she remembered she had been dreaming of Brother Edvin. She couldn't recall what it was about, but she kissed the hands of the kneeling monks and asked them to bless her companions.

Because of the beaver fur cape, the other pilgrims realized that Kristin was not a commoner. And when she happened to mention that she had traveled the king's road over the Dovre Range twice before, she became a sort of guide for the group. The men from Dovre had never been farther north than Hjerdkinn, and those from Vikvær did not know this region at all.

They reached Hjerdkinn just before vespers, and after the service in the chapel Kristin went out into the hills alone. She wanted to find the path she had taken with her father and the place beside the creek where she had sat with him. She didn't find the spot, but she thought she did find the slope she had climbed up in order to watch as he rode away. And yet the small, rocky hills along that stretch of path all looked much the same.

She knelt down among the bearberries at the top of the ridge. The light of the summer evening was fading. The birch-covered slopes of the low-lying hills, the gray scree, and the brown, marshy patches all melded together, but above the expanse of mountain plateaus arched the fathomless, clear bowl of the evening sky. It was mirrored white in all the puddles of water; scattered and paler was the mirrored shimmer of the sky in a little mountain stream, which raced briskly and restlessly over rocks and then trickled out onto the sandy bank of a small lake in the marsh.

Again it came upon her, that peculiar feverlike inner vision. The river seemed to be showing her a picture of her own life: She too had restlessly rushed through the wilderness of her earthly days, rising up with an agitated roar at every rock she had to pass over. Faint and scattered and pale was the only way the eternal light had been mirrored in her life. But it dimly occurred to the mother that in her anguish and sorrow and love, each time the fruit of sin had ripened to sorrow, that was when her earthbound and willful soul managed to capture a trace of the heavenly light.

Hail Mary, full of grace. Blessed are you among women and blessed is the fruit of your womb, Jesus, who gave his sweat and blood for our sake . . .

As she said five *Ave Marias* in memory of the painful mysteries of the Redemption, she felt that it was with her sorrows that she dared to seek shelter under the cloak of the Mother of God. With her grief over the children she had lost, with the heavier sorrows over all the fateful blows that had struck her sons without her being able to ward them off. Mary, the perfection of purity, of humility, of obedience to the will of her Father—she had grieved more than any other mother, and her mercy would see the weak and pale glimmer in a sinful woman's heart, which had burned with a fiery and ravaging passion, and all the sins that belong to the nature of love: spite and defiance, hardened relentlessness, obstinacy, and pride. And yet it was still a mother's heart.

Kristin hid her face in her hands. For a moment it seemed more than she could bear: that now she had parted with all of them, all her sons.

Then she said her last *Pater noster*. She remembered the leave-taking with her father in this place so many years in the past, and her leave-taking with Gaute only two days ago. Out of childish thoughtlessness her sons had offended her, and yet she knew that even if they had offended her as she had offended her father, with her sinful will, it would never have altered her heart toward them. It was easy to forgive her children.

Gloria Patri et Filio et Spiritui Sancto, she prayed, and kissed the cross she had once been given by her father, humbly grateful to feel that in spite of everything, in spite of her willfulness, her restless heart had managed to capture a pale glimpse of the love that she had seen mirrored in her father's soul, clear and still, just as the bright sky now shimmered in the great mountain lake in the distance.

The next day the weather was so overcast, with such a cold wind and fog and showers, that Kristin was reluctant to continue on with the ill child and Brother Torgils. But the monk was the most eager of them all; she saw that he was afraid he would die before he reached Nidaros. So they set off over the heights, but now and then the rain was so heavy that Kristin didn't dare head down the steep paths with the sheer cliffs both above and below, which she recalled lay all the way to the hostel at Drivdal. They made a fire when they had climbed to the top of the pass and settled in for the night. After evening prayers Brother Arngrim told a splendid saga about a ship in distress that was saved through the intercession of an abbess who prayed to the Virgin Mary, who made the morning star appear over the sea.

The monk seemed to have developed a fondness for Kristin. As she sat near the fire and rocked the child so the others could sleep, he moved closer to her and in a whisper began talking about himself. He was the son of a poor fisherman, and when he was fourteen years old, he lost his father and brother at sea one winter night, but he was rescued by another boat. This seemed to him a miracle, and besides, he had acquired a fear of the sea; that was how he happened to decide that he would become a monk. But for three more years he had to stay at home with his mother, and they toiled arduously and went hungry, and he was always afraid in the boat. Then his sister was wed, and her husband took over the house and share of the fishing boat, and he could go to the Minorites in Tunsberg. At first he was subjected to scorn for his low birth, but the guardian was kind and took him under his protection. And ever since Brother Torgils Olavssøn had entered the brotherhood, all the monks had become more pious and peaceful, for he was so pious and humble, even though he came from the best lineage of any of them, from a wealthy farming family over in Slagn. And his mother and sisters were very generous toward the monastery. But after they had come to Skidan, and after Brother Torgils had fallen ill, everything had once again become difficult. Brother Arngrim let Kristin understand that he wondered how

Christ and the Virgin Mary could allow the road to be so full of stones for his poor brothers.

"They too chose poverty while they lived on this earth," said Kristin.

"That's easy for you to say, being the wealthy woman that you surely must be," replied the monk indignantly. "You've never had to go without food. . . ." And Kristin had to agree that this was true.

When they made their way down to the countryside and wandered through Updal and Soknadal, Brother Torgils was allowed to ride part of the way, but he grew weaker and weaker, and Kristin's companions changed steadily, as people left them and new pilgrims took their place. When she reached Staurin, no one remained from the group she had traveled across the mountain with except the two monks. And in the morning Brother Arngrim came to her, weeping, and said that Brother Torgils had coughed up a great deal of blood in the night; he could not go on. Now they would doubtless arrive in Nidaros too late to see the celebration.

Kristin thanked the brothers for their companionship, their spiritual guidance, and their help on her journey. Brother Arngrim seemed surprised by the richness of her farewell gift, for his face lit up. He wanted to give her something in return. He pulled from his bag a box containing several documents. Each of them was a lovely prayer followed by all the names of God; a space had been left on the parchment in which the supplicant's name could be printed.

Kristin realized that it was unreasonable to expect the monk to know anything about her: the name of her husband or his fate, even if she mentioned her family name. And so she simply asked him to write "the widow Kristin."

Walking down through Gauldal, she took the paths on the outskirts of the villages, for she thought if she met people from the large estates, it might turn out that they recognized the former mistress of Husaby. She didn't fully know why, but she was reluctant for this to happen. The following day she set off along the paths through the woods on the mountain ridge to the little church at Vatsfjeld, which had been consecrated to John the Baptist, although the people called it Saint Edvin's Church.

The chapel stood in a clearing in dense forest; both the building and the mountain behind were mirrored in a pond from which a curative spring flowed. A wooden cross stood near the creek, and all around lay crutches and walking sticks, and on the bushes hung shreds of old bandages.

There was a small fence around the church, but the gate was locked. Kristin knelt down outside and thought about the time she had sat inside with Gaute on her lap. Back then she was dressed in silk, one of the group of magnificently attired noblemen and women from the surrounding parishes. Sira Eiliv stood nearby, holding Naakkve and Bjørgulf firmly by the hand; among the crowd outside were her maids and servants. Then she had prayed so fervently that if this suffering child would be given his wits and health, she would ask for nothing more, not even to be freed from the terrible pain in her back which had plagued her ever since the birth of the twins.

She thought about Gaute, so stalwart and handsome he looked on his huge blue-black horse. And about herself. Not many women her age, now close to half a century, enjoyed such good health; that was something she had noticed on her way through the mountains. Lord, if only you would give me this and this and this, then I will thank you and ask for nothing more except for this and this and this. . . .

Surely she had never asked God for anything except that He should let her have her will. And every time she had been granted what she asked for—for the most part. Now here she sat with a contrite heart—not because she had sinned against God but because she was unhappy that she had been allowed to follow her will to the road's end.

She had not come to God with her wreath or with her sins and sorrows, not as long as the world still possessed a drop of sweetness to add to her goblet. But now she had come, after she had learned that the world is like an alehouse: The person who has no more to spend is thrown outside the door.

She felt no joy at her decision, but it seemed to Kristin that she herself had not made the choice. The poor beggars who had entered her house had come to invite her away. A will that was not her own had put her among that group of impoverished and ill people and invited her to go with them, away from the home she had managed as the mistress and ruled as the mother of men. And when she had consented without much protest, she knew that she did so because she saw that Gaute would thrive better if she left the estate. She had bent fate to her will; she had obtained the circumstances she wanted. Her sons she could not shape according to her will; they were the way God had created them, and their obstinacy drove them. With them she could never win. Gaute was a good farmer, a good husband, and a faithful father, a capable man and as honorable as most people. But he did not have the makings of a chieftain, nor did he have the inclination to long for what she had desired on his behalf. Yet he loved her enough to feel tormented because he knew she expected something else of him. That was why she now intended to beg for food and shelter, even though it hurt her pride to arrive so impoverished; she had nothing to give.

But she realized that she *had* to come. The spruce forest covering the slopes stood drinking in the seeping sunlight and swayed softly; the little church sat silent and closed, sweating an odor of tar. With longing Kristin thought about the dead monk who had taken her hand and led her into the light emanating from the cloak of God's love when she was an innocent child, who had reached out his hand to lead her home, time after time, from the paths on which she had strayed. Suddenly she remembered so clearly her dream about him the night before, up in the mountains:

She dreamed that she was standing in the sunshine in a courtyard of some grand estate, and Brother Edvin was walking toward her from the doorway to the main house. His hands were full of bread, and when he reached her, she saw that she had been forced to do as she envisioned, to ask for alms when she came to the villages. But somehow she had arrived in the company of Brother Edvin, and the two of them were traveling together and begging. But at the same time she knew that her dream had a double meaning; the estate was not merely a noble manor, but it seemed to her to signify a holy place, and Brother Edvin belonged to the servants there, and the bread which he offered her was not simply flatbread the way it looked; it signified the Host, *panis angelorum*, and she accepted the food of angels from his hand. And now she gave her promise into Brother Edvin's hands.

CHAPTER 5

FINALLY SHE HAD arrived. Kristin Lavransdatter sat and rested in a haystack on the road beneath Sion Castle. The sun was shining, and the wind was blowing; the part of the field that had not yet been cut undulated with blossoming straw, red and shiny like silk. Only the fields of Trøndelag were ever that color red. At the bottom of the slope she could see a glimpse of the fjord, dark blue and dotted with foam; fresh white sea swells crashed against the cliffs of the shore for as far as she could see below the green-forested promontory of the town.

Kristin let out a long breath. All the same, it was good to be back here, good even though it was also strange to know that she would never leave here again. The gray-clad sisters out at Rein followed the same rules, Saint Bernard's rules, as the brothers of Tautra. When she rose before dawn and went to church, she knew that Naakkve and Bjørgulf would also be taking their places in the monks' choir. So she would end up living out her old age with some of her sons after all, although not in the way she might have imagined.

She took off her hose and shoes to wash her feet in the creek. She would walk to Nidaros barefoot.

Behind her on the path leading up over the castle's summit several boys now appeared, gathering around the portal to see if they could find a way into the fortress ruins. When they caught sight of Kristin, they began shouting crude words at her while they laughed and hooted. She pretended not to hear until a small boy—he couldn't have been more than eight—happened to roll down the steep incline and nearly rammed into her, uttering several loathsome words he had boldly learned from the older ones.

Kristin turned around and said with a little laugh, "You don't need to scream for me to know you're a troll child; I can see that by the tumbling pants that you're wearing."

When the boys noticed the woman was speaking, they came bounding down, the whole pack of them. But they fell silent and grew shamefaced when they saw she was an older woman wearing pilgrim's garb. She didn't scold them for their coarse words but sat there looking at them with big, clear, calm eyes and a secretive smile on her lips. She had a round, thin face with a broad forehead and a small, curving chin. She was sunburned and had many wrinkles under her eyes, yet she didn't look particularly old.

Then the most fearless of the boys started talking and asking questions in order to conceal the confusion of the others. Kristin felt so merry. These boys seemed to her much like her own daredevils, the twins, when they were small, although she hoped to God that *her* sons had never had such filthy mouths. These boys seemed to be the children of smallholders from town.

When the moment came that she had longed for during the whole journey, when she stood beneath the cross on Feginsbrekka and looked down at Nidaros, she wasn't able to muster her soul for prayers and devotion. All the bells of the town began pealing at once, summoning everyone to vespers, and the boys all started talking at once, eager to point out to her everything in sight.

She couldn't see Tautra because a squall was blowing across the fjord toward Frosta, bringing fog and torrents of rain.

Surrounded by the group of boys, she made her way down the steep paths through the Steinberg cliffs, as cowbells began ringing and herders shouted from all sides. The cows were heading home from the town pastures. At the gate in the town ramparts near Nidareid, Kristin and her young companions had to wait while the livestock was driven through. The herders hooted and yelled and scolded, the oxen butted, the cows jostled each other, and the boys told her who owned each and every bull. When they finally went through the gate and walked toward the fenced lanes, Kristin had more than enough to do watching where she set her bare feet between the cow dung in the churned-up track.

Without asking, a few of the boys followed her all the way to Christ Church. And when she stood amid the dim forest of pillars and looked toward the candles and gold of the choir, the boys kept

tugging at Kristin to show her things: from the colored patches of
light that the sun on the rose window cast through the arches, to
the gravestones on the floor, to the canopies of costly cloth above
the altars—all things that were most likely to catch a child's eye.
Kristin had no peace to collect her thoughts, but every word the
boys uttered aroused a dull, deep longing in her heart: for her
sons, above all else, but also for the manor, the houses, the out-
buildings, the livestock. A mother's toil and a mother's domain.

She was still feeling reluctant to be recognized by people who
might have been friends with Erlend or her in the past. They always used to spend the feast days at their town estate and have
guests staying with them. She dreaded running into a whole entourage. She would have to seek out Ulf Haldorssøn, for he had
been acting as her envoy with regard to the property shares she
still owned up here in the north and that she now wanted to give
to the Rein Convent in exchange for a corrody.[1] But she knew that
a man who had served as one of Erlend's guardsmen while he was
sheriff was supposed to be living on a small farm out near Bratør;
he fished for white-sided dolphins and porpoises in the fjord and
kept a hostel for seafarers.

All the lodgings were full, she was told, but then Aamunde, the
owner himself, appeared and recognized her at once. It was
strange to hear him call out her old name.

"If I'm not mistaken . . . aren't you Erlend Nikulaussøn's wife
from Husaby? Greetings, Kristin. How is it that you've come to
my house?"

He was more than happy if she would accept such lodgings for
the night as he could offer, and he promised that he himself would
sail to Tautra with her on the day after the feast.

Late into the night she sat outside in the courtyard, talking
with her host, and she was greatly moved when she saw that Erlend's former subordinate still loved and esteemed the memory of
his young chieftain. Aamunde used that word about him several
times: young. They had heard from Ulf Haldorssøn about his unfortunate death, and Aamunde said that he never met any of his
old companions from the Husaby days without drinking a toast to
the memory of their intrepid master. Twice some of them had collected money and paid for a mass to be said for his soul on the

anniversary of his death. Aamunde asked many questions about Erlend's sons, and Kristin in turn asked about old acquaintances. It was midnight before she went to bed, lying down beside Aamunde's wife. He had wanted both of them to give up their bed for her, and in the end she had to agree to take at least his half.

The next day was the Vigil of Saint Olav. Early in the morning Kristin went down to the skerries to watch the bustle along the wharves. Her heart began pounding when she saw the lord abbot of Tautra come ashore, but the monks who accompanied him were all older men.

Just before midafternoon prayers the crowds began heading toward Christ Church, carrying and supporting the ill and the lame, to find room for them in the nave so they would be close to the shrine when it was carried past in procession the following day after high mass.

When Kristin made her way up to the stalls that had been put up near the cemetery wall—they were mostly selling food and drink, wax candles, and cushions woven from reeds or birch twigs to kneel on inside the church—she happened to meet the people from Andabu again. Kristin held the child while the young mother went to get a drink of local ale. At that moment a procession of English pilgrims appeared, singing and carrying banners and lighted tapers. In the confusion that ensued as they passed through the great crowds around the stalls, Kristin lost sight of the people from Andabu, and afterward she couldn't find them.

For a long time she wandered back and forth on the outskirts of the throngs, hushing the screaming child. When she pressed the girl's face against her throat, caressing and consoling her, the child would put her lips to Kristin's skin and try to suckle. She could tell the child was thirsty, but she didn't know what to do. It would be futile to search for the mother; she would have to go into the streets and see if she could find some milk. But when she reached Upper Langstræte and tried to turn north, there was again a great crush of people. An entourage of horsemen was coming from the south, and at the same time a procession of guardsmen from the king's palace had entered the square between the church and the residence of the Brothers of the Cross. Kristin was pressed back into the nearest alleyway, but there too people on horseback and on foot were streaming toward the church, and the crowds grew so fierce that she finally had to save herself by climbing up onto a stone wall.

The air above her was filled with the clanging of bells; from the cathedral the *nona hora*[2] was rung. At the sound the child stopped screaming; she looked up at the sky, and a glimmer of understanding appeared in her dull eyes; she smiled a bit. Touched, the old mother bent down and kissed the poor little thing. Then she noticed that she was sitting on the stone wall surrounding the hops garden of Nikulaus Manor, their old town estate.

She should have recognized the brick chimney rising up from the sod roof, which was at the back of their house. Closest to her stood the buildings of the hospital, which had vexed Erlend so much because it had shared the rights to their garden.

She hugged the stranger's child to her breast, kissing her over and over. Then someone touched her knee.

A monk wearing the white robes and black cowl of a friar. She looked down into the sallow, lined visage of an old man, with a thin, sunken mouth and two big amber eyes set deep in his face.

"Could it be . . . is that you, Kristin Lavransdatter?" The monk placed his crossed arms atop the stone wall and buried his face in them. "Are you here?"

"Gunnulf!"

Then he moved his head so that he touched her knee as she sat there. "Do you think it so strange that I should be here?"

She remembered that she was sitting on the wall of the manor that had been his first home and later her own house, and she had to agree that it was rather odd after all.

"But what child is this you're holding on your knee? Surely this couldn't be Gaute's son?"

"No . . ." At the thought of little Erlend's healthy, sweet face and strong, well-formed body, she pressed the tiny child close, overcome with pity. "This is the daughter of a woman who traveled with me over the mountains."

But then she suddenly recalled what Andres Simonssøn had said in his childish wisdom. Filled with reverence, she looked down at the pitiful creature who lay in her arms.

Now the child was crying again, and the first thing Kristin had to do was ask the monk if he could tell her where she might find

some milk. Gunnulf led her east, around the church to the friars'
residence and brought her some milk in a bowl. While Kristin fed
her foster child, they talked, but the conversation seemed to halt
along rather strangely.

"So much time has passed and so much has happened since we
last met," she said sadly. "And no doubt the news was hard to
bear when you heard about your brother."

"May God have mercy on his poor soul," whispered Brother
Gunnulf, sounding shaken.

Not until she asked about her sons at Tautra did Gunnulf become more talkative. With heartfelt joy the monastery had welcomed the two novices who belonged to one of the land's best
lineages. Nikulaus seemed to have such splendid spiritual talents
and made such progress in his learning and devotions that the abbot was reminded of his glorious ancestor, the gifted defender of
the Church, Nikulaus Arnessøn. That was in the beginning. But after the brothers had donned cloister attire, Nikulaus had started
behaving quite badly, and he had caused great unrest in the
monastery. Gunnulf wasn't sure of all the reasons, but one was
that Abbot Johannes would not allow young brothers to become
ordained as priests until they were thirty, and he refused to make
an exception to this rule for Nikulaus. And because the venerable
father thought that Nikulaus prayed and brooded more than he
was spiritually prepared for and was thereby ruining his health
with his pious exercises, he wanted to send the young man to one
of the cloister's farms on the island of Inder; there, under the
supervision of several older monks, he was to plant an apple
orchard. Then Nikulaus had apparently openly disobeyed the
abbot's orders, accusing his brothers of depleting the cloister's
property through extravagant living, of indolence in their service
to God, and of unseemly talk. Most of this incident was never reported beyond the monastery walls, Gunnulf said, but Nikulaus
had evidently also rebelled against the brother appointed by the
abbot to reprimand him. Gunnulf knew that for a period of time
he had been locked in a cell, but at last he had been chastened
when the abbot threatened to separate him from his brother Bjørgulf and send one of them to Munkabu; it was no doubt the blind
brother who had urged him to do this. Then Nikulaus had grown
contrite and meek.

"It's their father's temperament in them," said Gunnulf bitterly. "Nothing else could have been expected but that my brother's sons would have a difficult time learning obedience and would show inconstancy in a godly endeavor."

"It could just as well be their mother's inheritance," replied Kristin sorrowfully. "Disobedience is my gravest sin, Gunnulf, and I was inconstant too. All my days I have longed equally to travel the right road and to take my own errant path."

"Erlend's errant paths, you mean," said the monk gloomily. "It was not just once that my brother led you astray, Kristin; I think he led you astray every day you lived with him. He made you forgetful, so you wouldn't notice when you had thoughts that should have made you blush, because from God the Almighty you could not hide what you were thinking."

Kristin stared straight ahead.

"I don't know whether you're right, Gunnulf. I don't know whether I've ever forgotten that God could see into my heart, and so my sin may be even greater. And yet it was not, as you might think, that I needed to blush the most over my shameful boldness or my weakness, but rather over my thoughts that my husband was many times more poisonous than the venom of snakes. But surely the latter has to follow the former. You were the one who once told me that those who have loved each other with the most ardent desire are the ones who will end up like two snakes, biting each other's tails.

"But it has been my consolation over these past few years, Gunnulf, that as often as I thought about Erlend meeting God's judgment, unconfessed and without receiving the sacraments, struck down with anger in his heart and blood on his hands, *he* never became what you said or what I myself became. He never held on to anger or injustice any more than he held on to anything else. Gunnulf, he was so handsome, and he looked at peace when I laid out his body. I'm certain that God the Almighty knows that Erlend never harbored rancor toward any man, for any reason."

Erlend's brother looked at her, his eyes wide. Then he nodded.

After a moment the monk asked, "Did you know that Eiliv Serkssøn is the priest and adviser for the nuns at Rein?"

"No!" exclaimed Kristin jubilantly.

"I thought that was why you had chosen to go there yourself," said Gunnulf. Soon afterward he said that he would have to go back to his cloister.

The first nocturn had begun as Kristin entered the church. In the nave and around all the altars there were great throngs of people. But a verger noticed that she was carrying a pitiful child in her arms, and he began pushing a path for her through the crowds so that she could make her way up to the front among the groups of those most crippled and ill, who occupied the middle of the church beneath the vault of the main tower, with a good view of the choir.

Many hundreds of candles were burning inside the church. Vergers accepted the tapers of pilgrims and placed them on the small mound-shaped towers bedecked with spikes that had been set up throughout the church. As the daylight faded behind the colored panes of glass, the church grew warm with the smell of burning wax, but gradually it also filled with a sour stench from the rags worn by the sick and the poor.

When the choral voices surged beneath the vaults, the organ swelled, and the flutes, drums, and stringed instruments resounded, Kristin understood why the church might be called a ship. In the mighty stone building all these people seemed to be on board a vessel, and the song was the roar of the sea on which it sailed. Now and then calm would settle over the ship, as if the waves had subsided, and the voice of a solitary man would carry the lessons out over the masses.

Face after face, and they all grew paler and more weary as the vigil night wore on. Almost no one left between the services, at least none of those who had found places in the center of the church. In the pauses between nocturns they would doze or pray. The child slept nearly all night long; a couple of times Kristin had to rock her or give her milk from the wooden flask Gunnulf had brought her from the cloister.

The encounter with Erlend's brother had oddly distressed her, coming as it did after each step on the road north had led her closer and closer to the memory of her dead husband. She had given little *thought* to him over the past few years, as the toil for her growing sons had left her scant time to dwell on her own fate, and yet the thought of him had always seemed to be right behind her, but she simply never had a moment to turn around. Now she seemed to be looking back at her soul during those years: It had lived the way people live on farms during the busy summer half of the year, when everyone moves out of the main house and into the lofts over the storerooms. But they walk and run past the winter house all day long, never thinking of going inside, even though all it would take was a lift of the latch and a push on the door. Then one day, when someone finally has a reason to go inside, the house has turned strange and almost solemn because it has acquired the smell of solitude and silence.

But as she talked to the man who was the last remaining witness to the interplay of sowing and harvesting in her life together with her dead husband, then it seemed to her that she had come to view her life in a new way: like a person who clambers up to a ridge overlooking his home parish, to a place where he has never been before, and gazes down on his own valley. Each farm and fence, each thicket and creek bed are familiar to him, but he seems to see for the first time how everything is laid out on the surface of the earth that bears the lands. And with this new view she suddenly found words to release both her bitterness toward Erlend and her anguish for his soul, which had departed life so abruptly. He had never known rancor; she saw that now, and God had seen it always.

She had finally come so far that she seemed to be seeing her own life from the uppermost summit of a mountain pass. Now her path led down into the darkening valley, but first she had been allowed to see that in the solitude of the cloister and in the doorway of death someone was waiting for her who had always seen the lives of people the way villages look from a mountain crest. He had seen sin and sorrow, love and hatred in their hearts, the way the wealthy estates and poor hovels, the bountiful acres and the abandoned wastelands are all borne by the same earth. And he had come down among them, his feet had wandered among the lands, stood in castles and in huts, gathering the sorrows and sins of the rich and the poor, and lifting them high up with him on the cross. Not my happiness or my pride, but my sin and my sorrow, oh sweet Lord of mine. She looked up at the crucifix, where it hung high overhead, above the triumphal arch.

The morning sun lit the tall, colored panes of glass deep within the forest of pillars in the choir and a glow, as if from red and brown, green and blue gemstones, dimmed the candlelight from the altar and the gold shrine behind it. Kristin listened to the last vigil mass, matins. She knew that the lessons of this service were about God's miraculous healing powers as invested in His faithful knight, King Olav Haraldssøn. She lifted the ill child toward the choir and prayed for her.

But she was so cold that her teeth were chattering after the long hours spent in the chill of the church, and she felt weak from fasting. The stench of the crowds and the sickening breath of the ill and the poor blended with the reek of candle wax and settled, thick and damp and heavy, upon those kneeling on the floor, cold in the cold morning. A stout, kind, and cheerful peasant woman had been sitting and dozing at the foot of a pillar right behind them, with a bearskin under her and another one over her lame legs. Now she woke up and drew Kristin's weary head onto her spacious lap. "Rest for a little while, sister. I think you must need to rest."

Kristin fell asleep in the woman's lap and dreamed:

She was stepping over the threshold into the old hearth room back home. She was young and unmarried, because she could see her own thick brown braids, which hung down in front of her shoulders. She was with Erlend, for he had just straightened up after ducking through the doorway ahead of her.

Near the hearth sat her father, whittling arrows; his lap was covered with bundles of sinews, and on the bench on either side of him lay heaps of arrowpoints and pointed shafts. At the very moment they stepped inside, he was bending forward over the embers, about to pick up the little three-legged metal cup in which he always used to melt resin. Suddenly he pulled his hand back, shook it in the air, and then stuck his burned fingertips in his mouth, sucking on them as he turned his head toward her and Erlend and looked at them with a furrowed brow and a smile on his lips.

Then she woke up, her face wet with tears.

She knelt during the high mass, when the archbishop himself performed the service before the main altar. Clouds of frankincense billowed through the intoning church, where the radiance of colored sunlight mingled with the glow of candles; the fresh, pungent scent of incense seeped over everyone, blunting the smell of poverty and illness. Her heart burst with a feeling of oneness with these destitute and suffering people, among whom God had placed her; she prayed in a surge of sisterly tenderness for all those who were poor as she was and who suffered as she herself had suffered.

"I will rise up and go home to my Father."

CHAPTER 6

THE CONVENT STOOD on a low ridge near the fjord, so that when the wind blew, the crash of the waves on the shore would usually drown out the rustling of the pine forest that covered the slopes to the north and west and hid any view of the sea.

Kristin had seen the church tower above the trees when she sailed past with Erlend, and he had said several times they ought to pay a visit to this convent, which his ancestor had founded, but nothing had ever come of it. She had never set foot in Rein Convent until she came there to stay.

She had imagined that life here would be similar to what she knew of life in the convents in Oslo or at Bakke, but things were quite different and much more quiet. Here the sisters were truly dead to the world. Fru Ragnhild, the abbess, was proud of the fact that it had been five years since she had been to Nidaros and just as long since any of her nuns had set foot outside the cloister walls.

No children were being raised there, and at the time Kristin came to Rein, there were no novices at the convent either. It had been so many years since any young maiden had sought admittance to the order that it was already six winters ago that the newest member, Sister Borghild Marcellina, had taken her vows. The youngest in years was Sister Turid, but she had been sent to Rein at the age of six by her grandfather, who was a priest at Saint Clement's Church and a very stern and somber man. The child's hands had been crippled from birth, and she was misshapen in other ways too, so she had taken the veil as soon as she reached the proper age. Now she was thirty years old and quite sickly, but she had a lovely face. From the first day Kristin arrived at the convent, she made a special attempt to serve Sister Turid, for the nun reminded her of her own little sister Ulvhild, who had died so young.

Sira Eiliv said that low birth should not be a hindrance for any maiden who came to serve God. And yet ever since the convent at Rein had been founded, it was usually only the daughters or widows of powerful and highborn men from Trøndelag who had sought refuge there. But during the wicked and turbulent times that had descended upon the realm after the death of blessed King Haakon Haalegg, piety seemed to have diminished greatly among the nobility. Now it was mostly the daughters of merchants and prosperous farmers who considered the life of a nun. And they were more likely to go to Bakke, where many of them had spent time learning their devotions and womanly skills and where more of the sisters came from families of lower standing. There the rule prohibiting venturing outside the convent was less strict, and the cloister was not as isolated.

Otherwise Kristin seldom had the chance to speak with Sira Eiliv, but she soon realized that the priest's position at the convent was both a wearisome and troubled one. Although Rein was a wealthy cloister and the order included only half as many members as it could have supported, the nuns' money matters were in great disarray, and they had difficulty managing their expenses. The last three abbesses had been more pious than worldly women. Even so, they and their convent had vowed tooth and nail not to submit to the authority of the archbishop; their conviction was so strong that they also refused to accept any advice offered out of fatherly goodwill. And the brothers of their order from Tautra and Munkabu, who had been priests at their church, had all been old men so that no slanderous gossip might arise, but they had been only moderately successful at managing the convent's material welfare. When King Skule built the beautiful stone church and gave his ancestral estate to the cloister, the houses were first built of wood; they all had burned down thirty years ago. Fru Audhild, who was abbess at the time, began rebuilding with stone; in her day many improvements had been made to the church and the lovely convent hall. She had also made a journey to the general chapter at the mother cloister of the order, Tart in Burgundy. From that journey she had brought back the magnificent tower of ivory

that stood in the choir near the high altar, a fitting receptacle for
the body of the Lord, the most splendid adornment of the church,
and the pride and cherished treasure of the nuns. Fru Audhild had
died with the fairest of reputations for piety and virtue, but her ignorance in dealing with the builders and her imprudent property
ventures had damaged the convent's well-being. And the abbesses
who succeeded her had not been able to repair that damage.

How Sira Eiliv happened to come to Rein as priest and adviser,
Kristin never knew, but this much she did know: From the very beginning the abbess and the sisters had received a secular priest with
reluctance and suspicion. Sira Eiliv's position at Rein was such that
he was the nuns' priest and spiritual adviser; he was also supposed
to see about putting the estate back on its feet and restoring order
to the convent's finances. All the while he was to acknowledge the
supremacy of the abbess, the independence of the sisters, and the
supervisory right of Tautra. He was also supposed to maintain a
friendship with the other priest at the church, a monk from Tautra. Sira Eiliv's age and renown for unblemished moral conduct,
humble devotion to God, and insight into both canonical laws and
the laws of the land had certainly served him well, but he had to
be constantly vigilant about everything he did. Along with the
other priest and the vergers, he lived on a small manor that lay
northeast of the convent. This also served as the lodgings for the
monks who came from Tautra from time to time on various er-
rands. When Nikulaus was eventually ordained as a priest, Kristin
knew that if she lived long enough, she would also one day hear
her eldest son say mass in the cloister church.

Kristin Lavransdatter was first accepted as a corrodian. Later she
had promised Fru Ragnhild and the sisters, in the presence of Sira
Eiliv and two monks from Tautra, to live a chaste life and obey the
abbess and nuns. As a sign that she had renounced all command
over earthly goods she had placed in Sira Eiliv's hands her seal,
which he had broken in half. Then she was allowed to wear the
same attire as the sisters: a grayish white woolen robe—but without the scapular—a white wimple, and a black veil. After some
time had passed, the intention was for her to seek admittance into
the order and to take the vows of a nun.

But it still was difficult for her to think too much about things of the past. For reading aloud during meals in the refectory, Sira Eiliv had translated into the Norwegian language a book about the life of Christ, which the learned and pious Doctor Bonaventura had written. While Kristin listened, her eyes would fill with tears whenever she thought about how blessed a person must be who could love Christ and his Mother, the cross and its torment, poverty and humility, in the way the book described. And then she couldn't help thinking about that day at Husaby when Gunnulf and Sira Eiliv had shown her the book in Latin from which this one had been copied. It was a thick little book written on such thin and dazzling white parchment that she never would have believed calfskin could be prepared so finely, and it had the most beautiful pictures and capital letters; the colors glowed like gemstones against gold. All the while Gunnulf had talked merrily—and Sira Eiliv had nodded in agreement with his quiet smile—about how the purchase of this book had made them penniless, so they had been forced to sell their clothes and take their meals with those receiving alms at a cloister until they received word of some Norwegian clerics who had come to Paris; from them they could borrow funds.

After matins, when the sisters went back to the dormitory, Kristin always stayed behind in the church. On summer mornings it seemed to her sweet and lovely inside, but during the winter it was terribly cold, and she was afraid of the darkness among all the gravestones, even though she steadily fixed her eyes on the little lamp which always burned in front of the ivory tower containing the Host. But winter or summer, as she lingered in her corner of the nuns' choir, she always thought that now Naakkve and Bjørgulf must also be praying for their father's soul; it was Nikulaus who had asked her to say these prayers and psalms of penance as they did every morning after matins.

Always, always she would then picture the two of them as she had seen them on that gray, rainy day when she went out to the monastery. Nikulaus had suddenly appeared before her in the parlatory, looking oddly tall and unfamiliar in the grayish white monk's robes, with his hands hidden under his scapular—her son—and yet he had changed so little. It was mostly his resemblance to his father that seized her so strongly; it was like seeing Erlend in a monk's cowl.

As they sat and talked and she told him everything that had happened on the estate since he left home, she kept waiting and waiting. Finally she asked anxiously if Bjørgulf would be coming soon.

"I don't know, Mother," replied her son. A moment later he added, "It has been a hard struggle for Bjørgulf to submit to his cross and serve God. And it seemed to worry him when he heard you were here, that too many thoughts might be torn open."

Afterward she felt only deadly despair as she sat and looked at Nikulaus while he talked. His face was very sunburned, and his hands were worn with toil; he mentioned with a little smile that he had been forced to learn after all to guide a plow and use a sickle and scythe. She didn't sleep that night in the hostel, and she hurried to church when the bells rang for matins. But the monks were standing so that she could see only a few faces, and her sons were not among them.

The following day she walked in the garden with a lay brother who worked there, and he showed her all the rare plants and trees for which it was renowned. As they wandered, the clouds scattered, the sun emerged, and a fragrance of celery, onion, and thyme rose up; the large shrubs of yellow lilies and blue columbine that adorned the corners of the beds glittered, weighted down with raindrops. Then her sons appeared; both of them came out of the little arched doorway in the stone building. Kristin felt as if she had been given a foretaste of the joys of paradise when she saw the two tall brothers, dressed in light-colored attire, coming toward her along the path beneath the apple trees.

But they didn't talk much with each other; Bjørgulf said almost nothing the entire time. He had become an enormous man, now that he was full-grown. And it was as if the long separation had sharpened Kristin's sight. For the first time she understood what this son of hers had had to struggle with and was doubtless still struggling with as he grew so big and strong in body, and his inner astuteness grew, but he felt his eyesight failing.

Once he asked about his foster mother, Frida Styrkaarsdatter. Kristin told him that she was now married.

"May God bless her," said the monk. "She was a good woman; toward me she was a good and faithful foster mother."

"Yes, I think she was more of a mother to you than I was," said

Kristin sadly. "You felt little trace of my mother's heart when such harsh trials were placed upon you in your youth."

Bjørgulf answered in a low voice, "And yet I thank God that the Devil never managed to bend me to such unmanliness that I should test your mother's heart in such a manner, even though I was close to it. . . . But I saw that you were carrying much too heavy a burden, and aside from God it was Nikulaus here who saved me those times when I was about to fall to temptation."

No more was said about that, or about how they were faring at the monastery or that they had acted badly and brought disfavor upon themselves. But they seemed quite pleased when they heard of their mother's intention to join the convent at Rein.

After her morning prayers, when Kristin walked back through the dormitory and looked at the sisters, sleeping on the beds, two to each straw mattress, and wearing their robes, which they never took off, she would think how unlike these women she must be, since from their youth they had devoted themselves solely to serving their Creator. The world was a master from whom it was difficult to flee once a person had submitted to its power. Surely she would not have fled either, but she had been cast out, the way a harsh master chases a used-up vassal out the door. Now she had been taken in here, the way a merciful master takes in an old servant and out of compassion gives her a little work while he houses and feeds the worn-out and friendless old soul.

From the nuns' dormitory a covered gallery led to the weaving room. Kristin sat there alone, spinning. The sisters of Rein were famous for their flax. Those days during the summer and fall when all the sisters and lay sisters went out to work in the flax fields were like feast days at the convent, especially when they pulled up the ripe plants. Preparing, spinning, and weaving the flax and then sewing the cloth into clerical garments were the main activities of the nuns during their work hours. None of them copied or illustrated books as the sisters in Oslo had done with such great skill under the guidance of Fru Groa Guttormsdatter, nor did they practice much the artful work of embroidering with silk and gold threads.

After some time Kristin was pleased to hear the sounds of the estate waking up. The lay sisters would go over to the cookhouse to prepare food for the servants; the nuns never touched food or drink until after the morning mass unless they were ill. When the bells rang for prime, Kristin would go over to the infirmary if anyone was sick, to relieve Sister Agata or one of the other nuns. Sister Turid, poor thing, often lay there.

Then she would begin looking forward to breakfast, which was served after the third hour of prayer and the mass for the convent's servants. Each day, with equal joy, Kristin would look forward to this noble and solemn meal. The refectory was built of wood, but it was a handsome hall, and all the women of the convent ate there together. The nuns sat at the highest table, where the abbess occupied the high seat, along with the three old women besides Kristin who were corrodians. The lay sisters were seated farther down. When the prayer was over, food and drink were brought in and everyone ate and drank in silence, with quiet and proper manners. While one of the sisters read aloud from a book, Kristin would think that if people out in the world could enjoy their meals with such propriety, it would be much clearer to them that food and drink are gifts from God, and they would be more generous toward their fellow Christians and think less about hoarding things for themselves and their own. But she herself had felt quite different back when she set out food for her flock of spirited and boisterous men who laughed and roared, while the dogs sniffed around under the table, sticking up their snouts to receive bones or blows, depending on what humor the boys were in.

Visitors seldom came to Rein. An occasional ship with people from the noble estates might put in when they were sailing into or out of the fjord, and then men and their wives, with children and youths, would walk up to the cloister to bring greetings to a kinswoman among the sisters. There were also the envoys from the convent's farms and fishing villages, and now and then messengers from Tautra. On the feast days that were celebrated with the most splendor—the feast days of the Virgin Mary, Corpus Christi Day, and the Feast of the Apostle Saint Andreas—people from the nearest villages on both sides of the fjord would come to the nuns' church. Otherwise only the convent's tenants and workers who lived close by would attend mass. They took up very little space in the vast church.

And then there were the poor—the regular charity cases who received ale and drink on specific days when masses were said for the souls of the dead, as provided for in the testaments of wealthy people—and others who came up to Rein almost every day. They would sit against the cookhouse wall to eat and seek out the nuns when they came into the courtyard, telling the sisters about their sorrows and troubles. The ill, the crippled, and the leprous were always coming and going. There were many who suffered from leprosy, but Fru Ragnhild said that was always true of villages near the sea. Leaseholders came to ask for reductions or deferments in their payments, and then they always had much to report about setbacks and difficulties. The more wretched and unhappy the people were, the more openly and freely they talked to the sisters about their circumstances, although they usually gave others the blame for their misfortunes, and they spoke in the most pious of terms. It was no wonder that when the nuns rested or while they worked in the weaving room, their conversation should turn to the lives of these people. Yes, Sister Turid even told Kristin that when the nuns in the convent were supposed to deliberate about trade and the like, the discussion would often slip into talk about the people who were involved in the cases. Kristin could tell from the sisters' words that they knew little more about what they were discussing than what they had heard from the people themselves or from the lay servants who had been out in the parish. They were very trusting, whether their subordinates spoke well of themselves or ill of their neighbors. And then Kristin would think with indignation about all the times she had heard ungodly lay people, yes, even a mendicant monk such as Brother Arngrim, accuse the convents of being nests of gossip and the sisters of swallowing greedily all rumors and unseemly talk. Even the very people who came moaning to Fru Ragnhild or any of the sisters who would speak to them, filling their ears with gossip, would berate the nuns because they discussed the cries that reached them from the outside world, which they themselves had renounced. She thought it was the same thing with gossip about the comfortable life of convent women; it stemmed from people who had often received an early breakfast from the sisters' hands, while God's servants fasted, kept vigil, prayed, and worked before they all gathered for the first solemn meal in the refectory.

Kristin served the nuns with loving reverence during the time before her admittance to the order. She didn't think she would ever be a good nun—she had squandered her abilities for edification and piety too much for that—but she would be as humble and faithful as God would allow her to be. It was late in the summer of A.D. 1349, she had been at Rein Convent for two years, and she was to take the vows of a nun before Christmas. She received the joyous message that both her sons would come to her ordination as part of Abbot Johannes's entourage.

Brother Bjørgulf had said, when he heard of his mother's intention, "Now my dream will be realized. I've dreamed twice this year that before Christmas we both would see her, although it won't be *exactly* as it was revealed to me, since in my dream I actually *saw* her."

Brother Nikulaus was also overjoyed. But at the same time Kristin heard other news about him that was not as good. He had laid hands on several farmers over by Steinker; they were in the midst of a dispute with the monastery about some fishing rights. When the monks came upon them one night as they were proceeding to destroy the monastery's salmon pens, Brother Nikulaus had given one man a beating and thrown another into the river, at the same time sinning gravely with his cursing.

CHAPTER 7

A FEW DAYS later Kristin went to the spruce forest with several of the nuns and lay sisters to gather moss for green dye. This moss was rather rare, growing mostly on toppled trees and dry branches. The women soon scattered through the forest and lost sight of each other in the fog.

This strange weather had already lasted for several days: no wind, a thick haze with a peculiar leaden blue color that could be seen out over the sea and toward the mountains whenever it lifted enough so that a little of the countryside became visible. Now and then it would grow denser, becoming a downpour; now and then it would disperse so much that a whitish patch would appear where the sun hovered amid the shrouded peaks. But an odd heavy bathhouse heat hung on, quite unusual for that region down by the fjord and particularly at that time of year. It was two days before the Feast of the Birth of Mary. Everyone was talking about the weather and wondering what it could mean.

Kristin was sweating in the dead, damp heat, and the thought of the news she had heard about Naakkve was making her chest ache. She had reached the outskirts of the woods and come to the rough fence along the road to the sea; as she stood there, scraping moss off the rails, Sira Eiliv came riding toward home in the fog. He reined in his horse, said a few words about the weather, and they fell to talking. Then she asked the priest whether he knew anything about the incident with Naakkve, even though she knew it was futile. Sira Eiliv always pretended to know nothing about the private matters of the monastery at Tautra.

"I don't think you need to worry that he won't come to Rein this winter because of that, Kristin," said the priest. "For surely that's what you fear?"

"It's more than that, Sira Eiliv. I fear that Naakkve was never meant to be a monk."

"Do you mean you would presume to judge about such things?" asked the priest with a frown. Then he got down from his horse, tied the reins to the fence, and bent down to slip under the railing as he gave the woman a steady, searching glance.

Kristin said, "I fear that Naakkve finds it most difficult to submit to the discipline of the order. And he was so young when he entered the monastery; he didn't realize what he was giving up or know his own mind. But everything that happened during his youth—losing his father's inheritance and the discord that he saw between his father and mother, which ended with Erlend's death— all this caused him to lose his desire to live in this world. But I never noticed that it made him pious."

"You didn't? It may well be that Nikulaus has found it as difficult to submit to the discipline of the order as many a good monk has. He's hot-tempered and a young man, perhaps too young for him to have realized, before he turned away from this world, that the world is just as harsh a taskmaster as any other lord, and in the end it's a lord without mercy. Of that I think you yourself can judge, sister.

"And if it's true that Naakkve entered the monastery more for his brother's sake than out of love for his Creator . . . Even so, I don't think God will let it go unrewarded that he took up the cross on his brother's behalf. Mary, the Mother of God, whom I know Naakkve has honored and loved from the time he was a little boy, will doubtless show him clearly one day that her son came down to this earth to be his brother and to carry the cross for him.

"No . . ." The horse snuffled against the priest's chest. He stroked the animal as he murmured, as if to himself, "Ever since he was a child, my Nikulaus has had remarkable capacities for love and suffering; I think he has the makings of a fine priest.

"But you, Kristin," he said, turning toward her. "It seems to me that you should have seen so much by now that you would put more trust in God the Almighty. Haven't you realized yet that He will hold up each soul as long as that soul clings to Him? Do you think—child that you still are in your old age—that God would punish the sin when you must reap sorrow and humiliation because you followed your desire and your pride along pathways God has forbidden His children to tread? Will you say that *you* punished your children if they scalded their hands when they picked up the boiling kettle you had forbidden them to touch? Or the slippery ice broke beneath them when you had warned them not to go out there? Haven't you noticed when the brittle ice broke beneath you? You were drawn under each time you let go of God's hand, and you were rescued from the depths each time you called out to Him. Even when you defied your father and set your willfulness against his will, wasn't the love that was the bond of flesh between you and your father consolation and balm for the heart when you had to reap the fruit of your disobedience to him?

"Haven't you realized yet, sister, that God has helped you each time you prayed, even when you prayed with half a heart or with little faith, and He gave you much more than you asked for. You loved God the way you loved your father: not as much as you loved your own will, but still enough that you always grieved when you had to part from him. And then you were blessed with having good grow from the bad which you had to reap from the seed of your stubborn will.

"Your sons . . . Two of them He took when they were innocent children; for them you need never fear. And the others have turned out well—even if they haven't turned out the way *you* would have liked. No doubt Lavrans thought the same about you.

"And your husband, Kristin . . . May God protect his soul. I know you have chastised him in your heart both night and day because of his reckless folly. It seems to me that it must have been much harder for a proud woman to remember that Erlend Nikulaussøn had taken you with him through shame and betrayal and blood guilt if you had seen even once that the man could act with cold intent. And yet I believe it was because you were as faithful in anger and harshness as in love that you were able to hold on to Erlend as long as you both lived. For him it was out of sight, out of mind with everything except you. May God help Erlend. I fear he never had the wits to feel true remorse for his sins, but the sins that your husband committed against you—those he did regret and grieve over. That was a lesson we dare to believe has served Erlend well after death."

Kristin stood motionless, without speaking, and Sira Eiliv said no more. He untied his reins and said, "May peace be with you." Then he mounted his horse and rode away.

Later, when Kristin arrived back at the convent, Sister Ingrid met her at the gate with the message that one of her sons had come to see her; he called himself Skule, and he was waiting at the speaking gate.

He was conversing with his fellow seamen but leaped to his feet when his mother came to the door. Oh, she recognized her son by his agile movements: his small head, held high on his broad shoulders, and his long-limbed, slender figure. Beaming, she stepped forward to greet him, but she stopped abruptly and caught her breath when she saw his face. Oh, who had done such a thing to her handsome son?

His upper lip was completely flattened; a blow must have crushed it, and then it had grown back flat and long and ruined, striped with shiny white scar tissue. It had pulled his mouth askew, so he looked as if he were always sneering scornfully. And his nose had been broken and then healed crooked. He lisped slightly when he spoke; he was missing a front tooth, and another one was blueblack and dead.

Skule blushed under his mother's gaze. "Could it be that you don't know me, Mother?" He chuckled and touched a finger to his lip, not necessarily to point out his injury; it might simply have been an involuntary gesture.

"We haven't been parted so many years, my son, that your mother wouldn't recognize you," replied Kristin calmly, smiling without restraint.

Skule Erlendssøn had arrived on a swift sailing ship from Bjørgvin two days before with letters from Bjarne Erlingssøn for the archbishop and the royal treasurer in Nidaros. Later that day mother and son walked down to the garden beneath the apple trees, and when they could finally talk to each other alone, Skule told his mother news of his brothers.

Lavrans was still in Iceland; Kristin hadn't even known that he'd gone there. Oh yes, said Skule, he had met his youngest brother in Oslo the previous winter at a meeting of the nobles; he was there with Jammælt Halvardssøn. But the boy had always had a desire to go out and see the world, and so he had entered the service of the bishop of Skaalholt and left Norway.

Skule himself had accompanied Sir Bjarne to Sweden and then on a war campaign to Russia. His mother silently shook her head; she hadn't known about that either! The life suited him, he said with a laugh. He had finally had a chance to meet all the old friends his father had talked so much about: Karelians, Ingrians, Russians. No, his splendid scar of honor had not been won in a war. He gave a chuckle. Yes, it was in a brawl; the fellow who gave it to him would never have need to beg for his bread again. Otherwise Skule seemed to have little interest in telling her any more about the incident or about the campaign. He was now the head of Sir Bjarne's guardsmen, and the knight had promised to regain for him several properties his father had once owned in Orkedal that were now in the possession of the Crown. But Kristin noticed that Skule's big steel-gray eyes had a strange look in them as he spoke of this.

"But you think that such a promise cannot be counted on?" asked his mother.

"No, no." Skule shook his head. "The documents are being drawn up at this very time. Sir Bjarne has always kept his promises, in all the days I've been in his service; he calls me kinsman and friend. My position on his estate is much like that of Ulf back home with us." He laughed. It didn't suit his damaged face.

But he was the handsomest of men in terms of bearing, now that he was full-grown. The clothing he wore was cut according to the new fashion, with close-fitting hose and a snug, short *cotehardi,* which reached only to mid-thigh and was fastened with tiny brass buttons all the way down the front, revealing with almost unseemly boldness the supple power of his body. It looked as if he were wearing only undergarments, thought his mother. But his forehead and handsome eyes were unchanged.

"You look as if something were weighing on your heart, Skule," ventured his mother.

"No, no, no." It was just the weather, he said, giving himself a shake. There was a strange reddish brown sheen to the fog as the veiled sun set. The church towered above the treetops in the garden, eerie and dark and indistinct in a liver-red haze. They had been forced to row all the way into the fjord in the becalmed sea,

said Skule. Then he shifted his clothes a bit and told her more
about his brothers.

He had been sent on a mission by Sir Bjarne to southern Norway in the spring, so he could bring her recent news from Ivar and
Gaute because he had traveled back north through the countryside
and over the mountains from Vaagaa, home to Vestland. Ivar was
well; he and his wife had two small sons at Rognheim, Erlend and
Gamal, both handsome children. "At Jørundgaard I arrived for a
christening feast. And Jofrid and Gaute said that since you were
now dead to the world, they would name their little maiden after
you; Jofrid is so proud of the fact that you're her mother-in-law.
Yes, you may laugh, but now that the two of you don't have to live
on the same manor, you can be sure that Jofrid thinks it splendid
to speak of her mother-in-law, Kristin Lavransdatter. And I gave
Kristin Gautesdatter my best gold ring, for she has such lovely eyes
that I think she will come to look much like you."

Kristin smiled sadly.

"Soon you'll have me believing, my Skule, that my sons thought
I was as fine and grand as old people always become as soon as
they're in their graves."

"Don't talk like that, Mother," said the man, his voice strangely
vehement. Then he laughed a little. "You know quite well that my
brothers and I have always thought, ever since we wore our first
pair of breeches, that you were the most splendid and magnanimous woman, even though you clutched us tightly under your
wings so many times that we had to flap hard before we could escape the nest.

"But you were right that Gaute was the one with the makings
of a chieftain among us brothers," he added, and he roared with
laughter.

"You don't need to mock me about that, Skule," said Kristin,
and Skule saw that his mother blushed, looking young and lovely.

Then he laughed even harder. "It's true, my mother. Gaute Erlendssøn of Jørundgaard has become a powerful man in the northern valleys. He won quite a reputation for himself by abducting
his bride." Skule bellowed with laughter; it didn't suit his ruined
mouth. "People are singing a ballad about it; yes, they're even
singing that he took the maiden with iron and steel and that he
fought with her kinsmen for three long days up on the moors. And

the banquet that Sir Sigurd held at Sundbu, making peace among kin with gold and silver: Gaute is given credit for that too in the ballad. But it doesn't seem to have caused any harm by being a lie. Gaute rules the entire parish and some distance beyond, and Jofrid rules Gaute."

Kristin shook her head with a sad little smile. But her face looked young as she gazed at Skule. Now she thought that *he* looked most like his father; this young soldier with the ravaged face had so much of Erlend's lively courage. And the fact that he had been forced to take his own fate into his hands early on had given him a cool and steadfast spirit, which brought an odd sense of comfort to his mother's heart. With the words Sira Eiliv had spoken the day before still in her mind, she suddenly realized that as fearful as she had been for her reckless sons and as sternly as she had often admonished them because she was tormented with anguish for their sakes, she would have been less content with her children if they had been meek and timid.

Then she asked again and again about her grandson, little Erlend, but Skule had not seen much of him; yes, he was healthy and handsome and used to having his own way at all times.

The uncanny fog, tinged like clotted blood, had faded, and darkness began to fall. The church bells started ringing; Kristin and her son rose to their feet. Then Skule took her hand.

"Mother," he said in a low voice, "do you remember that I once laid hands on you? I threw a wooden bat at you, and it struck you on the forehead. Do you remember? Mother, while we're alone, tell me that you've fully forgiven me for that!"

Kristin let out a deep breath. Yes, she remembered. She had asked the twins to go up to the mountain pastures for her, but when she came out to the courtyard, she found their horse still there, grazing and wearing the pack saddle, and her sons were running about, batting a ball. When she reprimanded them sternly, Skule threw the bat at her in fierce anger. What she remembered most was walking around with her eyelid so swollen that it seemed to have grown shut; her other sons would look at her and then at Skule and shun the boy as if he were a leper. First Naakkve had beat him mercilessly. And Skule had wandered around, boiling with defiance and shame behind his stony, scornful expression. But that evening, as she was undressing in the dark, he came creep-

ing into the room. Without saying a word, he took her hand
and kissed it. When she touched his shoulder, he threw his arms
around her neck and pressed his cheek to hers. His skin felt cool
and soft and slightly rounded—still a child's cheek, she realized.
He was just a child, after all, this headstrong, quick-tempered boy.

"Yes, I have, Skule—so completely, that God alone can understand, for I can't tell you how completely I've forgiven you,
my son!"

For a moment she stood with her hand on his shoulder. Then he
seized her wrists and squeezed them so tight that she cried out; the
next instant he put his arms around her, as tender and frightened
and ashamed as he had been back then.

"My son . . . what is it?" whispered his mother in alarm.

In the dark she could feel the man shaking his head. Then he let
her go, and they walked back up to the church.

During the mass Kristin happened to remember that she had once
again forgotten about the cloak for the blind Fru Aasa when they
were sitting on the bench outside the priest's door that morning.
After the service she went around the church to get it.

In the archway stood Skule and Sira Eiliv, holding a lantern in
his hand. "He died when we put in at the wharf," she heard Skule
say, his voice full of a peculiar, wild despair.

"Who?"

Both men started violently when they saw her.

"One of my seamen," said Skule softly.

Kristin looked from one man to the other. In the glow of the
lantern she caught sight of their faces, incomprehensibly strained,
and she uttered a little involuntary cry of fear. The priest bit his
lip; she saw that his chin was trembling faintly.

"It's just as well that you tell your mother, my son. It's better if
we all prepare ourselves to bear it if it should be God's will for our
people to be stricken with such a harsh—" But Skule merely
moaned and refused to speak. Then the priest said, "A sickness has
come to Bjørgvin, Kristin. The terrible pestilence we've heard rumors about, which is ravaging countries abroad."

"The black plague?" whispered Kristin.

"It would do no good if I tried to tell you how things were in
Bjørgvin when I left there," said Skule. "No one could imagine it

who hasn't seen it for himself. Sir Bjarne took stern measures at first to put out the fire where it broke out in the buildings around Saint Jon's Monastery. He wanted to cut off all of Nordnes with guardsmen from the castle, even though the monks at Saint Michael's Monastery threatened him with excommunication. An English ship had arrived with sick men on board, and he refused to allow them to unload their cargo or leave the ship. Every single man on that vessel perished, and then he had it scuttled. But some of the goods had already been brought ashore, and some of the townsmen smuggled more off the ship one night, and the brothers of Saint Jon's Church demanded that the dying be given the last rites. When people started dying all over town, we realized it was hopeless. Now there's no one left in Bjørgvin except for the men carrying the corpses. Everyone has fled the town who could, but the sickness follows them."

"Oh, Jesus Christus!"

"Mother . . . Do you remember the last time there was a lemming year back home in Sil? The hordes that tumbled along all the roads and pathways . . . Do you remember how they lay dying in every bush, rotting and tainting every waterway with their stench and poison?" He clenched his fists. His mother shuddered.

"Lord, have mercy on us all. Praise be to God and the Virgin Mary that you were sent up here, my Skule."

The man gnashed his teeth in the dark.

"That's what we said too, my men and I, the morning we hoisted sail and set off for Vaag. When we came north to Moldøsund, the first one fell ill. We tied stones to his feet and put a cross on his breast when he died, promising him a mass for his soul when we reached Nidaros; then we threw his body into the sea. May God forgive us. With the next two, we put into shore and gave them the last rites and burial in a proper grave. It's not possible to flee from fate after all. The fourth one died as we rowed into the river, and the fifth one died last night."

"Do you have to go back to town?" asked his mother a moment later. "Can't you stay here?"

Skule shook his head and laughed without mirth. "Oh, I think soon it won't matter where I am. It's useless to be frightened; fearful men are half dead already. But if only I was as old as you are, Mother!"

"No one knows what he has been spared by dying in his youth," said his mother quietly.

"Silence, Mother! Think about the time when you yourself were twenty-three years old. Would you have wanted to lose all the years you've lived since then?"

Fourteen days later Kristin saw for the first time someone who was ill with the plague. Rumors had reached Rissa that the scourge was laying waste to Nidaros and had spread to the countryside; how this had happened was difficult to say, for everyone was staying inside, and anyone who saw an unknown wayfarer on the road would flee into the woods or thickets. No one opened the door to strangers.

But one morning two fishermen came up to the convent, carrying between them a man in a sail. When they had gone down to their boats at dawn, they found an unfamiliar fishing vessel at the dock, and in the bottom lay this man, unconscious. He had managed to tie up his boat but could not climb out of it. The man had been born in a house belonging to the convent, but his family had since moved away from the region.

The dying man lay in the wet sail in the middle of the courtyard green; the fishermen stood at a distance, talking to Sira Eiliv. The lay sisters and servingwomen all had fled into the buildings, but the nuns—a flock of trembling, terrified, and bewildered old women—were clustered near the door to the convent hall.

Then Fru Ragnhild stepped forward. She was a short, thin old woman with a wide, flat face and a little, round red nose that looked like a button. Her big light brown eyes were red-rimmed and always slightly teary.

"*In nomine Patris et Filii et Spiritus Sancti,*" she said clearly, and then swallowed hard. "Bring him to the guesthouse."

Sister Agata, the oldest of the nuns, elbowed her way through the others and, unbidden, followed the abbess and the fishermen who carried the sick man.

Kristin went over there that night with a potion she had prepared in the pantry, and Sister Agata asked if she would stay and tend the fire.

She thought she would have been hardened, familiar as she was with birth and death; she had seen worse sights than this. She tried to recall the very worst she had ever witnessed. The plague patient sat bolt upright, for he was about to choke on the bloody vomit he coughed up with every spasm. Sister Agata had strapped him up with a harness across his gaunt, sallow red-haired chest; his head hung limply, and his face was a leaden grayish blue. All of a sudden he would start shaking with cold. But Sister Agata sat calmly, saying her prayers. When the fits of coughing seized hold of him, she would stand up, put one arm around his head, and hold a cup under his mouth. The ill man bellowed with pain, rolling his eyes terribly, and finally thrust a blackened tongue all the way out of his mouth as his terrible cries ended in a pitiful groan. The nun emptied the cup into the fire. As Kristin added more juniper and the wet branches first filled the room with a sharp yellow smoke and then made the flames crackle, she watched Sister Agata straighten the pillows and comforters behind the sick man's back and shoulders, swab his face and crusted brown lips with vinegar water, and pull the soiled coverlet up around his body. It would soon be over, she told Kristin. He was already cold; in the beginning he had been as hot as an ember. But Sira Eiliv had prepared him for his leave-taking. Then she sat down beside his bed, pushed the calamus root back into her cheek with her tongue, and continued praying.

Kristin tried to conquer the ghastly horror she felt. She had seen people die a more difficult death. But it was all in vain. This was the plague—God's punishment for the secret hardheartedness of every human being, which only God the Almighty could see. She felt dizzy, as if she were rocking on a sea where all the bitter and angry thoughts she had ever had in this world rose up like a single wave among thousands and broke into desperate anguish and lamenting. Lord, help us, we are perishing. . . .

Sira Eiliv came in later that night. He reprimanded Sister Agata sharply for not following his advice to tie a linen cloth, dipped in vinegar, around her mouth and nose. She murmured crossly that it would do no good, but now both she and Kristin had to do as he ordered.

The calm and steadfast manner of the priest gave Kristin courage, or perhaps it aroused a sense of shame; she ventured out of the juniper smoke to lend Sister Agata a helping hand. There was a suffocating stench surrounding the sick man which the smoke could not mask: excrement, blood, sour sweat, and a rotten odor coming from his throat. She thought of Skule's words about the swarms of lemmings; she still had a dreadful urge to flee, even though she knew there was nowhere to flee from this. But after she had finally persuaded herself to touch the dying man, the worst was over, and she helped as much as she could until he breathed his last. By then his face had turned completely black.

The nuns walked in procession carrying reliquaries, crosses, and burning tapers around the church and convent hill, and everyone in the parish who could crawl or walk went with them. But a few days later a woman died over by Strømmen, and then the pestilence broke out in earnest in every hamlet throughout the countryside.

Death and horror and suffering seemed to push people into a world without time. No more than a few weeks had passed, if the days were to be counted, and yet it already seemed as if the world that had existed before the plague and death began wandering naked through the land had disappeared from everyone's memory—the way the coastline sinks away when a ship heads out to sea on a rushing wind. It was as if no living soul dared hold on to the memory that life and the progression of workdays had once seemed close, while death was far away; nor was anyone capable of imagining that things might be that way again, if all human beings did not perish. But "we are all going to die," said the men who brought their motherless children to the convent. Some of them spoke with dull or harsh voices; some of them wept and moaned. They said the same thing when they came to get the priest for the dying; they said it again when they carried the bodies to the parish church at the foot of the hill and to the cemetery at the convent church. Often they had to dig the graves themselves. Sira Eiliv had sent the men who were left among the lay servants out to the convent fields to bring in the grain, and wherever he went in the parish, he urged everyone to harvest the crops and help each other tend to the livestock so that those who remained wouldn't suffer from hunger after the scourge had spent its fury.

The nuns at the convent met the first trials with a sense of desperate composure. They moved into the convent hall for good, kept a fire going day and night in the big brick fireplace, and ate and slept in there. Sira Eiliv advised everyone to keep great fires burning in the courtyards and in all the houses, but the sisters were afraid of fire. The oldest sisters had told them so often about the blaze thirty years before. Mealtimes and work regimens were no longer adhered to, and the duties of the various sisters were no longer kept separate as children began to arrive, asking for food and help. The sick were brought inside; they were mostly wealthy people who could pay for gravesites and masses for their souls in the convent, as well as those who were destitute and alone, who had no help at home. Those whose circumstances were somewhere in between stayed in their own beds and died at home. On some farms every single person perished. But in spite of everything, the nuns had still managed to keep to the schedule of prayers.

The first of the nuns to fall ill was Sister Inga, a woman Kristin's age, almost fifty, and yet she was so terrified of death that it was a horror to see and hear. The chills came over her in church during mass; shaking, her teeth chattering, she crawled on her hands and knees as she begged and implored God and the Virgin Mary to spare her life. A moment later she lay prostrate with a burning fever, in agony, with blood seeping out of her skin. Kristin's heart was filled with dread; no doubt she would be just as pitifully frightened when her turn came. It was not just the fact that death was certain, but it was the horrifying fear that accompanied death from the plague.

Then Fru Ragnhild herself fell ill. Kristin had sometimes wondered how this woman had come to be chosen for the high position of abbess. She was a quiet, slightly morose old woman, uneducated and apparently without great spiritual gifts. And yet when death placed its hand on her, she showed that she was a true bride of Christ. In her the illness erupted in boils. She refused to allow her spiritual daughters to unclothe her old body, but the swelling finally grew as big as an apple under one arm, and she had boils under her chin; they turned hard and blood-red, becoming black in the end. She endured unbearable agony from them and burned with fever, but each time her mind would clear, she lay in bed like an example of holy patience—sighing to God, asking forgiveness for her sins, and uttering beautiful, fervent prayers for her convent and her daughters, for all those who were sick and sorrowful, and for the peace of everyone's soul, who would now

have to leave this life. Even Sira Eiliv wept after he had given her
the viaticum; his steadfast and tireless zeal in the midst of all the
misery had otherwise been a thing of wonder. Fru Ragnhild had already surrendered her soul into God's hands many times and
prayed that He would take the nuns under His protection when
the boils on her body began to split open. But this turned out to be
a turn toward life, and later others experienced the same thing:
Those who were stricken with boils gradually recovered, while
those stricken with bloody vomiting all died.

Because of the example of the abbess and because they had
witnessed a plague victim who did not die, the nuns seemed to
find new courage. They now had to do the milking and chores in
the cowshed themselves; they cooked their own food, and they
brought back juniper and fresh evergreen branches for the cleansing smoke. Everyone did whatever task needed doing. They nursed
the sick as best they could and handed out healing remedies: their
supplies of theriac and calamus root were gone, but they doled
out ginger, pepper, saffron, and vinegar against the sickness, along
with milk and food. When the bread ran out, they baked at night;
when the spices were gone, people had to chew on juniper berries
and pine needles against the sickness. One by one the sisters suc-
cumbed and died. Night and day the bells for the dead rang from
the convent church and from the parish church in the heavy air, for
the unnatural fog hung on; there seemed to be a secret bond between the haze and the pestilence. Sometimes it became a frosty
mist, drizzling down needles of ice and half-frozen sleet, covering
the fields with rime. Then mild weather would set in, and the fog
returned. People took it as an evil omen that all the seabirds had
suddenly disappeared. They usually flocked by the thousands
along the stream that flows through the countryside from the fjord
and resembles a river in the low stretches of meadow but widens
into a lake with salt water north of Rein Convent. In their place
came ravens in unheard-of numbers. On every stone along the water sat the black birds in the fog, uttering their hideous shrill cries,
while flocks of crows more numerous than anyone had ever seen
before settled in all the forests and groves and flew with loathsome
shrieks over the wretched land.

Once in a while Kristin would think of her own family—her
sons, who were spread so far and wide, the grandchildren she

would never see; little Erlend's golden neck would hover before her eyes. But they seemed to grow distant and faded. Now it almost seemed as if all people were equally close and distant to each other in this time of great need. And she had her hands full all day long; it now served her well that she was used to all sorts of work. While she sat and did the milking, starving little children whom she had never seen before would suddenly appear beside her, and she seldom even thought to ask where they were from or how things were back home. She gave them food and took them into the chapter hall or some other room where a fire was lit or tucked them into bed in the dormitory.

With a feeling of wonder she noticed that in this time of great misfortune, when it was more necessary than ever for everyone to attend to their prayers with vigilance, she never had time to collect her thoughts to pray. She would sink to her knees in front of the tabernacle in the church whenever she had a free moment, but she could manage nothing more than wordless sighs and dully murmured *Pater nosters* and *Ave Marias*. She wasn't aware of it herself, but the nunlike demeanor and manners she had assumed over the past two years swiftly began to fall away; she again became like the mistress she had been in the past, as the flock of nuns diminished, the routines of the convent were abandoned, and the abbess still lay in bed, weak and with her tongue partially paralyzed. And the work mounted for the few who were left to tend to everything.

One day she happened to hear that Skule was still in Nidaros. The members of his crew had either died or fled, and he hadn't been able to find new men. He was well, but he had cast himself into a wild life, just as many young people, out of despair, had done. They said that whoever was afraid would be sure to die, and so they blunted their fear with carousing and drinking, playing cards, dancing, and carrying on with women. Even the wives of honorable townsmen and young daughters from the best of families ran off from their homes during these evil times. In the company of wanton women they would revel in the alehouses and taverns among the dissolute men. God forgive them, thought Kristin, but she felt as if her heart was too weary to grieve over these things properly.

And apparently even in the villages there was plenty of sin and depravity. They heard little about it at the convent because there they had no time to waste on such talk. But Sira Eiliv, who went everywhere, ceaselessly and tirelessly tending to the sick and dying, told Kristin one day that the agony of people's souls was worse than that of their bodies.

Then one evening they were sitting around the fireplace in the convent hall, the little group of people left alive at Rein Convent. Huddled around the fire were four nuns and two lay sisters, an old beggar and a half-grown boy, two women who received alms from the convent, and several children. On the high seat bench, above which a large crucifix could be glimpsed in the dusk hanging on the light-colored wall, lay the abbess with Sister Kristin and Sister Turid sitting at her head and feet.

It was nine days since the last death had occurred among the sisters and five days since anyone had died in the convent or the nearest houses. The plague seemed to be waning throughout the countryside as well, said Sira Eiliv. For the first time in three months a glimmer of peace and security and comfort fell over the silent, weary people sitting there. Old Sister Torunn Marta let her rosary sink into her lap and took the hand of the little girl standing at her knee.

"What do you think she could mean? Well, child, now we seem to be seeing that Mary, the Mother of God, never withdraws her mercy from her children for long."

"No, it's not the Virgin Mary, Sister Torunn. It's Hel. She'll leave the parish, taking her rakes and brooms, when they sacrifice an innocent man at the gate of the cemetery. By tomorrow she'll be far away."

"What can she mean?" asked the nun, again uneasy. "Shame on you, Magnhild, for spreading such loathsome, heathen gossip. You deserve to taste the rod for that. . . ."

"Tell us what you mean, Magnhild. Don't be afraid." Sister Kristin was standing behind them; her voice sounded strained. She had suddenly remembered that in her youth she had heard Fru Aashild talk about dreadful, unmentionably sinful measures which the Devil tempted desperate men to try.

The children had been down in the grove near the parish church at twilight, and some of the boys had wandered over to a sod hut that stood there; they had spied on several men who were making plans. It seemed that these men had captured a small boy named Tore, the son of Steinunn from down by the shore. That night they were going to sacrifice him to Hel, the plague giantess. The children began talking eagerly, proud to have sparked the attention of the grown-ups. It didn't seem to occur to them to feel pity for this poor Tore; he was a sort of outcast who roamed the countryside, begging, but never came near the convent. When Sira Eiliv or any of the abbess's envoys went looking for his mother, she would flee or refuse to talk to them, no matter whether they spoke to her kindly or sternly. She had spent ten years living in the alleyways of Nidaros, but then she acquired a sickness that disfigured her so badly that finally she could no longer earn a living in the manner she had before. And so she had come to the parish and lived in a hovel out on the shore. Occasionally a beggar or the like would move in and share her hut for a time. Who the father of her boy might be, she herself didn't know.

"We must go out there," said Kristin. "We can't just sit here while Christian souls sell themselves to the Devil right on our doorstep."

The nuns whimpered. They were the worst men of the parish, coarse, ungodly fellows, and surely the latest calamity and despair must have turned them into regular demons. If only Sira Eiliv was home, they lamented. Ever since the onset of the plague, the priest's position had changed, and the sisters expected him to do everything.

Kristin wrung her hands. "If I have to go alone . . . Mother, may I have your permission to go out there myself?"

The abbess gripped her arm so tightly that she gave a little cry. The old woman, who was unable to speak, struggled to her feet; by gesturing she made them understand that she wanted to be dressed to go out. She demanded to be given the gold cross, the symbol of her office, and her staff. Then she held on to Kristin's arm since she was the youngest and strongest of the women. All the nuns stood up and followed.

Passing through the door of the little room between the chapter hall and the church choir, they stepped out into the raw, cold winter night. Fru Ragnhild began shivering, and her teeth chattered. She still sweated incessantly from the illness, and the sores left by the plague boils were not fully healed; walking caused her great pain. But she snarled angrily and shook her head when the sisters implored her to turn around. She gripped Kristin's arm harder, and shaking with cold, she trudged ahead of them through the garden. As their eyes grew used to the dark, the women glimpsed light patches of withered leaves scattered beneath their feet and a pale scrap of cloudy sky above the bare crowns of the trees. Drops of cold water trickled down, and gusts of wind murmured faintly. Sluggish and heavy, the drone of the fjord sighed against the shore beyond the cliffs.

At the bottom of the garden was a small gate; the sisters shuddered at the shriek of the rusted iron bolt as Kristin struggled to shove it open. Then they crept onward through the grove, down toward the parish church. They caught a glimpse of the tarred timber shape, darker against the night, and they saw the roof and ridge turret with its animal-head carvings and cross on the top against the pale gleam of the clouds above the slopes on the other side of the fjord.

Yes, there were people in the cemetery; they sensed their presence rather than saw or heard anything. Now a low, faint gleam of light appeared, as if from a lantern standing on the ground. Something moved in the darkness nearby.

The nuns huddled together, whimpering faintly under their whispered prayers; they took several steps forward, stopped to listen, and moved forward again. They had almost reached the cemetery gate.

Then out of the darkness they heard the shrill cry of a child's voice: "Hey, stop, you're getting dirt on my bread!"

Kristin let go of the abbess's arm and ran forward, through the churchyard gate. She pushed aside several shadowy men's backs, stumbled on piles of shoveled dirt, and came to the edge of the open grave. She fell to her knees, bent down, and pulled out the little boy who was standing in the bottom, still complaining because there was earth on the good piece of *lefse* he had been given for sitting still in the pit.

The men were frightened out of their wits and ready to flee. Several were stomping in place; Kristin could see their feet in the light from the lantern on the ground. Then she thought that one of them seemed about to leap at her. At that moment the grayish-white habits of the nuns came into view, and the group of men stood there, in confusion.

Kristin still held the boy in her arms; he was crying for his *lefse*. She set him down, picked up the bread, and brushed it off.

"Here, eat it. Now your bread is as good as ever. And you men should go on home." The quaver in her voice forced her to pause for a moment. "Go home and thank God that you were saved before you committed an act you might never be able to atone for." Now she spoke the way a mistress speaks to her servants: kindly, but as if it would never occur to her that they might disobey. Without thinking, several of the men turned toward the gate.

Then one of them shouted, "Wait a minute, don't you see it's a matter of life itself, maybe even all we own? Now that these overstuffed monks' whores have stuck their noses in it, we can't let them leave here to talk about what went on!"

None of the men moved, but Sister Agata began shrieking and yelling, with sobs in her voice, "Oh, sweet Jesus, my bridegroom. I thank you for allowing us, your servant maidens, to die for the glory of your name!"

Fru Ragnhild shoved her sternly aside, staggered forward, and picked up the lantern from the ground. No one raised a hand to stop her. When she lifted it up, the gold cross on her breast glittered. She stood leaning on her staff and slowly shone the light down the line, giving a slight nod to each man as she looked at him. Then she gestured to Kristin that she wished her to speak.

Kristin said, "Go home in peace, dear brothers. Have faith that the worthy Mother and these good sisters will be as merciful as God and the honor of His Church will allow them to be. But move aside now so that we might take away this child, and then each of you should return to your own home."

The men stood there, irresolute. Then one of them shouted in the greatest agitation, "Isn't it better to sacrifice *one* than for all of us to perish? This boy here, who belongs to no one—"

"He belongs to Christ. Better for all of us to perish than for us to harm one of his children."

But the man who had spoken first began yelling again. "Stop saying words like that or I'll stuff them back into your mouth with this." He waved his knife in the air. "Go home, go to bed, and ask your priest to comfort you, and keep silent about this—or I swear

by the name of Satan that you'll find out it was the worst thing
you've ever done, trying to meddle in our affairs."

"You don't have to shout so loudly for the one you mentioned
to hear you, Arntor. Be assured that he isn't far away," said Kristin
calmly. Several of the men seemed to grow fearful and involuntarily crept closer to the abbess holding the lantern. "The worst thing,
for both us and for you, would have been if we had stayed home
while you went about building your home in the hottest Hell."

But the man, Arntor, cursed and raged. Kristin knew that he
hated the nuns because his father had mortgaged his farm to them
in order to pay penalties for murder and blood guilt with his wife's
niece. Now he continued slinging out the Fiend's most hateful lies
about the sisters, accusing them of sins so black and unnatural that
only the Devil himself could have put such thoughts into a man's
mind.

The poor nuns, terrified and weeping, bowed under the vicious
words, but they stood stalwartly around the old abbess, and she
held the lantern in the air, shining it at the man and gazing calmly
at his face as he raged.

But anger flared up inside Kristin like the flames of a newly lit
fire.

"Silence! Have you lost your senses? Or has God struck you
blind? Should we dare breathe a word under His admonishment?
We who have seen His wedded brides stand up to the sword that
was drawn for the sake of the world's sins? They kept vigil and
prayed while we sinned and forgot our Creator every single day;
they shut themselves inside the fortress of prayer while we roamed
through the world, urged on by avarice for treasures, both great
and small, for our own pleasure and our own anger. But they came
out to us when the angel of death was sent among us; they gathered up the ill, the defenseless, and the poor. Twelve of our sisters
have died from this sickness; all of you know this. Not one of
them turned away, not one of them refused to pray for us all with
sisterly love, until their tongues dried up in their mouths and their
life blood ebbed out."

"How beautifully you speak about yourself and those like
you—"

"*I* am like *you*," she screamed, beside herself. "I'm not one of
the holy sisters. I am one of you."

"How submissive you've become, woman," said Arntor derisively. "I see that you're afraid. When the end comes, you'll be saying you're like *her*, the mother of that boy."

"God must be the judge of that; he died for her as well as for me, and he knows us both. Where is she? Where is Steinunn?"

"Go out to her hovel, and I'm sure you'll find her there," replied Arntor.

"Yes, someone should send word to the poor woman that we have her boy here," said Kristin to the nuns. "We can go out to see her tomorrow."

Arntor snickered, but another man shouted reluctantly, "No, no . . . She's dead." He told Kristin, "Fourteen days ago Bjarne went out to her place and bolted the door shut. She was lying there, close to death."

"She was lying there?" Kristin gave the men a look of horror. "Didn't anyone bring a priest to her? Is . . . the body . . . still lying there? And no one has had enough mercy to put her into consecrated ground? And her child you were going to . . ."

Seeing her horror seemed to make the men lose their wits from fear and shame; they began shouting all at once.

Above all the other voices, one man cried out, "Go and get her yourself, sister!"

"Yes! Which of you will go with me?"

No one answered.

Arntor shouted, "You'll have to go alone."

"Tomorrow, as soon as it's light, we will go to get her, Arntor. I myself will pay for her resting place and a mass for her soul."

"Go out there now. Go there tonight. Then I'll believe that you're all full of holiness and virtue."

Arntor had thrust his face close to hers. Kristin raised her clenched fist up before his eyes; she uttered a loud sob of fury and terror.

Fru Ragnhild came over and stood at Kristin's side; she struggled to speak. The nuns cried that the next day the dead woman would be brought to her grave.

But the Devil seemed to have robbed Arntor of all reason; he kept on screaming, "Go now. Then we'll believe in the mercy of God."

Kristin straightened up; pale and rigid, she said, "I will go."

She lifted up the child and put him into Sister Torunn's arms; she shoved the men aside and began running swiftly toward the gate, stumbling over hillocks and heaps of earth, as the wailing nuns raced after her and Sister Agata yelled that she would go with her. The abbess shook her fists to say that Kristin should stop, but she seemed completely beside herself.

At that moment there was a great commotion in the darkness over by the cemetery gate. In the next instant Sira Eiliv's voice asked: "Who is holding a *ting* here?" He stepped into the glow of the lantern; they saw that he was carrying an axe in his hand. The nuns crowded around him; the men made haste to disappear into the darkness, but at the gate they were met by a man holding a drawn sword in his hand. A tumult ensued, with the clang of weapons, and Sira Eiliv called out: "Woe to any man who breaks the peace of the cemetery." Kristin heard someone say it was the mighty smith from Credoveit. A moment later a tall, broad-shouldered man with white hair appeared at her side. It was Ulf Haldorssøn.

The priest handed him the axe—he had borrowed it from Ulf—and then took the boy, Tore, from the nun as he said, "It's already past midnight. All the same, it would be best if you all came back to the church. I want to tend to these matters tonight."

No one had any other thought but to comply. But when they reached the road, one of the pale gray figures slipped away from the flock of women and headed for the path leading into the woods. The priest shouted, ordering her to come with the others.

Kristin's voice replied from the dark; she was already a good way down the path: "I can't come, Sira Eiliv, until I've kept my promise."

The priest and several others set off running. She was leaning against the fence when Sira Eiliv reached her. He raised the lantern. Her face was dreadfully white, but when he looked into her eyes, he realized that she had not gone mad, as he first had feared.

"Come home, Kristin," he said. "Tomorrow we'll go with you, several men. I will go with you myself."

"I've given my word. I can't go home, Sira Eiliv, until I have done as I promised."

The priest stood in silence for a moment. Then he said softly, "Perhaps you are right. Go then, sister, in God's name."

Strangely shadowlike, Kristin slipped into the darkness, which swallowed up her gray-clad figure.

When Ulf Haldorssøn appeared at her side, she said in a halting and vehement voice, "Go back. I didn't ask you to come with me."

Ulf laughed quietly. "Kristin, my mistress, haven't you learned yet that things can happen without your request or orders? And I see you still don't realize, no matter how many times you've witnessed it, that you can't always manage alone everything that you've taken on. But I will help you to undertake this burden."

There was a rushing sound in the pine forest all around them, and the roar of the waves out on the shore grew louder and then fainter, carried on the gusts of wind. They were walking in pitch-darkness.

After a while Ulf said, "I've accompanied you before, Kristin, when you went out at night. I thought I could be of some help if I came with you this time as well."

She was breathing hard in the dark. Once she stumbled over something, and Ulf grabbed hold of her. Then he took her hand and led the way. After a moment he noticed that she was weeping as she walked along, and he asked her what she was crying about.

"I'm crying because I was thinking that you've always been so kind and loyal toward us, Ulf. What can I say? I know that it was mostly for Erlend's sake, but I almost think, kinsman . . . you've always judged me less harshly than you had the right to, after what you first saw of my actions."

"I have always been fond of you, Kristin—no less than I was of him." He fell silent. Kristin saw that he was overcome by great emotion. Then he continued, "That's why it was so hard for me as I sailed over here today. I came to bring you news that I find difficult to tell you. May God give you strength, Kristin."

"Is it Skule?" asked Kristin in a low voice after a moment. "Is Skule dead?"

"No, Skule was fine when I spoke to him yesterday, and now few people are dying in town. But I received news from Tautra this morning—" He heard her give a deep sigh, but she did not speak.

After a moment he said, "It's already been ten days since they died. But there are only four brothers left alive at the monastery, and the island is almost swept clean of people."

They had now reached the edge of the woods. Over the flat expanse of land before them came the roaring din of the wind and sea. Up ahead in the darkness shone a patch of white—sea swells in a small inlet, with a steep pale sand dune above.

"That's where she lives," said Kristin. Ulf noticed that slow, fitful tremors passed over her. He gripped her hand hard.

"You've chosen to take this burden upon yourself. Keep that in mind, and don't lose your wits now."

Kristin said in an oddly thin, pure voice, which the wind seized and carried off, "Now Bjørgulf's dream will come true. I trust in the mercy of God and the Virgin Mary."

Ulf tried to see her face, but it was too dark. They walked across the tide flats; several places were so narrow beneath the cliff that a wave or two surged all the way up to their feet. They made their way over tangled seaweed and large rocks. After a while they glimpsed a bulky dark shape against the sand dune.

"Stay here," said Ulf curtly. He went over and threw himself against the door. She heard him hack away at the osier latches and then throw himself at the door again. She saw it fall inward, and he stepped inside the black cave.

It was not a particularly stormy night. But it was so dark that Kristin could see nothing but the sea, alive with tiny glints of foam rolling forward and then sliding back at once, and the gleam of the waves lapping along the shore of the inlet. She could also make out the dark shape against the hillside. She felt as if she were standing in a cavern of night, and it was the hiding place of death. The crash of the breaking waves and the trickle of water ebbing between the tidal rocks merged with the flush of blood inside her, although her body seemed to shatter, the way a keg splinters into slats. She had a throbbing in her breast, as if it would burst from within. Her head felt hollow and empty, as if it were leaking, and the gusts of wind swirled around her, blowing right through her. In a strangely listless way she realized that now she must be suffering from the plague herself—but she seemed to be waiting for the darkness to be split by a light that would roar and drown out the crash of the sea, and then she would succumb to terror. She pulled up her hood, which had been blown back, drew the black nun's cloak closer, and then stood there with her arms crossed underneath, but it didn't occur to her to pray. Her soul had more than enough to do, working its way out of its collapsing house, and that was what made her breast ache as she breathed.

She saw a flame flare up inside the hovel. A moment later Ulf Haldorssøn called to her. "You must come here and light the way for me, Kristin." He stood in the doorway and handed her a torch of charred wood.

The stench of the corpse nearly suffocated her, even though the hut was so drafty and the door was gone. Wide-eyed, with her lips parted—and her jaw and lips felt as rigid as wood—she looked for the dead woman. But she saw only a long bundle lying in the corner on the earthen floor. Wrapped around it was Ulf's cape.

He had pulled loose several long boards from somewhere and placed the door on top. As he cursed the clumsy tools, he made notches and holes with his axe and dagger and struggled to bind the door to the boards. Several times he cast a quick glance up at her, and each time his dark gray-bearded face grew stonier.

"I wonder how you thought you would manage to do this all alone," he said, bending over his work. He looked up, but the rigid, lifeless face in the red glow of the tarred torch remained unchanged—the face of a dead woman or a mad creature. "Can you tell me that, Kristin?" He laughed harshly, but it did no good. "I think it's about time for you to say a few prayers."

In the same stiff and listless tone she began to pray: "*Pater noster qui es in celis. Adveniat regnum tuum. Fiat voluntas tua sicut in celo et in terra.*" Then she came to a halt.

Ulf looked at her. Then he took up the prayer, "*Panum nostrum quotidianum da nobis hodie . . .*" Swiftly and firmly he said the words of the *Pater noster* to the end, then went over and made the sign of the cross over the bundle; swiftly and firmly he picked it up and carried it over to the litter that he had made.

"You take the front," he said. "It may be a little heavier, but you won't notice the stench as much. Throw the torch away; we'll see better without it. And don't stumble, Kristin; I would rather not have to touch this poor corpse again."

The raging pain in her breast seemed to rise up in protest when she lifted the poles of the litter over her shoulders; her chest *refused* to bear the weight. But she clenched her teeth. As long as they walked along the shore, where the wind blew, she hardly noticed the smell of the body.

"I'd better climb up first and pull the litter up after me," said Ulf when they reached the slope where they had come down.

"We can go a little farther," said Kristin. "Over to the place where they bring down the seaweed sledges; it's not as steep."

The man could hear that her voice sounded calm and composed. And now that it was over, he started sweating and shivering; he had thought she was going to lose her wits that night.

They struggled onward over the sandy path that led across the clearing to the pine forest. The wind blew freely but not as strongly as it had on the shore, and as they walked farther and farther away from the roar of the tide flats, she felt as if it was a journey home from the uttermost terrors of darkness. The land was pale on both sides of the path—a field of grain, but there had been no one to harvest it. The smell of the grain and the sight of the withering straw welcomed her back home, and her eyes filled with the tears of sisterly compassion. Out of her own desperate terror and need she had come home to the community of the living and the dead.

From time to time the dreadful stink of decay would wash over her if the wind blew at her back, but it wasn't as foul as when she was standing inside the hut. Here the air was full of the fresh, wet, and cold purity of the breeze.

And stronger than the feeling that she was carrying something gruesome on the litter behind her was the sense that Ulf Haldorssøn was walking along, protecting her back against the living and black horror they had left behind; its crashing sound became fainter and fainter.

When they reached the outskirts of the pine forest, they noticed lights. "They're coming to meet us," said Ulf.

A moment later they were met by an entire throng of men carrying torches, a couple of lanterns, and a bier covered with a shroud. Sira Eiliv was with them, and Kristin was surprised to see that the group included several men who had been in the cemetery earlier that night; many of them were weeping. When they lifted the burden from her shoulders, she nearly collapsed. Sira Eiliv was about to catch her when she said quickly, "Don't touch me. Don't come near me. I can feel that I have the plague myself."

But Sira Eiliv put his hand under her arm all the same.

"Then it should be of comfort for you to remember, woman, what Our Lord has said: That which you have done unto one of my poorest brothers or sisters, you have also done unto me."

Kristin stared at the priest. Then she shifted her glance to the men, who were moving the body to the bier from the litter Ulf had made. Ulf's cape fell aside; the tip of a worn shoe gleamed, dark with rain in the light of the torches.

Kristin went over, knelt down between the poles of the litter, and kissed the shoe.

"May God bless you, sister. May God bathe your soul in His light. May God have mercy on all of us here in the darkness."

Then she thought it was life itself working its way out of her—an unthinkable, piercing pain as if something inside, firmly rooted to the utmost ends of her limbs, had been torn loose. All that was contained within her breast was ripped out; she felt it fill her throat. Her mouth filled with blood that tasted of salt and filthy copper; a moment later her entire robe was covered with glistening, dark wetness. Jesus, can there be so much blood in an old woman? she thought.

Ulf Haldorssøn lifted her up in his arms and carried her.

In the convent portal the nuns met the procession, carrying lighted tapers in their hands. Kristin no longer had her full wits about her, but she sensed that she was half carried, half supported through the doorway. The white-plastered vaulted room was filled with flickering light from yellow candle flames and red pinewood torches, and the stomping of feet roared like the sea—but for the dying woman it was like a mirror of her own sinking life flame, and the footsteps on the flagstones seemed to be the crash of death's current, rising up toward her.

Then the glow of light spread outward to a larger space; she was once again under a dark, open sky—out in the courtyard. The light played over a gray stone wall with heavy pillars and tall windows: the church. Someone was carrying her—it was Ulf again—but now he became one with all those who had ever carried her.

When she put her arms around his neck and pressed her cheek against his prickly bearded neck, she felt like a child again, with her father, but she also felt as if she were taking a child in her own arms. Behind his dark head there were red lights, and they seemed to be shining from the fire that nourishes all love.

Some time later she opened her eyes and her mind was clear. She was sitting propped up in a bed in the dormitory; a nun stood leaning over her, wearing a linen cloth on the lower half of her face, and she noticed the smell of vinegar. It was Sister Agnes; she could tell by the eyes and the tiny red wart on her forehead. And it was daytime. A clear gray light entered the room through the little windowpane.

She was not suffering now, but she was soaked with sweat, terribly weak and tired, and she had a sharp, stabbing pain in her breast when she breathed. Greedily she drank a soothing potion that Sister Agnes held to her lips. But she was freezing.

Kristin leaned back against the pillows, and now she remembered everything that had happened the night before. The wild shimmer of a dream had vanished completely; she realized that she must have been slightly out of her wits. But it was good that she had done what she had: rescued the little boy and prevented those poor people from being burdened with such a misdeed. She knew she should be overjoyed that *she* had been fortunate enough to do this before she died, but she didn't have the strength to rejoice as she ought to. She had more a sense of contentment, the way she felt lying in bed back home at Jørundgaard, weary from a day's work well done. And she had to thank Ulf. . . .

She had spoken his name, and he must have been sitting in the shadows near the door and heard her, for he crossed the room and stood before her bed. She stretched out her hand to him, and he took it, clasping it firmly and warmly in his.

Suddenly the dying woman grew uneasy; her hands fumbled under the folds of bedclothes around her neck.

"What is it, Kristin?" asked Ulf.

"The cross," she whispered, and pulled out her father's gilded cross. She recalled that she had promised the day before to offer a gift for the soul of poor Steinunn. But she had forgotten that she owned no more earthly possessions. She owned nothing more than this cross, which her father had given her, and her wedding ring. She still wore that on her finger.

She took it off and looked at it. It lay heavy in her hand, pure gold and set with large red stones. Erlend, she thought. And she realized that now she should give it away; she didn't know why, but she felt that she should. She closed her eyes in pain and handed the ring to Ulf.

"Who do you want to leave it to?" he asked softly. When she didn't reply, he said, "Should I give it to Skule?"

Kristin shook her head, keeping her eyes closed tight.

"Steinunn . . . I promised . . . masses for her. . . ."

She opened her eyes and looked at the ring lying in the dark palm of the smith. And her tears burst forth in torrents, for she felt as if she had never before fully understood what it signified. The life to which this ring had married her, over which she had complained and grumbled, raged and rebelled. And yet she had loved it so, rejoicing over it, with both the bad and the good, so that there was not a single day she would have given back to God without lament or a single sorrow she would have relinquished without regret.

Ulf and the nun exchanged a few words that she couldn't hear, and he left the room. Kristin tried to lift her hand to wipe her eyes but didn't have the strength; her hand remained lying on her breast. It hurt so terribly inside, her hand seemed so heavy, and she felt as if the ring were still on her finger. Her mind was becoming confused again; she *must* see if it was true that the ring was gone, that she hadn't merely dreamed she'd given it away. She was also becoming uncertain. Everything that had happened in the night, the child in the grave, the black sea with the small, swift glimpses of the waves, the body she had carried . . . she didn't know whether she had dreamed it all or been awake. And she didn't have the strength to open her eyes.

"Sister," said the nun, "you mustn't sleep yet. Ulf has gone to bring the priest to you."

Kristin woke up with a start and fixed her eyes on her hand. The gold ring was gone; that was certain enough. There was a shiny, worn mark where it had sat on her middle finger. On the brown, rough flesh it was quite clear—like a scar of thin white

skin. She thought she could even make out two round circles from
the rubies on either side and a tiny scratch, an *M* from the center
of the ring where the holy symbol of the Virgin Mary had been
etched into the gold.

The last clear thought that took shape in her mind was that she
was going to die before the mark had time to fade, and it made her
happy. It seemed to her a mystery that she could not comprehend,
but she was certain that God had held her firmly in a pact which
had been made for her, without her knowing it, from a love that
had been poured over her—and in spite of her willfulness, in spite
of her melancholy, earthbound heart, some of that love had *stayed*
inside her, had worked on her like sun on the earth, had driven
forth a crop that neither the fiercest fire of passion nor its stormi-
est anger could completely destroy. She had been a servant of
God—a stubborn, defiant maid, most often an eye-servant in her
prayers and unfaithful in her heart, indolent and neglectful, impatient toward admonishments, inconstant in her deeds. And yet He
had held her firmly in His service, and under the glittering gold
ring a mark had been secretly impressed upon her, showing that
she was His servant, owned by the Lord and King who would now
come, borne on the consecrated hands of the priest, to give her release and salvation.

As soon as Sira Eiliv had anointed her with the last oil and viaticum, Kristin Lavransdatter again lost consciousness. She lay
there, violently vomiting blood, with a blazing fever, and the priest
who was sitting with her told the nuns that the end would come
quickly.

Several times the dying woman's mind cleared enough that she
could recognize one face or another: Sira Eiliv or the sisters. Fru
Ragnhild herself was there once, and she saw Ulf. She struggled to
show that she knew them and that it was good they were with her
and wished her well. But for those who stood at her bedside, it
merely looked as if she were flailing her hands in the throes of
death.

Once she saw Munan's face; her little son was peeking at her
through a crack in the door. Then he pulled back his head, and his
mother lay there, staring at the door to see if the boy would look
through it again. Instead Fru Ragnhild appeared and wiped her

face with a damp cloth, and that too felt good. Then everything disappeared in a dark red haze and a roar, which at first grew fearfully loud, but then the din gradually died away, and the red fog became thinner and lighter, and at last it was like a fine morning mist before the sun breaks through, and there was not a sound, and she knew that now she was dying.

Sira Eiliv and Ulf Haldorssøn left the deathbed together. In the doorway leading out to the convent courtyard, they stopped.

Snow had fallen. None of them had noticed this as they sat with her and she struggled with death. The white sheen was strangely dazzling on the steep slant of the church roof opposite them; the tower was pale against the murky gray sky. The snow lay so fine and white on all the window frames and all the jutting gray stones of the church walls. And the two men seemed to hesitate, not wanting to mar the new snow in the courtyard with their footprints.

They breathed in the air. After the suffocating smell that always surrounded someone stricken with the plague, it tasted sweet and cool, a little empty and thin, but as if this snowfall had washed sickness and contagion out of the air; it was as good as fresh water.

The bell in the tower began ringing again; the two men looked up to the movement behind the sound holes. Tiny snowflakes were shaken loose, rolling down to become little balls; some of the black shingles could be seen underneath.

"This snow won't last," said Ulf.

"No, it will melt away before evening," replied the priest. There were pale golden rifts in the clouds, and a faint, tentative ray of sunshine fell across the snow.

The men stayed where they were. Then Ulf Haldorssøn said quietly, "I've been thinking, Sira Eiliv . . . I want to give some land to this church . . . and a goblet she gave me that once belonged to Lavrans Bjørgulfsøn . . . to establish a mass for her . . . and my foster sons . . . and for him, Erlend, my kinsman."

The priest's voice was equally quiet, and he did not look at the man. "I think you might also mean that you want to show Him your gratitude for leading you here last night. You must be grateful that you were allowed to help her through this night."

"Yes, that was what I meant," said Ulf Haldorssøn. Then he

laughed a little. "And now I almost regret, priest, that I have been such a pious man—toward her."

"It's useless to waste your time over such futile regrets," replied the priest.

"What do you mean?"

"I mean that it's only a man's sins that it does any good for him to regret."

"Why is that?"

"Because no one is good without God. And we can do nothing good without Him. So it's futile to regret a good deed, Ulf, for the good you have done cannot be taken back; even if all the mountains should fall, it would still stand."

"Well, well. That's not how I see things, my Sira. I'm tired . . ."

"Yes . . . and you must be hungry too. Come with me over to the cookhouse, Ulf," said the priest.

"Thank you, but I have no wish to eat anything," said Ulf Haldorssøn.

"All the same, you must come with me and have some food," said Sira Eiliv, placing his hand on Ulf's sleeve and pulling him along. They headed across the courtyard and over toward the cookhouse. Without thinking, they both walked as lightly and carefully as they could in the new snow.

EXPLANATORY NOTES

References Used

Blangstrup, Chr., ed. *Salmonsens Konversations Leksikon*. 2d ed. Copenhagen: J. H. Schultz Forlagsboghandel, 1928.

Knudsen, Trygve, and Alf Sommerfelt, eds. *Norsk Riksmåls Ordbok*. Oslo: Det Norske Akademi for Sprog og Litteratur og Kunnskapsforlaget, 1983.

Mørkhagen, Sverre. *Kristins Verden: Om norsk middelalder på Kristin Lavransdatters tid*. Oslo: J. W. Cappelens Forlag, 1995.

Pulsiano, Phillip, ed. *Medieval Scandinavia: An Encyclopedia*. New York: Garland Publishing Co., 1993.

Sawyer, Birgit and Peter. *Medieval Scandinavia: From Conversion to Reformation, circa 800–1500*. Minneapolis: University of Minnesota Press, 1993.

PART I

CHAPTER 1

1. *high seat:* The place of honor, reserved for the male head of the family or an honored guest. The high seat was usually in the middle of the table, on the side against the wall. Servants often sat on the opposite bench.

CHAPTER 2

1. *try to lure her inside:* In medieval Norway people believed that the forests and mountains were populated by many types of supernatural beings, which were both unpredicatable and menacing.

2. *the transparent hide:* Both window openings and smoke vents were often covered with a transparent membrane, usually made from a cow's stomach.

CHAPTER 3

1. *His two motherless daughters had been taken in:* An arrangement by which a number of neighboring estates agreed to provide a certain amount of food for the poor. Each manor fulfilled its obligations either by distributing food to needy individuals or by taking in charity cases for a specified length of time.

2. *Convertere, Domine . . . :* Return, O Lord, how long? and let it repent thee concerning thy servants. Psalms 30:13. Be not wroth very sore, O Lord, neither remember iniquity for ever: behold, see, we beseech thee, we are all thy people. Isaiah 64:9.

CHAPTER 4

1. *ting:* A meeting of free, adult men (women rarely attended) which met at regular intervals to discuss matters of concern to a particular community. On the local level, the *ting* might consider such issues as pasture rights, fencing, bridge and road construction, taxes, and the maintenance of the local warship. A regional *ting,* attended by chieftains or appointed deputies, would address such issues as defense and legal jurisdiction. The regional *ting* also functioned as a court, although its authority diminished as the power of the king grew. In addition to its regular meetings, a *ting* could be called for a specific purpose, such as the acclamation of a new king.

CHAPTER 5

1. *Duke Skule when he rallied the forces:* In 1238 the Norwegian Duke Skule Baardssøn challenged King Haakon Haakonssøn's right to the throne by having himself proclaimed king at the

Øre *ting*. He and his army of followers waged war in several parts of Norway, but after losing a battle in Oslo, he fled to Nidaros. Skule was eventually slain at Elgeseter Cloister. His death brought to an end the century-long strife over succession to the throne.

2. *offering the land to the heirs:* In accordance with the laws of the time, ancestral land had to be offered for sale to the descendants of the original owners before it could be sold to anyone else.

3. *his father had acknowledged him as his own:* Not until 1270 did celibacy for priests become part of Norwegian Church law. Even then, it was not strictly enforced, particularly in the countryside.

4. *the murder of the dukes:* In 1318 the Swedish dukes Eirik and Valdemar were murdered by their older brother, King Birger Magnussön, after a long-standing power struggle.

5. *a letter of reprieve:* Permission, granted by the king, for a man to remain in Norway even though he either had been sentenced to banishment or had committed acts punishable by banishment.

CHAPTER 6

1. *merchants of Bjørgvin:* Medieval name for Bergen, which was the royal and ecclesiastical center of West Norway. In the twelfth century it became the first port in Scandinavia to have international commercial importance, and it was the main market for the export of dried cod, or stockfish. By the fourteenth century Bjørgvin was the largest Norwegian town.

2. *woodpile dance:* Dance often performed around a large woodpile on the day after a wedding. First the bride and groom and then other couples, by turn, would share a piece of bread and drink from the same cup and then dance around the woodpile.

3. *Abishag the Shunammite:* A beautiful young woman who came under David's care when he was an old man. Adonijah sought in vain to make her his wife.

PART II

CHAPTER 1

1. *the Gandvik coast:* The Gandvik Sea was the medieval name for the White Sea, near present-day Arkhangel'sk, Russia.

2. *mare:* A supernatural female creature which, according to folk belief, torments people in their sleep by perching heavily on their chests.

CHAPTER 2

1. *prime:* The second of the seven canonical hours, usually about 6 A.M. According to Church law, specific prayers were to be recited at seven prescribed times of the day.

2. *chapter:* An assembly of the canons of a cathedral. Canon was an ecclesiastical title for a member of a group of priests who served in a cathedral and who were usually expected to live a communal life.

CHAPTER 3

1. *Venite: revertamur . . . :* Come, and let us return unto the Lord: for he hath torn, and he will heal us; he hath smitten, and he will bind us up. . . . Then shall we know, if we follow on to know the Lord: his going forth is prepared as the morning; and he shall come unto us as the rain, as the latter and former rain unto the earth. Hosea 6:1 and 3.

2. *Salvator mundi . . . :* Savior of the world, save us all.

3. *turnover day:* The day on which tenants and servants were allowed to give up their positions and move to new ones. The exact day varied by area, but was often Summer Day (April 14) and Winter Day (October 14) of each year.

CHAPTER 7

1. *with either five or eleven others:* Two types of oath could exonerate a person from a charge brought against him. One required five people to swear to the person's veracity; the other required eleven people. In the case of an accused woman all the others had to be women.

2. *King David and Bathsheba:* Old Testament story about the beautiful Bathsheba, wife of Uriah the Hittite. She was seduced by King David and conceived a child who later died. After the death of Uriah, Bathsheba married David and gave birth to Solomon.

PART III

CHAPTER 1

1. *the farmer in the mound:* A commonly held pagan belief that the spirit of the original owner of an estate continued to offer protection from the grave.

2. *Quid mihi . . . :* Woman, what have I to do with thee? mine hour is not yet come. John 2:4.

CHAPTER 2

1. *Winter Day:* October 14, considered the beginning of the winter half year.

2. *an unredeemable offense:* A crime that could not be absolved through the payment of fines; a crime punishable by unconditional banishment.

CHAPTER 4

1. *Jesus Kristus Soter . . . :* Jesus Christ the Savior. The lion of the tribe of Judah is victorious.

CHAPTER 5

1. *corrody:* A pension or allowance granted by a cloister in exchange for donated land or property; it permitted the holder to retire into the cloister as a boarder.

2. *nona hora:* The fifth of the seven canonical hours set aside for prayer, usually the ninth hour after sunrise.

LIST OF HOLY DAYS

Saint Paal's Day	January 15
Saint Gregor's Day	March 12
Holy Cross Day	May 3
Midsummer (Saint Jon's Day)	June 24
Saint Margareta's Day	July 20
Feast of Mary Magdalena	July 22
Saint Olav's Day (Feast of Saint Olav)	July 29
Saint Bartholomew's Day	August 24
Feast of the Birth of Mary	September 8
Holy Cross Day	September 14
Saint Matthew's Day	September 21
Saint Michael's Day (Michaelmas)	September 29
Winter Day	October 14
Saint Simon's Day	October 28
The Feast of Saint Jude	October 28
All Saints' Day	November 1
Corpus Christi Day	November 9
Saint Clement's Day	November 23
Saint Catherine's Day	November 25
Feast of the Apostle Saint Andreas	November 30
Saint Lucia's Day	December 13
Ascension Day	Fortieth day after Easter
Whitsunday	Seventh Sunday after Easter
Whitsuntide	The week beginning with Pentecost, the fiftieth day after Easter
Advent	December (varies annually)

FOR THE BEST IN PAPERBACKS, LOOK FOR THE

In every corner of the world, on every subject under the sun, Penguin represents quality and variety—the very best in publishing today.

For complete information about books available from Penguin—including Penguin Classics, Penguin Compass, and Puffins—and how to order them, write to us at the appropriate address below. Please note that for copyright reasons the selection of books varies from country to country.

In the United States: Please write to *Penguin Group (USA), P.O. Box 12289 Dept. B, Newark, New Jersey 07101-5289* or call 1-800-788-6262.

In the United Kingdom: Please write to *Dept. EP, Penguin Books Ltd, Bath Road, Harmondsworth, West Drayton, Middlesex UB7 0DA.*

In Canada: Please write to *Penguin Books Canada Ltd, 10 Alcorn Avenue, Suite 300, Toronto, Ontario M4V 3B2.*

In Australia: Please write to *Penguin Books Australia Ltd, P.O. Box 257, Ringwood, Victoria 3134.*

In New Zealand: Please write to *Penguin Books (NZ) Ltd, Private Bag 102902, North Shore Mail Centre, Auckland 10.*

In India: Please write to *Penguin Books India Pvt Ltd, 11 Panchsheel Shopping Centre, Panchsheel Park, New Delhi 110 017.*

In the Netherlands: Please write to *Penguin Books Netherlands bv, Postbus 3507, NL-1001 AH Amsterdam.*

In Germany: Please write to *Penguin Books Deutschland GmbH, Metzlerstrasse 26, 60594 Frankfurt am Main.*

In Spain: Please write to *Penguin Books S. A., Bravo Murillo 19, 1° B, 28015 Madrid.*

In Italy: Please write to *Penguin Italia s.r.l., Via Benedetto Croce 2, 20094 Corsico, Milano.*

In France: Please write to *Penguin France, Le Carré Wilson, 62 rue Benjamin Baillaud, 31500 Toulouse.*

In Japan: Please write to *Penguin Books Japan Ltd, Kaneko Building, 2-3-25 Koraku, Bunkyo-Ku, Tokyo 112.*

In South Africa: Please write to *Penguin Books South Africa (Pty) Ltd, Private Bag X14, Parkview, 2122 Johannesburg.*